THE PENDULUM
FILES

THE PENDULUM FILES
By p.m.terrell

Published by
Drake Valley Press
USA

This novel is a work of fiction. Any resemblance to actual persons, living or dead, is entirely coincidental. The characters, names (except as noted under "Special Thanks"), plots and incidents are the product of the author's imagination. References to actual events, public figures, locales or businesses are included only to give this work of fiction a sense of reality.

ISBN 978-1-935970-09-5 (Trade Paperback)
ISBN 978-1-935970-10-1 (eBook)

Author's website: www.pmterrell.com

Special Thanks

To all the fans, friends and family who encourage me to continue writing and who eagerly await each new novel. Without you, I'd have to get a real job.

And to Arnold West, the proprietor of The Village Station Restaurant in Lumberton, North Carolina, for permission to use his restaurant in scenes throughout this series.

1

Vicki screamed as the oversized truck clipped the rear of the car, sending them into a gut-wrenching tailspin. As the rear wheels ground in protest against the spongy mud shoulder, the front of the vehicle curled sideways into the roadway. She glanced behind them as the truck backed off, but before she could catch another jagged breath it gained speed once more and rammed into the driver's side door. The sound of metal against metal was deafening in its intensity, ferocious in its onslaught.

The two vehicles were locked together while the truck continued its forward momentum, crumpling the driver's side as Brenda shrieked in terrifying agony. Then it shook them off like a lioness loosening its grip on prey too weak to fight. As the truck sped past them, their vehicle crisscrossed the roadway before coming to an abrupt halt.

The air was forced out of their lungs as though they'd both been violently punched in the gut. Then there was nothing but silence.

Vicki stared out the cracked windshield at the flat terrain and straight, two-lane road. The truck was visible less than a mile in front of them, but only because the truck's stark white color stood out against the darkening sepia skies. Nighttime was approaching fast and she had no clue where they were or how they could find help.

Then the car began to drift of its own accord. She shook Brenda by the shoulder, urging her to open her eyes. Blood trickled down her face in a silent response. As Vicki looked down, she realized her sister's body was covered in blood, as was the steering wheel that was wedged against Brenda's abdomen.

Frantic, she swung around to peer out the passenger side window. The car was almost completely off the road, the rear wheels sinking ever deeper into thick muck above a ravine. The swamps were sucking them down; the water swirling around the cypress knees below them as if waiting to consume them. The car tilted and as Vicki hurled back around, she realized the tires on the driver's side were lifting up.

"Brenda!" she shouted, punching her sister's arm in a frantic attempt to awaken her.

Her eyes skimmed the terrain just outside the door in her growing frenzy: the water cypress rose high on either side of the road, their giant branches twisting in the growing wind like gnarled fingers; the swamp just feet from the vehicle, gaping as if ready to swallow them whole. There were no homes in sight; no sign of life. Her screams simply evaporated in the intensifying wind.

Looking down at the console where they'd both laid their cell phones just moments earlier, she realized they'd been violently ejected, landing somewhere else in a vehicle that now resembled an accordion. She turned around to search the floorboard and back seat, but as the car began to slide, she froze. With her heart in her throat, she realized every moment brought them closer to the sharp ravine above an untamed swamp that stretched as far as the eye could see.

Whirling back around, she realized the white truck had stopped and was turning around.

"He's coming back!" she shouted.

Brenda murmured something incomprehensible, her eyes still shut and the blood still seeping from wounds on her forehead.

Fighting against a rising hysteria, Vicki grabbed her by the arm and tried unsuccessfully to pull her across the console. But her sister remained wedged between the crumpled door and the dashboard, which now rested on her bloody knees.

"He's coming back!" she shouted again, shaking Brenda. "We've got to get out!"

The truck was now facing them. It seemed to sit there, calmly watching them with intense headlights that felt like unblinking, evil eyes.

"Save yourself," Brenda managed to croak, the effort so labored that Vicki could feel the anguish in her voice.

"I won't leave you," Vicki argued, her own voice raspy. "You have to get out. You have to find the strength!"

"I can't," her sister said in an uncharacteristic sigh of resignation. Her head lolled forward so she could no longer see her face but only a mountain of copper hair drenched in blood. In a brief moment of lucidity, she continued, "He's after me, not you. Get out. Follow the swamps—they'll lead you to a farmhouse on the other side. He won't follow you."

"I won't leave you," Vicki repeated.

"Think of the baby!" Brenda urged, gritting her teeth against the agony. "For God's sake, think of your baby!"

Vicki sucked in her breath sharply as her eyes, now widened with surprise, were drawn to her belly. Her unborn child kicked within her as if to spur her to action.

She glanced up as the truck lurched forward. It rushed toward them as she stared wide-eyed, clearly gaining in speed as it barreled straight for them. Yet in her mind, it felt as if it was moving in slow motion. Her sister or her unborn child—

Then somehow she was sliding feet-first against the uneven bank, the mud propelling her away from the car. She caught a glimpse of her shoe wedged above her, yet she didn't remember opening the door or climbing out. As she continued to peer upward, she caught sight of the small vehicle sitting helplessly, its rear wheels now dangling precariously above her.

With a start that jolted her heart, she realized the car would be pushed over the bank and directly atop her. She tried to scramble out of the way as sheer panic swept over her but something slapped her back into place. The cypress trees had somehow grown closer until they surrounded her, and now they taunted her unmercifully with heavy, wet branches that reached down to strike her. Somewhere in the back of her mind she realized her cheeks were soaked from her own tears and yet she was powerless to stop them.

The storm had grown to a fever pitch. It seemed to shout her name over and over again as sobs wracked her body. And as the roar of the truck's engine grew in terrifying intensity, the violent screams that escaped her lips were drowned out by the excruciating sound of metal against metal.

Vicki's head lolled from side to side, the branches that had buffeted her face now taking on the feel of strong, rough hands.

"Vicki!" The voice was insistent. "Vicki, Darlin'! Wake up!"

She bolted upright, nearly bumping her head into Dylan's. Only his quick evasive action prevented a painful collision. A realization began to creep over her that she was not in a desolate swamp escaping from a madman, but she was sitting in the middle of the bed, drenched in perspiration, her chest heaving while Dylan stared at her wide-eyed.

"You were havin' y'self a nightmare," he stated.

"Brenda," she said, throwing off the covers.

He reached out and with one muscular arm around her waist he prevented her from bounding off the bed. "She's asleep in 'er room, no doubt," he said calmly. "But if you go about rushin' in to see to 'er, she's likely to pop a cap in you."

She settled back to the mattress. As she caught her breath, her surroundings sank in. She was in the large master bedroom on the third floor of their rambling old home. The moonlight peered around the edges of the curtains, casting lengthy fingers of muted light across the floor. The familiar furniture took shape until finally she looked back at Dylan, who was still watching her intently.

"Must 'ave been a helluva dream," he said. His voice was husky with sleep, his hazel eyes tired. "Come," he said, "lay back down w' me."

Silently, she lay on her back as he draped an arm and a leg across her. His black hair tumbled across his forehead as he moved to kiss her cheek. "Not sayin' I told you so, but I cautioned against eatin' so late."

"That's saying 'I told you so'," she said, a slow smile forming despite her abrupt awakening.

"You must be avoidin' anythin' that causes nightmares, Darlin'. You know what they say."

She waited for him to continue.

He ran his large hand across her belly, which was barely beginning to round. "If you 'ave nightmares while you're expectin' the baby will be born w' a fear o' the dark."

Her eyes met his.

"It's true," he added. He settled in beside her, snuggling her against his powerful chest.

"I saw—"

"Shhh," he whispered tiredly. "Twas just a dream, 'tis all. Don't worry about a thin'. I'm here. I won't be allowin' anythin' to harm you."

She rested her hand atop his arm. His breathing slowed and became rhythmic. But as she lay in his arms, she knew beyond a shadow of a doubt, it hadn't been a dream.

It was a premonition.

2

Dylan knelt next to the box, his fingers caressing the miniature amber statue dwarfed by his large hands. The door behind him was open wide and as he returned the statue to the box and lifted another, slightly larger one, he heard the murmur of voices from the adjacent room. The crisp fragrance of gurgling water and fish tank chemicals permeated everything, it seemed, everything except the figurines, trinkets and jewels.

Behind him and just beyond the door were rows of fish tanks in which freshwater angelfish were busy breeding or caring for their young. Vicki's voice was soft and melodious against the constant hum of the tanks as she taught her sister how to care for the fish. Every now and then Brenda's husky voice interjected and the voices would go back and forth, soft against husky, but he wasn't paying close enough attention to decipher their words.

Since Brenda had returned to live with them, she'd been a fast learner, helping to care for the angelfish as expertly as Vicki or himself. It would come in handy if she managed to remain out of trouble, he thought; though Vicki's due date was still months away, time would march quickly and soon they both would be caring for their newborn. Brenda would be a welcome hand in the fish house.

A few feet away was his black and white border collie Shep, curled as though sleeping; but as he glanced in her direction, he caught her blue eyes open and her ears pricked as she kept her attention focused on everyone's activities. She'd arrived in America from Ireland no worse for the wear and had settled in as if her adventure had been the most natural thing in the world. Though Sam had dutifully taken her to North End Veterinary Clinic for her shots and grooming, he hadn't boarded her there but had taken her home with him until their return from the Emerald Isle. She'd even managed to make friends with Sam's cat.

Dylan turned back to the boxes: eight columns of four boxes each, the cardboard splitting on most while a few sported water stains. All had come from Laurel Maguire's home; many he'd found in a makeshift attic space in the garage he'd demolished just before departing for his homeland. A few he'd found in the remnants of the coal cellar and a few more in an unfinished room on the third floor.

From the beginning, his instinct told him they were not pieces of junk. But now, as he withdrew a piece of gold leaf from another box, he knew beyond a doubt that they were priceless.

As if to confirm his instinct, his eyes landed on newspaper clippings heralding the start of World War II in Great Britain. There could only be one reason why artifacts were carefully arranged in between newspapers, blueprints and hastily scribbled plans that included locations and dates throughout Europe.

Laurel Maguire's husband had assisted the Nazis in hiding the stash.

It had come to him on the long plane ride back home from Ireland. As Vicki and Brenda napped in their reclined seats, he'd closed his eyes and seen the riches that lay beneath the bogs. The amber walls with their gold leaf and embedded figurines had spoken to him. The voices in his head were soft at first but as the hours had crept past, they grew louder and more insistent.

The portrait that had hung in the front hallway had long ago been taken down and placed with the boxes. Now his eyes moved from the newspaper to the portrait. As he stared into the hard, cold eyes of Jonathan Maguire, he calculated his approximate age. He would have been around thirty years old at the end of World War II, he surmised, certainly not too old to have been involved in one way or another with the fight between the Germans and the English.

And if his hunch proved correct, he'd loathed the English and he'd worked with the Germans—not only against the Brits in war, but also to hide the valuable items the Germans pilfered as they overran Europe.

Two male voices joined in the conversation outside his door, breaking his concentration. As he looked to the spot where Shep had lain, it was empty; the dog had been as silent and stealthy as she'd always been, disappearing and reappearing like a ghost.

"Dylan!"

"In here," he answered as he rose to his feet and hastily returned the items to the nearest box. He ran his hand through his black hair, combing it with his fingers as he made his way through the store room and into the brighter radiance of the fish room.

As his eyes adjusted to the light, they fell upon Brenda's mountain of copper hair cascading down her back as she pressed her body close to Christopher Sandige's lean frame. His hands encircled her hair, grasping it in a manner that caused Dylan to clear his throat and look away.

Sam had kneeled in the floor to scratch Shep behind her ears. The dog pawed at him and nuzzled his face as though they were old friends. At the sight of Dylan, he stood and catching a glimpse of Brenda and Chris engaged like two teenagers at a drive-in movie, he barked, "We're working here, for Christ's sake."

Reluctantly, Chris relinquished his hold on her and their lips parted. Brenda backed away unhurriedly while a slow, sly smile inched across her face.

"Is a pregnant woman supposed to be working in here?" Sam asked Vicki.

She rolled her eyes. "Dylan researched it to death. He couldn't find any reason for me not to continue working."

"That's true," Dylan said. "And you know what they say."

All eyes turned to him.

"If you spend a lot o' time w' the fishies, the child will learn to swim much faster."

The room remained silent.

"It's true," he added.

Sam cleared his throat. "Got some news a short while ago," he said. He looked pointedly at Chris and Brenda. "I thought it best to tell everybody at the same time."

"Why am I thinkin' this isn't good news you 'ave 'ere, Sam?" Dylan asked, moving to stand behind Vicki.

"It's not good," Sam answered. "Not necessarily bad. Just news. Take it at face value."

"Well, what is it?" Vicki prodded.

Dylan stepped forward so her back rested against his chest.

"When you two lovebirds met," Sam said, pointing at Chris and then at Brenda, "there was the little matter of a double homicide."

"We were both cleared," Chris said. His eyes narrowed. "In fact, a man was arrested and convicted for those murders."

"Joseph Gabucci," Sam offered.

"That's him." Brenda's voice took on a strained quality.

"He received two life sentences. The plan, theoretically, was for him to die in prison."

"They're not letting him go?" Chris' voice was hushed and urgent.

Sam hesitated. "Officially, he was not released."

"Officially? What does that mean, 'officially'?"

Sam crossed his arms and looked at each of them in turn. "He broke out of prison."

"When?"

"How?"

"Sometime during the night, as best they can determine. They don't know how."

"He couldn't have just walked out," Chris said, incredulous.

"It happens all the time," Brenda offered. "That is, when you have someone on the inside helping you."

"And you should know," Sam said.

"I'll be beggin' your pardon," Dylan interjected. "I'm comin' in a bit late in the game 'ere and I'm not quite certain I'm understandin' you. If the man was convicted and is servin' time, the fact that he escaped doesn't reopen the case. These two should remain in the clear. Unless," he added as an afterthought, "they think they had somethin' to do w' his departure."

"Oh, everybody's quite certain they *didn't* help him," Sam said wryly.

"That's right," Brenda said, turning to Vicki and Dylan. "Because Joseph Gabucci was trying to kill me and Chris."

"What?" Vicki's and Dylan's voices answered in unison.

"It's a long story."

"I've got plenty o' time for this one, I'll be tellin' you that," Dylan said.

Brenda looked at Chris, who nodded for her to continue. Taking a deep breath, she said, "I was working with a banker to move some money off-shore."

"An illegal pursuit, no doubt," Dylan said.

"Are you going to let me tell the story or what?"

He waved for her to proceed.

"It doesn't really matter what we were doing or why. The fact is, somebody hired Joseph Gabucci to kill the banker and his wife. Actually, his wife was collateral damage."

"Oh, well then, the wife was just an accident," Dylan responded with thinly veiled sarcasm.

"Which is why," Sam interjected, "he was convicted of one count of premeditated murder and one count of manslaughter."

"Then he came after me," Brenda continued. "Chris was just in the wrong place at the wrong time."

"I was in the right place at the right time," Chris corrected. "I like to think I had a little something to do with Brenda escaping him."

"Chris held him off so I could get away. Alec—"

"Alec Brodie, our next door neighbor?"

"One and the same. He arrested Joseph and continued to look for me."

"Did he think you were in cahoots with 'im, perhaps?" Dylan asked.

"It all came out at trial that I was not. Not that I was there," Brenda added hastily. "As everybody here knows, I was 'vacationing' in Argentina."

"But," Sam interrupted, "they never did find out who the man was working for. They could link him to the murders but nothing—and nobody—else."

"So," Vicki said slowly, "now that he's escaped from prison, do they think he'll try to kill Brenda?"

"No," Sam said.

"Of course not," Brenda stepped over his words in her haste to reply. "There's no reason for him to come after me. I've turned over all the evidence of the scheme I was involved in to the FBI." She lifted her leg to show off her ankle bracelet. "It was part of my conditional release while awaiting trial on the other schemes."

"Last night I had a dream," Vicki stated flatly. The room became hushed as all eyes turned to her. "I dreamed a man was trying to kill Brenda."

"What?" Sam said.

"It was only a nightmare, Darlin'," Dylan said, wrapping his arms around her.

"When one of my psychic spies has a vision—even if it's a dream," Sam said, "I take it seriously."

When Dylan looked at Sam, his brows were knit and his face darkened. "Are you sayin' that Vicki here, in addition to bein' able to travel around the world w' her visions—she can also see into the future?"

Sam stroked his chin and peered at Vicki for a moment before answering. "Psychics can be highly effective at seeing into the past or even the present," he said. "But they are less effective at seeing into the future."

"Why is that?" It was Brenda's voice now, and as Dylan glanced in her direction, he noted her face had grown paler.

"Scientifically—which is what I deal in," Sam responded, "everyone on the planet has what is known as 'free will'. Every decision you make, regardless of how minor or insignificant you believe it to be, places you on a certain path. At any time, another decision can veer you slightly off that path or even on a different one entirely."

"Meaning?"

"Meaning there are too many variables—hundreds, even thousands—that can be changed at any instant. Once that occurs, any predictions of the future can fly out the window. Suppose, for example, one of you is told that you'll be involved in a car accident. You make a decision not to go out to dinner one evening; maybe you don't feel so well. So you stay home. Or you've misplaced your keys and you're getting a later start than intended. Meanwhile, the drunk driver predicted to hit you is passed out, or a bartender calls him a ride, or he's picked up by the cops and spends the night in jail. Or maybe, just weeks or months before, he's had an intervention and he's not drunk at all. Each one of those factors is enough to change the future."

Dylan placed his chin atop Vicki's head. She was silent and he wondered if she was thinking about her own destiny and the fact that when she was twelve years old, she had accurately predicted her own parents' death in an airplane accident. She'd tried to warn them but was ignored by her parents, school teachers and even counselors. Their death changed her life in ways she could never have imagined—from the CIA learning of her psychic abilities to being separated from her sister and two brothers. And though Vicki and Brenda had reunited, she had yet to find her brothers.

Chris reached for Brenda's hand. "What danger are we in?"

Sam shrugged. "My guess? None."

"Your guess?" Dylan asked. "You come here tellin' us a murderer has escaped, you say you take Vicki's dream seriously and then you tell us no one here is in any danger a'tal?"

"Of course I came to warn you. Keep your eyes open. Go about your business but be aware of your surroundings at all times."

"What are the authorities doing?" Chris asked.

"It's FBI jurisdiction. He'll most likely end up on their Most Wanted list."

"That's it?"

"No; it isn't." Sam took a deep breath. "They'll get the word out to national media. His case won't get buried. I can guarantee you that. They're working to find him." He turned to Dylan. "Anyway, I've got more business to discuss. Dylan?"

—•—   —•—   —•—

The air outside was crisp and cool as autumn settled into coastal North Carolina. As Dylan joined Sam under the giant oak tree in the middle of the back yard, they were met with a wave of multi-colored leaves that fluttered to the ground.

"So what danger is Vicki in w' her sister stayin' here?" Dylan asked.

"You heard me back there," Sam answered. "None."

"I'm not thinkin' that's correct." His eyes narrowed. "It wasn't that long ago that a group o' rogue agents came after 'em. And if you don't know who this Joseph fellow works for, who's to know he isn't connected w' 'em somehow? What makes you certain he won't finish the job the others started?"

"Do you want me to put Brenda back in FBI custody?"

"That's not m' call, Sam. It's the FBI's if they believe she's in danger. Otherwise, it's up to Vicki and her sister."

Sam pulled out a cigarette and placed it in his mouth.

"No smokin'," Dylan said. "On account o' I don't want Vicki breathin' the fumes in 'er condition."

"We're outside." Sam had his hand in his pocket but relinquished his hold on the lighter. He kept the cigarette in his mouth as he answered. "If the FBI thought Brenda would be compromised, you'd already have had a visit from them."

"So it's up to Vicki and Brenda."

"It's not public knowledge that Brenda turned over the files to the FBI."

"Are you jokin' me?"

"Think about it. They don't want to give the folks on the list time to establish alibis. They want to complete their investigations first—so when arrests are made, it comes as a surprise."

"So. Where would that be leavin' us?"

Sam looked beyond him at the back yard before his eyes rested on Alec Brodie's house. "Here's what we're gonna do. I'll check with the FBI; they're in charge of the case against Brenda and they'll have to agree to this. And so would the girls, if they want her to remain here. But if they agree, we'll have the locals issue a press release that Brenda has been apprehended for a computer scheme in conjunction with that double homicide."

"The locals meanin' Alec Brodie."

Sam shrugged. "Local law enforcement. Then we'll put out a bit of misinformation."

"Oh?"

"She'll have to lay low. Stay inside the house." He gestured toward the fish house. "Or in there. We'll say she's serving time in a federal prison awaiting trial."

"And that's supposed to keep Vicki safe?"

Sam studied the rambling old home. "Not too many know that Brenda and Vicki are sisters. I didn't even know until recently. If they think Brenda is behind bars, they won't be looking for her here."

"And you're willin' to risk Vicki's life on this, are you?"

"Hey. I care about her, too, you know. I'll get some guys out here to install cameras all the way around the house. You'll have a security system to rival the best. We'll get remote control devices for you, Vicki and Brenda so all you'll have to do is punch a button and it will alert the police—and me—that you need help."

Dylan nodded. "I don't want anythin' to happen to 'er."

"Neither do I. I wouldn't place her in harm's way." Sam removed the unlit cigarette from his mouth and rolled it between his forefinger and thumb as he studied Dylan. "You gonna marry her and make my grandchild legit?"

"Your grandchild, 'eh?" Sam had adopted Vicki after her parents died. But instead of being placed in his home, she'd gone to live at Langley and indoctrinated into the psychic spy program. "Aye. I've got a ring. Haven't asked 'er yet."

"Well, what's keeping you?"

"I want it to be special, you know. I don't want to waltz into the fish house and say, 'ey, woman, put this on."

Dylan could have sworn Sam started to smile but just as quickly, he cleared his throat. "Anyway, that's not why I wanted to see you."

Dylan propped his foot on an exposed root. "Well, 'ave at it, then."

"A sixth ship was bombed this morning."

"Six ships," Dylan breathed. "Another merchant ship from China, headin' to the United States, I presume?"

"That's right. These attacks are monopolizing the news."

"As they should."

"Not when the President is running for reelection. He wants to know who is bent on destroying goods bound for America. He wants to be able to show the American public somebody's face. He wants to tell them we're hunting them down."

"Why am I thinkin' this has somethin' to do w' me?"

"I'm picking you up in front of the house at 4 am. Be ready."

"For what?"

"I'll fill you in tomorrow. Anyway, you'll be back around midnight."

Dylan nodded. "Will I be needin' to bring anythin' in particular w' me?"

Sam started toward the driveway. "I'll have everything."

"A'fore you go," Dylan said abruptly.

"Yeah?" He turned back to look at him.

"When the CIA purchased this house," he nodded toward the three-story structure, "did you purchase e'erythin' in it?"

"Of course we did. You know that."

"I mean, e'erythin'? Even if I was to find somethin' in the attic or whate'er, somethin' mayhap the nephew didn't know Laurel Maguire owned. Would it still be mine?"

Sam studied him curiously. "The nephew sold the house and all its contents without restriction."

"I see."

"You find something valuable?"

"Ooh, perhaps an antique or two."

"Yeah. Well, it's yours. Do what you want with it."

Before Dylan could respond, the older man made his way to the dark sedan in the driveway. Shep stood at the hedges along the side yard to watch him depart. He hadn't noticed her milling about, and when he glanced away for the briefest of time before looking back, the dog was gone.

Behind him, the door to the fish room opened. Vicki's soft laughter wafted through the back yard, and he turned to watch her tossing out Brenda and Chris with a wide smile on her face.

"Get a room!" she was ordering.

Brenda and Chris held hands as they hurried across the yard to the house. Chris glanced at Dylan with a telltale grin just before they rushed up the steps to the kitchen door. As they disappeared inside, Dylan turned back toward the fish house to see Vicki watching him. Her skin glowed and her strawberry blond hair caught the breeze and fanned out around her. She was smiling; despite the bad news Sam had brought, she was content, he thought; as she should be.

And with the fish taken care of and Brenda and Chris occupied, there was no time like the present to show her how very much he loved her.

3

It was barely seven o'clock but the skies had been pitch black for more than an hour. Dylan made his way into the living room, switching on some lamps as Brenda followed with a tray of coffee and cups, which she set on the coffee table. Chris was right behind her with another tray of warm apple pie slices cradled by scoops of vanilla ice cream.

"I don't know why you won't let me carry anything," Vicki said as she plopped onto the couch.

"I've told you a'fore," Dylan said as he joined her, "and you know what they say."

All eyes turned to him.

"If you carry a lot o' heavy thin's while you're expectin', the baby will be born w' a bad back."

Vicki, Brenda and Chris exchanged glances.

"It's true," Dylan added as he switched on the television.

Vicki passed the plates of apple pie to each of them as they settled in. At Dylan's exhale, she glanced up. "What is it?"

"Our show's been preempted." He leaned forward to stare into the screen. "Looks like your President is about to speak."

Chris took a healthy gulp of coffee. "Mind if we watch this?"

"Dylan hates politics," Brenda muttered.

"I do," Dylan agreed. "But if it's all the same to you, I'd like to hear what the President has to say."

"Really?" Vicki leaned toward him to look into his eyes. "You do?"

"Just this once, mind you."

They grew silent as they waited for the President to appear. For a few moments, the only sound was the four of them eating their pie and remarking on Benita's culinary achievement. The Mexican housekeeper and cook had made herself an invaluable member of the household; she went about her work quietly and diligently and always seemed to have everything clean and in place—and fabulous food awaiting them. And in the off-chance they'd experience an Apocalypse, the freezer was packed with enough prepared food to last months.

The announcement was made, returning everyone's attention to the television to watch the President make his way down a hallway to a waiting podium.

"Turn it up," Dylan directed Chris.

"This morning," the President began, "at approximately seven fifteen Eastern Standard Time, a sixth cargo ship bound from China to the United States was attacked and destroyed. These ships were unarmed. The attacks were unprovoked. They came without warning, destroying all goods on board and killing all members of the ship's crew on impact.

"All six attacks occurred in international waters along a route well known to merchant vessels. In proximity to each of these ships were other merchant ships leaving China for destinations all over the world. In each instance, only ships bound for the United States were destroyed."

Dylan took a sip of his coffee. He found himself staring into the President's eyes and wishing he could read his mind.

"We will not stand idly by," the President continued, "and allow such unprovoked attacks. We will investigate fully. We will identify the cowardly criminals. And we will hunt them down and bring them to justice."

"How many times have I heard that?" Chris muttered.

"But this brings to light another issue. An issue I brought up during my campaign. An issue I continue to believe is the right path for America and her citizens. We cannot control what happens in another country. International shipping lanes are not the sole jurisdiction of the American government and her peoples. And with unemployment at record highs, with so many of our own citizens wanting work, needing work and unable to find work, I reiterate a campaign promise. We must bring these jobs back home."

"The other party is going to pounce all over that," Brenda said wryly.

"I can't believe he's politicizing the bombing of those ships," Vicki added.

"I can," Chris said bluntly.

Only Dylan remained silent as he continued watching the President's facial expressions, his hand gestures, and those eyes that remained fixed on the camera.

"I call on every business owner in America who has moved their operation to a foreign country to close them down and to open them back up here in America, among your fellow citizens. If you are patriotic, if you believe in the future of America, if you believe in its citizens, if you believe in our country, you will bring those jobs back home!"

The last word was punctuated with his fist on the podium. His eyes narrowed as he continued staring into the camera. His mouth was set, his spine erect.

"I repeat. Bring - those - jobs - back - home!"

With that, he turned and began the brief walk away from the cameras. They listened to reporters' questions clamoring over one another, but the President continued walking as if he didn't hear them.

"Well, he does have a point," Vicki said, breaking the silence in the room. "They've closed down one factory after another and moved the operations overseas."

"I remember," Chris said, "when tax breaks were given to the wealthiest citizens. The theory was that those people created the companies that created the jobs that kept America moving. Now they have their tax breaks and they're employing people all over the world—except here at home."

"But you have to remember," Brenda said, "each one of those wealthy individuals is in business for one reason and one reason only: to make more money for themselves. If they have to pay minimum wage for a factory worker here but they can pay fifteen cents an hour for one in a third world country, that's potentially millions more in their own pockets."

Dylan set his coffee cup on the tray in front of him. The show they'd intended to watch began and soon the political talk dissolved into laughter as the comedy unfolded. Only Dylan was not laughing. He was too busy thinking and wondering what Sam had in mind for them tomorrow. For some reason he couldn't quite put his finger on, he didn't have a good feeling about it.

4

A full moon and a teasing mist greeted Dylan as he stepped onto the front porch. He paused for a brief moment to inhale a fresh floral scent. No doubt it was the witch hazel bushes, he thought, their yellow, ribbon-like autumn flowers coming to life under the gentle precipitation.

He locked the door and made his way to the porch swing. He was five minutes early and Sam was almost always right on time.

The street was quiet; dawn was still a few hours away. He longed to return to bed with his arms wrapped around Vicki's soft, yielding body, his hand on her slightly rounded belly as if protecting their unborn child. A chilly breeze whistled around the corner of the building, tussling his hair, and he felt goose bumps forming on the back of his neck. Aye, he thought. What he wouldn't do to be back in their warm bed right now.

He'd kissed her gently before leaving, but she hadn't awakened. He'd pulled the covers over her naked shoulder and quietly tucked her in. Then he'd made his way downstairs with his boots in his hands, past the closed door where Brenda and Chris lay sleeping, and into the kitchen to grab a muffin. He was tempted to eat two, as he didn't know what the day ahead of them would bring, but he hadn't known Sam to ever miss a meal.

As if on cue, he spotted headlights heading south on Elm Street. He remained seated until it grew closer and he recognized the dark sedan. He was down the steps, his long legs striding down the sidewalk briskly, and ready to open the passenger door before Sam had come to a full stop.

His car smelled of coffee and as he pulled away from the curb, Sam nodded toward the cup holders in front. "Hope you like hazelnut."

"Thank you," Dylan said, wrapping his fingers around the warm travel cup. "I do."

"So, I'll fill you in on some of our mission on the drive to the airport," Sam said, taking a healthy swig of his coffee. "Then the rest once we get there."

"The airport, 'ey?"

Sam ignored him as he continued. "The agency has secret prisons all over the world. They're known as Black Sites. You know why they're secret?"

"I'm thinkin' you'll be tellin' me."

"Because every country we're in looks the other way. Until we bring them to our shores, we're not bound to the same laws and regulations we have here."

"Is that the way of it, then?"

Sam turned the car to the right and took another sip of coffee as they moved toward the river. "The agency has a new method for interrogation. That's where you come in."

Dylan warmed his hands on the cup and tried to keep his face expressionless. Truth be known, he hated torture. Giving it or receiving it. Both were loathsome activities.

"We're supposed to be nice," Sam went on.

Dylan chuckled. "Oh? Is that so?"

"We're supposed to befriend them. Make them like us. Get a comradery going with them." His voice took on an edge of sarcasm.

"Are you jokin' me now?"

"Americans are hated."

"Not by everybody."

"By the guys we've got in prison, they are. But the Irish aren't."

"Ooh." They reached the river and Sam drove across the deserted bridge before heading down Second Street toward the airport.

"So here's the deal. We've rounded up the usual terrorists. Your mission is to get one in particular to talk."

"Sure, and you've given me the whole day in which to do it, 'eh?" Now it was his turn to use a little sarcasm.

"We've got scores of analysts in Washington," Sam continued as if he hadn't heard him. "Some of them are tracking on one specific individual. That's all they do, day after day. They know what that person ate for breakfast, lunch and dinner. They know who they saw and where they went and who they phoned. Hell, they even know when they've crapped."

"Scintillatin' job, I'm sure."

"Others have a target group. The Russians. The Chinese. The Eastern Bloc. Then those are divided into sections, reaching down to groups of three and then to one."

"So who will I 'ave the pleasure o' meetin' today?"

Sam gestured to the glove compartment. "You'll find the file in there."

Dylan removed a thick file from the glove compartment and leafed through it.

Sam flipped on a light that illuminated Dylan's lap and the file. "But here's the rub," he said. "Just before something big happens—like a ship being bombed—we usually have chatter. Phone calls. Emails. Communication of one sort or another."

Dylan nodded but continued reading through the file.

"After a bombing, somebody comes forward and takes the credit. Imagine. Bombing millions of dollars worth of goods heading to the United States. Then doing it six times. Around half the world, the group would be heroes. They should be celebrating in the streets."

"Well?" Dylan said, glancing up. "And are they?"

"No."

He waited for him to continue. Sam seemed focused on the street before them; it stretched out, wide and long, and completely deserted.

"There was no chatter. Before, during or after. And no one has taken credit."

Dylan stared at the picture of a middle-aged man. His skin was the color of molasses, his short hair more salt than pepper, and his ebony eyes cold; they were the eyes of a man without a soul, he thought. "Then this man—?"

"One of the usual suspects. In fact, it's a coup that we apprehended him."

"It must be difficult to live to middle age in Somalia," he said as he perused the file.

Sam chuckled. "Yeah. When you do what he does."

"Which is?"

"Modern day pirate. Oh, he doesn't get in the boat and prey on unsuspecting ships himself. No; he recruits young men to do it for him."

"And what does he get out o' it?"

"Money. Goods. Prestige." Sam cut him a sideways glance. "Especially when he can claim he's bested the United States." He turned the car onto the road leading to the airport.

"And you're thinkin' he's somethin' to do with the ship bombin's, I take it."

"That's what you're going to find out."

One more turn and they headed for the main terminal. It was a small airport, one used only for private aircraft and no commercial flights. The road was empty, as all of them had been, and though lights kept the airport runways visible, the hangars sat quietly, their doors closed. It would be some time, he surmised, before they came to life.

Sam parked near the front entrance.

"Am I takin' this w' me?" Dylan asked.

"It's yours. I want him to see how thick a file we have on him. He thinks he's been operating in the dark. It's time he knows he's been watched."

As they made their way to the terminal, Dylan's eyes scoured the glass and brick building. There might have been a dim glow inside, he thought, but if so, it was more emergency lighting than office lights. Or it might have simply appeared that way from the outside lamps shining their way inside. Either way, it looked closed and empty.

As they reached the front door, however, it swung open. A trim man with short hair and a blond mustache gestured them inside. No sooner had Dylan stepped foot inside the building than he heard the deadbolt locking behind him.

The man strode through the building from front to back, opening a door onto the tarmac. Again, once they'd passed through, the door behind them was locked.

A short distance away with the engine idling was a small passenger plane. He counted just four windows on a white aircraft with a wide blue stripe down the side. The man stopped at the base of the opened steps and wordlessly gestured toward them. Once Sam and Dylan were aboard, he followed, drawing up the steps before settling into the pilot's seat.

"Is he always so chatty?" Dylan asked as he selected a seat on the empty plane and buckled in.

Sam cast a sideways glance toward him before settling into a seat on the other side of the aisle.

Dylan turned back to the file. "Well," he said more to himself than to Sam, "we're off to meet me new friend then."

5

It looked like a warehouse. Only the armed guards encircling it silently proclaimed that it was not. Dylan glanced at the high barbed wire fences; and then there's that, he thought.

He was led down the side of the building to the last door. It was open, allowing flies the size of wasps to gather in droves. He brushed them away from his face as he made his way inside.

He found himself in a large room, empty except for three metal chairs, a metal table and a floor fan. The building was also metal and just stepping inside caused the perspiration to break out across his forehead and between his shoulder blades. Though the fan blades were rotating, the air felt heavy and still.

Behind the table was a scruffy man with unkempt hair and bags under his eyes that spoke of many a sleepless night. He was the thinnest man Dylan had ever seen; his face didn't appear to be more than five inches wide and his neck seemed to bleed right into his chest and arms as if his shoulders didn't even exist. His clothing was filthy but as Dylan studied him, he realized his shoes were expensive Versace's. The black leather was covered in dirt but as his eyes swept upward, he realized the cut of the shirt and the trousers were also those of a successful businessman.

"Are you just a mite warm in 'ere?" Without waiting for a response, he moved the fan closer to the table and directed the air flow toward the chairs. "Ah, that's much better.

"Me name's Dylan Maguire," he continued as he sat in the hard metal chair across from Shar ma arke Galaid. He casually dropped the hefty file on the desk and leaned back to look at the man he'd studied on the flight from America. His eyes appeared harder and more callous in person than they had in the surveillance photographs. His wrists were cuffed together with barely three inches between them.

Galaid didn't respond but continued staring at him as if he'd relish the thought of slitting Dylan's throat.

"I work w' An Garda Síochána," he continued smoothly, allowing more of his Irish accent to flow. "Are you aware o' 'em?"

The man rolled his eyes and looked away.

"The thin' is, I might be able to remove you from this place 'ere unless o' course, you'd prefer to remain w' the Americans." When he didn't respond, Dylan gestured toward the open door behind him. "Lovely beaches out there. I can hear the ocean from here. Must 'ave beautiful sunsets."

He waited a moment but the man was obviously intent on remaining silent.

"It's a long flight from Ireland," Dylan continued. "As you can imagine, I'm sure. And the food on the plane was atrocious. Have you eaten yet? Are you hungry?"

Galaid continued to stare at a point somewhere to the left of them, away from the door.

Dylan dropped his pen and bent to pick it up. He glanced under the table as he did so. Good; it was just as he'd been told. Both of Galaid's ankles were cuffed to his chair.

"No?" Dylan asked. "Then perhaps a smoke?" He pulled a half-empty pack of cigarettes from his shirt pocket and offered it to the man.

Begrudgingly, he accepted it and Dylan silently thanked Sam for the prop. He pulled out a lighter and politely helped him light it. Galaid drew in a long breath as Dylan returned the items to his pocket. The man's eyebrow rose slightly.

"I'm attemptin' to quit meself," Dylan lied. "I suppose I should toss 'em but I hang onto 'em instead." He was thankful he'd positioned the fan the way he had; it kept the smoke from encircling his head as Galaid exhaled.

"Would you care for 'em?" he said suddenly. He withdrew the cigarettes and left them on the table just out of Galaid's reach. He kept the lighter in his pocket.

Galaid eyed the pack hungrily. Ah, Dylan thought, now he knows I can be a friendly sort. Another smoke, somethin' cool and wet to drink, a little food... It will all be forthcomin' as I get to know you better.

It was approaching ten o'clock when Dylan stepped onto the boardwalk beside Sam. The sun had long ago disappeared beyond the horizon. With its warmth gone, the building had been transformed into a chilly, drafty and shadowy fortress.

He brushed a stray lock from his forehead as he watched Galaid being led away by one of the other operatives. He now wore an orange jumpsuit and no shoes, the chain between his shackled ankles so short that he was forced to shuffle along.

"I got nowhere," Dylan murmured to Sam. Though it hadn't been for lack o' tryin', he thought. He'd chatted with him until Sam had motioned for him at noon. While they took a lunch break, Galaid had been strip searched, removed of all his possessions, hosed down and given a prison uniform. When Dylan returned an hour later, the man had a cut above his brow that hadn't been there earlier as well as fresh blood between his toes, which remained bare.

He'd resumed his chat by reiterating that Galaid could leave with him and be treated fairly, if only he answered his questions. But though the man had begun to talk, he'd steadfastly denied having had any involvement in the ship bombings.

The scene was repeated a few hours later, when Dylan was relieved by two men with chiseled faces, muscular biceps and what looked to be a cattle prod. He'd heard a scuffle behind him and an agonized scream before he left, once more with Sam, though his dinner felt more like rocks going down.

Back and forth they'd gone until Dylan was tired and Galaid was exhausted.

Now Sam watched as they led the man around the corner of the building. "I wouldn't say that."

"But I didn't manage to get a single piece o' useful information."

Sam held up a CD. "We've got it all recorded. This will go to the analysts in Washington. They'll analyze every twitch, every movement of his eyes, every word he uttered. They'll know if he was lying."

"Do they 'ave the other blokes' interrogation as well?"

Sam began walking in the opposite direction from where Galaid had been taken and Dylan fell into step beside him. "Of course not."

"What will become o' him now?"

He shrugged. "He'll be held here indefinitely. They've got him on other charges."

"And where exactly are we?"

They crossed a barren courtyard. Once on the other side, he could hear an airplane as it was coaxed to life.

"Best you don't know."

As he glanced at the ocean, now murky under darkened skies, and mentally calculated the time in flight, he had a good idea where they were; he didn't really need Sam's confirmation, he told himself. "So, you don't think it was a wasted day then?"

Sam stopped beside a chain link fence. On the other side, the pilot sat in the cockpit with a clipboard, apparently going through a preflight checklist. "Do you think he was involved?"

Dylan stroked his chin. "To be quite honest w' you, no. I don't."

"Why not?"

"He was a braggart, once we got goin'. He claimed all sorts o' thin's, atrocities against all manner o' people. But he was particularly proud o' the crimes against Americans. It was clear he hates 'em." He grasped the fence and leaned into it as he thought through his day. "I truly believe if he'd had anythin' to do w' it, he would 'ave wanted to claim credit. I think there's a bit o' Somali honor in it, if you want to know me thoughts on the matter."

Sam nodded slowly.

"And I'm thinkin' whate'er those blokes did while I was gone and whate'er they plan on doin' to him now, it could result in a confession. But I'm not quite sure I'd be buyin' it."

Sam reached past him to open the gate. "You'll be back," he said over his shoulder as he started toward the plane. "He'll be broken down some more. Next time you see him, he'll be ready to be rescued by the Irish."

"And what will be done w' him then?" Dylan asked, following Sam across the tarmac.

"Nothing that wouldn't happen anyway. He'll stay right here." He glanced at Dylan out of the corner of his eye. "It's not like you really do work for An Garda Síochána. Nice touch, by the way."

"You know," Dylan said as they reached the plane, "I could serve time for impersonatin' the Garda."

Sam laughed out loud and slapped Dylan on the back. "Don't worry. What happens at a Black Site stays at the Black Site."

Before he could respond, Sam climbed aboard the plane and settled into a seat. Once more, it was just the two of them. As Dylan popped open a soft drink, the pilot secured the steps inside the aircraft. A few minutes later, they were airborne.

It was a cloudless night, so dark that he had a difficult time finding the moon and when he did, it was barely more than an emaciated crescent. The stars should have been bright and he should have been able to make out various constellations, but it was as if they'd been wiped away, leaving only a black void behind them. He placed the soft drink can in a cup holder and leaned back.

Sam switched on his overhead lamp and laid a briefcase full of papers across his lap tray. He was clearly engrossed in paperwork so Dylan closed his eyes. They felt gritty and they stung, as if assaulted by salty air and blowing sand. Soon the monotonous drone of the airplane lulled him to sleep.

6

Dylan buttered his blueberry muffin while he half-listened to Chris' and Brenda's good-natured banter. The kitchen was cheerfully bright; the trees had lost their leaves and more of the sun's warm rays made their way through the side window. It was, Dylan thought, as if the sun was teasing him into thinking it was temperate outside, though he knew better. It would be a chilly day, although it would feel balmy in the eighty degree temperature they maintained in the fish house.

"The polls may have him down for now," Chris was saying, "but he won't be there for long."

"Don't underestimate the female vote," Brenda shot back. "He's lied to two wives, cheated on them both, and now he's been found with a prostitute. You think any woman in their right mind would trust him with the country when he can't be trusted by his own family?"

"Voters' memories are short. It's something every politician counts on."

"I don't get it," Brenda said, her eyes narrowing although her lips curled into a smile. "Some of these guys act like we're still in the nineteenth century when the average voter didn't have a trail of evidence at their fingertips."

"But you have to want to find the trail," Chris said before leaning forward and pecking her gently on the lips.

Dylan sighed loudly and both turned to look at him.

"You have an opinion?" Chris asked.

"Aye. I do. M' opinion is politics should ne'er be spoken in polite company. Or at the breakfast table. Come to think o' it, at any table."

"But you have to be concerned about the future of the country. Where America goes, so goes the rest of the world." Chris leaned back and took a liberal sip of coffee.

"I'm sure the future o' the country will be just fine w'out me input." Before either of them could retort, he pointed his half-eaten muffin at them both. "Somethin' I learned growin' up in Ireland. Don't talk politics. Don't talk religion. And don't give your opinion unless you've specifically been asked. And *then*, consider where you are and who you're talkin' to a'fore answerin'."

"Sorry if we offended you," Chris said.

"I guess we'll have to watch the pundits in the privacy of the bedroom," Brenda added, a devious smile creeping across her face.

"Frankly, I don't want to know what you do in your bedroom. Pundits or otherwise." He turned toward Vicki, who was quietly listening to their conversation. "Darlin'," he said, leaning over her to lift a tray filled with meats, "you've hardly eaten a thin'. You must eat." He grabbed a couple of slices of bacon and two sausage patties and plopped them onto her plate. "You're eatin' for two now, you know."

Before Vicki could respond, Chris asked, "When are you due?"

"April 15," Vicki and Dylan answered simultaneously.

"Tax day," Chris said with a chuckle.

"Aye," Dylan laughed. "Tax day seems appropriate, don't you think? He should be a nice deduction o'er the next couple o' decades."

"*He?* Do you know—?"

"No," Vicki answered.

"Aye," said Dylan. "I make boys." At their raised eyebrows, he added, "I do."

Brenda took a sip of hot green tea as she peered over the cup's rim at them.

"Dylan, I have a favor to ask of you," Chris said, turning serious. He slipped his arm around Brenda's shoulders.

"Ask away."

"I don't want to impose on you, but I wondered if I might stay here for awhile." Before Dylan could respond, he hastily added, "I'd compensate you, of course. And I'd be happy to help out around the house with whatever you'd like me to do."

He finished the muffin before responding. "You're welcome to stay as long as you want. And I do 'ave a job for you. I meant to discuss w' you, somethin' Sam spoke to me about the other day—"

"Did I hear my name?"

They turned as Sam made his way into the kitchen. He started to place his briefcase on the kitchen counter, but at Vicki's slight shake of the head, he removed it and placed it on the floor instead. He poured himself a cup of coffee before filling a plate with sausage, bacon, eggs and a muffin.

"Why don't you join us for breakfast?" Dylan asked.

"Thank you," Sam said, pulling out a chair and making himself comfortable. "I think I will." He glanced around the kitchen. "Where's Benita?"

"Mexico," Vicki answered. "Her mother is ill."

"Any idea how long she'll be gone?"

"Just a few days. She's helping to move her into her sister's home for long-term care."

Sam bit into the muffin. "Who made breakfast?"

All eyes moved to Dylan.

"Pretty good," Sam said. "Pretty good."

"Dylan was just about to tell me what he'd like for me to do around here," Chris said.

"Aye. I was. Here's the thin'. W' the news o' that man breakin' out o' prison—"

"Joseph Gabucci," Sam offered.

"Aye. Him. It's been decided, Miss Carnegie," he looked pointedly at Brenda and waited for their eyes to meet before continuing, "that you should not be seen outside o' this house or the fish house. That's your world."

"Do I have to remind you that I am still wearing this ankle bracelet?" Brenda said humorlessly.

"It's for your own protection," Sam interjected. "Speaking of which, I spoke to the FBI agent in charge of your case this morning."

"Oh?" The color rose in Brenda's cheeks.

"They're issuing a press release about your capture. It's going to allude to the fact that you are behind bars."

"Are you here to take me back?"

"Not if you remain in this house. You can go into the back yard only to access the fish house. Nothing else. You do that, and you can stay here. Cross the line and you'll be back in prison—for your own protection."

"Where do I fit into all this?" Chris asked.

"You," Dylan said, pointing a finger at his chest, "are *her* babysitter."

"Excuse me?" Brenda said.

"And don't go thinkin' it's an easy task, either. It's the toughest job a man could 'ave. You've got to keep 'er in this house, even if she wants to go out to dinner, buy new clothes, get out an' about. You think you can handle it?"

To Dylan's surprise, Chris leaned back in his chair and steepled his hands.

"Aren't you going back to Washington?" Sam said after a moment of silence.

Chris shook his head. "After my boss was implicated in— shall we say, a questionable set of transactions—I was fired. Which is just as well, since I testified before a congressional subcommittee on the improprieties."

"I never meant for you to lose your job," Brenda said quietly.

"It's better than working for a crooked politician," Chris answered. "Anyway, it's too late in this election cycle for me to find another position as a political strategist. So I'll have to wait this one out, see who's elected, and start floating my resume after the first of the year."

"Even if they've just been elected?" Vicki asked, breaking her relative silence.

"Best time in the world. A good campaign takes years of strategizing. It's a full-time job for more than one person."

"Incredible," Dylan breathed.

"So what's your hesitation?" Brenda asked. "You don't think you can handle me?" She raised her chin. It was difficult to tell whether she was joking.

Chris turned to Dylan. "I'm up for the challenge."

"Excuse me," Brenda said. "I'm sitting right here. You'd think I wasn't in the room, the way you guys are talking about me."

"That's grand," Dylan said, rising from the table. He took his plate to the sink and rinsed it before adding it to the dishwasher.

"Don't go anywhere yet," Sam said in between bites. "I came to talk to you two." He motioned toward Vicki.

"It's time for me to do some babysitting," Chris said, pushing back his chair. He reached for Brenda's hand. "Upstairs."

Brenda started to pick up her plate but Dylan waved them on. "I'll take care o' it."

Sam waited until they'd left the room before continuing. "We're stumped on these bombings," he said.

"The ship bombings?" Vicki asked.

He nodded. "Dylan's already working on it. I need you on it, too."

"What do you need me to do?"

"Spy on the ocean," Sam answered.

Dylan nearly spewed his coffee. "Is that all?"

Vicki looked from Dylan to Sam. "He's right, Sam. What you're asking me to do is spy on an area larger than all seven continents combined."

"It's not quite that bad," Sam said. He wiped his mouth and dropped his napkin on his plate before rising. "Hand me that briefcase over there," he directed Dylan.

Dylan grabbed the briefcase. Sam pushed the breakfast dishes out of the way before opening it and pulling out a large map of the world. Spreading it before them, he pointed to a series of "x" marks. "Six marks," he said. "One for each ship that went down."

Vicki and Dylan leaned in closer.

"The path a ship takes from their point of origin to their destination is called a trade route. It might look to the untrained eye as if a ship just heads in a general direction but in fact, they travel an internationally recognized trade route." He pulled a ruler from his briefcase and placed one end at China's coast. "The Port of Tianjin is the largest port in Northern China, shipping over 476 million tons of cargo last year alone. With cargo headed to the U.S.," he continued, moving the ruler so the other end touched the United States, "Los Angeles is the most common destination. Other than a jog around Japan, it's pretty much a straight shot."

"So it appears," Dylan said, "as though the attacks occurred once the ships were almost dead center between the two continents."

"There's only four marks," Vicki pointed out.

"The other two," Sam said, dropping the ruler down slightly, "were on this shipping lane, from Hong Kong to L.A."

"But the distance between the two routes," Dylan said, placing his left thumb on the lower route and his forefinger on the upper one, "is not that far apart at this longitude."

"You got it," Sam said. "Los Angeles is roughly at a 34 degree latitude. Tianjin is at 39 degrees and Hong Kong is at 22. But when the upper and lower trade routes reach this point, they're within ten degrees of each other."

"How many kilometers are in a degree, I wonder?"

"Each degree of latitude is roughly a hundred and eleven kilometers—about sixty-nine miles."

"So if the attacks are within ten degrees latitude," Vicki said, "the area in question encompasses around six hundred and ninety miles."

"That's roughly the same distance as New York to South Carolina," Sam said. He raised his eyes to look at each of them in turn.

"You want 'er to spy on an area about half the length o' this country? 'ave you lost your mind?"

"That would be roughly six hundred and ninety miles between latitudes and four hundred miles wide," Sam continued. "Or, roughly, two hundred and seventy-six thousand square miles."

"You're completely off your nut." Dylan took a step back to straighten his spine and stare at Sam, wide-eyed.

"Sam," Vicki said, "Dylan's right. There's no way—"

"There's more," Sam said. "I can get a schedule of each ship as it leaves port. So we'll know when they're reaching that area. We'll know whether to target the upper or lower shipping lane."

"Then why not just train a satellite on it?"

"That's why I need you," Sam said. "I need to know where to train the satellite."

"But—"

"Give it a try. I wouldn't ask you if it wasn't important."

7

When Vicki was a young girl, long before a plane crash would take the lives of her parents and change her life forever, she used to stand in front of the hulking china cabinet in the formal dining room, silently studying the depression-era cobalt blue glasses.

"They'll be yours some day," her mother would say with a gentle smile.

She loved those glasses though she couldn't imagine why. They were thick, the glass imperfect. To a small child, the rim seemed endlessly fat and clumsy. But they had stems. She could envision herself holding them as a beautiful, grown woman, her fingers wrapped around those stems in a tantalizing manner, her lips pressed to the rim as she peered over the glass at her husband or lover. He would use them, too, and one day she would stand in her own dining room and tell her daughter that someday they would be hers.

She never knew what happened to them, a thought that occurred to her with sadness. One day she was ogling them. The next, she was homeless, unwanted, an orphan with nowhere to go.

She didn't know why she thought of those glasses now as she lay atop her bed, one arm slung over her eyes to prevent any fragment of light from entering. She could hear her own measured breathing and the steady tick, tock of the wall clock heralding the gentle passing of time. Then the sound of the clock faded and only her own breath filled the air, swirling around her in growing gusts.

When she opened her eyes, she was floating just above the surface of the water. She gasped as she realized the endless ocean that surrounded her on all sides was the color of those cobalt blue glasses. The surface was imperfect like the glass; bending and roiling and dancing with the rising wind.

She rose higher, bringing her hand to her brow to shield her eyes from the sun's relentless rays. Glancing to the compass she now held in her hand, she looked to the east toward the United States, but she could see nothing but the glassy blue surface of the ocean. As far as the eye could see, there was nothing but water meeting the sky, and where they met was anyone's guess. They blended seamlessly; the sporadic clouds reflected in the water so flawlessly that she wondered if it was really a reflection at all or twin sets of swirling puffs.

She turned slowly to the south and again, as far as the eye could see, there was nothing but water and sky. The air was thick with salt; she could smell the fresh perfume of the ocean water and could taste the salt on her lips. It seemed to cling to her lashes and invade her nostrils, repelling her senses even as she sought to breathe in deeper and inhale more of the pungent scent.

Again, she turned. The west appeared identical to the east and the south, broken only by occasional whitecaps that appeared out of nowhere and disappeared just as quickly. The roar of the ocean filled her ears—and nothing else. Shading her eyes further from the glaring sun, she looked to the skies for signs of life but there were none. No birds sang out. No planes ventured past. No sounds of thunder rolled by her. There was nothing but the solid, all-encompassing noise of the ocean surface meeting the air.

When Sam spoke to her, the roar lessened and she wondered if her senses had been at a heightened state or if the ocean had really spoken so loudly. Now she honed in on his voice and the numbers he gave her in a monotonous tone.

Instinctively, she glanced back at her palm. Now it held a GPS. She registered the latitude and longitude and adjusted her coordinates, flying upward and moving just above the water's surface. Back and forth she moved, constantly checking the GPS to ensure that she was turning outward in a growing circle, searching, searching...

A few minutes might have passed or a few hours. She grew ill and closed her eyes to the constant cobalt blue that now threatened to invade her senses. The mission, she reminded herself. I must complete the mission.

Sam read another set of coordinates to her and again, she adjusted. There was nothing as far as the eye could see.

Just as she was ready to report a lack of findings yet again, she thought she spotted something bobbing along the surface. She zoomed closer and closer still, until she realized she was staring at a cargo ship.

The broad surface of the ship was covered with metal rectangular boxes, each the size of a railroad car. She counted ten across at the narrowest point and fourteen across at the broad center. Row after row, they stretched—eighteen rows in all. The ship was massive, and yet as she glanced away, she realized it was nothing but a speck in the wide expanse of ocean.

She reported her findings to Sam, her voice sounding disembodied to her own ears as she spoke.

There were only two crew members moving inside a bridge that loomed over the rest of the ship, but she knew there would be more below deck. Logic dictated it.

After describing the ship that clearly bore China's flag and lettering, she moved outward, searching for any additional signs of life. But there was none. For hundreds of miles in every direction, there was absolutely nothing else.

She returned to the ship, checking her GPS and reporting back to Sam.

"I don't know what I thought we would find," he said. The monotonous tone he seemed to reserve for her psychic missions was now inflected with more than a little frustration. "It's like finding a needle in a haystack. Come on back, Vicki."

She felt her feet touching the deck, her clothes billowing out around her like thin gauze caught by the breeze. The gentle wind lapping against the surface of the water was the only sign of life outside of the bridge. What a lonely, desolate way to earn a living.

"Time to come back," Sam directed again.

She checked her GPS and turned toward the States, spiraling upward and away from the ship as she readied herself to return to North Carolina. She had just begun to move beyond the ship when a roar the likes of which she'd never experienced before enveloped her in a deafening, fierce explosion.

Instinctively spinning back to the ship, she was met with a wave of heat so brutal that she could feel her hair singeing. Her cheeks were scorched, and in an instant, she could no longer breathe.

"Vicki," Sam said, his voice rising. "Listen to me. Focus on the sound of my voice. Focus on me, Vicki."

She struggled to breathe but with every breath she took, she felt as if she was inhaling flames. They seared her throat as they leapt through her body into her lungs. She was dying. She was dying. The words became a refrain, shutting out everything else around her.

"Vicki." The Irish accent was insistent. "Don't leave me. Turn around. Come to me, Vicki. I'm waitin' for you. Do you feel m' hands?"

She couldn't feel his hands. She couldn't feel anything but charred skin. Her eyes were burned. She struggled to open them, but every movement was now excruciating. She wanted to scream, to moan, to cry out with the overwhelming pain, but her throat was scorched.

"Take me hand, Vicki. Take me hand and I'll pull you to safety. Do you feel me? Come to me, Vicki. You can do it. *You can do it.*"

She fought to open her eyes and with a sickening realization sweeping over her, she discovered her eyes had been open all along. There was nothing but flames in every direction. They shot upward without end, blocking out the sun and the sky. The ocean was ablaze, the inferno sweeping across the surface like the flow of lava across solid ground, unchecked and all consuming.

"Vicki!" He was shouting now. But where was he?

She struggled to see him, tried vainly to speak to him, but she was too far away. She couldn't reach him. The flames were too high, and nothing she did, no direction she turned, would take her away from the hell she would die within.

The slap across her cheek forced the air from her lungs. Before she could orient herself, she was grabbed unceremoniously and slapped again.

"Stop it!" she managed to croak.

The world stilled around her. Painfully, she opened her eyes and fought the dizziness that threatened to overwhelm her. She groaned and the hands lowered her to the soft confines of a thick comforter.

"Do you hear me?"

"Stop shouting," she moaned. She was going to be sick to her stomach.

"What happened?" Sam demanded.

She opened her eyes against the intensity of sudden light. "Turn off the light," she pleaded.

"There are no lights on," Dylan answered.

"What happened?" Sam demanded loudly.

"Jesus feckin' Christ," came Dylan's thundering voice.

Vicki opened her eyes once more and struggled against the sharpness of a room that seemed to glow.

Dylan grabbed Sam. In an instant, he'd raised him to his feet and punched him square in the jaw. Sam reeled backward, crashing against the dresser on the far wall. "I'll tell you what happened!" Dylan bellowed. "You near about killed 'er, that's what happened!"

Sam stared at Dylan with his mouth agape. "What did you do that for?"

"You're lucky I don't kill yer sorry arse!"

Sam raised both hands in a defensive gesture. "I'm not doing anything to her. She's okay. Look." He pointed. "She's okay."

"She's *not* okay!" Dylan shouted.

"Please." Vicki struggled to sit up.

"Stay right where you are," Dylan warned.

"Dylan, listen to me," Vicki said, her voice growing stronger. "I am okay. Look."

Dylan ran a trembling hand through his hair, but she didn't know whether it was trembling due to anger or fear. Then he was at her side, pulling her toward him and encircling her with his arms. "I've ne'er felt so damn helpless in all me life," he said, his voice still filled with boiling emotion.

Sam's cell phone rang and Dylan whirled around to face him.

"I'm just answering my phone," Sam said. "That's all I'm doing." He kept his palms open as though Dylan had pointed a gun at him before groping for the phone inside his pocket. Finally finding it, he brought it to his face as he answered. "Yeah. What? When? Are you sure?"

Vicki sat up straighter and despite Dylan's efforts to keep her firmly on the bed, she tossed her legs over the side and stared at Sam.

He took a deep breath, his eyes landing on Vicki as he listened to the voice on the other end of the phone. Then abruptly, he clicked off the phone and rose to his feet.

Dylan wiped the sweat off his brow and fought to calm his ragged breath.

"We're taking you to Fort Bragg," Sam said.

"Oh, no—" Dylan started.

"Don't do this," Sam warned. "She needs medical attention."

"You need medical attention!" Dylan repeated, turning to Vicki.

"She needs the doctors at Fort Bragg. Ones who understand our mission."

"What the—?"

"I don't have time to explain it now." Sam stopped a short distance from them, his eyes appealing to Dylan's sense of reason. "The ship she was on was just blown up. We don't know how she might have been affected. She's got to get checked out."

"Then get out o' me way, man!" Dylan roared.

Before Vicki could protest, he lifted her into his arms and raced down the steps, Sam on his heels.

8

The waiting room was empty except for the two men sitting side by side, uneasily watching the clock's minute hand tick so slowly it felt excruciating. Vicki had been in the exam room for nearly an hour.

"I should be there with 'er," Dylan's low voice broke the silence.

"Better that you're not. You—or I—would just be in the way."

Another five minutes crept past before Dylan spoke again. "Me apologies for punchin' you."

Sam rubbed his jaw, which was still red. "Apology accepted."

He turned to fix the older man with narrowed eyes. "But if you ever do anythin' else to hurt Vicki or me child, I swear to God I'll kill you w' me bare hands."

Sam studied Dylan's large hands before answering. "Respectfully, I didn't hurt her."

"What the h'ail happened back there?"

"It's hard to explain."

"Try."

Sam rubbed his eyes and leaned back in his chair. "During Vicki's mission, I received a series of text messages."

"I saw that you did."

"They were coordinates, the same coordinates I gave to Vicki. We had been tracking several ships in route to the States and the coordinates I gave her were the same ones the satellites were being redirected to."

"So if you had satellite technology, what did you need Vicki's spyin' for?"

"Vicki's vision is one more piece of the puzzle. She could move inside the bridge, if needed, or below deck. If anyone boarded the ship, she could overhear their conversation. She could give us a level we don't have with satellites."

"But how did you know that ship was bein' targeted?"

"We didn't. All we knew was the ship left China en route for Los Angeles. There are dozens more out there right now, following the same trade route."

"Then—"

"If she had spotted another ship—say, a pirate ship—she could have redirected her focus to them. She could have listened to their conversation and overheard their plan of attack. But there was nothing else there. Nothing for a hundred miles or more. The blast came without any warning."

"Well, it seems perfectly obvious to me what happened."

Sam waited for Dylan to continue. After a moment, he prodded, "Would you care to share it with me?"

"Why, a submarine, of course."

Sam began shaking his head but Dylan continued undaunted. "Your satellite wouldn't see a submarine submerged under the water; might not even be able to pick up a periscope in an ocean as vast as the Pacific. The submarine located the ship and bombed it. End o' story."

"That all sounds very logical," Sam said, "but we have our own submarines in the area. Where do you think the coordinates originated?"

Dylan leaned forward, resting his elbows on his knees as he thought. "So you're tellin' me that you had American submarines in that exact area?"

"Yep."

"And they spotted the cargo ship."

"Yep."

"And they relayed the coordinates to—?"

"Washington."

"And Washington redirected the satellites and also sent you a series o' texts with coordinates."

"Yep."

Dylan was silent for a moment. "And I suppose if there had been any other submarines in the area at'al, ours would 'ave known about it?"

"Yep."

"So where the h'ail did the bomb come from?"

"That's the question we're all asking right now." Sam sighed heavily. "That's the piece of the puzzle we have to solve."

"It wasn't a pirate ship," Dylan mused. "Nobody boarded the ship. Nobody fired on it from underwater. What about from the sky?"

"We were watching the skies also. For a bomb to hit that ship, they had to have been well within range for the satellites to pick up."

"What about stealth technology?"

"Nobody has it except us."

"Are you sure?"

"I'm sure."

"You'd stake your life on it."

Sam didn't answer.

"I said—"

"If—and this is a big *if*—a stealth bomber hit that ship, we're talking a superpower."

"Well, there's your suspects."

"Not quite. Since the Cold War ended, there's only one country who fits the definition of a world superpower, and that's the United States."

"Well, I'd adjust the definition if I were you because someone we can't see bombed that ship."

"The question is, why? Suppose China is able to develop a stealth bomber. Why would they bomb their own ship? They won't get paid for shipments that don't reach their destination."

"What about Russia?"

Sam waved his hand as if dismissing the idea. "The Russians don't have the technology."

"Then who—?"

"There are three recognized powers that are expected to claim superpower status in the 21st century. China—and it makes no sense for them to bomb their own ships—India and the European Union. India and the EU are allies."

"And what is China?"

"Worth watching."

Dylan rose from his seat and looked pointedly at the clock. "Still, I don't think they did it."

"What are they doin' to Vicki back there?" Dylan asked impatiently.

"That's the other piece of this whole puzzle."

"What do you mean?"

"You and I both know that Vicki's body never left the bedroom."

"Aye."

"Physically, from all that we could see and observe her body was never in any danger."

"I'm hearin' what you're sayin' and it's makin' perfect sense to me. But it doesn't explain what happened to 'er."

"The mind is a powerful thing," Sam said as he watched Dylan begin to pace. "Vicki's mind—some would say her soul— left her body and was transported to the exact location I gave her. When she's there, she can look down at what she believes is her own body—her own hands, for example. She might look at her palm and magically, there's a tool there—GPS, a watch, a compass, whatever she needs in her mission—and it feels as real as if I was sitting here holding it myself."

"Are you sayin' that Vicki can also imagine bein' hurt?"

"Yes. She can."

"So when she's on one o' these missions—"

"If she doesn't focus on the sound of my voice and my directives, she can feel as if she is physically threatened."

"Meanin'?"

"Let's say she had been on the ship when it exploded around her. She would have seen debris flying all around her, a tornado of destruction. Fire. Perhaps the screams of the crew, if they didn't perish instantly. She would have felt the heat. Perhaps would have felt it singeing her skin or her hair. If she went down with the ship, she could have felt as though she was drowning."

"But she wasn't burnin' and she wasn't drownin'. She looked to be asleep in our bed—until she began havin' breathin' problems."

"You know that. And I know that. But haven't you ever experienced a nightmare? One in which you woke up in a cold sweat, your heart pounding, unable to catch your breath—"

"Of course. But it didn't actually harm me. I didn't 'ave to go to an emergency doctor."

"But psychologically, Vicki was there. She knew it wasn't a dream. And when I ordered her to come back, to return to us in that room, for whatever reason, she was rooted at that bomb site."

Dylan stopped pacing and locked eyes with Sam. "Are you sayin' she could 'ave perished there?"

"I'm saying that," Sam spoke more slowly as if carefully choosing his words, "she could have been in such a level of shock as to put herself in cardiac arrest."

"So that's what they're checkin' back there?"

"That's what they're checking."

"Don't you think," Dylan said, his voice rising, "if she'd been in cardiac arrest, we should 'ave transported 'er to a hospital five minutes from the house?"

"And tell them what?"

"To check the damn heart!"

"Look. If she'd been in cardiac arrest, I could have performed CPR on the spot."

"Then why are we here checkin' 'er heart?"

"It's a precaution. They've got all her medical records on file here. They're just putting her through the paces to make sure she's not going to suffer any consequences."

"What about me son?"

"Your—do you know it's a boy?"

"I know it's a boy, even if the doctors don't know it yet."

"How?"

"Because I make boys."

Sam stared at him.

"It's beside the point," Dylan said in frustration. "If she could put 'erself into cardiac arrest, don't you think she could 'ave placed our child in jeopardy? A spontaneous miscarriage or somethin'?"

"Is there such a thing?"

"The h'ail if I know! I'm not a physician and I'm not a psychic, either. All I know is the woman I love is—" he waved his arms convulsively "—somewhere back there with me child in 'er belly. And if somebody doesn't come out 'ere pretty damn fast, I'm goin' through every room until I find 'er."

"Jesus," Sam said. "Get a grip. What're you gonna be like during delivery?"

"I won't be leavin' 'er side."

"You won't be sitting in a waiting room?"

"That's right. I'm deliverin' me child meself."

"You're delivering it."

"You heard me."

"A doctor—"

"Oh, I'll want a doctor to be there. You can rest assured o' that. But it'll be *my* hands on 'er, coaxin' 'er along, helpin' 'er with the pain. And it'll be *my* hands that catches our son when he makes 'is entrance."

"Well," Sam said. "You're a better man than I am."

Dylan began his pacing again.

After a moment, Sam stood up and patted Dylan on the shoulder. "Come on. Let's go find Vicki."

9

Sam's sedan blended into the muted rays of dusk as Vicki reached the bottom step to the front porch. Though it was still early—barely five o'clock—the light on the porch was already turned on as if welcoming them home.

Dylan stopped in the front yard to pick up the afternoon newspaper. He took a moment to peruse the headlines but the waning light was too dim. It's just as well, he thought. It had been a long day, an emotionally exhausting day, and he wasn't up to reading the news after all.

He had just turned around to follow Vicki into the house when a car pulled alongside the curb. He hesitated as the passenger side window was rolled down and the driver leaned across to speak to him.

"Excuse me," the man said, "I'm a bit lost. Can you tell me where the Comfort Inn is located?"

Dylan stepped to the side of the vehicle. Within a matter of a few seconds, his mind registered an older gentleman with graying hair and impossibly black eyes, an easy smile on his lips while he waited for Dylan's response. He was alone; the back seat was empty and the front filled with a mishmash of possessions.

"Ooh," Dylan said, leaning on the door, "you most certainly are lost. The Comfort Inn is back the way you came." He pointed to the north. "Elm Street here is a one-way street, so you'll need to take the next turn and take Chestnut, the next street over, back to the north." As he continued providing directions, the man listened intently, his eyes casually moving from Dylan's face to the house behind him and back.

"I don't know how I could have taken such a wrong turn," the man said when Dylan finished.

"Fortunately, it's a small town," Dylan said, his eyes dropping to the passenger seat. "You'll be there in no time at'al... Are those baby booties on your seat there?"

"Yes," the man answered. "I'm knitting them for my grandchild."

"Well, congratulations to you. Me own child is due in a few months as well."

"Is it?"

"Aye. A strappin' baby boy."

"Congratulations."

Dylan looked up from the tiny booties to find the man still smiling but his eyes seemed eerily emotionless. He began to feel a chill creep up his back. He straightened, removing his hand from the door. "Well, I won't be keepin' you then."

"Thanks for the directions." With that, the vehicle pulled away from the curb and the window was rolled up. Dylan waited until the car turned as he'd directed him before moving toward the house.

The sound of the television reached him as he stepped into the front hall. Striding to the living room door, he found Vicki already curled into an armchair and Brenda and Chris on the sofa. Brenda stared at a smartphone screen until Dylan wrenched it from her.

"Hey," she exclaimed. "What're you doing?"

He looked at the screen before answering. It was filled with the latest political poll results. "This your phone?" he asked Chris.

"Yes." Chris remained seated but his eyes narrowed as if he was trying to read Dylan's mind.

He tossed the phone into his lap. "She's prohibited from usin' the Internet. Part of 'er conditions."

"Sorry," Chris said, stuffing it into his pocket. "Why didn't you tell me?" he asked Brenda.

Before she could answer, Dylan said, "Ooh, she won't be volunteerin' information such as that, I can tell you that much. She isn't to use a computer at'al, and that includes phones, iPads, and other devices."

"I was just looking at polling with Chris," she pouted.

Though her lips were full as they curled downward into a frown, he wasn't buying it. "I don't trust you," he said bluntly.

She glanced at Vicki. "You've got a smart man there."

As Dylan made his way to Vicki's chair, she moved so he could perch on the arm. He leaned down and planted a quick kiss on the top of her head.

"Another ship bombing," Chris said, pointing at the television.

"Oh?" Dylan said.

"It's completely turned the upcoming elections upside down."

"How so?" Vicki asked.

"Before, the issues were all over the place—interest rates, tax structures, foreign policy... Now it's all about jobs."

"How could ships bein' bombed turn into that, I wonder?"

"Because they're ships loaded with goods bound for America," Chris continued, leaning forward. He clearly relished the chance to talk politics. "There's a movement underway for the factories built overseas to come home. Employ Americans for a change. Keep the manufacturing right here among the very people who buy the products."

"Is that right?"

"And those who are for it are getting a tremendous bump in the polls. Those against it are taking dramatic hits."

"Well." Dylan looked at Chris intently.

"It's all about the jobs," he continued.

The noise from the television grew as several men's voices rose in vain efforts to drown out their opponents. "Will you turn that off?" Dylan asked.

Chris muted it. "Political pundits."

"I've yet to talk politics or hear politics without feelin' the worse for it when it's over."

Brenda glanced at Vicki. "Where have you two been anyway?"

"I had a mission this morning," Vicki answered, avoiding their eyes.

"I thought you guys were here."

"We were," Dylan said, squeezing Vicki's shoulder. "And then we were called away to Fort Bragg."

"Without even saying good-bye?" Brenda asked.

"It wasn't as if we were leavin' you for good," Dylan said. "And don't try tellin' me you've gotten all squishy on me."

"All squishy?" Brenda laughed.

"I'm starvin'," Dylan said. "And I'd wager Vicki is famished as well."

"I don't have much of an appetite," she said softly.

"Ooh, but you must eat." Turning toward Chris and Brenda, he asked, "'ave you discovered any food Bennie left us?"

"Tons. There's a whole baked chicken in the frig."

"Ah, just what me stomach's been wantin'." He wrapped his arm around Vicki's shoulder. "Would you care to join me? You know what they say."

"Here it comes," Brenda said in a stage whisper.

"If you don't eat properly when you're pregnant, the child will be born fightin' anemia 'is whole life." She didn't answer and after a moment, he said, "It's true."

The bed was softly lit with candles on each of the nightstands. Dylan slipped a pillow underneath Vicki's head before lying on his side facing her. His fingertips followed her contours from her neck to her breasts before lazily moving down her hips.

"Are ya feelin' alright?" he asked.

She gazed into his eyes for a moment before answering. He smiled as he waited, his eyes turning into merry crescents. The hazel color was tinged with gold flecks, his large black pupils matching a thin ring of black at the edges of his irises. She pressed her finger to his lips and sighed as he gently kissed them. "Yes," she whispered. "Couldn't you tell?"

He laughed, his voice filling the room. "You were moanin' so loud, I half thought your sister would come bargin' in to see if I was killin' you."

Vicki felt the heat rising in her cheeks as she giggled.

"Would you care for somethin' to drink? I have red grape juice and white grape juice. In a wine glass, o' course."

"I'm fine."

"You're sure? It's no problem at'al."

She followed his gaze to the coffee table a few feet away, where the remnants of their dinner still sat. It had been a beautiful evening. Dylan had whisked her upstairs for a romantic dinner for two before making love to her. He'd been especially gentle since she'd told him of her pregnancy, which made her love him all the more.

"You're not feelin' dizzy or faint, I hope?"

"Not at all," she answered. She grew serious. "What happened to me this morning—it's never happened before."

"What was it like?"

"I thought I was going to be killed in the explosion."

"Couldn't you hear me callin' you?"

"Yes. But you sounded so far away. And I was surrounded by flames."

His brow creased as his hand squeezed her hip.

"You must have slapped me?" Vicki asked.

"I apologize. I most certainly would ne'er 'ave meant to hurt you. Especially with child. With or without child, come to think o' it. I didn't know what else to do. I was frantic."

"I've had some near brushes," she went on, allowing her fingers to follow his jawline, "and Sam has always been able to talk me back. But this time…"

Dylan waited through a few seconds of silence. "I don't like what you do, Vicki."

Her eyes had been following her fingers but now they locked onto his eyes. "What do you mean?"

"Sam 'as always informed me that you couldn't get hurt, that you went places only in your mind. But today I found out there is some danger to it. And I felt helpless watchin' you clearly suffer, not knowin' what to do. Then when Sam said we had to take you to the doctor, I could 'ave killed 'im with me bare hands for puttin' you in danger."

"That was a once-in-a-million experience. I'm sure it will never happen again."

"I can't lose you, Vicki. And I can't lose our child. I hope you understand that."

She smiled reassuringly. "You won't lose me. And we won't lose the baby."

He rolled onto his back and stared at the ceiling. "I plan to 'ave a chat w' Sam. Certainly he can place you on maternity leave."

She laughed. "Maternity leave is a matter of weeks, usually after the baby arrives."

"I don't care."

She inched closer to him, dropping her head against his chest. He ran his fingers through her long hair before caressing the back of her neck.

"It can't be good for the baby," he went on. "Whate'er symptoms your body was feelin'—heart palpitations, fear—our child would 'ave felt that too, don't you think?"

"I hadn't thought about it."

"Well, don't you think you should now?" His voice was tinged with impatience. "I'm sorry, Darlin'," he said in a softer tone. "It's clearly upsettin' me."

"Then talk to Sam," she said. "Maybe he can put me on less dangerous missions."

"I'll 'ave a word w' 'im tomorrow then."

"Do you have to go back to Fort Bragg tomorrow?" She lifted one leg over him and ran her hand along his muscled chest.

"I don't know. But I understand the new alarm system w' be installed tomorrow. I forgot to tell you earlier; I received a message on me cell. The men will be arrivin' by mid-mornin'. Cameras, motion-sensored lights, even the ability to see all around our grounds on the telly."

"Is that so?"

"Aye. It is."

She waited for him to continue but he remained silent. After a moment, she realized his chest was moving rhythmically. She glanced at his face to find that he'd turned his head to the side. His eyes were closed and his lips were slightly open. She watched him as he slept; his black hair was tousled from their lovemaking, one lock falling over his forehead to touch his brow.

Quietly, she slipped away from him. He murmured something and she hesitated until his breathing resumed a deep cadence. Then she leaned to each nightstand and blew out the candles. As the darkness descended, she snuggled against him once more, drawing the covers over them as they lay intertwined.

10

Dylan closed the door behind him and stepped onto the boardwalk, deep in thought. The air was stifling hot and so humid he could feel the moisture on his skin. The air didn't seem to move at all but languished over the prisoners. He peered down the walk at the row of cages at the far end. And they *were* cages, he thought. They weren't cells but cages like those found in old-fashioned zoos. They had no cover, no protection against the searing heat of the sun. Their inhabitants' only defense was to lie on concrete floors and try to outlast the hours stretched before them.

"Been waiting long?"

He turned as Sam strolled up the walk, his arms filled with papers.

"No."

"Come on," Sam said, brushing past him. "Let's go somewhere private."

He followed the older man around the corner of the building and past another row of baking men in stark cages, before entering a second building. The doors were open, revealing a lack of air conditioning, and fans in each room did less than a fair job of keeping the air moving.

Sam entered a snack room and headed straight for the coffee pot. "Care for some?" he asked as he poured himself a cup.

Dylan shook his head.

"There's soft drinks and bottled water in the frig there."

Dylan grabbed a bottle of water. He turned around just as Sam was disappearing into the hallway. He took long strides to catch up with him as he wandered to the end of the hall before turning into another. Finally, he stepped into an unused office and closed the door.

"There," Sam said. "That's better."

As he pulled out a chair at a small round work table, Dylan pulled up another.

"So," Sam said before Dylan had barely seated himself, "what's your assessment?"

Dylan took a deep breath. "You know I met w' Shar ma arke Galaid again. Spent all mornin' w' 'him, in fact." He leveled his eyes at Sam. "He might very well be playin' me for a fool. But I don't believe he had anythin' to do w' the ship bombin's."

"Why not?"

"He begged me to take 'im out o' this place."

Sam chuckled. "I bet he did."

"And I believe he would 'ave told me what I wanted to hear—what I needed to hear—for the chance to be in m' custody and not…" He waved his hand toward the door. "He's worn down. He's weak. And he's sick. And if he knew anythin', I believe he would 'ave informed me, even if the information was too little to do anythin' with."

Sam didn't respond but kept his eyes leveled on Dylan's.

"I also interviewed an Iranian. In theory, it makes a lot o' sense to think the Iranians are behind this." He paused.

"Go on."

"I know we discussed the superpowers in depth. But let's take another look at 'em, shall we?" Without waiting for an answer, he continued, "First, the European Union. They're allies. They have nothin' to gain by bombin' goods headed to America. Suppose I was a businessman in Ireland and I wanted the factory in me own back yard that's currently now in China. I'd still 'ave the challenge of gettin' me goods overseas. Bombin' a ship—or seven o' 'em—wouldn't help me own cause."

Sam nodded.

"India. They're also an ally. But given the same scenario, they'd have the same challenge o' gettin' their goods to America. So what good would destroyin' a few ships do 'em? Nothin' that I can see. Though India, I would think, would be—or could be—the most likely competitor for Chinese factories."

"Okay. So if we mark those two off the list, that leaves only China."

"And what good would it do 'em to bomb their own ships? Their people wouldn't want to board a ship headed to America on account o' the danger. Their factories wouldn't be paid for goods they couldn't deliver. And now we've got politicians clamorin' for the jobs to come home. None o' which helps the Chinese cause."

Sam steepled his hands and remained uncharacteristically silent.

"But there are countries who might be poised to become a superpower, one that we 'aven't considered as yet."

"And you're thinking Iran."

"I am."

"Did the Iranian give you any information to go on?"

"Not a damn thin'."

"Then why—?"

"He's cagey, that one. I know he's hidin' somethin'. I can feel it in me bones. You know how they say you can see a man's soul through 'is eyes? 'is are soulless. They're depths o' hatred and nothin' else."

"You want to stay on him?"

Dylan took a long swig of water and savored the refreshing feeling as it moved down his parched throat. "What would you 'ave me do?"

"You could stay here. It may take a few days or a few weeks, depending how tough he is to crack. He's been in here for eight months at least. He's either near the breaking point or he's hardened to the point where he'll never be."

"But if he's been 'ere for eight months, what could he know o' the bombin's?"

"Those things are planned sometimes years in advance. A lot of our enemies are very patient. They bide their time and strike when the timing's right."

"I also interrogated two men from Yemen. They 'ate America, that's pretty damn clear. But they don't 'ave the resources to 'ave pulled that off. Neither did the one from Pakistan or the Ukraine. They all 'ate the west. And if they could 'ave bombed ships headed to America, they certainly would not 'ave hesitated to do so."

"But you think the Iranian could have."

"Do we know what Iran 'as available to 'em? Do we know what their capabilities are?"

"I'm not on the Iranian task force. But I can get those answers for you."

Dylan stood up and walked to a small window in the far wall, where he peered out at another row of cages. This place was depressing. "I don't think leavin' me 'ere for weeks or months is the answer."

Sam didn't respond.

"If I provide a list o' the men I'm most interested in, what would be the likelihood o' gettin' the seasoned interrogators to break 'em down for me? Try the same tactic we did w' Galaid?"

"Say the word."

"I'll 'ave a list ready for you a'fore we leave."

"I still want Galaid questioned."

"Even after what I told you?"

Sam nodded. "He's important to the Somalis. I want to find out why."

"Fair enough."

The room fell silent as Dylan turned back to the window. The sun would soon set and as hot as it was at the moment, in another couple of hours the absence of the sun would herald a night of unbelievable cold. There was nothing to hold the warmth in; no trees and, he noted, no cloud cover. He wondered if the men would be left in the cages overnight.

"There's still somethin' eatin' at me insides," Dylan said, turning back to Sam.

Sam gestured, directing him to continue.

"How did they actually bomb the ship? With an American submarine patrollin' the waters, reportin' back that there were no other ships or submarines in the vicinity, what could 'ave blown a ship that size out o' the water? With the satellite focused on that exact longitude and latitude, they most certainly would 'ave seen a plane, had the bomb come from the air."

"We've got a team of analysts trying to figure that out."

"Could it 'ave been a mine?"

"Not possible."

"And why not?"

"It's Russian roulette. The chances of striking seven ships all bound from China to the United States is astronomically low. Those same waters are used by a variety of ships from battleships and carriers to goods heading all over the world."

"You've told me the probability but not why it's impossible."

Sam rubbed his chin thoughtfully. "I'll float the idea up the chain."

"It would be worth lookin' into, if you want me honest opinion about it."

Sam stood up and crumbled his empty coffee cup into the nearest wastebasket. "So what we've got so far is a hunch the Iranians did it with navy mines."

"Do you 'ave any better ideas?"

He opened the door. "We have hundreds of personnel working on this, from interrogators to analysts to strategically placed spies. Every snippet of information—including yours—is fed into supercomputers, where probabilities are analyzed and statistical conclusions are drawn."

"I'm not quite certain what you just said," Dylan said as he joined him. "But me question wasn't answered. Do you 'ave any better ideas?"

"Not a one," Sam said as he started down the hall.

11

It was after eleven when Dylan opened the front door and tiredly stepped inside. Sam was on his heels and though both had eaten at the Black Site, the food was undeniably lacking in taste and quantity. Bennie would, no doubt, have left something tantalizing in the freezer and whatever it was, Dylan was hoping it would convince his stomach that his throat hadn't been slit.

Before Sam had closed the door behind them, Dylan was lured to the living room by dancing blue lights that implied the television set had been left on. As he drew near, he found Chris sitting on the edge of the sofa cushion. His eyes were riveted on the television screen and his face had the same expression as one watching the final moments of a close Super Bowl game. He was so engrossed in what he was watching that he didn't seem to have noticed Dylan at the door and Sam coming up behind him.

Dylan's eyes moved through the otherwise dim room until they landed on Brenda. She was curled into an overstuffed chair, her long legs underneath her as they supported a laptop. Just as Chris' attention was held rapt by the television, Brenda's seemed immersed in the computer screen.

Dylan swore under his breath.

Chris turned toward him. "Oh, Dylan," he said pleasantly, "I didn't hear you come in."

"Obviously," he answered as he crossed the room and grabbed the laptop out of Brenda's lap.

"Hey," she complained, "what are you doing?"

Dylan turned toward Chris. "Did I not tell you that Brenda is forbidden from usin' any computer devices?"

"Oh, yeah. I—"

"Did I not tell you that meant smartphones, iPads and tablets?"

"Yeah, I—"

"Did I neglect to inform you that meant computers as well?"

"I'm sorry, I—"

"Computers, meanin' laptops, desktops or come to think o' it, any device at'al that 'as the ability to access the Internet?"

"You did."

"Are you understandin' that failure to keep 'er off the Internet could mean she gets imprisoned again?"

Chris' face turned white. "It's all my fault." He stood up and muted the television.

"It's clearly not all your fault, 'cause as I see it, you weren't exactly shovin' the laptop down 'er throat as I came in. Seemed to me, she was on it o' 'er own accord while you were completely oblivious to 'er breakin' the terms o' 'er release."

"I should have been paying closer attention."

"Will you two stop talking about me like I'm a two-year-old and he's my babysitter?" Brenda said in disgust.

"He *is* your babysitter," Dylan retorted. "And if he can't or won't do a better job o' keepin' you from the only thin' I asked o' 'im, then I'll have no recourse but to send you back to a jail cell."

Brenda bit her lip as the color rose in her cheeks.

"And chewin' your lip half off won't make thin's any better."

"I said I was sorry, Dylan," Chris said. His brows were beginning to knit and despite his words, Dylan could tell his patience was waning.

He spun on his heels and moved to a card table in the corner of the room. Without another word, he turned on a light and sat down with the laptop in front of him.

"What are you doing?" Brenda said, moving swiftly from the armchair to stand behind him. She made a move to close the cover but Dylan blocked her.

"I'll be seein' what's so damn important to you that you'd risk goin' back to prison to see."

"It's nothing—"

"Oh, it's somethin' alright." Dylan stared at the screen as Brenda seemed to hold her breath behind him. Sam quietly moved in beside Brenda and peered over his shoulder. "Are you understandin' this?" Dylan asked him.

Sam studied it for a moment before responding. When he spoke, he turned to stare at Brenda. "You'd better explain what's going on."

"Is it—?" Chris stopped himself and looked at Brenda. "You're not doing something illegal, are you?"

Dylan snorted.

"No," Brenda said indignantly. "I was not."

"What is this?" Sam said, his face reddening.

"It doesn't matter. You've all condemned me."

"He's givin' you the chance to explain y'self. Which is precisely what I'd be doin' if I were you."

"Will you listen?"

Sam and Dylan each crossed their arms in front of them as they waited. Chris perched on the edge of the table. The silence grew uncomfortable.

"Well?" Sam said.

"We were watching the news," Brenda began.

Dylan groaned.

"You might not care what goes on in the world around you," Brenda said hotly. "But I do."

"How did watchin' the news put the computer in your hands, I wonder?"

"Are you going to let me talk or not?"

"Everybody, silence," Sam directed. "Except Brenda."

"Another ship was hit this evening."

Sam and Dylan inhaled in unison.

"It wasn't destroyed—the crew was saved, at least. But it's sinking and it's doubtful they'll recover much of the cargo. So as

Chris and I were watching, of course representatives of both parties came on, pointing fingers at this or that extremist..."

Her voice faded and after a moment, Sam said, "Go on."

"So, I know just before a strike—the World Trade Center, an Embassy, whatever—there's chatter."

Sam straightened.

"Directly afterward, there's chatter. Even if the responsible party doesn't choose to call up NBC or CNN or FOX, they're taking responsibility among their own people. It raises them to hero status. It's like winning a decisive battle—the victor wants their supporters to know. If for no other reason, it proves they should continue."

"So what did you find?" Sam asked icily.

Brenda took a deep breath. "There is no chatter."

"There is none, or you were interrupted before you found it?"

"There is none. Trust me, I know where to look."

"*Trust me?*" Dylan scoffed.

"Bad choice of words, okay? The bottom line is, nobody is taking responsibility for it."

Sam moved to the edge of the sofa, where he sat heavily on the arm.

"You knew that already, didn't you?" Brenda asked.

"Yes. I knew it."

"Can someone fill me in 'ere?" Dylan asked.

"What she's saying is significant. There should be an Intelligence trail so wide and so obvious that we should know by now exactly who is committing these acts of terrorism." Sam sounded tired. "But whoever is doing it doesn't want the world to know who they are—not even their own supporters."

"Well," Dylan said, closing the laptop and standing up. "That's all well an' good, and the government is workin' on the issue. But the last time I checked, you, lassie, were not on the list o' employees." He tucked the laptop under his arm. "If I 'ave to lock up every damn piece o' electronic equipment in this house, I'll do it. Or you'll go back to prison and await your trial there. Take your pick. But I'll not be comin' into me own house again and findin' your felon arse abusin' me good nature."

"I'm really sorry," Chris said. "I should have been paying closer attention."

"You shouldn't 'ave to be sorry. And the truth o' the matter is you shouldn't 'ave to babysit 'er. She should be adult enough to understand the terms o' 'er release and abide by 'em." He reached the door to the living room. "You and your sister couldn't be more dissimilar." He hesitated and turned back to them. "Where is Vicki, by the way?"

"She went to bed a few hours ago," Brenda said.

"Is she ill?"

"She said her head was pounding from all the noise."

He felt the blood drain from his face. "What noise?"

"The alarm system was installed today."

"Ooh, that's right," Dylan said.

"It was?" Sam asked. "That was awfully fast."

"They knew exactly what you wanted—cameras, motion sensors… We didn't want to set it until you both knew the code."

Sam shook his head. "I just placed that order a day or two ago. Our guys are obviously getting faster."

"Oh, and that dog of yours wouldn't shut up. I thought she was going to attack the installer," Brenda added.

"What did you do w' 'er?"

"Locked her in the storage room in the fish house."

"What?"

"I didn't know what else to do with her, and the guy said he was only alarming the house."

Dylan felt his face redden. "Is she there now?"

"Of course not. The minute the guy left, I let her out."

"Where is she now?"

"With Vicki. She wouldn't leave her side."

Dylan didn't respond. He took the stairs two at a time to the third floor. He'd entered the darkened bedroom where Vicki lay sleeping before he realized he still had the laptop under his arm. As he turned to set it down, he spotted Shep lying on the floor beside the bed, curled as though sleeping but with one eye open and one ear pricked.

12

The intensity of the overhead fluorescent lamps coupled with the stark tiled floor provided an impersonal, dispassionate atmosphere that was in direct contrast to Dylan's and Vicki's mood. They'd spent the better part of an hour exploring color swatches in the vast hardware store before moving on to stenciling patterns.

"I love this," Vicki said, pointing to a pattern of ducks, giraffes and other creatures in a whimsical pattern. "We could paint the walls this shade of yellow—" she held up a pale yellow swatch "—and paint this border along the top, all the way around the nursery."

"Well now, Darlin'," Dylan said, swallowing. "Now that I've informed you that I make boys, don't you think it would work much better if we painted the walls this shade o' blue—" he held up his own swatch next to hers "—and used this pattern 'ere, w' the baseball bats, footballs and basketball hoops?"

Vicki smiled before rising up on her tiptoes to plant a soft kiss on Dylan's lips. "How can you be so sure it's a boy?"

"A man knows these thin's."

"He does, does he?"

"Aye. He does."

"And what if we decorate the room for a boy and find out it's a girl?"

"It won't happen. You must trust me on this, lass."

She studied the assortment of sports patterns. "We could wait until after the ultrasound is done and then we'll know for certain."

"And when will that be, I wonder?"

"I think it's around the sixteenth week."

"Ooh, Darlin'. Why wait nearly two months for a stranger to tell you what I already know?"

"Just to be on the safe side. It would still give us plenty of time to get the nursery ready—"

"I must respectfully disagree. I ne'er know where Sam is goin' to be sendin' me nor how long it will take. And I don't want to be rushin' through the whole process o' preparin' the nursery at the last moment."

"If we wait until the sixteenth week, it still gives us a good four or five months," Vicki said gently.

"Then we must compromise."

"How?"

"Well, from a purely male point o' view, the cute little giraffes and ducks there are—emasculatin'."

"For an infant?" She cocked her head. "Really."

"That's just me point o' view, if you want to know the honest truth o' the matter."

Vicki returned the stencils to their original place on the shelf. "I see."

"Ooh. You're angry w' me now."

"No… But how do you suppose a girl is going to feel if we paint the room blue and the border has all that sport stuff on it?"

"But I told you—"

"I know what you told me. But humor me, okay? What if there is the slightest chance that it's a girl?"

Dylan sighed. "Okay. 'ere's what I'll do for you. But only because I love you more than anythin' and I want to see you happy."

Vicki tried to suppress a smile.

"I'll paint the walls yellow. It's a nice, neutral color. And I'll even help you w' the stencilin' o' the wee animals. And I suppose when the child is born, it'll be awhile a'fore he'll even be able to focus on what's around 'im. But promise me, when it's a boy, as I know it's goin' to be, you'll allow me to redecorate and do a proper job for me son."

Vicki sighed. "Maybe we'll just paint the walls yellow and leave it at that."

"But what about the stencil?"

"We don't have to do it before the birth…" Vicki's eyes moved beyond Dylan.

He waited a moment for her to continue. When she didn't, he turned to follow her gaze. At the end of the aisle stood the man who had asked for directions in front of their house. He was of average height and he wore an overcoat that seemed a bit too large for him. Both hands were placed inside his pockets and for some reason Dylan couldn't quite put his finger on, that made him distinctly uncomfortable. He was also watching them intently with black eyes that didn't blink and which showed no emotion.

Dylan instinctively placed a hand on Vicki's shoulder. He glanced at her as he stepped in front of her to place himself in between her and the strange man. When he glanced back toward the end of the aisle, the man was gone.

"I don't care," Dylan said as he followed Vicki into the house. "Your safety is my responsibility."

He immediately turned to set the alarm. As the system began to beep, he glanced up to see Brenda coming down the stairs with Shep on her heels. "What's up?" she asked.

"Dylan thinks some guy is stalking us," Vicki said, removing her jacket.

"What?"

"I didn't say that," Dylan said. "I just thought it was peculiar, is all, that he stopped 'ere o' all places to ask for directions. And then we see 'im watchin' us in the store."

"Maybe he recognized you and had planned to say hello and thanks for the directions," Vicki said.

"I don't think so. Otherwise, he wouldn't 'ave disappeared the way he did."

Brenda stopped at the bottom of the stairs. Her knuckle grew white as she hugged the newel post. "You don't think it was…?" Her voice was dry.

Dylan's eyes met hers. "I'm not takin' any chances. I've phoned Sam. And from now on, the alarm stays on even when we're at home." He started down the hall toward the kitchen.

"We've been turning it on before we go to bed at night," Brenda said, following him as Vicki took up the rear.

"It will stay on durin' the day as well, until this bloke has been captured."

They found Chris in the kitchen, digging into a warm bowl of banana pudding. "How do you all manage not to weigh a ton?" he asked as they entered. "All this delicious food—"

"Dylan thinks he's seen Joseph Gabucci."

Chris stood up abruptly. "What?"

"I didn't say that," Dylan said.

"Then who do you think he is?" Vicki asked.

He exhaled sharply. "I just want to discuss the matter w' Sam. And as a protective measure, I want the alarm on all the time."

"What happens when we have to go back and forth to the fish house?" Vicki asked.

"You turn off the alarm at the kitchen door." Dylan strode to a second newly installed keypad. "Take the remote w' you and if there's anybody about, hit the key 'ere w' the picture o' a police badge. That'll set off the alarm. And if you reach the fish house w'out an issue, close the door immediately and reset the alarm on the remote."

Vicki let out an exasperated sigh.

"Better yet," Dylan continued, "neither o' the ladies are allowed out o' the house without Chris or I accompanyin' you."

"But—" Brenda began.

"I agree," Chris interjected.

"Dylan," Vicki said, her voice rising, "don't you think you're going a bit overboard?"

"That's me child you're carryin' there. And I love you and I love 'im. And I won't stand by and allow anythin' to happen to either o' you. Not when I could 'ave prevented it."

"Stop it, everybody." Brenda's voice was forceful. "Sit down." She pointed to the chairs around the table. With her jaw locked and her eyes narrowed, they all complied silently while she remained standing. Once they were seated, she stared at each of them in turn. "Let's assume for just a minute that this guy you've seen *is* Joseph Gabucci. Why is he here?"

They looked at her and then at each other. Finally, Chris said, "Why don't you tell us?"

Her jaw dropped. "I don't know."

"Don't play these games w' us," Dylan said. "If any one o' us knows why he's here, it's you."

"What I'm saying," Brenda continued, undaunted, "is there's no reason for him to be here. The whole bank scheme I was involved in is over. It was front page news, most especially here. It should be the last place he'd want to be."

"Okay," Vicki said, trying to keep her voice even, "let's think this through. Are you absolutely positive that he was after you two because of a bank scheme?"

"Absolutely positive," Brenda answered. "My partner was a bank employee. He had a touch of conscience and was going to go public with the whole thing. He said some things to the wrong person—got himself on a hit list, and me, too. You heard Sam the other day; this guy Gabucci was convicted. He should die in prison."

"He should 'ave," Dylan agreed. "A'fore he broke out."

"So the question," Brenda said more insistently, "is why would he come back here? With a double homicide all over the media, it blew the case wide open. Everything was laid out there for the whole public to see. It wasn't a secret anymore."

Dylan rested his arms on the table. "What else are you hidin'?"

"Hey—" Chris said, his brows furrowing.

"He's right," Brenda said, resting her hand on Chris' shoulder to keep him seated. "He must think I've got more information. Something that hasn't been made public."

"The list?"

"The list o' crooked politicians is w' the FBI now," Dylan said. "Surely, he would know that. Whether you lived or died, the list is in the hands o' the authorities."

"How would he know that if he's been in prison?" Vicki asked. "Sam even said the list hasn't been made public."

"And you haven't exactly seen a long line of politicians marched out of the Capitol, have you?" Brenda added.

Dylan cocked his head. "Go on."

"Each case requires additional investigation. Even when I've handed over everything I know, the feds have to build air-tight cases."

"So they'll arrest the politicians one at a time," Chris added.

"That's right. They could be days apart, weeks apart—even years apart. I've agreed to answer all the questions the feds put in front of me. But I have no idea how many investigative teams are involved."

"So this guy Gabucci could be tied to any one of those politicians," Vicki breathed.

"It's a crap shoot which one."

"Do you think he still wants you dead?" Dylan's question sounded painfully blunt.

Brenda swallowed. "Of course he does. I'm unfinished business. And I've brought nothing but trouble down on you guys ever since I've been here."

"That's not true—" Vicki protested.

"You're an enabler, Vicki," Brenda said, brushing off her objection. "And you two have a baby to think about now. I'm beginning to think the best place for me to be is locked away in a federal prison."

"But how do you know he won't find you there? If he's got friends on the inside—"

Dylan stood. "Brenda's right. We can't risk it. In federal protection is the best place for 'er to be. And not in our protection," he added before Vicki could interject. "Let's face it straight-on—you go places in your mind, Vicki. And you're pregnant. You're in no shape to protect a federal witness. And I've got me own cases to work. They're takin' me out o' this house and I've a feelin' they're about to get more time-consumin'. And don't even bother sayin' you'll take care o' 'em both," he added, turning to Chris. "She's obviously important to the FBI. They need to step up to the plate and protect 'er."

The room fell silent and as Dylan glanced from one to the other, each one in turn dropped their eyes. "You know I'm right," he said. "We'll wait until Sam is 'ere and we'll discuss exactly how we should make this happen."

13

Dylan remained a few feet from the door, his eyes shifting from the murky silhouette on the other side of the stained glass sidelights to the man in the living room peering around the drawn curtain. The clean-cut agent kept his fingers inches from his service weapon and nodded to Dylan to open the door.

He stepped to the door. Taking a deep breath, he inched it open, shielding his body with the heavy wood as he peeked around the edge. Then he sighed with relief. "Alec," he said, pushing open the screen door, "get in here."

Alec Brodie had barely made it into the foyer before Dylan was closing the door behind him, locking it securely.

Alec glanced into the living room through the open doorway. He was dressed in a suit, his sheriff's department pistol creating a bulge under his jacket. His sandy hair was a bit unruly as if the wind had caught it but the bags that once appeared under his eyes were dissipating. And so, Dylan noted, was his hefty midsection. He supposed moving in with his next-door neighbor Sandy had been a good decision for him.

"I saw all the vehicles outside," he said slowly, his eyes moving over the crowd gathered, "and I thought I'd see if you needed any help."

"I'm glad you're here," Dylan said, motioning for him to enter the room. "Everyone," he said in a louder voice, "this is m' neighbor, Alec Brodie. He's a detective workin' with the sheriff's department."

"We've met," the agent who had been peering around the curtain said, stepping forward and extending his hand. "Jim Beard. FBI."

"Yes," Alec said, shaking his hand. "We worked that hate crime together."

"And you remember Agent Roy Berkley."

Alec stepped forward to shake the other agent's hand. "I do." His eyes moved through the room, falling in turn on Sam, Vicki and Chris before stopping at Brenda.

"Come on in," Sam said. "Have a seat. You should hear what's going on."

"I didn't mean to pry," Alec said as he moved further into the room and took a seat. "It's just—when I saw the cars out front—well, FBI vehicles are easy to spot. I thought something might be wrong."

"Maybe not," Sam said, leaning back against the sofa. "You remember Miss Carnegie."

"Yes," Alec said, looking in her direction. Brenda kept her eyes cast downward, uncharacteristically subdued.

"She's been charged with multiple computer crimes," Sam continued. "While she's awaiting trial, the FBI was kind enough to release her into our custody."

"She's agreed to cooperate with some cases we're working on," Jim added. "In return, we'll recommend fewer charges or a lesser penalty."

"Things were pretty much going according to plan…"

Dylan nearly snorted but caught himself and coughed awkwardly.

"But then Joseph Gabucci escaped from prison."

"You remember him, don't you?" Roy asked.

"I was the one who arrested him," Alec said. "I testified at his trial."

"Dylan here," Sam said with a half-wave of his hand toward Dylan, "thinks he spotted him in town."

"Oh?" Alec sat up a bit straighter and peered at Dylan.

Dylan stepped to the coffee table and pointed at a picture they'd been studying a few minutes before Alec's knock on the door. "That's the bloke alright," he said. "W'out a doubt."

Alec glanced at the picture. "I see."

"Miss Carnegie has already turned over all the evidence involving the computer scheme," Sam said.

"I testified in Gabucci's murder trial," Chris offered. "I seemed to be the only eyewitness since…"

"Since Brenda had fled the country," Dylan finished abruptly.

"Anyway," Sam continued, "we were meeting to discuss our next course of action. It's unclear to any of us why this guy should come back here—"

"Unless he thinks he's got unfinished business," Alec concluded.

They all nodded. Only Vicki remained silent and still. As Dylan glanced at her, he thought she had clenched her eyes in an attempt to keep tears at bay. He made his way around the room to stand by her chair but when she opened her eyes, they were dry and she appeared resolved.

"So let's cut to the chase," Brenda said. Her voice was husky and strained. "I obviously need to be moved from here. The only question is where you guys are going to take me."

"I don't want you to go," Vicki argued.

"She's right," Jim said, motioning toward Brenda. "This was considered a safe house. Now that cover may have been compromised. The only way we can keep any of you safe is to move her to another location."

"And the sooner the better," Roy added.

"What about the press release you guys were going to do?" Sam asked.

"It was done two days ago. We reported that she'd been picked up and charged in a computer scheme. We also reported that she was in a federal prison awaiting trial." He cleared his throat. "She's considered a flight risk."

"Gee, wonder why," Brenda said.

"I've been—busy," Sam said, averting his eyes. "Do you know if the media picked up on it?"

Jim nodded. "Especially in the local news."

"We don't know whether Gabucci saw it," Roy offered. "And with him on the run, we can't be sure."

"Have you put out an APB on him?" Alec asked.

"He's on our Most Wanted. But whatever else you can do locally, we'd appreciate it," Jim said. "Especially since Maguire has positively identified him. We need local law enforcement on high alert."

"I'll do it right away."

"The question now is how to remove Carnegie from this house—and where to take her."

"I suggest that Detective Brodie get a couple of marked cars over here," Jim said. "Park them right in front so they're highly visible. Maguire, you got a camera?"

"On m' phone."

"Take pictures or video. We'll make sure the media gets it and we'll raise the hype so they're more likely to run it on television. We want the public—including Gabucci—to know she's been apprehended and she's in federal custody."

"Hold on," Dylan said.

All eyes turned to him.

"Are you tellin' me that you'll waltz 'er out o' here in handcuffs?"

"That's right."

"And the marked cars will be in front o' me house here?"

"Yes."

"That won't do."

"Excuse me?" Jim leaned forward, his eyes narrowing.

"This is me home. I've got a business in m' back yard here." He squeezed Vicki's shoulder. "And Vicki here's pregnant w' me child. I can't 'ave a spectacle in front o' our home. I can't 'ave the neighbors thinkin' we've been harborin' a fugitive. I can't 'ave a child brought into this world w' rumors circulatin' o'er his head."

"He's right," Sam said. "Vicki and Dylan work with me." He glanced at Alec, whose face was expressionless. "We can't risk blowing their cover. The community believes they raise freshwater angelfish. They don't know these gals are related. And for now, I want to keep it that way."

The room fell silent. After a few moments, Jim asked the obvious. "So, how are we going to do this?"

"I can see your back door from the driveway," Alec said to Dylan. "Ever since you tore down that old garage, there's a clear view from the side street."

"And?" Sam prompted.

"We can pull a vehicle almost to the back door. We can take her out of the house without anyone seeing her."

"What about the video and the media?" Dylan asked.

Alec stroked his chin thoughtfully.

"You drive a marked vehicle, don't you?" Jim asked him.

"Yes."

"And you live next door?"

"That's right."

"We want you in on the pickup. Even if the neighbors see you, they're probably accustomed to your vehicle in the neighborhood."

They all began to nod in agreement.

"Where's the county jail?" Roy asked.

"A few miles from here."

"We'll take her to the county jail. We'll get it on video as she's removed from the car and escorted into the jail. Once she's inside, we'll take her right back out and put her in one of the FBI vehicles."

"And take her where?" Vicki asked.

"To an undisclosed location."

"But—"

"It's best you don't know where."

"He's right," Jim said. "The fewer the people who know where she's being kept, the more secure she will be. You'll all be," he added.

"I like the plan," Dylan said. "It takes the media attention away from this house. And she'll be in safe custody every moment. I take it that you blokes will arrange to get the video to the media?"

"They'll have it in time for the late night news."

"You mean—" Vicki started.

"We can't waste any time," Jim said. "The longer she's here, the more danger you're all in."

14

The hotel room was dark but that's the way Joseph liked it. It was a welcome respite from the never-ending brilliance of overhead lights in the prison, lights that were never turned off even as they slept. Their rude intensity had penetrated his lids until he became accustomed to sleepless nights, nights in which he'd lain awake listening to the arguments of others and the cries of grown men.

The only light in this room came from two laptop screens that sat nearly side by side on the corner desk. One was opened to the Internet, a research tool he'd referred to in the best and the worst of circumstances. The other was split into multiple views, each one focused on a single room, hallway or stairwell. He zoomed into one of them, opening it so it encompassed his entire screen. Then he leaned back in his chair and allowed a slight smile to tug at the corners of his mouth.

They were all there, he thought; all the players in one small space—Brenda Carnegie, Christopher Sandige, the FBI and the CIA. Even the man who'd arrested him, Detective Alec Brodie, was there.

It had been too easy. The work request for the alarm system had been intercepted by one of his associates and passed along to him. He glanced at the chair in the far corner where a blond wig, cap and beard lay beside an alarm company uniform. He'd been a bit apprehensive at approaching the house; Chris, Brenda and the Irishman would have recognized him if they looked close enough. But luck had been with him.

Early that morning, he'd watched as the CIA department head had picked up the Irishman. Then he'd driven down the street, stolen an alarm company van and parked it in a far corner of the hotel parking lot, where it remained while he'd eaten breakfast, returned to his room, changed into his disguise and returned to the rambling house on Elm Street.

A car was missing from the driveway and the Irishman's live-in girlfriend had answered the door. He'd spent the better part of the day installing cameras around the perimeter of the house as well as his own hidden surveillance cameras in the kitchen, living room, two bedrooms, the stairwell and the downstairs hallway. He'd programmed the system and then instructed the young woman named Vicki how to use it.

He'd taken his time once he'd discovered that Chris had spirited Brenda out of the house. He'd hoped they would return while he was there; it would have made his job infinitely easier.

Now he cracked his knuckles while he listened to them discuss their plans. On the other laptop, he pulled up Google Earth and zoomed in on their house and neighborhood. Now his job would be slightly more difficult—but he would be successful. Of that he was certain.

He'd waited at the house until he could no longer justify his presence there, and they still had not returned. So he'd come back to the hotel and had been watching ever since.

Chris and Brenda had arrived home in the late afternoon, seemingly giddy in each other's proximity. They'd retired to her bedroom, where Joseph had been treated to quite a show. His cheeks flushed with the thought of it. Afterward, they'd gone downstairs and turned on the television and a short time later, the Irishman had arrived home. They'd never mentioned that they'd left the house; most likely, Joseph thought, because they were bending the rules.

Well, he might have missed them then. But he wouldn't allow them to slip through his fingers again.

So, he thought as he sipped coffee that had long ago chilled, they intended to take her out of the house within minutes. He cocked his head and weighed his options. He had night vision goggles and he might be able to find a suitable spot to lay in wait until she exited the house; then he could dispose of her sniper-style. But, he debated himself, he was on the south side of town— the opposite direction from the Comfort Inn, the hotel he'd asked directions to. It had been a name pulled out of a hat; a name on a sign the same as a dozen other hotels he might have used instead. But he knew, even as he asked the Irishman for directions, that he was already checked into a hotel on the south side, miles away.

It might take him fifteen minutes to reach their house and another ten to get set up, if all worked according to plan. He hated a rush job, though. He was methodical and preferred to be well-prepared for any contingency. Rushing to their house now, climbing a tree or clambering to a roof while hoping some idiot neighbor wouldn't walk their dog at an inopportune time, wasn't his style.

He continued to listen to their conversation, the back and forth between them triggering a mental note as to the hierarchy. Clearly, Sam was in control even though Brenda was under the jurisdiction of the FBI. Interesting, he thought. He might be able to use that information later, should the situation warrant it.

When they decided to take her to the county jail for the video and the swap, he turned to the other laptop and pulled up the sheriff's department website. Then he switched back to Google Earth. Although the sheriff's department had a Lumberton address, it was situated in a more rural area, one that appeared to be outside of the town proper. He zoomed in on the facility.

No, he thought. It was too risky. There were wooded areas nearby; close enough for him to easily shoot her as she was removed from the vehicle. That wasn't the problem. He'd been able to play at this game for so many years because he always had an exit strategy. And shooting her in front of the county jail would bring too much attention. They would swarm the woods and even if he managed to outmaneuver those on the ground, they would certainly call in reinforcements—dogs or helicopters.

He panned the image between the jail and the house. But, he thought, that left a bit of rural area in between. They would be in a vehicle with perhaps one in front and one behind. He'd have to separate them… Or would he?

With one eye on the screen monitoring their conversation, he unplugged the other laptop and slipped it under his arm. Crossing the hotel room, he pulled an innocuous looking piece of luggage from the closet. Everything he needed would be right in there—sniper rifle, pistols, and even improvised explosive devices. He left the room silently, making his way down a darkened hallway to the parking lot behind the hotel.

15

Dylan watched uneasily as the two dark sedans backed down the driveway. Alec's marked car was at the curb; to the neighbors, it would look completely natural, he thought, sandwiched in between his house and the home Alec shared with Sandy. He recognized the first vehicle backing down the driveway as Sam's; it pulled ahead and stopped at the corner. The second one contained the two FBI agents in the front seat; as it passed under the streetlight, Dylan caught a glimpse of Brenda's red hair in the back.

As they paused in the street to switch gears, Dylan fought the rising sensation in his gut. It felt like a rock growing. It became harder and larger until he was having difficulty swallowing.

Sam pulled away from the stop sign, turning south on Elm Street. As he passed in front of the house, the door behind him opened and Chris stepped out. Shep trotted to the top step but didn't descend from the porch.

The second car was barely a car length behind Sam. Dylan glanced behind him as Vicki joined them.

"I thought I told you it would be easier on you if you didn't see 'er off," Dylan said. His voice seemed to catch in his throat. He hoped they hadn't noticed but when he peered at Chris out of the corner of his eye, he was looking at him strangely.

Alec pulled his car behind the FBI vehicle. Dylan watched them travel down Elm Street—a convoy without appearing as such.

"I know," Vicki was saying. "But I just have this strange feeling."

"Oh?" Dylan felt as though he was only half-listening. He wished he knew why his stomach was turning summersaults inside him.

"This doesn't feel right," Vicki said, shivering in the night air.

"What do you mean?" Chris asked.

"I can't put my finger on it. But I just have the feeling that this isn't right. It's not the right time. Or the right place. Or… something."

The first vehicle turned the corner. Dylan slipped his hand in his pocket and fingered his truck key.

The air around them grew tense as if static electricity hovered just above their heads, waiting to jolt them.

The second vehicle turned the corner behind the first.

"Get in the truck," Dylan ordered. Before they could answer, he was down the steps and heading to the driveway.

He might have been surprised to know that both Vicki and Chris hadn't hesitated to follow him, but he was too focused on the truck to notice they were right on his heels. By the time he reached the driver's door, Chris was rounding the truck bed on his way to the passenger side. And once Dylan opened the door, Vicki was there, climbing up before he could even raise a hand to help her.

He had the engine started and was backing down the driveway before their doors were closed.

"Sam," he said, cradling the cell phone between his cheek and his shoulder, "this isn't right."

"We discussed it. It's a done deal."

"Vicki has a feelin'," he pushed. "Somethin's not right."

"Sam, don't do it," Vicki shouted to be heard.

"You want us to turn around and go back?" Sam asked. His voice was mellower and Dylan could almost feel the wheels turning.

"Where are you now?" Dylan asked.

"Crossing the Lumber River."

"There's a KFC on the left."

"I see it."

"Stop there in back o' the restaurant. I'll be there in less than a minute."

"We can't have a meeting in a parking lot—"

"No meetin'. We're switchin' Brenda to me truck."

"We're—?"

"Call the others. You'll have to hurry."

———   ———   ———

The sky was black and though it appeared completely cloudless, Dylan couldn't see any stars at all. He pulled in front of the three vehicles at the far side of the parking lot. He left the door open as he strode quickly to the FBI vehicle.

Jim was out of the car and had the back door open before Dylan reached them. "You're the lead vehicle," he said as Brenda climbed out of the car.

Without a word, Dylan grabbed her hand and escorted her abruptly to the waiting truck. "Where's Vicki?" he asked as he peered inside.

"She's riding with Sam," Chris answered.

"Get in," Dylan ordered. Brenda slipped in without a word and without her usual bravado. He thought her face appeared paler but he didn't have time to ponder it. He climbed in behind her and closed the door, placed the truck in gear and headed for the road. The entire switch took less than one minute.

He was about two car lengths in front of Sam's car as he turned down Martin Luther King Boulevard. He glanced in his rear view mirror as the FBI vehicle turned. He could see the front end of Alec's car before he focused on the road in front of him. Something still wasn't right.

"You're too far ahead," Sam said as if reading his mind.

Chris held the cell phone in front of them, the speaker loud and clear.

"I don't want you too close to me," Dylan responded. His voice sounded even but his insides were still churning. He could hear voices in the background. The communications radio, he thought.

"Alec has called ahead," Sam said. "They're waiting for us at the jail."

"Isn't that risky, doin' that on the radio?"

"Secure channel."

"It's too risky," Dylan insisted.

"We're almost there."

The traffic was sparse. As they moved further from the heart of town, it grew thinner until only the four vehicles remained. The houses and storefronts were behind them now, replaced by trees. Something was very, very wrong.

They were nearing the intersection where he would make the final turn as instinct kicked in. His foot slammed the gas pedal, causing Brenda and Chris to lurch in their seats. The vehicle accelerated rapidly and he gripped the steering wheel with both hands. He heard Chris' and Brenda's voices tumbling over each other but he couldn't concentrate on their words. The cell phone Chris gripped in front of them bounced up and down and from left to right as the vehicle strayed from the inner lane to the outer and then took the turn back to the right in a wide, chaotic arc.

The road was dark and he kept his eyes focused on the swath of pavement the headlights panned in front of him. He saw a hubcap hugging the line down the center of the road, as if it had fallen off a passing vehicle.

Then his eyes glimpsed something else a car length ahead of the hubcap—something larger, like a carburetor. He passed the hubcap when he spotted a third piece of metal, also in the center of the roadway, an equal distance from the second one.

He swerved onto the shoulder of the road, nearly hitting the ditch in his fervor. Brenda let out a poorly stifled scream as the cell phone catapulted out of Chris' hand.

"Right!" Dylan shouted. "Go to the right!"

He glimpsed into the rear view mirror as Sam followed him onto the shoulder of the road. They were lined up, Dylan thought as his eyes remained riveted on the mirror, lined up like sitting ducks.

The third device he'd spotted and the one closest to them, was even with Sam's vehicle when it exploded, sending flames twenty feet into the air. For a moment, he couldn't see the vehicle, and he slammed his foot on the brake as he continued staring.

"Don't stop!" Brenda screamed. "It's a trap!"

"Vicki's back there!" Dylan yelled. His voice reverberated through the cab. He turned around, his eyes scanning the smoke behind them.

"Go!" Brenda and Chris both shouted in unison. "Go!"

The corner of Sam's car became visible as it veered back onto the roadway. It was accelerating and before Dylan could turn back around, they swerved to the far side of the road and then back into the center as it passed them. He caught a glimpse of Vicki holding onto the handle above the door before he slammed his foot onto the gas pedal.

Behind him, another explosion sounded, sending another plume of smoke and flames into the air, followed by a third.

"Who's behind us?" he demanded as he glued his eyes to Sam's bumper in front of him.

Chris turned around. "I can't see anyone," he said in a hoarse voice. Then a moment later, "It's too much smoke. It looks like the whole road is on fire."

Sam's taillights were rapidly disappearing and Dylan leaned into the steering wheel as he accelerated to close the gap.

"Someone's coming out of the smoke," Chris said nervously.

"Keep your eyes on 'im," Dylan demanded grimly.

Seconds passed that felt more like minutes. Dylan was acutely aware of the sound of their breathing: Brenda's, ragged and low; Chris', filled with anxiety as if he was catching it in his throat; and his own, heavy with rage that was growing inside him.

"It's Alec," Chris said, his voice loud in the close confines of the truck cab.

"Is 'e followin' us, then?"

"No. He's pulled around in front of the fire and stopped his car."

More seconds passed. Dylan glanced in the rear view mirror. They would soon be out of sight.

"I think he's gotten out of the car and he's going back on foot," Chris said. His voice was tinged with disbelief.

Dylan exhaled sharply. That's what he would do, he thought. He's seen us speed off and he knows we'll do our best to keep Brenda safe—keep all o' us safe. But if Jim and Roy are in need o' assistance, his trainin' will cause 'im to go back for 'em. "Call 9-1-1," he said suddenly.

"What?"

"Tell 'em about the explosive devices. Tell 'em there could be two and possibly three officers injured."

Brenda and Chris began scrounging around the floorboard in search of the cell phone while Dylan leaned further into the steering wheel and tried to keep from getting too far behind Sam. He saw the taillights disappear suddenly and his eyes roamed from right to left, searching for the sedan. Then he spotted the glow from the headlights as it traveled along a perpendicular road. He barely slowed as he took the turn. The truck bed whipped too far to the left and he found himself fishtailing along the country road. His knuckles were white as he gripped the steering wheel, his eyes unblinking and focused on the taillights ahead of him.

He barely heard Chris' voice as he made the phone call. Somewhere in the back of his mind he heard sirens that sounded miles away, the sound traveling across the open fields and cloudless skies.

He didn't see Brenda wrench the phone from Chris' hands but in the next moment, it was her voice filling his ears. And as she placed the call on the speakerphone, he heard Vicki's voice in response. She was measured and calm and the sound of her voice began to slow the frenetic beating of his heart.

"Does Sam have a destination?" Brenda was saying.

There was a slight lapse. "No," Vicki said.

"Then tell him to take the next right turn and an immediate left."

In front of him, Dylan saw the taillights swerve to the right. Then through nearly naked tree branches, he spotted them swerving back to the left. He followed a few seconds later, his mind focused on remaining on the road as the truck again began to fishtail.

They were traveling at a 45-degree angle through fields of cornstalks that had turned brown in the autumn season.

"In about a mile, you'll see another road on the right," Brenda was saying. "Turn there and then take another left in a quarter of a mile."

"Okay," Vicki answered. Dylan could only assume she also had the speakerphone on and Sam was following her instructions without wasting his energy or focus to speak. "Where are we going?" Vicki added as they took the first turn.

"Lumberton Police Department," Brenda said.

Dylan's concentration was nearly broken as he jerked his head toward her. Just as quickly, he turned back to the road to make the turn after Sam's sedan.

"I'm taking you around the outskirts of Lumberton. We'll enter from the east."

They took the next turn a quarter of a mile later. Brenda continued issuing curt instructions and both Sam and Dylan followed them without question. The two women sounded completely calm, which astonished him. Perhaps he expected tears or hysteria, but he was thankful neither manifested itself.

The city lights loomed in front of them. Sam reached the first stoplight, slowed so briefly that Dylan wondered how he could have known it was clear, and then breezed right through the red light.

"Clear!" Chris yelled as they entered the intersection.

Dylan also ran the light. A siren split the air and as he glanced into the rear view mirror, he spotted a marked police car pulling out of a parking lot, the blue lights flashing.

"I've got an officer on me tail," he said.

"Don't stop." It was Sam's voice now, husky and tense, as the sedan sped up once more.

With Brenda directing them, they maneuvered through sleepy neighborhoods at the speed of NASCAR drivers. Another police car joined the pursuit and up ahead a third was approaching from the opposite direction.

"Next left!" Brenda yelled.

Sam took the next turn with Dylan on his heels, missing his bumper by mere feet.

"Right!" Brenda yelled.

They made the next turn at breakneck speed. Ahead, Dylan could see the police station looming. Two more blocks, another turn and they both careened into the parking lot with four police cars in hot pursuit.

Sam didn't slam on his brakes until he was almost over the sidewalk. Dylan stopped so suddenly, he thought for certain he was going to ram Sam's sedan but the truck managed to stop inches from his bumper.

The police cars surrounded them and as Dylan looked out his driver's side window, he saw them approaching now on foot with their guns drawn.

16

Joseph closed the door to his hotel room. Wasting no time, he retreated down the corridor and slipped out the side entrance where his car waited just outside. He tossed the luggage into the back seat, climbed into the front, and headed toward the interstate.

He should have removed his belongings before the hit, he thought. It was a stupid mistake. A hired man always left his temporary lodgings before striking; one never knew if the destination afterward would be changed out of necessity. Roads could suddenly have police blocks, someone could have been in hot pursuit, or he'd simply need to leave town quickly.

Just as he was doing now.

He checked his speedometer, careful to remain under the posted speed limit as he entered the highway and merged with traffic. He wouldn't go far; the South Carolina border was just twenty miles away. He would find a place to hold out until he could regroup and form a new plan.

He cursed under his breath as he drove, the sound of his own voice sounding foreign to him in the confinement of the vehicle. His plan should have worked, even though it had been hastily carried out.

He had an arsenal of improvised explosive devices. The more robust they were, the larger and bulkier they tended to be. He usually had a few auto parts, things that might easily fall off a vehicle—like a hubcap, though the carburetor had been a stretch. The IED was then placed under it—or in the case of the carburetor, carefully planted inside of it. Then there was nothing left to do except wait.

He'd driven to the road he thought they would certainly take en route to the county jail. He'd quickly but methodically marked off the spot where the first vehicle, the lead car, would pass. The second IED was the largest one, the one he designated for *her*. It was carefully placed two car lengths behind the first vehicle. The third device was placed two car lengths behind that one.

He didn't know for certain that there would be three cars, but he figured on a lead vehicle to smooth the way and a follow-up vehicle to protect the rear. The target would be in the center vehicle. They always were. It was supposed to be the safest position.

He'd then moved nearly a mile away, parked his vehicle into a wooded area well out of range of any lights, climbed a tree and waited with his three remote control devices. Each device was the size of a cell phone—and had actually been constructed out of cell phones. It was an ingenious device, one he'd used many times before.

Where the hell the truck had come from, he didn't know but it had certainly screwed up his plans royally. He'd watched through high-powered binoculars as it drove the stretch of road ahead of the three in the convoy. Whether the driver had thought the debris in the road was suspicious, he didn't know. Maybe the guy was drunk. Next thing he knew, the truck was swerving off the road, kicking up a mountain of gravel and dirt.

He'd waited until the first convoy vehicle was at the spot he'd carefully identified and detonated it. But the car had followed the truck off the roadway and the device he'd so carefully planted just on the right side of the center line, did not cause the damage he'd anticipated.

Still, it had resulted in the desired effect. The two vehicles behind the first one came to a screeching halt. When that occurred, he set off the third explosive device, striking the sheriff's vehicle in the rear. That simple step prevented the rear vehicle from backing up and allowing the target vehicle to spin around and retreat in the opposite direction.

A split second later, he detonated the center device. There was nowhere for the target vehicle to escape; in front of them and behind them, the air was filled with flames and smoke. The nails he had added to the IEDs had done their job as well; spinning in every direction, they would have flattened the tires and embedded themselves into the glass and metal on the vehicles.

But the target device—oh, that had been lovely. He could see the car parts flying through the air, the sound reverberating through the still night. The tree in which he'd perched shook with the violence of the explosions, the first from the detonated device and the second from the gasoline tank.

So why did he have this strange feeling that something was wrong?

Maybe it was the way the truck had stopped briefly before speeding away. He would have expected them to pull off to the side, perhaps get out and approach the other vehicles. Sometimes there's a wannabe hero who will attempt to brave the flames to pull out the victims. But almost always a witness will phone 9-1-1 from the side of the road, their eyes riveted to a horror they can't bring themselves to turn away from.

Or maybe it was the lead vehicle. It was part of the convoy; he was certain of it. He could spot a government vehicle any time, any place. The purpose of the lead vehicle was to make certain the protected individual reached their designated rendezvous. But it had pulled away.

He felt the blood draining from his face, leaving his cheeks ice-cold.

She hadn't been in the center car.

The lead vehicle had not hesitated to get away from the explosions. They hadn't stopped to lend assistance. And as he'd followed it through his binoculars, he'd not only seen its pace increase at a breakneck speed but once it had passed the truck, the truck had sped up as well.

Brenda Carnegie had been in one of those two vehicles.

He crossed over the state line into South Carolina and immediately began searching the road signs for a motel. This time, he was looking for a place with exterior room doors. No more corridors or passing through the lobby, he thought. He needed a quick getaway when the time came.

He took the first exit off the interstate, his mind already a dozen steps ahead of himself. He needed to set up those laptops. And he needed to check every room in that rambling old house. If she was there, he would get her. And if she wasn't, he would find her. It was only a matter of time.

17

Dylan stood on the front porch, his arms surrounding Vicki's small frame as he pulled her close. Despite their plans, he'd still ended up with a marked police car in front of the house. Thankfully, he thought, they'd had the sense not to turn on their blue lights though if any of the neighbors glanced out their windows, they wouldn't be able to miss the vehicle just a few yards from the front porch. Another one was parked along the side street. Both were empty, the officers busy inside the house, presumably going from room to room to search for any sign of an intruder.

He wove his fingers through Vicki's long, strawberry blond hair until his fingertips found her scalp. He massaged it idly as he peered over her head at Alec's house next door. He felt as if he'd been kicked in the gut; the porch light was on next door, no doubt waiting for Alec to arrive home. And he had no idea whether he'd been injured.

His eyes moved steadily over his neighbor's house, stopping momentarily on the kitchen window before moving upward to the second floor. A dim light shone through the windows there; an indirect light, he thought, like a hallway light filtering into a bedroom.

He swore under his breath.

"Did you say something?" Vicki asked. Her voice was so low it was almost a whisper.

"No, Darlin'," he said. He took a deep breath. "The important thin' is you're unharmed."

It had been an experience he never wanted repeated. Not only had they narrowly escaped the explosions but he'd found himself in a police department parking lot surrounded by uniformed officers, all with guns pointed in his direction and yelling for him to put his hands in the air. He'd thought he was a goner for sure.

He didn't know what Sam said to them. He could barely see around the officers to notice that he, also, had his hands in the air. Brenda and Chris did as well, but for some reason, what bothered him the most was seeing Vicki forced to raise her hands as if she was a dangerous felon.

Then the officer beside Sam's door opened it, said a few words he couldn't hear and then reached inside. From where Dylan was sitting, it appeared as if the officer had reached to a pocket inside Sam's jacket while Sam still had his hands raised in the air.

Then in unison, all the officers holstered their weapons.

One had opened Dylan's door and asked for his identification. His hands shook as he pulled out both his driver's license and his CIA identification. They'd asked Vicki, Chris and Brenda to do the same.

Then apparently satisfied that they were government employees and Brenda was the only felon among them, they'd directed them into the police station, where they'd remained for the better part of an hour.

The best part of it was they learned the fate of the others. The worst part of it, he thought, was they learned the fate of the others.

Jim and Roy were dead; they'd never had a chance. It would take an autopsy to determine whether they died from smoke inhalation, the flames, or trauma from the explosion itself. He hoped it had been quick. The thought of them suffering and perhaps trying to get out of the vehicle while he sped away was enough to keep him awake at night. The guilt would weigh on him; he knew it would.

Sam's vehicle had avoided a direct hit because he'd swerved off the road away from the IED. The maneuver had saved him—and more importantly, it had saved Vicki and his unborn child.

The rear explosion had hit Alec's car. He'd apparently already begun to back up and because he wasn't following too closely, the front of the car had absorbed the brunt of the impact. He'd been skillful enough to circle the other vehicle even though his own was disabled, make certain those in front had escaped, and radio for assistance.

All that the officers were able to tell them was that Alec had been taken to the hospital; they didn't know the extent of his injuries.

A police officer stepped onto the front porch and Dylan reluctantly released his hold on Vicki as he turned toward him.

"All's clear," the officer said. "The dog is still inside but on its way down."

"There was no sign of forced entry?" Dylan asked.

"Everything looks good. You didn't have your alarm set?"

He shook his head. He wanted to add that in their haste he hadn't taken the time, but it seemed like a flimsy excuse at the moment.

Another officer stepped onto the porch, one hand loosely holding the leash of a large German shepherd.

"Well, I'd set it if I were you," the officer said.

Dylan started to respond with something witty and then realized it wasn't witty after all so he remained silent.

"Can we go in?" Vicki asked.

It wasn't until she spoke that he realized how chilly the night air had become. She shivered, her arms wrapping around her midriff as if to stave off the cold.

One of the officers held the door for them and Dylan motioned for Vicki to move inside. He started to follow her but stopped at the threshold. "What now?" he asked.

"Our orders are to remain here."

"Inside? Or—"

"Out," the officer answered. "I'll be out front. Simon," he motioned toward the officer with the dog, "will be on the side." He handed him a card. "That's my cell phone. If you need me, I'll be just steps away."

Dylan took the card and turned it over in his hand. "Thank you."

"Now set that alarm," Simon said, politely but firmly.

"Aye." He stepped inside and then turned back around. "When will you know about Alec Brodie?"

"We'll check with the hospital. You want us to call you?"

Dylan searched through his pockets until he found a scrap of paper. He wrote his phone number on it and handed it to the officer. "Thank you. Oh, and m' dog—a border collie—in me rush to leave, I left 'er on the front porch." He half-waved toward the porch. "She's gone. But she may be comin' back." When the officer didn't respond, he continued into the house and closed the door. She'd come back, he told himself. She always did.

Dylan turned on both showerheads before turning back to Vicki. She was slowly removing her clothing; her mouth was pursed as though her mind was wandering. Her shoulders were slumped and as she stepped out of her shoes and pulled off her jeans, she looked tired.

He unbuttoned his shirt as he watched her undress. His hands moved of their own accord, almost robotically. He sat on the chair in front of the dressing table as he pulled off his boots. He hadn't realized just how much his feet ached until they were free of their confines. Shedding his socks, he bent over his feet, massaging each in turn. Why did his feet hurt? He wondered.

The answer wasn't long in coming. Every muscle ached. As he stood, he felt Vicki's eyes on him as he unbuckled his belt and slipped off his jeans. His eyes met hers; he thought he detected longing and love… but also pain and worry.

He stepped toward her, pulling her into his arms. The
bathroom was beginning to steam up and he closed his eyes as
he breathed in the fragrance emanating from Vicki's hair. It
smelled of honeysuckle; light and fresh and floral. After a
moment, he reluctantly let her go. He pulled back the shower
curtain and managed a small smile as she stepped past him.

Once in the shower with the dual showerheads spreading
their warmth over them both, he was able to pull her back into
his arms and simply stand there with his chin resting on her
head. The water was almost too hot as it pounded across his
taut shoulders, but that was the way he wanted it. It beat against
his physique, across muscles that were stretched tight from
prolonged tension; muscles that felt too strained and too
inflexible.

"God, this feels good," Vicki murmured.

"I could stand here all night," Dylan agreed.

A moment passed with only the sound of the water beating
down upon them. Then he said, "Do you 'ave any idea how
frantic I was for your safety?"

She hugged him tight before answering. "Sam was great.
Something kicked in and he acted like he was on autopilot. He
was very calm, not flustered at all."

"And you?"

"Strangely, the same. I wasn't panicked at all."

"Good."

"And you?"

"Depends on who you ask, I suppose. I also remembered
m' CIA trainin'. But inside… I just knew I couldn't lose you."

He closed his eyes against the spray and remained in that
one spot until he was certain his shoulders and his back were
bright red from the assault. But finally, he began to feel the tension
subside. He breathed in Vicki's scent as he began to knead the
muscles around her shoulder blades.

She moaned and he opened his eyes. "Did I hurt you now?"

"No," she said softly. "Don't stop."

"Ah, now that's an order I love to hear." He reached beyond
her for the soap and lathered it between his hands before he
returned to massaging her. She leaned into him, pressing her

cheek into his chest as she continued to groan with pleasure under his hands. He could feel her tension melting away and could almost feel her body becoming more pliable. His hands moved from her back to her hips and as she stepped back slightly, his fingers traveled to her pelvis and up to her breasts.

"You know what they say is a great tension reducer," Vicki said quietly, a shy smile creeping across her face.

He bent his lips to hers, brushing over them lightly before fully tasting them. He kept his eyes open, watching hers crinkle with a soft grin. He pulled her close and as they embraced, he felt the sensuous lather from her breasts transferring to his broad chest.

"Why don't you show me?" he whispered.

⁙⁙⁙⁙

Dylan plopped onto his back with a satisfied exhale. "Oh, Darlin'," he breathed as she cuddled against his side.

"I should feel guilty," Vicki said.

He peered at her out of the corner of his eye. "We didn't do anythin' we've not done a'fore."

She giggled. "I should feel guilty for making love while my sister sits in a jail cell."

"A holdin' cell," Dylan corrected gently. "And the Lumberton Police Department is the safest place for 'er to be at this point."

"I know," Vicki conceded. She ran her fingers across his chest, tracing the muscles.

Dylan kissed her forehead. "The FBI is sendin' a task force to transfer 'er to a federal facility," he said. "She won't be in that cell for long."

"Then she'll just be in another cell."

"Maybe. Maybe not." He squeezed her shoulder. "They might transfer 'er to a safe house and she might be quite comfortable."

"I doubt it."

The phone rang and he groaned. "Who could—?" He peered at the caller i.d. "It's the police. 'alo? Aye, this is he… Oh… Oh, that's good news indeed… Oh, thank you. So he's to be home soon? Thank you." He clicked off the phone.

Vicki rolled over so she was resting almost atop of him. "Well?"

"They're keepin' Alec hospitalized but he's actually doin' quite well. He's a bit sore is all but he'll be fine." He sighed. "Thank the Good Lord."

"I wonder where Chris is?"

Dylan checked the clock on the nightstand. "He might still be w' Sam. He was hesitant to leave 'im, wasn't he?"

"He was hesitant to leave Brenda."

"Aye. He's a bit stuck on 'er, don't you think?"

She ran her lips across his. "Yes. He is."

"Anyway," he said, a sly smile crossing his face, "he's got a key to the house and the alarm code. He'll be fine on 'is own."

Vicki returned his smile. "What are you thinking?"

"I'm thinkin'," he said, running his hand over her skin, "how much I love your pale skin."

She laughed. "Never heard that before."

"You know, in times past, a woman w' a fair complexion such as yours would 'ave been considered a member o' the elite."

"Is that a fact?"

"That is a fact. Those w' tans would 'ave been those who had to work outside. A fair maiden was one who was pampered and cared for."

"I want to be pampered," Vicki whispered.

He placed his hands on the small of her back and looked deeply into the amber eyes he'd grown to love so much. They nearly glowed as she gazed back at him. "It would be m' pleasure," he answered as he gently pushed her off him and onto her back.

18

Joseph kept one eye on the television set and another on the laptop. He felt like a man who wanted to watch two shows at once and had to choose between the two. It was a particularly difficult decision.

On the television, a reporter informed the public of the explosions as film footage from a business' rooftop showed flames on the horizon—flames that were purportedly from the IEDs. Apparently, the fire had been seen for miles around and multiple calls had been placed to emergency operators.

They'd already determined that three IEDs had been placed in the roadway but they incorrectly identified the target as the two FBI agents and Alec Brodie, never mentioning Brenda Carnegie. Then they showed his prison photograph, a picture that was taken on one of the worst days of his life and it certainly showed. His jaw was tensed, his lips thin, and his eyes narrowed to near slits. His hair was clearly shown and instinctively, he ran his hand through the slick locks.

The reported motive was his capture after the double homicide; they assumed he was seeking revenge on the detective who had arrested him and helped to bring him to justice—and the FBI agents who had investigated the computer fraud.

He rose from his chair and dug out his electric razor from his luggage. The bathroom vanity and mirror were just a few steps from the bed in the decaying motel, and he stepped toward them with a critical eye focused on his hair. Then he plugged in his razor and ran it across his skull until a full head of hair was scattered in the sink, on the counter and on the floor. He stroked his smooth head as he peered at himself in the mirror.

His eyebrows were thick and black. He leaned in close to the mirror and carefully used the razor to cut them down to thin wisps. Then he studied his reflection again. Funny, how changing one's eyebrows could have such a dramatic effect.

He cleaned up the mess he'd made, placing the hair into a plastic bag meant for dirty clothes. He would discard it the next time he left the room—he wouldn't leave it here for the maid to find.

He tied it closed and then tossed it at the foot of the door where he wouldn't be likely to forget it. Then he returned to the chair.

The news had moved on to a storm out west and he turned toward the laptop.

What a show, he thought as he watched. He didn't often have the opportunity to be such a voyeur but the spectacle was difficult to turn away from. It almost made him wish he had a wife or a girlfriend—or anybody.

But his lifestyle had never permitted room for a meaningful relationship. He was a hired mercenary, just as likely to be sent to Europe or Asia as he was North Carolina or Washington, DC. He had no political ideology, no affiliations. Someone paid and he did the job. Simple as that.

He picked up the knitting he'd laid on the bed earlier and began to knit as he watched the young couple in their bedroom. Not surprising that she's pregnant, he thought. My God.

He glanced at the baby bootie in his hand; he was almost finished with it. He enjoyed the knitting and one day he hoped to open a crafts shop. He would stock it with the very best in materials and might even hold knitting classes.

This baby bootie was a delicate pink. He always got admiring comments when people thought he was knitting for a grandchild.

Years ago, he'd told people they were for his own children, though he'd never had any. He just knit them and when he was finished, they always seemed to find a home. Next, he might knit a pair of blue ones. He certainly had the yarn.

He glanced back at the screen which was split into blocks, each one depicting a room, a hall or the stairway in the old house. Everything else was silent and empty. It was clear that Brenda Carnegie had not yet returned. And neither had Christopher Sandige.

He turned off the television set. The hidden camera was providing more than enough to hold his attention. As he continued knitting, he kept one eye on the young couple and another flicking across the other rooms, looking for movement that never came.

When his cell phone rang, he muted the camera. He knew who was phoning him; only one person had his number. "Yeah?" he answered.

"Status."

"She got away."

There was a pause. Then, "She's wearing an ankle bracelet."

"Find out where she is, and I'll be there."

The phone clicked off. He turned the sound back on and resumed watching the two lovers.

19

She wasn't quite sure what roused her from sleep. But as Vicki slowly opened her eyes, she became aware of her nude body lying on one side with Dylan's larger, muscular form curled up behind her. One arm was stretched over her protectively and her derriere rested against his lap, their legs intertwined.

Normally some moonlight found its way inside, but the room was so murky that she wondered if there was any moon at all this night. She narrowed her eyes in an effort to adjust to the darkness as Dylan's measured, soft breathing remained against her ear.

She nearly gasped as her eyes fell upon a figure just a few feet from the bed. She frowned as it swayed in front of her; it was not flesh and blood—that much was obvious. It was almost opaque and as she continued to stare, it grew more luminous until a tiny woman stood in front of her with long, flowing white hair billowing about her as if blown by the wind.

She wore a thin nightgown that reached from the base of her neck all the way to her feet, and as Vicki continued to stare, she smiled.

"Mam," Vicki breathed as she recognized Dylan's grandmother.

Dylan murmured something incomprehensible and held her more tightly against him.

"Be careful what you do, child," Mam said in a clear voice. "There are eyes on you."

Vicki gasped and grabbed at the bed covering. "You shouldn't be watching us!" she exclaimed.

Dylan awakened and leaned over her to look at her face. "What is it, Darlin'?"

Vicki could feel the heat in her cheeks. She half-turned to Dylan to see him watching her with sleepy eyes. "I—" She turned back to where his grandmother had stood, but she was gone.

"Another bad dream, mayhap?" he asked before settling back. "There's nothin' at'al to be frightened of, Darlin'. I'll take good care o' you."

She tried to relax against his body once more. She kept her eyes open and her ears on alert but she was met only with silence and a darkness that reminded her that she'd had precious little sleep. Still, she pulled the bedcovers over them, covering their naked bodies.

The grandfather clock downstairs ticked off the seconds, the sound reminding her of just how silent the rest of the house really was. She finally felt herself snuggling into that warm cocoon of sleep.

She could feel Dylan's breath against the back of her neck; it was the steady breathing of a man deeply asleep. Then she became aware of something else, something against her nose as if someone was breathing on her face.

Her eyes flew open to find Mam leaning down in front of her, her face just inches from hers.

"It isn't me you need to be concernin' y'self with, child," she said. "Other eyes are watchin'."

20

Dylan had always been a light sleeper. Even though he'd drifted into a deep, comforting sleep, his eyes were open the moment the front door opened and the solid wail of the alarm system began to sound. He extricated himself from Vicki and was out of bed and slipping on his shorts when he heard the keypad downstairs, a tone sounding with each button that was pressed. A second later, the alarm was silent.

He stepped to the bedroom door and opened it silently, stealing a glance back at Vicki, who was still sound asleep. She'd sleep through anything, he thought.

Chris was resetting the alarm as Dylan made his way down the two flights of stairs. Shep met him halfway down, and Chris turned as the steps creaked under their weight, nodding his head tiredly. "Did I wake you?"

"No," Dylan lied. "The house is too quiet since the grandfather clock broke. I hadn't realized how the sound o' it helped to lull me to sleep."

Chris rubbed his eyes. "I hadn't noticed." He looked at the silent clock. "What happened to it?"

"Don't know. I'll be needin' to get it into a clock shop, I suppose... How did things go after we left?"

"Would you care to join me for a drink?"

Dylan grabbed a couple of Guinness from the refrigerator. Handing one off to Chris, he stepped to the kitchen table, pulled out a chair and sat down. He watched as Chris joined him. His eyes looked weary, dark bags forming underneath.

"So," Dylan said.

"She's spending the night in a holding cell."

"I figured as much."

"It isn't private."

"They rarely are."

Chris took a swig of the beer and stared for a moment at the bottle label as if it held a great deal of interest for him.

"She'll make do," Dylan said. "She's resilient, that one."

"More resilient than I am, I'm afraid."

"She's safe there."

Chris nodded. "There's that."

"Did Sam fill the police in on everythin', then?"

"Yeah. I stayed, too. Sam told them all about that guy Gabucci. Nobody knows why he's still after Brenda. She swears she's never met him."

"You believe 'er?"

Chris leveled his eyes at Dylan. "I do."

"Well, then."

"The FBI agents were killed."

Dylan nodded.

"If you hadn't gone after them," Chris said, his voice cracking, "she would have been in that car."

"But she wasn't," Dylan said. "That's the important thin'."

"You saved her."

"*We* saved 'er."

They sat for a moment in silence, each focused on their beer. Sometimes, Dylan thought, things were better this way.

"Like you said," Chris said, breaking the silence, "she's safe there."

"Aye… You been there all this time, 'ave you?"

He leaned back and rubbed the bridge of his nose. "Not the whole time. Maybe an hour or so." He sighed. "Then Sam drove me to his place and we sat and talked for a while."

"Oh?"

"Yeah. I think he wanted to know what I saw in Brenda… Why I fell in love with her."

"Was an explanation really necessary?"

Chris shrugged. "I think he was curious." He started to pull the label off his beer bottle.

Dylan took another swig.

"I don't know what the future's going to bring," Chris said suddenly.

"None o' us do."

"But you have Vicki. You'll soon be a father; she'll soon be a mother."

Dylan nodded.

"I don't know what I'll do," Chris continued. "I don't know what's going to happen with Brenda; whether she'll spend years in prison… She's so young."

He didn't know what to say so he took another deep drink.

"Sam seems to think she's got skills that our government could use. But he says Brenda isn't interested. She likes living her life on the edge."

"There's plenty o' 'edge' workin' for the CIA," Dylan grumbled.

"I think Sam wants me to convince her…" His voice faded.

"Convince 'er o' what? Cooperatin'? Goin' to work for 'im?"

"I don't know. It's all so up in the air."

"Do you 'ave a place in Washington?" Dylan asked.

"Do you want me out of here?"

"It's not that at'al. Just wonderin', is all."

"I have a condo. Funny. It was what I always wanted; a place I could step outside the door, lock it up, and leave for days, weeks or months at a time. No yard work, few home responsibilities. I could stay at work for as long as it took."

"I take it from your tone, that's not quite what you're wantin' anymore?"

He met Dylan's eyes as he shook his head. "She's changed all that."

"What does a political strategist do when he can't be in politics?"

Chris shook his head and stared at his beer again.

Dylan downed the rest of his drink. With a heavy sigh, he stood and crossed the kitchen to the wastebasket, where he plunked the bottle into the recycle side. "If you don't mind—"

"No, of course not," Chris said. "You mind if I stay up?"

"Not at'al. The police, I assume, were still watchin' the house?"

"One out front and one on the side. The guy out front had Shep sitting in the front seat with him."

Dylan instinctively reached to rub Shep behind one ear. "Well, then." He waited for a moment while he tried to think of something else to say. The moment passed and with Chris still focused on tearing the label off his bottle, Dylan turned and made his way down the hall to the stairs.

He hesitated at the bottom as he fingered the newel post. Then with fatigue beginning to wash over him, he climbed the two flights to the bedroom, his mind now focused on climbing back in bed with Vicki and wrapping his arms around her soft body once again.

21

Jails were seldom quiet. Even in the dead of night, they were barraged with a cornucopia of sounds and smells that assaulted the senses unmercifully. And sights, Brenda thought wearily, if one wasn't careful to keep the eyes averted—or better yet, closed.

She lay on the cot, the thin pad providing no cushion at all for her tired bones. It smelled of urine and vomit and disinfectant and there was no blanket or sheet to block the chilled air that escaped from the overhead vents. She laid an arm across her eyes to block the relentless glare of the overhead lights, her body trembling from the cold.

In the next cell, a woman repeatedly screamed for the guard. They'd answered her calls three times; the first, presumably to determine whether a monster really was attacking her and the second and third to stare at her as if she was comic relief. Now they simply ignored her, and Brenda was left wondering whether she was under the influence of some powerful drugs—or if she was in need of some.

On the other side, a young woman cried, her sobs echoing through the cells. She was clearly terrified; it wasn't difficult for anyone within range to deduce that it was her first arrest. Across from her, an older woman with a mouth like a sewer threatened her if she didn't shut up.

Down the hall, it sounded as if one woman was assaulting her cell mate while another one vomited loudly.

Jails were hell, Brenda thought. At least she knew what to do: shut up and stay out of anyone's crosshairs. And she had the cell to herself, at least for the time being.

It was impossible to sleep, though, and impossible to block the sounds from battering her nerves.

She hadn't realized she'd drifted off to sleep until the sound of keys clanking against a metal door jarred her awake. Though the cells did not contain windows, she knew it was too early to be daylight. She moved her arm just far enough for her to peer out from under it. A giant of a man stood in the doorway, his broad shoulders nearly reaching from one side of the entrance to the other. His features were in shadow from the bright hall lights behind him but from the turn of his head, it was obvious he was peering straight at her.

Shit, she thought. She continued to feign sleep, her eyes nearly closed, her arm allowing only a sliver underneath for her to watch him.

"Miss Carnegie," he said finally. His voice echoed through the close confines. The young woman's crying in the next cell became muffled, as if she was trying to subdue herself. The fight at the end of the hall ceased and she could feel all ears—except the drug addict next to her—listening.

When she didn't answer, he repeated her name.

It wouldn't be the first time she'd been raped in a jail cell, she thought.

Another guard came to stand beside him, just outside the cell door.

"Miss Carnegie," the first guard said in a louder voice, "you're leaving. Your ride's here."

This time, she stirred as if awakening. She lowered her arm and sat up. "And I was just beginning to like it here," she said.

"FBI is here to escort you," he said. He moved outside the cell and gestured for her to join them.

She ran her hand through her hair; though, come to think of it, she didn't actually care how badly she looked at the moment. She had no idea where she was going or how long it would take for them to get there. She just hoped it would be more pleasant than the holding cell.

She sauntered across the small cell, acutely aware that both men were watching her. As she joined them in the hallway, she said, "Thanks for the nice time, guys."

One managed a half-smile while the other remained solemn. They were both dressed in police uniforms and though she maintained a nonchalant demeanor, she wondered where the FBI agent was. They escorted her down one hall and up another, one in front and one behind, until they reached a door that required a code to open.

Once it buzzed open, they continued down yet another hall before moving into the main lobby. It was quiet; though the lighting was still bright, it *felt* like it was one o'clock in the morning.

They stopped between the front desk and the lobby door.

"Don't tell me I scared him off already?" she said.

"He's getting the car."

"Ah." She stepped forward to watch through the window. A dark sedan was making its way through the parking lot. They always drove dark sedans, she thought. It was like they got a special deal on them.

"You didn't have anything when you checked in?"

"No," she said, glancing toward a file on the counter that he was flipping through. "Sam Mazoli took everything when I 'checked in'."

The car stopped near the entrance and a man got out. He was dressed in a dark suit—standard issue FBI uniform, she thought—crisp, white shirt, a tie in muted colors, navy blue suit, shined shoes. He was bald; otherwise, he'd most likely sport the government-issue haircut.

One of the officers stepped to the door. Without a word, he opened it and nodded for her to follow.

"I signed the chain of custody," the agent was saying.

The officer nodded. "Stay safe."

"That's the plan," he answered. He glanced at Brenda and made his way around to the passenger side, opening the door for her.

"Aren't you sweet?" she purred as she joined him. "And what should I call you?"

His eyes were jet black and emotionless. "Try 'sir'," he answered.

"Yes, *sir*." She got into the car and watched as he closed her door and made his way back to the driver's side. He had a brief exchange with the police officers but she wasn't able to make out their words.

Then he climbed in, put the vehicle in gear and began driving. They remained silent as they maneuvered through town. At one point, they were only a few blocks from Dylan's and Vicki's home, and she wished wistfully that she was there, sleeping in Chris' arms. Or not sleeping, come to think of it.

They reached the interstate and he turned south.

"So," she said, "where are we going?"

He glanced at her out of the corner of his eye. He was an older man, she realized now that she was so close. He had deep lines around his eyes and his mouth was set in such a way that two parallel creases were permanently etched from the corners.

"A safe house," he said. His tone did not encourage conversation.

"Fine," she said, leaning back into the seat. "Wake me when we're there, okay?"

He didn't answer but she didn't care. It was quiet now and she much preferred the dull drone of the engine and the occasional interstate lights to the crying and cursing and drug-induced rages of cell-mates.

22

Dylan had just removed his shorts, climbed into bed and wrapped his body around Vicki's warm, soft curves when she bolted upright with a sudden shriek.

"Jaysus," he breathed, rolling onto his back. "You should warn a fella a'fore you do that."

"Brenda," she managed to say. She threw her legs over the side of the bed.

He gazed at her through the darkness. The room had taken on a deep blue undertone that permeated everything in it. "Brenda's fine, Darlin'."

"How do you know?"

"Chris is back. He was w' 'er until just a short while ago." He looked at her curiously. "Did you 'ave another bad dream?"

"Something's wrong with Brenda."

"No, it isn't, Vicki. I'm tellin' you. Now come back to bed. Please."

She stood up and turned back toward the bed. "I'm telling *you*, something is wrong with my sister."

He groaned. He was dead tired and all he wanted to do was curl up with her in his arms and sleep.

She started toward the door, apparently oblivious to her nudity.

"Get your robe on," he said with a resigned sigh. "We'll both go downstairs and ask Chris."

She glanced down at herself, looked back sheepishly, and continued wordlessly into the closet to don her robe. Dylan took advantage of the seconds to close his eyes. They felt like sandpaper.

"Well?" she asked.

He opened one eye.

"Are you coming?"

With another long groan, he reluctantly climbed out of bed. "You are goin' to owe me for this, I'm tellin' you."

"If she's okay and this is a false alarm, I'll do whatever you ask." She smiled slyly.

"Good. You'll allow me to sleep a full ten hours and threaten anyone wantin' to awaken me."

"Sexy."

He pulled on the same shorts he'd discarded only moments ago. She waited for him at the bedroom door; then they took the two flights of stairs to the main floor. They found him just as he was turning off the kitchen light.

"What's up?" His voice corroborated his exhaustion.

"Sorry to be disturbin' you, Chris. But Vicki wants to 'ave a word w' you."

He'd barely had a chance to focus on her before Vicki blurted, "Where is Brenda?"

He shook his head as if he didn't quite understand. "At the police department."

"What was to happen to her?"

He hesitated. "The FBI was sending someone to get her. They're taking her to a safe house."

"When?"

"Tomorrow." He looked from Vicki to Dylan and back to Vicki.

"Is there any chance they'd take her tonight?"

They moved toward the living room. Chris began speaking before he was completely through the door. "Do you have a premonition?"

"Yes," Vicki said. "I think she's in danger."

He pulled out his cell phone and dialed a number. A moment later, he said, "Sam. It's Chris. When was the FBI picking up Brenda?"

There was a pause. Dylan sat in the overstuffed chair and rubbed his eyes.

"Yeah," Chris was saying, "I know it's late. I'm sorry. But Vicki has a feeling—"

Another moment passed. "Okay. Thanks." He clicked off the phone and sat heavily on the couch.

"What did he say?" Vicki demanded.

"He's calling the police department."

They waited in silence. It was too silent, Vicki thought. Then, "Why isn't the grandfather clock ticking?"

"It's been broken for nearly a week," Dylan said tiredly. He seemed on the verge of falling asleep.

She felt as if her heart had grown heavier and her face began to tingle as though a cold wind was blowing over it. She opened her mouth to speak but realized Dylan's eyes were closed tight and Chris appeared to be struggling to stay awake.

It seemed as if they waited forever but in reality it might have been only five minutes before Chris' phone rang. "Yes?" He looked from Vicki to Dylan as he listened. "I see." There was a long pause. "Okay. I see." He averted his eyes from both of them. "Okay. Thanks."

When the phone clicked off, he stood for a long moment holding it absently, his eyes focused on an imaginary spot on the carpet.

"What's happening?" Vicki asked. Her voice shook.

"He said he was coming over. He said for Dylan and me to go back to bed. He wants to talk to you alone, Vicki."

23

Vicki lay on the couch with her arm over her eyes, despite the fact that the room was only dimly lit. She wished she could somehow filter the discussion between Dylan and Sam. If she was going to do this mission successfully, she needed to get in the right frame of mind, and their debate was hindering that process.

"I just don't think in 'er condition, she ought to be doin' this," Dylan was saying.

"We've already been through this," Sam said. "All I'm asking her to do is find her sister. If I can get some sort of location on her, the police and the FBI will do the rest."

"But we saw what happened last time."

"She's been doing this for years and that was the first time that ever happened. I'd venture to say it's most likely the last."

"Look, guys," Chris broke in. "Just look at the facts here. Sam said the guy who showed up at the police department had the whole fraud down pat, from the FBI identification to knowing exactly what paperwork was required to get her out—"

"Not to mention he knew where she was," Sam said gruffly. "She's obviously in danger. Every minute could count."

"Chris is right," Vicki spoke up. "I'm ready to do this thing, but not with you guys arguing over me." She moved her arm so she could see Dylan's face. "I'll be okay, Dylan. Really, I will."

"Get some sleep," Sam urged. "Vicki and I won't be long."

"I wouldn't be able to sleep," Chris said. "I'd rather stay here."

"I'll not be leavin' the mother o' me child," Dylan said, crossing his arms in front of him.

"Then please," Vicki said, "sit over there somewhere. And be quiet so I can do this. Please."

There was a grumble from Dylan but he moved to a chair across from the couch where he could keep an eye on her. Chris chose another chair, which left Sam beside the couch with Vicki.

"Okay," Vicki said. "Let's begin."

She took several deep breaths, trying to clear her mind by focusing on a white light that enveloped her. Gradually, everything in the room—from the furniture to the men watching her—faded into the light, and she felt herself drifting in that unique consciousness between reality and a plane beyond their sight.

Sam knew the telltale breathing pattern and began to direct her as a commander would do with an operative. "They left the police station less than an hour ago," Sam said. His voice was monotonous as if he was bored, but Vicki knew it was part of the persona he assumed for the psychic missions.

"Tell me which direction they went."

Vicki felt herself soaring upward above the police station. She turned to the north, then to the east. After a moment, she turned south. And then west. "Southwest," she said.

She found herself on the interstate. *Brenda,* she thought, *where are you? Where are you going?*

She was sleeping. She couldn't see her and yet she knew she was asleep. *Wake up, Brenda!* She urged. *Wake up!*

Brenda felt the steady movement under her, the constant drone of the engine that had lulled her to sleep now awakening her. She lay half-reclined in the passenger seat, her body completely still, as she oriented herself. Only her eyes moved, first from the dashboard and then to the view outside the windshield. They were still on the interstate and traffic was sparse; for as far as she could see, there were only a couple of tractor-trailers, their telltale yellow lights outlining their size.

They approached a road sign and she narrowed her eyes to see it more clearly as they passed; they were on Interstate 20. They'd already driven around sixty miles from Lumberton and turned west near Florence, South Carolina.

Something pulled at her psyche and she realized she'd been sleeping when she could have sworn she heard Vicki calling her name. It must have been a dream, she thought, as her attention moved back to the dashboard. Something about it bothered her but she didn't know why.

Her eyes continued to move until they landed on the driver. He looked as he did when he picked her up; two hands on the steering wheel at the two o'clock and ten o'clock positions, his eyes watching the road. He didn't seem to be aware that she was awake; or if he was, he didn't much care.

He was bald, she noted. His eyebrows were sparse and short. Wrinkles near his ear and his eye appeared pronounced, as if the lack of hair somehow highlighted them. Then she realized as they passed under a highway light that his scalp was lighter than his face. She kept her eyes narrowed so she could rapidly feign sleep as she waited for them to pass under the next light. It had to have been an optical illusion, she thought.

The next light came and went and she noted it again; there was a distinct pattern that included his scalp and the area where sideburns should have been. She felt her heart begin to quicken and she closed her eyes and breathed deeply, hoping he would think the steady breaths were simply sleep overcoming her.

Why did the dashboard bother her? She wondered. In her mind's eye, she went through each component in turn. The glove compartment. Check. The radio was off; silence, she thought, was better than music she detested. She opened her eyes to study the gauges in front of the driver. He was going seventy miles an hour and her own past experiences in South Carolina reminded her that the speed limit was most likely seventy. So he was going the speed limit. Imagine that, she thought. A fed going the speed limit. They usually drove like bats out of hell and why not? They didn't have to worry about speeding tickets.

Nothing else was out of the ordinary—the gas gauge showed nearly three-quarters; the tach was steady. Then why was she so worried all the sudden?

She turned her head slowly to look out the side window. There was a slope of grass that began at the edge of the shoulder before it leveled off and ended in groves of trees. Though the grass had turned brown with the season, the trees were primarily pine and stood branch to branch to provide a thick, shadowy cover against the night sky. The miles melted behind them and in front of them, there were no exits in sight.

He hadn't provided a name, she thought as she stared at the dark tree line. But then, she'd been tired and not quite her cocky self. She didn't remember asking him and she didn't remember the officers mentioning it.

He was dressed like the typical FBI agent; she often thought they all shopped at the same store. He drove a dark sedan…

There was that nagging tickle at the back of her mind. She was missing something. What was it?

The light from the dash created a reflection in the side window. Her eyes were open now, but with her head turned away from him, she wasn't sure if he knew she'd awakened. Why did that matter, anyway?

She looked at the dash's reflection. He was driving the speed limit on a straight road with no other traffic.

The radio wasn't on. Some people preferred silence, she thought. No. The radio wasn't on.

She felt the blood begin to drain from her face.

They all had police radios. Even the feds had them; they often coordinated with local law enforcement and they needed the radios for communication. Even Sam had one in an unmarked car.

She was leaning her head against the window as if asleep and now she began to move her fingers ever so slightly toward the door handle. She kept her eyes on his reflection; he was focused on driving, his eyes locked on the road just as it had been before. Only his right hand was holding the steering wheel now; it had slipped to a three o'clock position.

A slight movement caught her attention; it was so subtle, she almost thought she'd imagined it. Then she spotted the glint of metal across his body, though the road still held his attention. Her fingers locked onto the door handle as the metal rose slightly up and away from his body. He turned his head as his left hand snapped forward.

She jerked the door open as the shot rang out. She felt something sharp and hot against her shin as she kicked herself away from the car. She tumbled onto the pavement before hitting the shoulder, the gravel feeling like a million razors slicing through her flesh. She heard her own voice as if it was disembodied, screaming as she forced herself to roll across the sharp gravel before plummeting down the incline, compelling herself to continue rolling even as she realized she'd been shot in the leg.

She heard the car's brakes slamming, the tires squealing as the man struggled to bring the car to a stop. At seventy miles an hour, it should have taken the car further from her even as she rushed to escape. But when she came to her feet and looked back at the road, she estimated he was about three hundred feet further down the road—not far enough.

She ran toward the tree line, which now appeared too far away. As a second shot rang out, she knew his sights were set on her back, and she struggled to run straight, fighting the impulse to run opposite of him. It kept her profile smaller but when he shot a third and then fourth time, she could almost feel the bullets whizzing past her.

The third and fourth shots sounded increasingly louder and she knew he was running after her. Her breath was loud and labored, her blood pounding in her temples. Even as she drew closer to the shadows of the trees, she could feel herself slowing down. The adrenaline that propelled her down the slope and to her feet was fighting against the pain in her leg.

She could feel the blood oozing down her shin and pooling in her shoe, causing her to slip and slide along grass already slick with dew. Another shot rang out, whizzing so close to her hair that she thought it had passed through it.

She threw herself into the shadows, pushing herself beyond her leg's endurance to keep going, to get into the pine forest, weaving and bobbing forward and eastward, away from the car, away from the interstate. Hopefully, away from *him*.

She wanted to stop; she wanted to pull some article of clothing off herself and wrap it around her shin to keep the blood in, to keep the flesh together, but she didn't dare hesitate. She heard the branches cracking behind her; he was there and he was closing on her. Even as she propelled herself forward, she knew all he had to do was follow the movement of the branches ahead of him to know exactly where she was.

Vicki looked at her palm and read off the coordinates: latitude, longitude, degree. She looked to her compass and reported that she was traveling northeast. And though she struggled to remain with her, she felt herself moving away, Brenda's labored, jagged breaths replaced by Sam's monotonous voice on the phone, relaying the information she'd provided.

24

She couldn't be sure how far she'd traveled; it felt like a quarter of a mile, but she knew it had been much further. The fear had continued to thrust her forward, zigzagging through the pine forest like a jackrabbit.

The shots had long ago stopped. And she knew why.

She stopped when she could no longer breathe, when the throbbing in her sides had become excruciating, when the agonizing pain in her leg could no longer be denied. She sank behind a thick trunk, feeling for her shin in the gloom of night.

Her slacks were glued to her flesh and as she ripped the fabric away, she cried out with the torment despite her efforts to subdue herself. Her fingers searched for the wound and grew sticky with the effort; there were two holes, one in the back of her calf and one in front, barely missing the bone. The bullet had passed clear through.

With the amount of blood and no sign it was letting up, she worried it had hit an artery. Still seated and propped against the tree, she unbuckled her belt and struggled to take it off; even the loopholes in her slacks seemed to conspire against her. Finally, she had it off and she wrapped it around her calf, using her fingers to ensure the leather was pressed tightly against both bullet holes. The exit hole was the worst. She wasn't sure if the leather would hold once she stood, and in her concern, she pulled it tighter and wrapped it multiple times until she could fold the last piece through to keep it secure.

She wanted nothing more than to remain right where she was until morning, but she knew she didn't dare. She no longer heard her assailant because he'd returned to his car and was searching for her now. She knew his movements because she would have done the same thing. He could drive back and forth, covering twenty miles for every one she traveled on foot—if she ran.

She used the trunk to help haul her up, holding onto it as if it was a lifeline. Then she peered upward and tried to get her bearings from the stars. Behind her perhaps four or five miles back, she spotted the search light of a helicopter and heard the distinct sound of its rotor blades, but she couldn't be certain whether it was friend or foe.

She'd run away from the car at first, heading east because they had been traveling west. But once she'd reached the trees, she'd become disoriented. She hoped she'd continued to move toward the east, toward Interstate 95 and Florence, but she couldn't be certain. And now she began to worry about her vulnerability once daylight appeared.

As long as there was darkness, she could remain in the shadows of the trees, counting on the gloom of night to keep her hidden from view—as long as the helicopter didn't make its way in this direction. But once she emerged from the trees— whenever that was—she would be visible again. And if she remained in the forest, how did she know she wouldn't be fully visible when daylight found her?

She had no choice. Though her leg was throbbing and her head felt light, perhaps due to the loss of blood, she had to continue moving forward. She found the North Star and set her path toward the east, toward the interstate that would lead her home.

25

Joseph pulled his vehicle to the edge of the parking lot, where an oak tree's branches protruded like a canopy over two parking spots. He pulled across them both so he could see the roadway, the branches just inches from the car's roof. He didn't know why he preferred to be under them, but he felt a sense of security somehow with the little bit of concealment they offered.

He watched the truck stop for a few minutes and allowed himself time to observe the rhythm. On one side, tractor-trailers were parked, the lights on a few still on, their engines running. Others were noticeably dark, the cabs empty. The other side had smaller parking spaces and obviously catered to the automotive crowd but there were no customers at this hour of the morning. A service attendant walked outside just long enough to empty the trash cans into a larger barrel before rolling it to the nearby dumpster.

He wanted his heart rate to slow but even as he watched the unhurried pace of the attendant, he felt as though he was ready to boil over.

He'd driven back and forth along Interstate 20 in a wide loop, watching for any sign of her but there had been none. With traffic non-existent, he slowed to a crawl as he passed one set of trees after another, his eyes scanning the shadows, the grassy area that led to the highway, and even the highway itself.

He mentally calculated the distance he thought she could travel and broadened his scope in the event that she was faster than he anticipated, and still nothing.

He knew he'd shot her. He'd planned to pull off the deserted highway and force her outside the vehicle and down the slope so when he fired the fatal bullet, her body would be less visible to passing cars in the daylight hours. Then he'd get back in the car and drive hundreds of miles before darkness waned; with any luck at all, he would have been long gone before she was discovered.

He hadn't intended to shoot her while she was still in the car. Now there was blood splattered across the interior, which would create a problem as he covered his tracks. But though she was limping as she ran, he knew the shot hadn't been fatal. Which created another set of problems.

As he cleared his mind, he realized the most logical reaction would be for her to contact her sister. He could turn around and head for their house, set up and be waiting for her with a sniper rifle when she returned. But he'd be taking a big gamble. If they realized she'd been taken by someone other than an FBI agent, they could be looking for him and his vehicle at that very moment.

It was a big reason why he had to stop searching for her. On his last trip through, he spotted a state trooper in his rear view mirror. He studiously checked his speed to make sure he was within the posted limit and watched it, expecting it to speed past him and disappear on the horizon or at the next exit.

Instead, it pulled off to the shoulder of the road and stopped. The traffic was non-existent except for the two of them, so he couldn't be setting up his radar detector. Perhaps he was doing something no more exciting than paperwork. But it meant he could no longer drive in the circle he'd established; he couldn't risk the officer seeing the same car every few minutes. He couldn't risk getting stopped and questioned.

So Joseph had pulled off at the next exit, found the truck stop and stopped.

And now here he sat.

As he weighed his options, he pulled out his laptop. It still had a full charge so he logged on and went straight for the camera surveillance in the Irishman's house. The bedroom where the couple had been so amorous earlier was silent, the covers pulled back on the bed, and the bed conspicuously empty. He found the same thing in the bedroom Brenda had shared with Christopher Sandige. The upstairs hallway was dim and silent, as was the stairwell.

But when he clicked over to the living room, he was surprised to see Sam, Vicki, Chris and the Irishman gathered. He turned up the sound and backed up the recording to the point where Sam had emerged in the living room, obviously having just entered the house.

He listened intently, his eyes still wandering around the truck stop, watching and waiting. Then he jerked his head, stopped the tape and backed it up again. He listened a second time but this time his eyes were riveted on the scene unfolding in front of him. He felt his face grow cold and clammy as he listened to Vicki describing Brenda as she sat in his car; she gave accurate details of everything, including the make and model. She saw the interstate sign and knew they'd been on I-20 in South Carolina. And she knew when Brenda made a break for it, when the shot rang out, and how he had chased her down the embankment and into the woods.

She told in minute detail how Brenda had stopped to assess her wounds and wrap her calf with her belt to keep the blood from flowing out. And which direction she was traveling. Then he watched with astonishment as she told them the latitude, longitude and even the degree.

He pulled out his cell phone and called up an app to check his current coordinates. He wasn't far from where it had all unfolded—perhaps ten miles. And the officer might still be there on the shoulder of the road—and he might have been called to that position because of *her*.

He heard the faint sound of a helicopter and turned in his seat to stare out his back window. It was miles away, he figured, but the intensity of the search light was clearly visible above the treetops.

There weren't too many things that astounded him; he'd long ago decided that he'd seen just about everything. But this…

He dialed a number and waited.

"Yes?" The voice was curt.

"What do you know about psychic warriors?" Joseph asked.

There was hesitation on the other end of the line and for a moment, he thought they'd been disconnected. Then, "You mean like Stargate?"

"Exactly."

"That was discontinued in 1995."

"Just that project? Or did they move the operation?"

"No. The whole thing was dismantled."

"News flash. It hasn't been dismantled." He let that sink in for a moment and then, "We have a much larger problem than Brenda Carnegie. Find out everything you can about her sister, Vicki."

"I'm on it."

He clicked off the phone but continued staring at the computer screen. If this woman could see events unfold to that degree of accuracy, she could easily jeopardize his mission.

And he couldn't allow that to happen.

26

Brenda lay on her stomach on a bed of pine needles as she watched the sparse traffic on Interstate 95. In the distance, she could see the faintest pink glow on the horizon. If she was going to make her move, it had to be now while it was still dark and the use of headlights made the vehicles more easily spotted. She had to know when the coast was clear enough for her to make her way across six lanes of traffic to the other side of Interstate 95.

The belt had stopped the bleeding but the constriction had caused her leg to go numb. She took a ragged breath and used the trunk of a tree to support her weight as she came to her feet. It would take her at least three minutes to get across the interstate, she reasoned. That meant the coast had to be clear for at least three miles in each direction, a distance she couldn't see from one vantage point.

And if he came back around while she was crossing the highway, he could pick her off like she was a turkey at a turkey shoot. There would be no place to run and no place to hide.

She also didn't trust the police. The guy had been able to obtain FBI credentials and for all she knew, he was an FBI agent gone rogue. It might have already been reported that she'd escaped and perhaps the information being disseminated was that she was armed and dangerous.

A few months ago, she thought suddenly, she had no one she believed in. Now she had four she would trust her life to: Sam, Dylan, Vicki and Chris.

But she had to get to them.

Her first step was wobbly at best; her injured leg acted as if it wanted to collapse under her. She had nothing she could use as a crutch—the pine trees provided decent cover but even if she was able to break off a branch, they were too flexible to be able to support her weight.

So she took another step and another. As she moved away from the trees and toward the road, she realized her progress was painstakingly slow. At this rate, it would take her closer to ten minutes to cross the highway. It was too much to ask that there wouldn't be a vehicle in either direction for a twenty-mile stretch.

She half hobbled and half dragged her bum leg closer to the road. She stopped in the last vestiges of shadow to peer up and down the highway. A vehicle was approaching; she stood perfectly still, nearly holding her breath, as it drew closer. It seemed to slow and she silently prayed they were not looking in her direction. As it passed, she noted two adults in the front seat and a horde of kids in the back. One stared at her as they passed; it appeared to be a child around ten years old and hopefully if he said anything, his parents wouldn't believe him. Still, she waited until they were nearly out of sight before she began moving forward once again.

She had almost reached the road when a vehicle traveling at a high rate of speed came off the entrance ramp on the opposite side. Her heart nearly stopped as she recognized the blue lights on top and as if the trooper had read her mind, the lights began to flash and the siren blared. Stunned, she could only stand motionless.

But in the next instant, it pulled onto the interstate heading north as if the trooper hadn't seen her at all.

Again, she waited. She couldn't risk having the cop look in his rear view mirror and see her tottering across the highway covered in dried blood.

At last, she stepped onto the highway. Every step felt excruciating; her leg teetered between complete numbness and an agonizing sensation that her leg was on fire. She knew she was moving too slowly but she was now dragging her leg more than walking on it; the concern that she'd move too quickly and fall was too great to ignore. She didn't know if she'd be able to get back up again, and she'd be a sitting duck.

So she lumbered across, step by agonizing step. Halfway across the southbound lanes, she felt the trickle begin down her leg once more. As tight as the belt was, she was bleeding again.

The pink glow she'd spotted on the far horizon was growing more brilliant much too quickly. With dawn would come more traffic and her visibility would be increased exponentially.

She was perspiring now, the droplets coating her brow and her upper lip. She was filthy; between the blood and all the running through the forest, laying on pine needles, leaning against tree trunks—she was coated in grime. She was certain she had pine needles stuck in her hair; it was unruly on the best of days. Today it had to look like something out of a horror movie.

She reached the median and fought the urge to stop to catch her breath. A car was approaching in a northbound lane and she was stuck with nowhere to hide and without the ability to run.

At the same time, a tractor-trailer slowly made its way onto the entrance ramp, the gears shifting, audible from where she stood.

She had no choice. It was remain where she was, in full sight of both northbound and southbound lanes, or continue staggering across and hope she wasn't hit. She began crossing the first northbound lane as the car continued to approach two lanes over, blowing its horn as if she wasn't on the opposite side of the road. Any other time, she might have flipped them off or cursed them but she was too exhausted to do anything other than try to ignore them and keep going.

The tractor-trailer did not pick up speed on the entrance ramp and as she glanced across at the hulking vehicle, she realized he was not pulling into the lane but was moving from the acceleration ramp to the shoulder.

Please don't look this way, she thought as she continued to drag her leg across the highway. Please, God, let me be invisible!

She hadn't managed to get halfway across the first lane when the cab door opened and a muscle-bound man with thick brown hair climbed out. She glanced upward to see him move to the edge of the ramp, his eyes riveted upon her. She wanted to melt right into the pavement.

"Hey!" he called out.

She continued moving at her distressingly sluggish pace, but she peered upward to see him still watching her.

"Hey!" he called again. "Do you need help?"

———— ———— ————

The skies were blue, all vestiges of the night left behind as the tractor-trailer neared the main entrance at Fort Bragg.

Brenda had wanted him to drop her off at the last exit before the guard posts, but the driver, a man named Bo, had steadfastly refused. She was in no shape to walk, he'd said curtly, and she had to agree with him.

"Stay to the left," she said, directing him to the visitor gate. As they approached, she noticed all the other gates had long lines; they'd arrived during rush-hour traffic, no less, and all the military personnel who lived off-post as well as the civilian employees and contractors, were arriving to start a day of work.

She was bone-tired. She knew she smelled horribly and she had to look frightful but Bo had treated her as if she was the First Lady. He'd offered to take her to the closest hospital or police station or call 9-1-1 and wait with her until they arrived with an ambulance, but she hadn't wanted any of those options. She'd told him she had to get to Fort Bragg and God bless him, he'd driven out of his way to deliver her there.

As they approached the gate, a young man in uniform stepped out of the booth with a clipboard. He carried a vehicle under-mirror with him and approached the cab with a stern expression. Bo rolled down his window and leaned out.

"Hey, I've got a lady in here who needs help," he called out.

"What kind of help?" the uniformed man asked warily. He remained several feet from the cab so Bo had to continue to shout.

"Medical attention."

He shook his head. "You'll have to turn around and take her to Fayetteville."

Brenda leaned across Bo, despite the fact that she was getting his pants bloodied. "Private!" she called out.

His brows knit.

"Call Sam Mazoli," she shouted in her most no-nonsense voice. It was husky on a good day and now, with the tension of the moment and what surely must be dehydration, it sounded deep enough to be a man's voice.

He shook his head again. "I don't know—"

"CIA!" she shouted. She tried to ignore Bo's startled expression.

"Stay here," the private answered. He retreated into the booth and appeared to be looking through a directory of sorts. A moment later, he was on the phone. As the conversation ensued, he began staring at the two of them.

"You're not in any kind of trouble, are you?" Bo asked.

"Let me think. I've been shot in the leg and spent most of the night trying to get away. Yeah, I think I'm in a bit of trouble." As his face paled, she added, "But don't worry. I'm one of the good guys. For a change."

The young man returned to the truck. This time, he ventured to the window and his expression had softened. "Mr. Mazoli said you're to wait in the booth here. He's on his way."

Bo started to open his door.

"Not you, sir."

"I'm turning around this rig," Bo answered. "But this young lady can't get out of this thing by herself. She's injured."

He walked around the cab with the private in tow, arriving as Brenda opened the door.

"What happened?" the young man exclaimed as he took in her blood-soaked clothing.

"I've been shot," she answered curtly. "Now get me out of here."

Despite their efforts to help lift her to the ground, the movement was painful. Now that she'd arrived at her destination, she realized every bit of adrenaline that had propelled her forward had completely disappeared and she was left in a sort of purgatory between feeling completely and utterly drained and completely and utterly in agony.

"I'll call an ambulance," the private said tensely as they half-carried her to the booth. Other uniformed men began stopping to look at them from the other booths, and the cars entering the post slowed to gawk.

"No," Brenda said. "I don't want an ambulance. Not until Sam gets here."

"But—"

"It's classified," she said, leveling her eyes at him. "No questions. I'm waiting for Sam."

"Yes, ma'am."

A clean-cut man in a red sports car rolled down his window and asked if they needed additional help. Despite her injury, Brenda registered his square jaw, piercing eyes and broad shoulders. What a time for me to look like this, she thought.

They reached the booth. Though it was just large enough for one person, somehow all three squeezed into it as the two men labored to set her onto a stool.

"What do you need?" the man from the car asked. As Bo and the private backed away, she caught a closer look at his face. "I'll go get it."

She felt the blood draining from her face and as she looked toward the three men peering in at her, the booth began to tilt and whirl. She felt her body slipping off the stool like melted butter just as strong arms grabbed her to keep her from hitting the floor.

27

It might have been a hospital room but it felt more like a conference space as Vicki, Dylan, Chris and Sam gathered around the hospital bed. Chris held one of Brenda's hands in his, his attention riveted on her grimy, broken nails. Brenda's objections over Vicki brushing out her long hair were brief and superficial and as she saw the number of pine needles and debris mount, she wished she could take a long, hot shower.

That didn't seem to be in her immediate future, however. A nurse was busy placing a thick pillow under her leg, which looked twice its size due to the bandaging.

"You've got your pain medication right here," the nurse said as she pushed a device into her free hand. "Just push that button there when you need it."

"I won't need it," Brenda said.

She chuckled. "Just wait till the anesthetic wears off. Then you'll need it."

Brenda sighed and leaned back against the pillows, forcing Vicki to move to her bangs. "It's okay," she said in a low voice as she closed her eyes.

The nurse moved to the other side of the bed, where she checked the two intravenous drips—one consisting of clear liquid was, Vicki assumed, the pain medication. The other was blood and it was nearly empty.

"I'll be back with more plasma," the nurse said. "It's a wonder she's even lucid, between the blood loss and the anesthesia... My name's Gayle, by the way. I'll be taking care of her for the next few hours."

"How long will she be here?" Vicki asked.

"I can answer that," Sam said. He pulled a chair close to the bed and sat down heavily, rubbing his eyes before he continued. "She'll be here at least a week. Maybe longer." As Gayle left the room, he turned to the others. "Two men will remain stationed at her door around the clock. It's just a precaution—I can't think of any place safer than right here at Fort Bragg."

"I'd rather go back to Vicki's place," Brenda mumbled, her eyes still closed.

"You're safer here," Sam said, but the gruffness had left his voice. "And Vicki's safer with you here."

She mumbled something in response that they couldn't quite decipher and after another moment, Vicki stopped brushing her hair. "I think she's out," she said.

"Good. It's the best thing for her." Chris squeezed her hand tighter but she didn't respond.

"This is as good a time as any for me to tell you what we've found out," Sam said. He held a note pad in his lap but he didn't refer to his notes as he glanced from one to the other. Dylan had remained silent and appeared to be ready to doze off. As Sam continued, he rubbed the bridge of his nose between his thumb and forefinger before opening his eyes and focusing on his words.

"The police department supplied tapes that have already been sent to Washington—electronically, of course. They have cameras in their parking lot and we got a good look at the vehicle and the license plate. It's already been identified and it's already been tracked down."

"Did you catch him?" Vicki gasped.

"Not yet but it's just a matter of time. If you're interested in the particulars—"

"I am," Chris said.

"The vehicle was a Crown Victoria," Sam said. "Last year's model. It was reported stolen this morning from a car dealer's lot. The license plate was stolen off another vehicle; the owner didn't even know it was gone. He parked it in his driveway last night, got in it this morning and drove to work—which is where the cops found him when they investigated."

"I imagine he was surprised," Dylan said.

"To say the least. License was off a Honda Civic."

"But did you say you found the auto?" Dylan asked. "But you didn't find 'er assailant?"

"The vehicle was found at a truck stop in South Carolina. It had been pulled under some trees but a sharp-eyed officer found it this morning. They surrounded the truck stop—it'll be all over the news, if it hasn't been already—but there was no sign of him."

"Any evidence left in the vehicle?" Chris asked.

"They're processing it now. They tell me it was obvious that Brenda was shot as she attempted to escape."

Chris raised her knuckle to his lips and kissed it gently. Then he smiled. "I know she's out cold. Otherwise, she'd have had something to say about that."

They all chuckled but grew serious as Gayle reentered the room. She moved with precision to the IV unit, turning off and disconnecting the blood flow and then replacing it with the new bag. She glanced in their direction to find all eyes on her.

"She's been through quite an ordeal," Gayle said as she worked. "There are fragments of asphalt and gravel embedded in her skin, front and back as if she rolled in it."

Vicki inhaled sharply. "How could—?"

"Injuries like that, we normally see if someone's been dragged. We had an MP here once who stopped a drunk driver on post. He reached in to turn off the engine when the driver wouldn't comply, and the driver took off. The officer was stuck with his arm through the steering wheel and dragged…"

"You don't think she was—?"

Gayle shrugged. "All I'm saying is it's the same type of injury. Her body will be ejecting fragments for some time."

"You won't remove them?"

"Oh, no. There are way too many of them. But the body has a way of pushing them out of the skin. We see it all the time, especially with IEDs in war zones." She nodded toward her leg.

"That leg was a mess when she got here. The bullet went in through the back of her calf and came out the front, right next to the tibia. She's very lucky it didn't hit the bone; it would have shattered it. As it was, the exit wound was pretty large."

"Was it—did it have dirt in it?" Chris asked as he stared at her nails.

"Not too much. She'd put a belt around her leg, wrapped it pretty darn tight. She bled pretty heavily once it was taken off, so the belt probably saved her from bleeding to death." Vicki gasped but Gayle continued, "The belt kept the dirt and—" she glanced at her hair "—pine needles out of it."

"She's a tough lass," Dylan said. Even as he spoke the words, it felt like an understatement. The woman could definitely withstand a whole lot of pain.

"Yes, she is," Gayle said. She tested the blood flow from the new bag. Satisfied, she began cleaning up the materials from the last one. "I was here when she was brought in. Before they gave her pain meds, the doctor was poking his fingers into her wounds. She never even winced."

They all looked at Brenda's face, the tension lifted as she slept.

"Call me if you need anything," Gayle said. "I'll be right outside that door at the nurse's station." She stopped in the doorway. "She ought to sleep for several hours, if you've got something else to do… Between the anesthesia from the surgery and the pain meds we gave her, she might not wake up until dinnertime."

"Thanks," Sam said. "Oh, and I'll be stopping at the nurse's station and leaving a list of people who are cleared to visit her. Anyone not on that list and you contact me. They're not to come in."

"Gotcha. I saw the guards at the door, too. She must be an important lady."

Gayle left the room without waiting for a response, and Sam said, "Yeah. And we're trying to figure out why she's so important."

"I don't understand it," Vicki said. "The bank scheme—the list of crooked politicians—certainly, this guy knows that the authorities have all that information now."

"Yeah. I need to talk to you guys about that." Sam glanced toward the door. Satisfied no one was listening, he continued in a lower voice. "We have to be getting close to finding out the truth about something—what, I don't know. But they wouldn't have risked sending this guy into the police department if they didn't believe we were close to finding out their secret."

"What do you mean, 'they'?" Vicki asked.

"He means Gabucci isn't actin' on 'is own, I'd wager," Dylan said.

"That's right," Sam said. "The guy is a hired assassin. I've got a file four inches thick on him."

"You do?"

He shrugged. "Figuratively speaking. It's all electronic. Anyway, that's beside the point. The point is, I had Intel run everything they had on him when I learned he'd escaped. He's a professional, hired by the highest bidder. He doesn't seem to have any long-term affiliations, any alliances, so to speak. He also doesn't seem to act out of idealism or ideologies. It appears that he's in this business for the money, plain and simple."

"But who else—?" Chris began.

"Once they prosecuted him for the double homicide and the feds got the case, they started a full investigation on the guy. They've been taking their time—after all, he was locked up so he wasn't going anywhere—or so they thought. But they have a string of open cases and they were hoping to link him to some of them."

"And did they?" Dylan asked.

"They don't have enough concrete evidence for convictions, but they're still working on it. The guy's a professional. He rarely leaves prints or evidence of any kind. If it hadn't been for Chris' eye-witness testimony of the attempted murder of him and Brenda, he might have walked free."

"But that didn't tie him to the double homicide," Chris said.

"It was circumstantial but the jury was convinced, which is all that mattered." Sam cracked his knuckles and then rubbed the back of his neck. "Anyway, what we have to figure out is: who hired him to kill Brenda?"

Though they waited at the doors to the elevator, Vicki's attention was riveted to Brenda's room down the hall. The door was open and she could see Chris sitting beside her bed, holding her hand and talking. She had no way of knowing whether her sister had awakened and suspected that she had not; and she also suspected Chris was pouring his heart out to her anyway, from the look on his face.

He'd insisted on remaining with her, though he hadn't been able to get any more sleep the previous night than they had. But with nothing to do but sit and watch her sleep, Sam, Vicki and Dylan had opted to go home for a few hours of rest. They'd promised Chris they would return around dinnertime.

Outside her door sat two men with bulky shoulders and holstered pistols.

"So, listen," Sam was saying. "There's nothing either of you can do to help Brenda at this point."

"What will happen to her?"

"For starters, she'll remain right where she is. She's still in need of medical attention and I can't think of a better place for her to be. She's safe here."

"I agree," Dylan said, wrapping an arm around Vicki. "I know you'd much prefer 'er be at home. But she'll be receivin' the care she needs 'ere."

The elevator arrived and they waited for a nurse to get off before they entered. Sam pressed the button for the lobby. "And since you can't do anything for her," he continued, "I need you, Dylan, back on the ship bombings."

"I'd like to say I understand," he said, his eyes narrowing, "but there's still the matter of an escaped murderer roamin' about."

"I hope you're not proposing to find him."

"O' course not. But how precisely do you think he'd know that Brenda isn't back at home w' Vicki?"

"What are you getting at?"

"I'm gettin' at the fact that me girl 'ere might not be safe 'erself."

"You said they installed the alarm system."

"Aye. They did."

"So she carries the remote thingy around with her. She'll be fine."

"Do you really think so, Sam? Do you really think that we can leave your adopted daughter, pregnant as she is, at home whilst we don't know where a hired assassin is?"

They reached the ground floor. As they entered the lobby, Sam rubbed his chin. "You and I have to go back," he said with a sideways glance at Dylan. "There's no way around it. We've got a mission to perform and there are lives at stake."

"There are obviously lives a' stake 'ere, as well."

"Well, hell." They reached the front doors and Sam held the door open for Vicki. "We'll just bring her with us."

"I'm not so sure about that, either, to be perfectly honest about it. These little excursions make for some long days. Very long days. And she's in a very delicate condition."

"Will you two stop talking about me as if I wasn't right here?" Vicki demanded as they joined her on the sidewalk.

"Well, you solve the problem," Sam said.

They stopped to look at her expectantly.

"What's the problem again?" she asked.

Dylan groaned and started toward the car. "You're comin' w' me," he said. "You can sleep on the plane. We'll pack a cooler w' all sorts o' goodies for you and we'll put you in a nice, air conditioned room whilst we work… assumin' we can find one."

"Wonderful."

"Isn't that what I just suggested?" Sam muttered.

28

Vicki was about as comfortable as a person could get, considering the circumstances. She had an air conditioned office all to herself and while the desk chair left a lot to be desired, when she thought of the inmates at this facility, she knew she couldn't complain. She'd been reading books on her iPad most of the morning but frankly, she was getting bored. A glance at her watch and the memory of Dylan's warning that it would be a long day made her wish she'd stayed at home.

She rotated the chair so she was looking out the tiny window. The view should have reminded her of a beach vacation; palm trees swayed in a gentle breeze and a vivid blue ocean rolled in waves with frothy whitecaps that crashed against a pristine beach. The skies were a lighter blue but just as beautiful; a line of benign clouds appeared like fluffy balls of cotton as they meandered at a leisurely pace. It looked like the type of place she'd want to be, reclining in a beach chair with her toes planted in the soft, moist sand, her sunglasses shading her eyes against the brilliance of the sun while she sipped an exotic drink from a coconut...

But there, the fantasy ended; for as her eyes wandered from the unspoiled beach, she caught sight of a row of cages. She supposed each one might have been fifteen feet square, if that. They were open on all four sides and even the top was the same type of wire. It appeared as if blankets had been strewn across them, providing a sliver of shade for the men baking underneath.

Each one wore a bright orange jumpsuit. Most were lying on the concrete floor or sitting with their legs crossed under them. At least one was pacing.

The door opened behind her but she remained riveted to the scene before her. Even when Sam came to stand beside her, she kept her eyes fixed on the cages.

"Where are we?" she asked.

"It's a Black Site."

"Where?"

"You don't want to know."

"I don't want to know why those men are here?"

"No. You don't." He left her side and she heard the chair creak behind her.

After a moment of silence, he said, "Well, I hate to interrupt you because it's obvious you're real busy…"

She turned back to the room. He sat on the other side of the desk in a metal rolling chair that was quite rusted. In fact, most of the furniture in the room was in various degrees of rust, she realized.

"Since you're here anyway," Sam continued, "and I'm here, I thought we could do a mission."

"What do you need?"

"I need to know where Joseph Gabucci is."

She continued looking at him.

"You think you can find him?"

She hesitated as she tried to get her emotions under control. A psychic mission always meant that she was an observer, a disinterested party. Yet she couldn't think of Joseph Gabucci without remembering that he had tried to kill her sister not once, but twice. And he might be out there now planning a third attempt.

"What do you want to know?" she asked.

"Who he works for."

She swallowed. "I can try."

"Good. There's a room down the hall with a cot in it."

"You've already scoped it out, huh?" She smiled coyly.

"Of course. And I knew you'd say 'yes'."

"Well, let's do it."

"Now?"

"You got a better idea?"

———   ———   ———

She lay flat on her back on the aging cot and tried to ignore the musty odor that emanated from it. As she looked upward, she was met with a ceiling covered in mold, the thick layers of paint peeling off in sheets. The sooner she got this thing started, the sooner she could leave, she told herself.

The room was dim; unlike the office she'd been in earlier, this one had no window and only a naked bulb hanging from a wire that ran across half the ceiling and down the wall. The light was on but the bulb was either dingy or of low wattage—or both, she surmised—so that it did nothing to illuminate the room. There was no air conditioner here and the air felt stale and still.

Sam sat on a chair he'd pulled in from an adjacent office. He did not have his audio and video equipment so he tapped his notebook lightly as he waited for her to get situated.

She closed her eyes and rested her arms across her chest. She took several deep breaths that should have felt cleansing but for the amount of dust and decay in the air. A tickle began in her throat and she swallowed hard, trying to tamp it down.

"I want to know," Sam said in a low, even voice, "what Joseph Gabucci is afraid we'll find and who he works for."

It was called intention. Vicki knew that as her mind began to slip into an alternate consciousness, the person guiding the mission states what she should be searching for. The command becomes her psyche's intention, opening a path for her to follow.

She began to breathe rhythmically. After a few moments, she began to feel the familiar sensation of floating upward and away from her body. As always, she felt as if she had an earpiece and microphone attached to her; much like an operative embarking on a covert mission, tethered to her commander through the invisible line of communication.

"I'm over the ocean," Vicki said. Her voice was objective and strong. The water was crystal clear; she could peer into the depths and view schools of fish in a kaleidoscope of colors. It made sense, she thought; she was on an island and she would have to travel across an expanse of ocean to reach the mainland. But something wasn't right.

"I'm not over the Atlantic," she stated. She wasn't sure how she knew this, but she did. She felt as if she was much further west than she should be.

"Coordinates."

She looked at a GPS in her palm and read off the latitude, longitude and degree. "I'm off course," she said, incredulous.

"Stay with it," Sam said. His tone didn't change but remained almost detached. "Don't try to guide yourself to any specific location. Let yourself be guided instead to what you need to see."

"I'm moving closer to the water," she said.

"Do you see anything above the surface? Land? Ships?"

She hovered over the surface and turned in each direction, searching as far as her eyes could see. In her altered state, she felt as though she had eagle eyes, eyes that could see far greater distances than a human being. But she saw nothing; no birds, no land, no ships. Just the ocean, great and voluminous, shimmering in cobalt blue against an azure sky. She reported her findings— or lack of them—back to Sam.

"I feel pulled toward the water," she said. Though her voice remained calm, her heart felt as though it had begun beating faster and more vigorously.

"Toward the surface or underneath?"

"Underneath." It was, she thought, like she was being sucked in and though she tried to resist, the pull of the water was far stronger than herself.

"Listen to me, Vicki." Sam's voice was firm.

"I'm listening."

"I am going in with you. I'm going to walk you through this. Okay?"

"Yes."

"You are going to be fine. You're wearing a diving suit. Do you see it?"

She hadn't seen it; a moment ago, her palm had been naked as she'd peered at the GPS held within it. But now as she looked, her wrists were covered and as she studied her arms, legs and torso, she found she was dressed in a form-fitting diving suit. "Yes. I'm wearing it."

"What color is it?"

His question startled her; it seemed irrelevant. But even as she answered, something inside her said he needed to know how vividly she saw her protection. "Black," she said, "with blue trim along the outside of my arms and legs."

"Good. Now put the tank on."

She felt suddenly burdened with the weight of the tank on her back. "It's on."

"The tank is full. I checked it myself. You have 45 minutes."

She took a deep breath and was surprised to find that she now wore a diver's mask. She was breathing through her mouth now, connected to the tank with a hose. She nodded.

"This is new technology," Sam went on. "You can speak to me and still receive the air you need. Say something to me to test it."

She remained just on the surface of the water; inches from what she knew would be a deep dive. "I read you loud and clear," she said.

"You comfortable?"

"Yes."

"You have another piece of equipment," Sam said. "You won't even know it's there. But it will allow you to dive as deeply as you need to. You won't get the bends. You won't have any ill effects. Do you understand?"

"Yes." She knew, even as she accepted his instructions as gospel, what he was doing. He was ensuring that she didn't experience the same issues she had when the ship exploded. She had to have faith. She took a deep breath. "I'm ready."

"Go where your instinct takes you. Don't try to guide it."

She was pulled downward as if by an intense magnetic force. She could hear herself breathing in the confines of the mask; it sounded otherworldly. The ocean, so calm on the surface, was teeming with life underneath. Some of the fish were twice Vicki's size or more, and as a shark moved toward her, she found herself holding her breath. She debated within the space of a few seconds whether she should surface when the shark glided past her as if she wasn't there at all.

She turned to watch it move away from her when she spotted something large and hulking just beyond her scope of vision.

"How are you doing, Vicki?" Sam's voice was low but she had the sense that he'd moved closer to her.

"There's something down here," she said.

"Can you move closer to it? Describe it."

In an instant, she was within a few yards of it. Its shape was unmistakable. "It's a submarine."

"Whose?"

She shook her head. "I don't have a sense of danger."

"We're going to move inside it, Vicki. Close your eyes."

She obediently closed her eyes. She could feel herself drifting in the depths.

"When you open your eyes, you'll be inside. You'll find yourself in the control room. Do you understand?"

"Yes."

"Open your eyes."

She took a deep breath and as she exhaled, she opened her eyes. The amount of technology was mind-boggling; every direction she turned, there were gauges, buttons, screens and keyboards. They covered every wall, beginning at knee level and working their way over the crews' heads. At one end was a gigantic screen that reminded her of a large flat-screen television; but this had green and blue images on it that were clearly identifying their surroundings. The entire room was cast in a blue haze from the myriad of displays.

"Are you in the control room?" Sam asked.

"Yes."

"How many are in the room?"

"Four. One on each side. Those are wearing earphones. There is a chair in front of the large monitor at the front of the room. And another chair directly behind it, but about three yards back."

"There's a man in each of the chairs?"

"Affirmative. The other two are standing and conversing."

"What language?"

"English. They're Americans."

She could hear Sam swallow. "Can you hear what they're saying?"

"They've received orders. A vessel is approaching. They're to fire on the target."

"Why are they firing a missile?"

"They are transporting something dangerous—something radioactive? It has to be disposed of in the middle of the ocean."

"Are they getting ready to fire the missile now?"

"Yes."

"I want you to listen to me, Vicki. You're going to close your eyes again. When you open them, you're going to be hovering over the vessel they're about to bomb. You will not be harmed. Do you understand?"

"Yes."

"Close your eyes."

She dutifully closed her eyes. The voices began to fade as if they—or she—was walking away.

"Open your eyes."

She took a deep breath and as she exhaled, just as she had before, she opened her eyes.

She found herself in the exact spot she'd been in when the ship exploded in front of her. "It's the same ship I saw before," she said.

"What nationality is it?"

"Chinese."

"Pull back. Do you understand?"

"Yes."

"Pull back two miles."

Instantly, she moved back as if towed by a puppeteer. She hadn't had time to gauge her proximity before the ship blew up in front of her. But unlike the last time, she was continuing to move back—five miles, then ten. The flames were high and the debris was covering a broad range, but she couldn't feel the heat. "It's gone," she said simply. "Destroyed."

"Okay. That's all, Vicki. Return to me."

She felt the ocean disappearing. In its place was a relentless sun, pristine beaches, and rows of outdoor cells that were nothing more than animal cages. She was plucked back to the administrative building, back to the room with the naked bulb hanging overhead... back to Sam sitting next to her.

She opened her eyes to find him watching her closely. She felt completely drained.

"I'll get you some water," Sam said. "I want you to rest for a bit. Take a nap if you want."

She nodded. She wasn't about to argue; in fact, she felt as if she could slip into a deep sleep within seconds.

"When you wake up, I want sketches of that control room."

"Sure."

"Give me as much detail as you can."

"I'll do it now," Vicki said, struggling to sit up. "It's fresh in my mind now."

"I'll get you some paper," Sam said, coming to his feet. She watched him stride into the hallway with an urgency. She was reluctant to guess at the meaning of all the images she'd seen, but she had a deep feeling that she'd just grabbed a tiger by the tail.

29

Vicki finished the last sketch of the control room and set down her pencil. She was better than a decent artist, she thought as she studied it. She was able to retain even the most minute details and draw them just as she saw them in her mind's eye. While other remote viewers wrote lengthy reports, the agency had long ago discovered her illustrations were worth volumes. She only wished she'd brought her artist's kit with her; what everything needed—from the underwater submarine to the control room—was a watercolor swash of blue.

But as she gathered the pictures of the submarine and the control room, her heart sank and an uneasy feeling developed in the pit of her stomach. She couldn't help but think she'd failed on the mission Sam had given her. She didn't find Gabucci and she'd gathered no intelligence that could shed light on why he was so intent on killing her sister. And that bothered her; perhaps more, she thought, than it should.

"How's it going?" Sam asked as he strode into the room. He set a briefcase on the desk and reached for the sketches. Without waiting for an answer, he added, "These done?"

Vicki nodded. "It's all there."

He sat down in a chair on the other side of the desk. With his glasses perched on the end of his nose, he reviewed the illustrations. After a moment, he whistled. "Headquarters is going to love this," he said. "I'd be willing to bet my bottom dollar this is a US sub."

"I don't understand," Vicki said.

"What do you mean?" He peered at her over the rim of his glasses. "It's perfectly clear."

"No, it isn't. First of all, I should have been looking for Joseph Gabucci. Not maritime attacks."

He removed his glasses to look at her. "Remote viewing 101," he said without noticing her distress. "You can't direct where you're going to go and what you're going to see."

"You direct me with each mission."

"That's true—to a point. I tell you what I'm looking for. It's up to your subconscious to travel to wherever the answer lies. But sometimes, there is a more important message trying to get through. And you can't force it away from that message to find the answer to another."

"You're talking in circles."

"No I'm not. Look, I usually have you work on only one mission at a time. And I had you working on the ships. Even if you tried to clear your mind of that, the subconscious remembers it. So that's where it went."

"Then why even attempt to find Gabucci?"

He shrugged. "It was worth a try. And we'll try again."

He went back to studying the sketches while Vicki's mind wandered to her training where she'd received constant reminders that working on two cases at the same time could skew the results. She remembered well when remote viewers sketched elements of two different buildings in one blueprint or described facilities in Iran but placed them in North Korea. It was dangerous and she wondered at Sam's reasons for risking it.

"What if he commits another crime while my subconscious is hung up on the ships?" she asked with more than a twinge of frustration in her voice. "Brenda's life might depend on me."

Sam glanced up. "If he does commit another crime, it's not your fault, Vicki. He'd have done it anyway. So get that thought out of your head right now." His gaze scanned her face for a moment. "Brenda is safe," he added as if he saw something in her expression. "If you'd like, we'll call and check on her."

She thought of the security at Fort Bragg and the hospital room with Chris attentively watching over her while two officers stood guard just outside the door. He was right, of course; Brenda was safe. She would know it if she wasn't; she would sense it. "Even if my subconscious went where it was supposed to go," she said in an attempt to move the conversation back to a professional level, "obviously the submarine and the ship aren't what I should have been looking for. We know a US submarine isn't bombing the imports; I obviously tapped into a different mission."

"We'll know soon enough what you saw. I'll fax these to the analysts. Someone along the chain will be able to verify the exact submarine and its location. And they'll know when and why the missile was launched. Something like that would have required approval from the top."

"Meaning—?"

"The President. Radioactive material in the middle of the ocean—a nuclear sub launching a missile—that's some serious stuff." He rubbed his chin. "In fact, it doesn't make sense. They risk poisoning the ocean or radioactive particles escaping into our atmosphere. Either one could have catastrophic results… Maybe you locked onto a training mission."

"If so, it wasn't even a mission I'm assigned to. It has nothing to do with the import ships or Gabucci."

"Stop evaluating yourself," Sam said. "That's my job. And I say you did fine."

Before she could respond, Dylan popped his head into the doorway. "Well, so there you are. I've been searchin' for you for quite a while, I 'ave."

"What's up?" Sam tidied the pictures into a neat pile on his lap.

Dylan held up a sheet of paper. He wore a grin but it seemed a bit forced. "I 'ave a confession."

"Who?"

"Shar ma arke Galaid."

"Is that right?" Sam mused, taking the paper from Dylan. He examined the confession. "Quite a bit of detail here."

"At m' urgin'," Dylan said. "I wanted it to be thorough."

Sam read for a moment in silence while Dylan made his way around the desk to kiss Vicki on the forehead. He smoothed back her hair. "Are you doin' alright?"

"Doing fine," she smiled. "Just a little tired."

"You should rest then," he said, his brows beginning to knit together. "You know what they say."

Sam didn't move his head from the paper but he peered upward at Dylan. Vicki waited expectantly.

"If you don't nap when your body requires it, the child will be born narcoleptic."

Sam snorted.

"It's true," Dylan said, frowning. "The child will always be attemptin' to get the sleep the mother didn't."

Vicki forced herself to remain serious. "There's a cot down the hall. I plan to take a short nap."

"He said the reason he bombed the ships was because of American meddling in Somalia?" Sam said it as part statement and part question. They turned their attention from each other back to Sam.

"Aye." Dylan's eyes narrowed. "He was waitin' for me t'day. Said he'd been waitin' each day to see if I'd arrive. I didn't ask 'im for a confession. He was ready to give one as soon as he laid eyes on me."

"Is that so?" Sam continued to hold the confession in his hand but his eyes were fixed on Dylan. His glasses had slipped to the end of his nose again and he peered over the rim. "Did he say how they did it?"

"He did. It's all right there. But if you're askin' me opinion on the matter, I don't believe 'im."

"Why not?"

"Well. He said they bombed the ships from the air."

"In the middle of the Pacific Ocean."

"Aye. And I asked 'im what type o' technology they had. He said Russian-made bombs."

"Is that so?" Sam asked. His voice had become lower, his words more enunciated. "How'd they get hold of it?"

"He insisted the Russians sold 'em the aircraft and the bombs."

"What type of aircraft?"

"Said he didn't know. He said that part was above 'is standin'."

"Then he wouldn't know the type of bomb, either."

"Precisely."

"So he's saying he knows each of the ships was bombed from the air, that the Russians sold them the technology, but he doesn't know what type of aircraft or what type of bomb."

"Oh, you're a fast one," Dylan said. He rubbed Vicki's shoulder absent-mindedly. "I also asked 'im who trained the personnel. After all, you can't just take possession o' a bomber and know just how to use it."

"His answer?"

"The Russians."

Sam added the confession to the stack of sketches. "I may as well fax this, too, while I'm at it. It's one more piece of the puzzle." He made his way to the doorway.

"Aren't you a bit curious as to why he was ready to confess to me?"

He stopped and waited expectantly for Dylan to continue.

"He wants to go into Irish custody. As I'd promised 'im in those initial interrogations. Says he wants to be removed from the Americans."

Sam shrugged. "So?"

"So, what would you 'ave me do?"

"Nothing. We knew all along he wasn't leaving here."

"So that's it? I get a few sentences from 'im on paper and the mission is done and I turn me back on the whole affair?"

Sam studied Dylan's face for a moment before answering. "Tell him we need more. If he doesn't know the make and model of the aircraft, the type of bombs used, and where and how the bombers and pilots were trained, then give us the name of someone higher up the chain who does."

Before he could respond, Sam disappeared down the hall in search of a fax machine.

Dylan continued massaging Vicki's shoulder. "I don't mind tellin' you, Darlin', I've got meself a monster o' a headache."

"Have you taken anything for it?"

"Don't 'ave anythin'." He looked out the window. "It's this place that does it to me. It's a h'ail o' a way for a person to live, don't you think?"

"I try not to think about it."

"And you're successful at that, are you?"

"For the most part." She watched Dylan as he left her side to stand by the window. Just beyond was the beautiful beach she'd looked at only a short time ago. "I usually see these places in my mind's eye. But in addition to seeing it, I can feel the emotions. They can be very strong."

"This man, Galaid, the one I interrogated…" His voice faded off as he looked outside. Vicki remained silent and after a moment, he continued. "It's obvious they've tortured 'im."

"Did you ask?"

He shook his head. "I don't need to know. And I don't think I'd be wantin' to know… I could smell the fear on 'im, if that makes any sense at'al."

"It does. In a place like this, emotions are far stronger than anything we normally experience. And those emotions go on for far longer."

"What do you mean?"

"Well, you know the whole fight-or-flight syndrome."

"Aye."

"What does a man do when he's here, then? He can't fight back. And he can't flee."

"So the stress is sustained."

"And probably multiplies over time."

He turned back to her. "So how do you reconcile y'self to it all?"

Her eyes widened. "It's all for national security, of course. Imagine how many people this guy Galaid could kill or torture if he wasn't in here. He'd be back in Somalia running some criminal network. Consider the confession; he'd be part of the group who is bombing those ships, killing all the people on board."

"But I don't think he's part o' those bombin's."

"You said—"

"I know I got a confession. But I think he'd confess to just about anythin' just to get out o' this place. I don't think he's any angel, either, if you want me opinion about it."

"Well, then, focus on that, even if he's not involved in the bombings."

"I suppose."

Vicki yawned. "I need to lie down. Do you mind...?"

"O' course not. Do you need m' help to get there?"

She smiled tiredly. "No. It's just a few doors down. What will you be doing?"

"I suppose I'll be interrogatin' Galaid a bit more." He ran his hand through his hair. "You know what it is?" he said suddenly. "I've just put me finger on it. I do believe every pair o' eyes I look into 'ere—whether it's a man incarcerated or one o' the interrogators—their eyes look as if they 'ave no soul." He shivered. "I hope I never reach that point, I'll tell you that."

Vicki managed a smile. "Something tells me you never will."

30

Joseph closed the curtains in the hotel room before turning on a lamp. Then he returned for the bags he'd left just inside the door. He placed one bag on the counter in the bathroom and the second one on the closet floor. He carried the third to the desk and carefully unpacked the laptops, plugged them in and powered them up.

While he waited for both to boot, he stopped in front of the mirror and removed the white hair piece. It had been a decent disguise; it contained a silicone scalp to make it appear as if his hair was thinning, which was a far better camouflage than the overly thick rug of the typical toupee. Next, he removed the eyeglasses with the heavy black frames.

He debated a moment on whether to leave the mustache; it was dense, primarily white with a few silvery strands to make it look realistic. But the glue that held it in place was beginning to itch so after a brief hesitation, he peeled it off. He rubbed his upper lip as he peered into the mirror. He hoped he didn't develop a rash.

He removed the Valentino gray pinstripe suit jacket, the navy tie, and the crisp white shirt. Next came the Amedeo Testoni knock-offs and the pinstripe pants. Finally, he slipped off the Sky Moon Tourbillon look-alike watch and the palladium-like wedding band encrusted with fake diamonds.

He'd definitely looked the part of a successful businessman as he'd checked into the finest hotel he could find in Fayetteville, just half an hour from Lumberton and fifteen minutes to Fort Bragg. He'd requested a suite complete with a Jacuzzi and he'd inquired at the desk about upscale restaurants.

He wouldn't be mistaken for a killer.

Outside his hotel room window where he could easily keep an eye on it was a Mercedes coupe in silver metallic; not too showy but just enough to fit the persona he would need for the next phase of his plan.

The laptops both blinked at the login screens and he sat down in front of them in his underwear, completed the logon and dutifully entered the information to access the hotel's Wi-Fi.

He began the tedious task of scanning the tapes from the Irishman's house. He noted the time he left the house with his girlfriend in tow—3:45 am—and the time Christopher Sandige awakened, showered and changed, and ate breakfast. He did a quick job of feeding the fish in the building in their back yard before leaving at 9:15 am. After that, the tapes consisted of nothing but empty rooms.

His phone rang and he answered it while his eyes remained riveted to the screen. "Yeah?"

"About Sam Mazoli," the caller said simply.

"Go ahead," Joseph answered.

"His records are sealed. Only those with SCI clearances can get it."

SCI, he knew, stood for Sensitive Compartmented Information. It wasn't technically above Top Secret but it meant that anyone requesting that information would have to show proof that they were themselves part of the SCI project under a specified code name.

"Is there a code name?" Joseph asked.

"The code name is under a separate SCI."

"You're saying one SCI is required to obtain the name of the project he's assigned to, and another SCI for his personnel record?"

"That's correct."

Joseph leaned back in his chair. This would make it much more challenging to find out where he was assigned and what he was working on. "What about the girl?"

"There's no record of her."

"No record at all? Or no record within the agency?"

"The agency. There's no record she's ever worked for them, past or present."

"And the Irishman?"

"Same thing. Neither exists within the agency."

"Interesting."

"But we do have the information on their address."

"Continue."

"The house was purchased less than a year ago. It's held jointly by Victoria Boyd and Michael Dylan Maguire."

"Anything else?"

"DMV records. Both licensed in North Carolina."

"You get copies?"

"Affirmative."

"Email them to me."

There was a slight hesitation. "They're on their way."

"Excellent. Anything more to add?"

"Just their present location."

Joseph kept his eyes on the screen. The house was quiet as a tomb. "Which is?"

"Black Site 557."

He hesitated. "Where is that?"

"We're working on it."

"I want everything you can get on Boyd and Maguire."

"I'll call when we have more."

"And Brenda Carnegie?"

"She remains in the same hospital room at Fort Bragg. Christopher Sandige has been with her all day."

"Do we have one of the guards?"

"Affirmative."

"His schedule?"

"Eight p.m. to six a.m."

"Excellent. And I'm having a dinner meeting with—?"

"Colonel Beauchene. Eight o'clock tomorrow evening. We'll email his address at Fort Bragg."

"Excellent." With that, Joseph clicked off the phone. He had roughly thirty hours before he would drive through the gates at Fort Bragg to meet with the Colonel. His associates would, no doubt, provide the Colonel's office and home numbers in the event the soldier at the gate wanted verification. And once he was on post and had completed his obligatory dinner meeting, he would be free to wander… all the way to the post hospital. With one of the guards in their pocket, his visit to Miss Carnegie should not be problematic. Easy in, easy out. A quick shot of heart-stopping medicine in her IV and he could scratch her off his list.

Then he could turn his full attention to Sandige, Boyd and Maguire.

31

Vicki lay on her side with the covers pulled over her shoulder as she watched Dylan drying off through the open bathroom door. His thick black hair was damp from his shower and a few stray locks dropped onto his forehead, brushing his brow. Her eyes roamed from his muscular shoulders and arms down to his abdomen, flat and tight, before taking in his long, lean legs.

He tussled his hair once more before hanging up the towel and quickly combing his hair, though it did little good as the locks instantly dropped back onto his forehead.

When he turned off the bathroom light, it left the bedroom in a dark gray-blue haze. As her eyes adjusted to the dimmer light, she realized the moon was peaking around the curtain edges, providing her with an almost illuminated view of Dylan's body as he walked into the bedroom and pulled back the covers.

"Are you cold then?" he asked, eyeing the thick comforter she held onto and kept pulled to her neck.

"I'm fine," she murmured.

He climbed into bed but didn't bother pulling the covers over himself. He moved close to her, slipping his arms under the covers to wrap her in a loving embrace. Then he abruptly stopped and pulled the cover off her upper body.

"What the h'ail are you wearin'?" he asked, choking back laughter. Before she could answer, he added, "Those jammies look like somethin' me Mam would'a worn."

She pulled the covers back up to her neck. "Stop laughing at me. It's warm."

"Well, I'll turn the heat upta ninety if you'll agree to take that thin' off."

"What do you care what I wear?"

He sat up, his eyes wide and his mouth slightly open. "You've always slept in the nude, or in your panties. And you haven't caught a cold yet, now 'ave ya? Don't I 'old you close and keep you warm?"

She bit her lower lip.

"Okay," he said. "Out w' it."

"What do you mean?"

"I mean, somethin's about and I'd be wantin' to know what it is. Did I do somethin' to hurt you?"

"Of course not."

"Are you angry w' me then?"

"No. You've done nothing wrong."

He picked at the long cotton gown. "Then what's it w' this?"

She hesitated for a moment. "It's silly."

"I beg to differ w' you. Anythin' that causes me woman to dress like me Mam isn't silly. It's damn right serious, I'll 'ave you know."

She chuckled. "Now I really feel silly."

"So tell me what's what." He pulled the covers back further and straddled her, bending down to kiss her lightly before pulling back expectantly.

"I had a dream."

"Oh?"

"I dreamed... I dreamed that we were being watched."

He burst into laughter. "Is that all?"

She pushed at his chest. "Stop laughing at me."

"Well, I'm surprised you haven't dreamt that a'fore now."

"What do you mean?"

"Well, think about it, Darlin'. You spend your life spyin' on others. Don't you think it's quite natural for you to dream that someone is spyin' on *you*?"

"I never thought of it that way."

He rose up slightly and pulled her nightgown up before resting back down on her. "There's no one watchin' us, Darlin'. The drapes are drawn; the door is shut. It's just you and me."

He bent to kiss her but as he grew more passionate, she pulled back. "But—" she managed to say.

He looked at her patiently. "But what?"

"I don't know; I have this feeling…"

"Could it be the alarm cameras?" When she didn't answer, he said, "The cameras are installed around the perimeter o' the house. There are two cameras inside. One is starin' down the hallway *outside the closed door there*," he emphasized, "and picks up the stairs. The other is in the downstairs hallway. You can see it on the telly. There's nothin' to fear inside our own bedroom."

She knew he was speaking logically and she began to feel even sillier than before.

After a moment, he said, "Will you sit up and allow me to slip this thin' o'er your head and be done w' it?"

Sheepishly, she sat up and he gently slipped the gown off her, tossing it on the floor beside the bed. "I'll be most happy to turn up the heat for you, if that will make you warm. Or," he added with a sly smile, "you can allow me to heat you up quite nicely."

Before she could answer, he smothered her neck with kisses, his lips hot and moist against her skin. As he pulled back, she groaned in protest. Their eyes locked and as she moved her hands along his muscular arms to his chest, she tried to push Mam's image out of her mind. *Don't watch, Mam*, she thought as she raised her head and pulled down his to meet her lips. *Allow us this time alone.*

She slept on her side with her back to the bathroom door. Dylan lay curled behind her, his legs intertwined with hers and his arm protectively draped over her. His measured breathing was soft and warm against her ear, his face nuzzled into her strawberry blond hair.

All but the sheet was rumpled at the foot of the bed, a vestige from their lovemaking, and the sheet was only partway up their bodies, not quite covering their waists.

She dreamed she stood in a long hallway; so interminable that she could not see its end. The air was shrouded as if she was peering through a fog. As she looked for a light, she realized there were no windows through which sunlight might travel and there didn't appear to be any overhead lights or switches along the wall.

She groped her way along until she spotted movement up ahead. It appeared as if a door was open, but puzzled, she realized there was no light creeping from the room into the hall. Instead, it appeared as if apparitions moved through the gloom; shadows so black that she could distinguish them from the dark hall.

She felt a warm breath against her neck, and she swiveled her head to look behind her. But the hallway she had just negotiated was gone; there was no floor and no walls, only empty air swirled behind her as if she stood on a precipice. Startled, she turned back to find the remains of the hazy hallway still in front of her and the shadows still undulating at the open doorway.

She felt drawn to the ghostly presence, despite an internal struggle against a jittery, uneasy feeling that mounted within her as she grew closer. It was as if the key to a mystery was hidden just beyond the threshold and despite the possible dangers, she had no choice but to continue toward them—like a moth to a flame.

The air around her grew oppressive; perspiration trickled along her brow and upper lip. Her breath had grown ragged and labored as if the oxygen was diminishing as she grew closer. When she stopped once more to look behind her, she realized the hall—and her escape route—was disappearing with every step she took. She had no choice but to continue forward.

A steady, measured ticking reached her ears that grew louder as she arrived at the doorway and louder still as she moved into the room. She became obsessed with the sound. It filled her ears and her head until all other thoughts were blocked out, eradicated. She became consumed with finding the source but it echoed off the walls and through her brain, each *tick tock* reverberating through her body. The room was so dark that it appeared as though it had no ending and as she whirled around, even the door through which she'd entered was gone. All that was left was an empty void so black and so all-encompassing that she could not see her own hands as they groped blindly in front of her.

Then on the other side of the room, something flickered as if it was catching the rays from a spotlight. She was lured toward it as though her free will had been wrenched from her. She was fixated on reaching it.

The closer she moved to the object, the brighter the spotlight became until it was nearly blinding her. It cast a brilliance throughout until it appeared as though there was no room at all; instead, she was making her way through thick, choking clouds.

She was almost upon it before her brain could turn the form and the sound into something she recognized. It was a pendulum. It swung of its own accord, each *tick* and each *tock* vibrating to some unseen evil, as if it had developed a life of its own. It spoke to her, the volume growing louder and brasher until it seemed to be shouting at her. She covered her ears but the action did nothing to alleviate the agony that each measured sound made.

She reached out her hand to physically stop its movement but the pendulum swung through her palm as if it wasn't there at all. She gasped, pulling back in horror. The pendulum grew larger before her eyes and she backed away as she squeezed them shut to try and block out the image.

Open your eyes, the air whispered. Her eyes opened. Beneath the pendulum lay a plain manila file.

Vicki gasped as she awakened. The room was still and silent, except for Dylan's steady breathing against her ear.

She lay for a long while, wondering if his measured breath had somehow morphed into the sound of the pendulum. But she knew it had not; his breathing was soft and nearly imperceptible even though he was so close that he was wrapped around her. The sound of the pendulum had been louder than a freight train and it had hurt as much as a sonic boom.

Why had the innocuous object sent such terror through her? She wondered. Her heart still pounded, hurting her chest. Her breaths remained short and ragged as if she was fighting for oxygen and an icy cold had permeated through her body. Even the sheet she tried to wrap around them felt as if it had been stored in a freezer; it did nothing to warm her.

She pressed her back closer to Dylan. He responded by sleepily tightening his hold on her and drawing her nearer. She tried to calm herself with the knowledge that she was safe in his arms. But something in the pit of her soul screamed that she would not be safe until she found the source of the pendulum.

32

Dylan stepped outside the fish house. He waited for Shep to follow on his heels before gently closing the door behind them. The cool air hit him full in the face; it tingled against skin that was moist from a morning working in the 80 degree heat required for the angelfish. His hair was damp as it fell across his forehead and brushed his brow, and he instinctively swept it out of the way, only to have it fall back a moment later.

His eyes moved upward and rested on the bedroom window directly below the master suite. The ceiling light was on and as he watched, he could see Vicki moving through the room. A quick smile crossed his face; she was probably measuring for the infant furniture or planning in detail how she'd want to decorate. He thought back to their visit to the hardware store; he'd tried to steer her away from the border she'd selected but truth be told, he wouldn't have cared if she'd picked flaming monkeys, if that was what made her happy. He was going to have a son, and he couldn't have been more content.

"So. You'll do it, then?" he said into his cell phone.

"I would like nothin' better, Mick," Father Thomas Rowan said. "But I'd just not be knowin' if I could legally wed you in the States."

"What do you think o' this, then? We could 'ave a civil ceremony mayhap; I could inquire about it. Then you could officiate at a more formal service."

"So you've asked 'er already, 'ave you?"

Vicki moved to the window and stretched a measuring tape across the opening. Catching sight of Dylan, she stopped and smiled. He half-waved at her. Lord, she was beautiful. Her long, strawberry blond hair made his fingers itch for the fine strands and her delicate features called to his masculinity to protect her. "I 'aven't quite asked 'er yet," he said, "but I'll be takin' care o' that this evenin'. I'll be takin' 'er out to a romantic supper. It 'as to be special, you know, when I ask 'er."

"And you're certain she'll say 'yes'?" There was a hint of good-natured mockery in his voice.

"She'd better, I'll tell you that," Dylan said. Vicki went back to measuring but his eyes continued to follow her.

"And this formal weddin'—"

"Well, I'm not quite certain 'ow formal it will be, to be perfectly honest about it. We don't 'ave any friends 'ere. Just Chris and Brenda. Then Sam will o' course be givin' 'er away."

"Why don't you come back to Ireland for it? You know the whole village would be pleased as punch to attend the ceremonies."

"I'm afraid to take Vicki back home in 'er condition," Dylan said.

"You think Ireland will 'arm 'er?"

"I'm concerned, is all, about 'er needin' medical attention on account o' the baby, and there won't be medical care to be 'ad."

"Are you jokin' me? She's an American citizen. Any physician in the country will attend to 'er."

"Why is that?"

"She's got insurance, doesn't she?"

"Aye. It came w' the job."

"Well, there you 'ave it."

"But what if we can't find a suitable physician?"

"How about if I invite a couple to the ceremony? Would that please you?"

"I'll put some thought into it," he said reluctantly. "Does that mean you won't be comin' to the States to officiate?"

"I will if you don't come 'ere. Just give it a bit o' thought, 'eh? Either way, you could get married by the government to make it all official. Then by me to make it right a'fore God."

"Sure, then."

"Sure."

There was silence on the other end of the phone and Vicki moved out of his line of sight. A moment later, the light in the nursery was turned off.

"So," Dylan said. "On another subject."

A bell sounded in the background. "That's m' next appointment. My apologies, but I don't 'ave much time to continue speakin' to you, Mick."

"I'll get right to it, then. You remember the thin's you took from the Hoolihan brothers?"

There was a slight hesitation. "You 'aven't told a soul about that, 'ave you, Mick?"

"Of course not. I was just thinkin', is all, if a body came across somethin' valuable, say somethin' mayhap seized durin' the war that didn't belong to 'em but it didn't quite belong to anybody else, either, or at least they wouldn't 'ave known who it might belong to, or if the person was even still alive, or if they could even locate 'em…"

"Lord Almighty, get it out already."

"Are you usin' the Lord's name in vain, Father?"

"Just get to the point."

"If a body found somethin' like what you 'ave, who would it belong to? The body what found it, or some unknown entity from decades a'fore?"

"Well." There was silence on the other end of the line. Then, "Supposin' someone found somethin' like say, a piece o' gold. And it dated back to say, the war. I suppose if you could find the rightful owner, it would belong to 'em, even if they'd been separated from it for quite a time."

"But how would you go about findin' the rightful owner?" Dylan pressed. "And what if you didn't actually want to find 'em?"

"Are you sayin' you took somethin' you found 'ere in Ireland, Mick?"

"No. I'm sayin'…" He glanced around the yard but no one else was there. Shep would have alerted him if there was, he realized. She sat dutifully at his feet, her head bobbing in every direction, her eyes alert. "I'm sayin' this house I bought, everythin' in the house came w' the sale on account o' the owner's heir didn't want to be bothered w' it."

"Well, if you found it in the house, then, and you bought the whole entire thin', it's rightfully yours. You have the necessary papers to prove it?"

"Aye. But, 'ere's the thin'. Suppose the person who lived 'ere a'fore had taken somethin' that wasn't rightfully 'is. And I found it. And I know he didn't come by it honestly. What then?"

"Well, you could notify the local authorities."

"And what would they do? Say, if the objects in question came from, say, another country?"

"The only way to find out is to contact 'em. Whether they find the rightful owner or no, you'd have done what was right."

"But suppose—" Dylan swallowed and ran his hand through his hair. "Suppose it's rather valuable. And suppose it would leave Vicki and the baby—me son—in good stead, should anythin' 'appen to me. Suppose—"

"Suppose you're wantin' to keep what you found, and you're just lookin' for the priest to bless your action?"

"Oh, h'ail."

"Are you cursin' at the priest, Mick?"

"Forget I asked you."

"No. I won't forget. I found valuables and I stuffed 'em into a dark corner o' the church. You didn't see me handin' 'em over to the authorities, did you now?"

"I'm not judgin' what you did."

"Well, that's good, Mick, 'cause I expect the Lord to handle that chore when it's time. Are you in a hurry to get rid o' it, the thin' you found?"

"I suppose not."

"Then pray on the matter. Your conscience will guide you."

"You're no help at'al."

"And I won't be help to anyone else if I don't get off this phone." Father Thomas' voice turned softer. "Ring me up whene'er you want to talk, Mick. And give some thought to comin' 'ere for the ceremony. Your Mam would'a loved you comin' back 'ere for it."

"I'll think on it. Take care o' y'self, Thomas."

"Aye. And you as well."

With that, they clicked off. Dylan stood for a moment, absent-mindedly tossing his phone from one palm to the other while he continued to stare at the nursery window. Then he took a deep breath. He had work still to do in the fish house, and he'd promised Vicki he'd go with her to see Brenda and then shopping for the nursery afterward. He'd better get a move on.

33

Brenda's face was flushed and the scalp along her hairline was damp. She was leaning back against the pillows in her hospital room, surrounded by Chris, Sam, Vicki and Dylan. And she was shaking her head emphatically.

"I have no idea why he wants to kill me," she said. "I've told you repeatedly: I thought the whole ordeal was over once the computer fraud was exposed."

"You're not telling us something," Sam insisted.

She groaned. "The FBI was here all morning. They've threatened to send me back to prison to await my trial."

Vicki gasped. She sat down on the edge of the bed and took one of Brenda's hands in her own.

"There's nothing I can do to help you," Sam said. "FBI has jurisdiction."

She rolled her eyes.

"If you won't tell us, will you tell your sister?"

"Look," she said in exasperation. "Don't you think if I had any information on this guy, I'd be telling everybody? The creep's tried to kill me—not once, not twice—three times. I want him put away forever—probably a hell of a lot worse than anybody else around here."

"I trust what she's saying," Chris added. "She's got nothing to gain and everything to lose by withholding information."

"Just *think*," Sam urged. "Think about that list of crooked politicians you turned over. Who is on that list that would want you killed? Who has the most to lose?"

"I've *been* thinking," Brenda moaned. "I have nothing else to do in here but think." She waved her hand at the television screen. "And watch TV."

Dylan stole a glance at the screen. Four political pundits sat around a table; they were obviously shouting over each other but Sam had muted the sound when he'd arrived. And it was just as well. At the President's urging, companies were relocating their factories back to the United States, and two companies were returning to North Carolina. It was a boon to the economy with thousands going back to work, and more companies were expected within the coming months. His political opponents were saying his rhetoric was all for political gain, but even they could not deny the fact that no one could ensure safe passage of all the goods departing China for the United States.

"And what would you be watchin' all that political stuff for, anyways, I wonder?" Dylan broke in.

"What else am I going to watch? Don't know if you've noticed, but I'm not exactly an *'I Love Lucy'* kind of gal." She used her free hand to brush the hair back from her face. The strands were damp and her forehead was covered in perspiration.

"Are you watchin' it mayhap because you've got the dirt on one o' 'em? And mayhap you're busy watchin' the price go up on 'im?"

"A year ago, I'd have said 'yes'," she admitted. "But the feds have all the dirt on every one of them now. If I made a move, they'd intercept it." Vicki started to voice her objection, but Brenda spoke over her. "You don't think I know they're keeping tabs on me? I'm still wearing this lovely ankle bracelet, and I have no access to the Internet—no smartphone, no tablet, no laptop, *no nothing*. And if I dared try to logon, I'm sure they'd know it before I did."

"Just promise you'll *think*," Sam said. "There has to be a reason. He's not doing this just for the kicks. The stakes are high and he knows it. Whoever hired him knows it. And somewhere in that head of yours, you know it."

She groaned. "Yes, I'll think about it. Happy now?"

"Why are you sweating so much?" Vicki asked. Her brows furrowed. "Your hand is burning up."

"It's hot in this room," she grumbled.

"It isn't hot in here," Chris said. He leaned down and stroked her hair away from her face. "Vicki's right. You are burning up."

Dylan stepped to the door, opened it, and motioned for the nurse at the station. The two servicemen remained posted at the door, one on either side. He waited until the nurse approached and then said in a low voice, "Can you take 'er temperature, please? We think she's runnin' a bit o' a fever."

"Why, certainly," she responded. Her name badge said 'Nurse Penny'. "I'll be right back."

Dylan stepped back into the room and allowed the door to slowly close behind him.

"I'm telling you, it's nothing," Brenda insisted. But she closed her eyes and reclined into the pillows. Her eyes were sunken, her lids an odd shade of maroon.

The door opened as Penny swept into the room. She placed the thermometer in Brenda's mouth as she felt her pulse. She cocked her head and took a breath. Her mouth pursed and she pulled back the covers from Brenda's leg. "Everybody out."

"We're family," Dylan said. His tone was non-negotiable. "Vicki and I are stayin'."

Sam made his way to the door without a word. Chris appeared to be ready to argue but when the nurse began to unwrap the leg, he joined Sam in the hall.

Dylan couldn't say with any authority that he was accustomed to wounds and their various stages of decay or recovery. But he'd spent most of his life in a village where proper medical care was a luxury; if one had the relative wealth required for private insurance, a physician could be found in short order. But if one was dirt poor as he'd been raised, the government's guarantee of medical care meant weeks or months waiting for proper treatment.

So the villagers had done what they could themselves. It meant setting broken bones, sewing up wounds, reducing fevers and using whatever herbal or over-the-counter medications they could find—and pray for the best.

"I'll be right back," she said. "Don't touch anything."

As she left the room once more, Brenda said, "Can somebody hand me the remote? I want to hear this." Her eyes were fixed on the television screen.

"Are you crazy?" Vicki breathed.

"Give 'er the remote," Dylan said. When Vicki cast an inquisitive look at him, he added, "It'll keep 'er mind off 'er leg."

Vicki grabbed the remote and turned on the sound.

Penny moved into the room, her arms filled with supplies. "The doctor will be right here," she said. She laid the bandages on the bed beside Brenda and finished stripping her leg of the old ones.

They waited nearly half an hour, during which time they were subjected to clips from the President's last speech and new ones from the Governor's about the economic recovery, jobs creation and a return to pride in the "Made in the USA" mantra.

When the doctor arrived, Dylan and Vicki were urged toward the opposite side of the room while they worked. From his vantage point, he could not see her wound but he had a clear view of the medical team's faces. They were grim, their mouths set, while they cleansed the wound. As they inspected her body from the neck down, he turned away to give her privacy. He pulled Vicki close to him, but though she wrapped her arms around him, she kept her eyes on her sister.

Finally, the doctor addressed them. "You're Miss Carnegie's sister?" he asked.

"Yes." Vicki stepped forward and Dylan turned back around to see the nurse helping Brenda back into her gown.

"The wound is showing signs of infection," Doctor Dumas said as he removed the gloves from his hands. "I was concerned about this."

"What happens now?"

"We're catching it early but obviously, it's something that requires very close supervision. We're going to give her something to bring the swelling down in her leg and something to stop the infection from moving outside of the wound vicinity."

Dylan stole a look at Brenda. Her expression was completely impassive, as though they were discussing the weather. Something told him during the cleansing of the wound, she didn't flinch, either.

"We're also going to increase her pain medication—"

"No," Brenda said abruptly.

"Excuse me?" the doctor said, clearly taken aback by her opposition to his instructions.

"Do whatever you need to do to stop the infection," Brenda said calmly and evenly. "Do whatever it takes to save the leg. But I don't want any pain medication."

"You need to get some rest," Penny said. "The medicine will help with that."

Brenda looked pointedly at Dylan. "I don't want to take anything—*anything*—that will impair my abilities."

"Your abilities to do what?" Vicki breathed.

Dylan squeezed Vicki's shoulder. "Vicki's right, Brenda. Normally I'd agree w' you. But you've nothin' to fear here. There're guards posted outside your door twenty-four seven. You're safe here. Safe enough to get the rest you need so your body can do its healin'."

"I don't want it." She bit her lower lip in defiance.

"May we 'ave a word w' with 'er in private?" Dylan asked.

Doctor Dumas nodded. "I'm done here—for now. I'll leave instructions for the staff." He turned to Brenda as he reached the door. "You won't lose your leg. Not on my watch." With that, he was out the door, followed by the nurse.

"And just what do you think you're doin'?" Dylan asked as he reached her bedside.

"I know exactly what I'm doing," Brenda answered. "Get me some whiskey or rum and I'll take that. But I won't take anything that's going to knock me out. Not with a killer on the loose and my face on his target."

"What can I do to make you believe you're safe 'ere?"

"That's just it, Irish. There's nothing you can do. You think a hired hit man won't find a way to get on post? That he won't be willing to kill those guys outside my door to get to me?"

"First, he'd 'ave to know you're here. And I don't know how he'd be knowin' that."

"Dylan's right," Vicki said. Her voice was soft but her jaw was set.

"Second, just what do you think you'd be capable o' doin' to protect y'self if those men outside that door can't protect you?"

"Don't argue with me, Irish. No matter what you say, I will not take anything that could knock me out."

Dylan threw up his hands in exasperation. "It's your body," he said. "If you can deal w' the pain, then 'ave at it."

"Dylan!" Vicki said.

"He's right, Sis. I know how much pain I can tolerate. And it's more than you might think."

They remained for a long moment, eyeing each other as if they were three boxers in a ring. Then Dylan said, "Well. And so you need your rest, w' or w'out medicine. Darlin'," he took Vicki's hand, "let's join Sam and Chris."

"But—"

"We'll be back to check on you," he said, pulling Vicki toward the door.

———   ———   ———

Vicki wriggled out of Dylan's grasp as the door closed behind them. "Stop dragging me along like I'm a child!" she demanded, her face reddening.

He was so stunned he was speechless.

"You know," she continued, "just because I try to get along with everybody doesn't mean I don't have feelings—or opinions." She started back toward the door. "And I am not finished convincing my sister that she needs pain medicine and a good rest!"

"Darlin'," Dylan said, side-stepping in front of her. "Please, hear me out. I 'ave a plan, if you'd just listen to me. Just for a moment. That's all I'm askin' o' you."

The two guards stood. "Is there a problem?" one asked.

Vicki crossed her arms in front of her. "No," she said. One sat back down but the other remained standing. Sam and Chris were nowhere in sight. She turned back to Dylan. "Okay. What?"

"I don't think we're goin' to convince your sister to take medicine she doesn't want. She was rather emphatic."

"That's because I didn't get my chance to convince her."

"But," he continued undaunted, "you are 'er next o' kin, are you not?"

Her face relaxed a bit. "What does that have to do with anything?"

"Well, I'm thinkin', is all, that if your sister isn't able to make a coherent decision on account o' the pain she must be dealin' with, and the infection and all, that mayhap the medical staff would allow you to make the decision?"

"And what? Force it down her?"

"Oh, not at'al. They'll be givin' 'er medications for the infection and she is, after all, already on IV's... Isn't it possible they could drop a bit o' pain medicine into 'er IV?"

"That is *so* devious."

"I'll give you that. It is."

"It might just work." She abruptly turned toward the nurse's station with Dylan on her heels. "Nurse," she said as they approached, "is it possible for me to make a decision regarding my sister's care?"

"Do you have a power of attorney? A medical directive?"

"Not quite. But I am her only relative. Anyway, I'm wondering exactly what help the pain killers would do her?"

"To be honest," Penny answered, "I don't see how she's able to go all this time without any. She's had the morphine pump but she refuses to use it. She's got to be in tremendous pain."

"Yes," Vicki said, "but would it help her medical condition if she were to take the pain meds?"

"It would certainly allow her to get some rest. That, in itself, would help in her recovery. She doesn't sleep much, not even overnight. She just naps here and there."

"It's on account o' 'er not feelin' safe," Dylan mumbled next to Vicki's ear.

"Can I make the decision to give her something for the pain?" Vicki asked.

"I don't think so. Not without a medical power of attorney… The only way would be if she was unconscious or unable to make the decision herself."

"But wouldn't the pain itself color her ability to think rationally?" Vicki pressed.

The nurse sighed. "I'd really rather see her take it," she admitted. "I know she's got to be in tremendous pain. Like I said, I don't know how she can handle it…"

"Then you'll give 'er somethin'?" Dylan asked.

She looked from one to the other. "I could get in a lot of trouble…"

"She'll never have to know," Vicki said softly. "Perhaps it could be slipped in with the medicine for the infection and fever? She would simply fall asleep and when she wakes up, she'll have had some good rest and given her body more of a chance to heal…"

She glanced down the hallway, though it was perfectly clear except for the two guards. The second had returned to his seat and though they both kept a vigilant watch, their voices were too low for them to have heard the conversation.

"Okay," Penny said. "I'll slip it in. The doctor, after all, prescribed it… And if she doesn't ask me what each pill is for when I give them to her, she'd never have to know…"

"Thank you," Dylan said. "We'll all be restin' easy knowin' she's gettin' the best o' care."

"Yes," Vicki agreed. "We'll *all* rest easier."

34

Joseph would have preferred a restaurant more suitable for romantics; they tended to be dark with plenty of cubbyholes that provided privacy. In contrast, the one he found himself in now was open and brightly lit, affording no possibility for concealment. Oversized windows with roped back gold draperies further infringed on any desire for solitude. Though it was early evening, the skies were already the color of pitch, the somber mood heightened by a low, turbulent cloud cover. It meant that someone could be standing just a few yards from the window, plainly observing him while remaining completely undetectable themselves.

His eyes swept his surroundings; nearly every table was occupied. Instinctively, he weighed the possibility that a spy or another assassin was seated under the same roof, but as he studied each person with veiled eyes, he ticked each one off his list of probabilities. Still, he was uneasy with so many potential witnesses. Dinner had been a ruse to get him on post without raising suspicion but now he discovered himself checking his watch too frequently.

His eyes settled on Colonel Beauchene, who was busy nursing his whiskey sour.

Joseph took an unhurried sip of his rum and coke. He didn't often drink alcohol; it had the potential for muddling his instincts and worsening his aim, two things a hit man couldn't afford. There was a reason he'd managed to remain in a profession meant for much younger, fitter men. "Drone warfare is the future," he said in a low voice.

Colonel Beauchene looked up. "Where does that leave the average soldier?"

"Safely shielded from harm. Your men can be sitting at their desks right here at Fort Bragg, each one remotely controlling a drone in the Middle East. Our software is so precise that they can target a single individual. Using a joystick, they can simply push a button to lock onto the target and another button to release the weapon. It's as easy as playing a computer game." He sipped his drink while he studied the Colonel's expression.

"What can you give me that DARPA doesn't have?"

"We're in close contact with DARPA's scientists," he answered smoothly. He absent-mindedly caressed his diamond wedding ring while he wondered if the reference to the Defense Advanced Research Projects Agency had been meant to test him. "Not only are we assisting in the development of drones, but also of robotic warriors. Think about it: when the United States needs ground troops in the next conflict, we send androids instead of men. The enemy doesn't have a chance."

"And I suppose each one is remote controlled by a soldier at his desk?"

"We're moving far beyond that. One officer can control a hundred androids; soon it will be hundreds, perhaps thousands. Through the development of thinking robots, he can issue a command—through software, of course—that they will follow regardless of the obstacles thrown in their way."

Colonel Beauchene finished his drink and motioned to the waiter for another. The buffet was across the room, the line steady, and the aroma of beef, chicken and a variety of vegetables wafted under Joseph's nose. His stomach growled and he wished the man would suggest at least breaking momentarily for dinner, but he didn't appear to be interested in food.

"Give me an example," he said.

"The newest robot technology allows each one to detect a weapon pointed in their direction," Joseph said. "While humans are limited to seeing in front of them with a narrow peripheral view, robots don't have that restriction. Sensors can detect from three miles away; even long-range missiles can be identified by this advanced software."

Joseph leaned forward, his eyes locking onto the colonel's. "Suppose the officer issues an order for the androids to move into a village and disarm every resident there—and round them up. They will search for humans in every nook, issue a command in their own language to line up at a designated point, and as weapons are detected, they can melt them with laser weapon technology."

"So the androids will carry laser weapons?"

"They won't carry them. They're built into each finger. They can be fired one at a time or all ten can be fired at once for a deadly effect—or any combination can be used."

The waiter brought another drink and eyed Joseph's nearly full glass before withdrawing.

"And you say these lasers will *melt* the enemy's weapons?"

"That's right. Suppose you have an AK-47 trained on me, and I'm the android." Joseph lifted his forefinger on one hand. "Before you know what I'm about to do, I've done it: I've fired a laser that is melting your weapon—and if you don't let go of it, it will give you third degree burns—or worse. It has the power to take the skin off your fingers until only the bone is exposed."

Colonel Beauchene whistled. A few patrons looked in their direction, and Joseph inwardly winced. He didn't have to remind himself of the wig he wore with the exposed, lifelike silicone scalp; it was itching something terrible and he longed to remove it. So was his mustache but he eased the discomfort by smoothing down the hairs, a habit he'd seen men do with their facial hair. He only hoped the disguise would prevent any witnesses from correctly identifying him.

"I'd like a demonstration," the colonel said abruptly.

Joseph managed a smile that he hoped appeared sincere. "I'll be happy to oblige. In fact, we're very anxious to show off this new technology. It's far more advanced than anyone else in the world even comes close to."

"How can you be sure the Russians or the Chinese don't have something similar?"

He smiled a bit wider. "It's part of our job to know our enemies' capabilities."

The colonel nodded. "So when can you demonstrate it?"

"We can fly you to Washington," Joseph said, "where we can provide you with an unparalleled display of hundreds of androids acting on one man's command."

"I'd want my staff to see this as well."

"How many?"

"Oh, maybe nine or ten."

"We'll fly you all to Washington." Joseph thought he detected some reservation in the man's set jaw so he continued, "You can understand how difficult it would be to fly these androids here on a commercial aircraft." He chuckled. "I could manage one and we could demonstrate that here on post, but if you want to see some truly impressive stuff—and speak to the scientists themselves—I'd suggest a trip to Washington. All expenses paid, of course."

"We'd be able to speak to the scientists?"

"Absolutely. We'll give you a full tour… We'll demonstrate them running on treadmills at 60 miles per hour—the average speed of a cheetah. Jumping three stories high to land on a roof or jumping from three stories to land below—all without compromising the android's mission. There's a lot we can show you there."

There was a sparkle in his eyes now. "When can we make this happen?"

Joseph slipped his hand inside his Valentino suit jacket and pulled out a slim gold card case. He noticed the man's eyes on it as he removed one of his business cards and handed it to him. He was obviously estimating the cost of the fancy case, Joseph thought, as his eyes then traveled to his Sky Moon Tourbillon look-alike watch. "If I can get your business card," he continued, "I can give you a call tomorrow and we can set everything up. How does next week sound? We'll fly you up in the afternoon, have a nice evening on the town, and spend the next day touring the facilities and introducing you to our fleet of next-generation drones and robots."

Colonel Beauchene accepted Joseph's card and set it on the table in front of him while he rifled through his pocket for his own business card. The name was real but just not Joseph's, and the phone number and address were legitimate. Joseph had printed out the cards on his portable inkjet printer before leaving the hotel, and the number and address were those of a bona fide defense contractor. The name he used was that of a low-level administrator who would be quite surprised when the colonel phoned him. But it wouldn't matter by then. Joseph would be finished with dinner within the hour and within two, he will have taken out his target and set his eyes on the Irishman and his live-in psychic lover.

The next time he saw Fort Bragg—and he knew there would be a next time and another mission—he would have assumed the identify of someone else, and the disguise would be entirely different.

"Well," Colonel Beauchene said as he provided him with his card and placed Joseph's in his shirt pocket, "would you care to join me at the buffet?"

35

The hostess led Dylan and Vicki through the busy restaurant, past filled tables and into a back room nearest the bar. They settled into a cozy, private booth far from the chatter of others. It was just grand, Dylan thought, and it was exactly what he'd requested when he'd telephoned The Village Station earlier.

The server was beside their table and requesting their drink order almost as quickly as they'd settled in. Vicki ordered unsweetened iced tea and Dylan did the same; though he'd much prefer to order a bottle of wine, it was too risky for Vicki.

"It smells so good in here," she breathed. She inhaled deeply as if to reinforce her statement. "I hadn't realized how hungry I was."

He reached across the table to take Vicki's hand in his. The light was dim, which caused the amber color of her eyes to appear even more striking than usual. Just the feel of her soft skin against his, her fingers intertwined with his own, sent an electric charge through his body. But she'd always done that to him, from the first time they'd touched.

He'd had it all planned out: drinks, a nice entrée, dessert... And over coffee at the end of the meal, when both were feeling warm and full and relaxed, he would pop the question. But now, as he gazed into her eyes, he knew he couldn't wait.

"I have somethin' I want to say to you," he said. His mouth felt suddenly dry and almost on cue, the server returned with the tea.

"Are you ready to order?"

"We'll need just a few minutes to look over the menu," Dylan said. Turning to Vicki, he added, "If you don't mind?"

She nodded and the server moved away.

"I wanted to talk to you, too," Vicki said. "It seems like every time I've planned to, someone else has shown up and we haven't had the privacy…"

"Oh?"

"I wanted you to know," she said, squeezing his hand, "that I didn't plan to get pregnant."

"I've never asked you, 'ave I, now?" His voice was soft.

"No," she said, a shy smile crossing her face. "You never have. And I appreciate that." She swallowed. "But it's important to me that you know. I was taking the pill but, well, they say it isn't a hundred percent effective…"

"Well, I suppose I'm mighty potent then, 'ey?"

She burst out laughing. "That's one way of looking at it."

The server returned and Vicki glanced at the menu. "I suppose we should order," she whispered.

Dylan motioned for her to go first.

"I'll have the salad with grilled chicken," she said, handing the menu to the server.

"Darlin', you need more than a salad," Dylan chided.

"I'm getting grilled chicken with it."

"But you need somethin' more substantial. You're eatin' for two, you know."

"I'm fine."

He waited for her to change her mind. When she continued to gaze at him silently, he turned to the server. "I'll 'ave the filet, medium, w' a loaded potato and the salad bar. And please remember to return for our dessert order. We'll be wantin' one."

The server smiled. "Got it."

As she moved away, Vicki giggled. "We'll be wanting dessert, huh?"

"That's right. We will."

"Where were we?" Vicki pondered.

"You were sayin' you didn't intend to become pregnant. And I'm wonderin'," his face grew serious, "if you're regrettin' that you did?"

Her answer was instantaneous. "No. I'm not. I'm excited about it, actually. I just… Well, I just wanted you to know that I wasn't trying to trap you."

"I wouldn't 'ave minded if you had."

"I would."

The server started toward them with a basket of rolls, but Dylan caught her eye and waved her away. When he returned his attention to Vicki, he caught her watching him intently. "I wanted a moment w' you," he said by way of explanation.

He could see her Adam's apple as she swallowed hard.

"Vicki, from the very first time I laid me eyes on you, I knew I wanted us to be together."

She giggled. "The first time you ever told me that was when we were upstairs in the attic room, next to the freezer. Remember that?"

"You're not makin' this any easier by remindin' me o' the day you shot me."

"Oops. I'd forgotten about that."

"I haven't."

She sipped her tea impishly with her eyes still on him.

"But now that you brought it up, it was when Sam whisked me off to Langley and we were separated for a time that I… I knew I wasn't a happy bloke when you weren't in m' life."

"You make me happy, too," she said. She slipped both hands across the table.

He looked at her hands briefly before joining them in his own. They were so petite, with neatly manicured nails and silky smooth skin. Now he faced a quandary, he realized; with both hands on the table, he couldn't very well pull the tiny box from his pocket. "Well," he said, "I 'ave noticed you don't cry quite so often."

She laughed again. "I don't remember the last time I cried."

His throat was dry, and this felt as though it was taking far longer than he'd rehearsed. "The fact is, Vicki, darlin', I don't ever want to be separated from you again."

Her eyes locked on his but she remained silent.

"I'm askin' you if you'll agree to marry me so we can spend the rest o' our lives together."

She blinked.

It occurred to him immediately that she hadn't responded. He gently extricated one hand from hers and pulled the box from his pocket. Her face was flooded with color as he opened it. He watched her expression as her eyes dropped to the open box.

She swallowed. "You aren't doing this just because I'm pregnant, are you?"

"What? No... You'll notice there are two rings there, in fact."

She nodded.

"I'd purchased you the Claddagh ring a'fore we left for Ireland. A'fore I knew you were expectin' me child. Ironically," he added, "I'd ordered it from Dublin, not knowin' we'd be travellin' to Ireland."

She reached gingerly for the box, and he set it on the table. He pulled out the Claddagh ring and reached for her hand. "In Ireland, when a lass is engaged to be married, the ring goes on 'er left hand w' the heart pointed toward 'er fingertips. When she's married, the ring is turned around so the heart faces 'er wrist." He glanced toward her right hand. "If it's worn on 'er right hand w' the heart facin' the wrist, it means your heart 'as been captured. And if it's worn w' the heart facin' the fingertips on that hand, it means you're single and you're available."

He watched her as she visually examined the heart in the middle of the ring, the hand on either side of it, and the crown above the heart.

"So," he said. He tried to keep his voice light but when he continued, it came out hoarse and somewhat strained. "What'll it be? Which hand should I place it on, and which way do you want the heart to face?"

Her eyes rose from the ring to his face. The color had deepened in her cheeks and tears had formed in her eyes. "On my left hand, of course."

His fingers felt frozen around the ring he held.

"Yes," she said, "I will marry you, Dylan Maguire."

A thunderous applause erupted. Dylan nearly dropped the ring as their heads both turned toward the restaurant staff surrounding the table. Neither had noticed the group forming; now they looked into a sea of faces sporting broad smiles. Some of the women were as teary-eyed as Vicki. Arnold, the proprietor of The Village Station, stepped forward. "Congratulations!" he said, grinning from ear to ear.

Dylan realized he was still holding the ring and he turned back to Vicki to find tears rolling down her cheeks. Gently, he slipped the ring onto her left hand with the heart facing her fingertips. Then he stood up to shake hands with Arnold.

Vicki rose to accept a hug as Arnold declared, "I've never had a better day!"

One by one, the staff congratulated them before dispersing.

Vicki reached into her handbag for a tissue. "And we were just talking about how long ago it's been since I've cried!"

Something changed in that instant. Dylan could feel it as strongly as if someone had waved a magic wand over them. She'd agreed to be his wife. Now that it was really happening, his heart felt as though it was expanding to the point that his chest was going to explode. He would never again go through another day alone, he thought; he would be, from this day forward, half of a team, a partnership… a marriage.

He didn't realize until she'd dried her tears and then looked at his cheeks with wide eyes, that his face was wet. "I don't know what's come o'er me," he mumbled.

She offered him a tissue and he cleared his throat as he quickly wiped away the tears.

"So…?" She glanced at the box.

"Ah, yes." He gently removed the second ring from the box and held it up for her to see. "When Mam passed away, I thought… Well, this was 'er weddin' ring. And I know she'd be pleased to know you 'ave it."

"It's beautiful."

He slipped it onto her right hand. "I don't know which ring you want to wear on which hand, and it doesn't make any difference to me at'al." He continued to hold her hand, his eyes locked on the ring he'd seen his grandmother wear ever since he could remember. She'd never taken it off; not when she worked in the garden or dyed Easter eggs or worked bread dough or meat patties. It was sterling silver, the best his grandfather could afford, and the back had grown thin over the decades. It had been both her engagement ring and her wedding ring, a simple band of an interlocking Celtic weave symbolizing the never-ending circle—and the eternity—of Life itself. On top was a small diamond.

"It would be m' honor to get you a proper diamond for it, if you choose to keep it."

"Of course I'll keep it," Vicki whispered. "I can feel her presence through the ring." She felt of the diamond, her fingers racing over the small jewel and the Celtic pattern. "I don't want another diamond. I want the one that Mam always wore."

He felt his eyes begin to sting and he fought the tears that tried to form again. I'm as bad as a fresh-cheeked lass, he thought with embarrassment. He caught a glimpse of the server returning with their meal. Thankful for the interruption, he breathed in the rich aroma of steak and potato and quickly removed the box and his hands from the table to make room for their food.

36

Joseph parked on the back side of the hospital in a handicapped spot, dutifully hanging the special parking pass from his visor. Those spots were the closest to the entrance, which would allow for a quick escape. And no one would suspect someone with such a pass of being a hired assassin.

He took the medical bag from the front floorboard but left the blueprints of the hospital under the seat. He had it memorized and every step of his plan thought out.

The revolving doors opened into an expansive lobby. The offices were closed on both sides and the lights darkened. The lobby was opened to the two floors above, and as he peered upward he noted how empty and quiet it was. He found a janitorial sign leaning against a wall and he grabbed it as he walked past.

The men's room was partway down the hall. He placed the sign at the door. He was silent as he strolled in and casually glanced through all the stalls to make certain it was empty. Then he returned to the door and locked the deadbolt.

His movements quickened as he walked to the sink and placed his medical bag on the counter. He hastily removed the toupee and donned a dark blond hairpiece with a receding hairline. Then he removed the mustache and placed it, along with the old toupee, in the medical bag.

Next, he removed the jewelry and the business suit, replacing it with a pair of black slacks, a white shirt and a doctor's lab coat. He placed a stethoscope around his neck for good measure.

The old clothing and jewelry were shoved into the medical bag.

Then he pulled out a syringe and a small bottle. He pumped the fatal dose into the syringe and recapped it. He placed both in the pocket of his lab coat.

He did a quick inspection of his new disguise before moving to the door, unlocking the deadbolt, and slipping into the hallway.

———   ———   ———

He waited at the elevator until the minute hand was just right; if the nurses were on schedule, they would begin their hourly rounds. That would leave one nurse at the station, and the guard in their pocket would send her on an errand.

Then he pushed the button and waited.

Less than a minute later, he was stepping off the elevator. His eyes swept the hallway; a nurse at the far end was moving into a patient's room. A glance toward the other end yielded nothing but an empty hall. Directly ahead was Brenda Carnegie's room.

He moved toward it deliberately, his medical bag in his hand. Two guards were seated just outside her room, one on either side of the door. As he approached, one spotted him and slightly raised his head. He was the one.

Christopher Sandige moved into the open doorway, and Joseph stopped abruptly at the nurse's station, pulling a folder from the desk and opening it. He also grabbed a pen and made as if he was making notations in it while he kept an eye on the stainless cabinet directly in front of him, where he watched Sandige's blurred reflection as he spoke to the guards. He seemed reluctant to leave, but finally he closed the door. Then he made his way past Joseph to the elevator. In less than a minute, he was stepping onto the elevator and the doors were closing.

Joseph took the folder with him and continued to Brenda's door. Both guards rose as he approached.

"Make I help you?" one guard asked. He appeared to be in his mid- to late-thirties. His hair was cropped close and his eyes were a sharp blue; his chiseled look conjured images of morning sit-ups, lunch hours spent jogging, and evenings lifting weights.

Joseph glanced at the other one, the one who had briefly nodded. He appeared somewhat older. His face had a slightly puffy look about it that made him appear overweight; although, Joseph thought as he casually skimmed his eyes over him, he was probably as fit as the first man. "I'm here to check on Miss Carnegie."

"Your name?" the chiseled one asked.

"Hal," the second one said, "he's her doctor."

"I've not seen you before, sir," Hal said respectfully. "Your name, please?"

Joseph glanced at the folder in his hand. "I'm filling in for Miss Carnegie's regular physician," he said. "My name is—" he effortlessly recalled the name in the folder "—Dr. Wellstone. I should be on your list there."

"Ah," Hal said, checking the list, "yes. You are. I'm sorry, sir."

"No need to apologize," Joseph said. "You're just doing your job." He smiled. When neither made a move, he pointed toward the door. "May I?"

"Oh. Of course. Yes, Doctor." Hal pushed the door ajar.

"Thank you. I'll only be a moment; just doing my rounds to make sure everyone is healing as expected."

The guards remained standing until he was inside the room but as he turned to close the door, he noticed they were already sitting back down.

Once the door clicked shut, he turned toward the bed. The room was dim but slightly chilly; there seemed to be a breeze and he wondered briefly whether the air conditioner was on. He snapped his mind back to the job at hand and immediately, it didn't matter whether the room was fifty degrees or ninety.

She lay on her side, completely covered by the hospital bedding, the IV unit with its tubes dangling from the metal stand until they disappeared underneath the blanket. He moved to the unit and pulled out the syringe. She hadn't moved and appeared to be asleep.

Then he quietly disconnected the tube from the IV. If he'd been an actual doctor or nurse, he would have injected the fluid into a spot closer to the point of entry into her body, but he didn't want to risk disturbing her. It would kill her soon enough. He injected the entire amount into the tube and watched it travel down the tubing until it disappeared under the blankets. Then he quickly reattached the tube to the bag of plasma.

He was at the door with his hand on the handle when he stopped. Something troubled him. He turned back and stared at the lump; she hadn't appeared to have moved at all. He approached once again but on the other side of the bed, where he observed her body for a few seconds. She was not breathing; there was no telltale up-and-down motion under the covers.

He could leave right now and his job would be done. But something spurred him to slip his hand under the covers. It would be simple to check the pulse against her neck; even if she was not yet completely gone, the dose he'd given her would place her into a paralyzed state, unable to fight him.

His hand found the pillow but no hair and no head.

With one fluid movement, he pulled the blanket back.

The curse came instinctively as his heart began to pound rapidly. There, in place of Brenda Carnegie, was a twisted pillow with a bulge at the top, a twist where the neck should have been, and a larger bulge for the shoulder. He yanked the rest of the blanket down to find a series of pillows, expertly placed, tucked and fluffed to resemble hips and legs.

He whirled around to face the rest of the room. The closet door was open; empty hangers were visible and the floor underneath was vacant.

He strode to the bathroom door, swiftly opening it. It was empty.

Dumbstruck, he turned his attention back to the room. The air had grown chillier than when he first entered and as he stood there, examining the room with his eyes, he realized why: the curtains were pulled apart and the window was open.

He rushed to the window and stuck his head through the opening to peer outside. He scrutinized the area just below; she couldn't have jumped, he thought. She couldn't. As he stared at the ground below, there was no doubt that a jump like that would have broken bones, if it didn't kill her. There was a row of hedges which were neatly groomed; there were no signs of a body having fallen atop them. There was short, brown grass, dormant with the coming winter, and then a great expanse of asphalt.

Where the hell was she?

Instinct kicked in. He rushed back to the bed and pulled the blankets back up to cover the mounds of pillows. Then he returned to the door, took a deep breath, and opened it.

Neither guard stood up, though both acknowledged his presence.

"Have a good evening, gentlemen," Joseph said calmly as he moved past them. The door gently closed behind him with a soft click. He fought to keep his footsteps unhurried, even though he wanted to run through the hall; now it seemed as if the elevators were half a mile away and every second stretched into a minute. But he knew once he reached the end of the hall, it had taken him less than thirty seconds to get there. Instead of waiting at the elevators, he turned the corner. Once out of view of the guards, he sped toward the stairwell and took the steps two at a time. It was time for him to vanish—and only then could he stop to figure out what had gone wrong.

37

Vicki breathed a deep sigh of relief as Dylan closed and locked the front door.

"Isn't this grand?" Dylan said, sweeping her into his arms. "We 'ave the whole entire house all to ourselves! No Sam, no Chris…"

"I was just thinking the same thing myself," Vicki said.

He scooped her into his arms, burying his face against her neck as his lips swept over her skin. She inhaled his scent; a heady combination of the outdoors and musk that was uniquely his own. She wove her fingers through his thick black hair. He moved to her jawline, tantalizing her with his mouth until he'd reached her lips.

Their eyes were open and they locked onto one another: his hazel eyes shining like crescent moons as he smiled, the laugh lines crinkling at the edges of his eyes. And hers, she thought, must be filled with awe and love and a tremendous feeling of luck that she should have this man so in love with her.

His strong arms tightened around her as he pulled her so close that even their clothing could not buffer the heat that rose from each of them. He placed a hand on her cheek, his thumb teasing her skin as he leaned toward her.

"Ah, there you are!"

Vicki felt Dylan jump, his eyes wide, as he jerked his head upward. She followed his eyes to see Sam walking toward them from the kitchen, a fluffy white Persian in his arms.

"Where have you been?" Sam demanded.

Dylan did a double-take. Then he grasped Vicki's hand and held her ring finger up for Sam to inspect, a broad smile sweeping across his face. "Congratulate us."

"Well, it's about time," Sam said gruffly, though Vicki noted the smile that threatened to break out.

"May I call you 'Da' now?" Dylan teased.

He murmured something they couldn't decipher. Then, "So when's the date?"

"We haven't set it yet," Vicki said. She could feel her cheeks burning with the glow she was feeling inside.

"You planning a honeymoon?"

"Ireland," they both said.

"Hmm."

"So what's with the cat?" Vicki asked.

"It's my cat."

"We know it's your cat," Dylan said. "But why is she 'ere?"

"Chloe gets lonely when I'm gone."

" 'Chloe', 'ey?"

"Yes. Chloe. Classy cat like this needs a classy name."

"So, where's your car?" Vicki asked.

"I walked her down here. It's not far."

"You *walked* 'er, you say?"

Sam grimaced. "Yes. I walked her. She happens to enjoy a leash and a stroll around the neighborhood."

Dylan burst out laughing.

"What's so funny?" Sam asked.

"You Americans are hysterically funny. I can't even picture you waltzin' about the neighborhood w' a kitty on a leash."

"I said we *walked*," Sam said, his brows knitting, "not waltzed. Anyway, stop making fun of my cat. I don't poke fun at your fish or your dog."

"Where is Shep, by the way?" Vicki asked.

"Finishing up a bowl of milk in the kitchen."

"So," Dylan said, trying to grow somber, "what are you doin' down 'ere at this time o' night?"

"Looking for you two." He turned to Vicki. "You've got a mission."

Dylan and Vicki groaned simultaneously.

"Can't this wait until the mornin'?" Dylan moaned. "It's a special night for us."

"I wish it could."

"Oh, Sam, really—" Vicki began.

"It's Brenda," Sam interrupted. "She's gone."

Vicki lay on the living room sofa and closed her eyes. Dylan had retreated to the kitchen to make a pot of coffee, and Sam was settling into the chair nearest her head.

"Tell me what happened," Sam said simply.

She took a deep breath and tried to block everything out—the muffled noises coming from the kitchen, Sam's breathing, and the faint sound of a cat purring. She could feel herself slipping away and in an instant, she felt a brisk wind against her face.

As she looked out, she realized she was standing in front of an open window high above a parking lot. "The hospital at Fort Bragg," she murmured. She could hear the scratching of Sam's pencil, though she knew he was also audiotaping.

It took only a split second for her to realize she was standing beside Chris. His body was wedged against the wall as he used it to brace himself, and both his muscular arms were thrust out the window, holding onto a knotted sheet.

She moved outside and hovered just beyond the building as she watched Brenda climb down the sheet to another open window just below her hospital room. Her legs were wrapped around the sheet, which was knotted at regular intervals, and by the time she could heave her body through the window, she was panting heavily. Perspiration ran along her brow, and her scalp was damp, though the air outside was chilled.

Once inside, she tugged on the sheet twice and then let go. It was rapidly hauled upward. Caught between wanting to watch her sister and spy on Chris, she waited until Brenda had settled into a wheelchair to catch her breath before she moved back outside and to the floor above.

Chris quickly crammed the sheet into a disheveled ball and walked briskly to the bed, where he pulled the covers back and tucked the sheet alongside a series of pillows—and her house arrest ankle bracelet. The rivets had been busted off, and as Vicki relayed the information to Sam, she struggled to keep her emotions in check.

He finished tucking the blankets around the pillows and then walked to the door and opened it. Almost as soon as the door was open and the two guards were glancing at him, he looked back toward the open window. Vicki could see the confusion in his eyes; should he return and close the window? Or keep moving?

After a moment's hesitation, he closed the door behind him. He murmured a polite "good-night" to the guards and then forced himself to walk slowly toward the elevators. As he passed a doctor standing at the nurse's desk, Vicki felt as if she was drawn back to the man as Chris continued to move away.

She forced herself to remain with Chris, joining him on the elevator and then exiting just one floor below. This floor was laid out differently from the one above; she read off the signs to Sam as she followed him through a maze that eventually led to Radiology. There he stopped at an office, quietly opening the door to find Brenda seated inside.

"Are you okay?" he asked.

"I'm fine," Brenda answered, though she sounded winded. "Hurry and get downstairs."

"Back entrance?"

"Just like we planned."

Chris bit his lip as though he was holding back words. At her imploring expression, he backed out, closing the door behind him. Then he made his way to the staircase and rushed downstairs to the first floor.

He pulled out his cell phone as he navigated the revolving doors, moving quickly to an alcove just outside the doors. From there, his eyes wandered over the parking lot, stopping at the row of handicapped spots on the other side of the door.

His phone vibrated and he answered it immediately. "He's not here."

He was met with silence on the other end of the line.

"You're sure he's not at the front?"

"Too much activity there," Brenda whispered hoarsely. "No; if he's coming after me, he'll park at the back. Is the lot crowded?"

"No," Chris said, his eyes panning the lots on either side of the door. "Almost empty."

"Keep your eyes on the cars nearest the door. Then get your car and be ready to pick me up."

Vicki turned from Chris to survey the surroundings. Though Sam had been to the hospital countless times, she recited what she observed anyway; the recording would go up the chain and the analysts may never have visited the hospital at Fort Bragg. She described the wide entry and driveway that ended in a circle just beyond the revolving doors and as Chris made his way away from the doors, she described the covered walkway that separated expansive lots on either side. He moved swiftly to a blue Lincoln, sliding behind the steering wheel and starting up the engine before the door had even closed behind him.

Then he drove closer to the front doors, pulling through one row of parking spaces to another so he would not have to back out to make his getaway.

She remained with him for a brief moment, but reported back to Sam, "I'm feeling a lot of conflict. I need to be in Brenda's room; I feel drawn to the doctor I passed a moment ago... But Chris is waiting in his car and Brenda is on the floor just below her room..."

"Go back to Brenda's room."

In an instant, she was there, moving through the open window as the curtains billowed beside her. The doctor was standing beside Brenda's bed, disconnecting the unit of blood from the tube. She reported his actions back to Sam. She began to feel a chill creeping up the back of her neck as though she was in the presence of evil.

She moved around to the other side of the bed to watch him as he pulled a syringe from his pocket. "Almonds," she said.

"Excuse me?"

"Almonds. The liquid smells like almonds."

She could hear Sam's cell phone as he pressed the buttons but she tried to block him out. "Get the blood," she heard him say. "I want a toxicology report on it… Yeah, the blood they were giving her. Get the tubes, too, and anything else that came in contact with her." Then the phone clicked off.

She turned her attention back to the doctor and watched as he shot the liquid into the tube before reconnecting it. He moved beyond the bed, placing the syringe back into his pocket. "He's not a doctor," she said, her eyes moving to the hazardous waste container next to the bed.

"Who is he?" Sam asked.

She shook her head. "He didn't dispose of the syringe properly. He's put it back into his pocket." It was then that she noticed the white surgical gloves; they were so pale and the sleeves of the lab coat so long, that she almost missed them.

"Stay with him."

She watched as he turned back to the bed and quietly pulled back the blanket. The expression on his face was a mixture of rage and surprise, followed by confusion. He moved to the bathroom, checked it swiftly, and then his head pivoted toward the open window. He moved with unblinking black eyes to the window and peered down at the parking lot below where Chris sat idling his engine in between two other vehicles.

Then he was moving briskly through the room, pulling the blanket over the top pillow before reaching the door. He murmured something to the guards and then slowed his steps as he moved past the nurse's station and the elevators, turning down an adjacent hallway.

Once out of sight of the guards, he raced to the stairwell and took the steps two at a time down five flights, until he burst into the lobby on the ground floor.

The elevator doors opened as he moved past them, his eyes riveted on the revolving doors at the far end of the lobby. Vicki gasped as she saw Brenda in her wheelchair maneuvering out of the elevator as the man reached the doors, moving through them so swiftly that they were still spinning after he stepped out of them.

He made his way to the first car in the handicapped parking area. Vicki zoomed in on the license plate and relayed it to Sam as she watched him nearly jump into the car. He backed out of the space so quickly that his tires spun, and he didn't hesitate as he made his way onto the main road that would take him away from the hospital and away from Fort Bragg.

***

Vicki tried to catch her breath as she turned to find Chris' car zooming into the circular drive, stopping just inches from the revolving door as Brenda made her way through it. Hopping out, he rushed to the passenger side, opened the door and nearly lifted her out of the chair in an effort to get her in the car as rapidly as possible.

Then he raced back to the driver's side. The car was in gear and they were driving off before either door was closed.

As Vicki relayed the information back to Sam, she interrupted herself with a burst of frustration. "What are they doing?" she demanded. *"What are they doing?"*

38

Sam paced the living room floor, his ear glued to his cell phone. As Dylan held out a cup of hot coffee to him, he grabbed it without slowing his pace or pausing in his conversation.

"That's right," he said. "I know it's unusual. But we need all exits at Fort Bragg sealed, pronto. Complete ID check in progress... And run this tag," he added, looking up the license number in his notes. "Silver Mercedes coupe, late model...Yes, I'm leaving now." He clicked off the phone and took a healthy swig of coffee, then grimaced as the liquid burned his throat.

"What's goin' on?" Dylan asked. He stood at the doorway, his eyes moving from Sam to Vicki and back again.

"Gabucci is on Fort Bragg," Sam said.

"What?"

Sam waved away his concern. "We'll get him. I'm having all exits sealed. It was the flaw in his plan, coming onto a military installation. He won't escape us now." Without waiting for a reply, he punched in another phone number.

Dylan moved to Vicki's side. "Is your sister—?"

"I don't know," she said as he sat beside her. She'd come to a seated position but now gripped her head in her hands as the room began to spin. "I came out of my mission too quickly," she said in response to Dylan's quizzical expression.

"Is there anythin' I can be doin' for you?"

She shook her head. "I just need a couple of minutes to readjust."

He nodded and seemed to be chewing the inside of his mouth as he looked at her.

"What is it?" she asked.

He hesitated briefly before rubbing her back gently. "Does he 'ave 'er?"

She shook her head and then groaned with the effort. "I don't think so. It's impossible to tell whether what I was seeing was taking place as I was seeing it, or sometime before…" She glimpsed his face and smiled weakly. "I know it's confusing."

"Confusin' is an understatement, to be sure."

Sam's voice cut in on their conversation. "Yeah, Sam Mazoli here… I need Brenda Carnegie's hospital room completely sealed. Nobody gets in or out until I get there… I'm going to want to interview those two guards so they don't go anywhere…" He stopped pacing long enough to take another swig of coffee. "Yeah, I sent the technicians to get the blood, but don't let them leave, either. I want to see everybody personally. Oh, and do me a favor? Have the MP's put out an alert on this license plate…" Again, he referred to his notes, providing the make, model and license plate number. Then, "Yeah; I'll get you photographs right away. I'm working on it."

He clicked off the phone but immediately dialed another number. "Get me some more coffee, will you?" he asked as he waited.

Dylan was down the hall almost before he'd finished his request. A moment later, he was back with the coffee pot. He poured Sam another cup and peered at Vicki. "You want some, Darlin'?"

She shook her head. "I don't drink coffee."

"I know. I was just thinkin', under the circumstances…" His voice trailed off as Sam began to speak.

"Sam Mazoli here. Look, I need you to pull the information you got me on Joseph Gabucci… Yeah. Get that over to Fort Bragg MP's, Fayetteville and Lumberton. Hell, broadcast it to the whole state. The guy's at large and dangerous… Contact the

FBI; let them know he's on Fort Bragg and have them meet me at the hospital; room…" He hesitated while he looked up Brenda's room number. After providing it, he clicked off again.

"What can I do for you, Sam?" Dylan asked.

Sam held up a finger as he dialed another number. "Be right with you," he said.

Dylan set the coffee pot on a trivet and rejoined Vicki, wrapping his arm around her shoulders. "For a man who looks bored near 'alf the time," he muttered, "He can be quite the ball o' energy, now can't he?"

Vicki would have chuckled had the situation not been so dire. Their eyes met and she knew from the sudden somber expression on Dylan's face that he knew how worried she was. As if he was reading her mind, he said, "Don't worry, Darlin'. They'll find your sister. And they'll find this murderer Gabucci. It'll all work out just fine and dandy."

"Sam Mazoli here," Sam's voice broke in. "Look, I know every vehicle that goes in or out of Fort Bragg is caught on their video cameras… Yeah. I need you to get those tapes and look for this vehicle…" He rattled off the make, model and license plate once more, this time without referring to the notes. "I want to know how this guy got on post. Call me as soon as you have something." He clicked off and turned to Dylan.

"You wanna help? Give me a ride to my house. I've gotta pick up my car." He turned toward the front door and then stopped. "Where's Chloe?"

"I'll get her," Vicki said, going in search of the Persian.

Dylan pulled his keys from his pocket. "I'm ready to transport you whene'er you're ready to go," he said.

Sam nodded as his phone rang. "Sam Mazoli here… Yeah. Good. I'll be right there." He clicked off and made his way to the door. He appeared to be ready to begin tapping his foot as they waited for Vicki. He checked his watch and then checked it again.

"You want me to go in search o' 'er?" Dylan asked.

"On second thought," Sam said as if he hadn't heard him, "It might be best if you go with me to Bragg. There's no telling what we'll find there, and I might need you."

Dylan turned to find Vicki emerging from the back of the hall. They exchanged glances; it was apparent that she'd heard Sam's directive. "Chloe's not on this floor," she said to Sam. "I'll check upstairs."

"No," Sam interjected. Vicki stopped with her hand on the balustrade. "I'll pick her up when I'm done at Bragg. I'm wasting too much time as it is."

"Sure," she said, glancing again at Dylan. "She'll be fine."

Sam's phone rang again and he stepped onto the front porch as he answered it.

Dylan leaned down to brush his lips across Vicki's. "M' apologies, Darlin'," he whispered. "I promise I'll be back just as quickly as possible to finish what we started." He lingered longer as if he was reluctant to leave but with a frustrated groan, he pulled away and opened the door. Sam was already off the porch, his voice trailing off as he headed around the side of the house to Dylan's truck. He stopped at the threshold and turned back to Vicki. "Lock this door as soon as I leave. And set the alarm."

She nodded and stepped forward to place her hands on the door.

"Keep the remote w' you, as well as your mobile."

"Stay safe," she whispered. Her voice caught in her throat.

Then with another groan, he dropped his hand from the screen, letting it gently swing back to click into place. "I'll be back," he said as he hurried down the steps after Sam. "And it won't be a moment too soon!"

Vicki closed the heavy front door and locked the deadbolt before turning to the alarm pad and keying in the code. The telltale beeping began, heralding the activation of the alarm system. She stood for a moment, her back to the stairs, as she listened for the truck to start. Once the alarm system stopped beeping, she thought she detected the sound of the truck engine as it moved further from the house.

Sighing, she turned around to find Shep sitting at the base of the stairs, watching her with intent ice-blue eyes, her head cocked to the side as if trying to read her thoughts. Directly beside her was Chloe, her large, round eyes nearly cerulean in color, her mountain of white Persian fur tipped with the faintest silver. Her head was cocked in the same direction as Shep's and despite the empty feeling in her gut as Dylan drove away, she laughed.

"So there you are!" she exclaimed as she made her way toward the stairs. The cat meowed and bounded up the stairs, pausing at the second floor to look back at her. Vicki glanced into the living room, where a single lamp shone dimly. Turning, she noted the kitchen light obliquely lit the wide hallway just beyond the staircase; she debated for a split second whether to turn them both off and decided they would remain on—at least until Dylan returned home.

Shep seemed to be waiting for her to spring into action; she'd never before seen an animal stare with such intensity. She reached down to rub her behind her ears. "Let's go to bed," she said before heading up the stairs after Chloe.

She paused on the second floor as the cat had and looked back down the staircase. The floor below looked and felt so empty and vast; even the grandfather clock sat idly, the hands frozen. She had a strange sensation that seemed to move up from her chest into her throat as if something wasn't right. She hesitated, mulling over whether to return to the living room and nap on the couch or go into the kitchen for a late night snack to awaken her more fully.

Turning again, she spotted both Chloe and Shep at the top of the next set of stairs, watching her from near her bedroom door. They seemed to be silently asking what was keeping her from joining them. She thought it odd; to her knowledge, Chloe had never been in the house before and yet there she stood, just outside the master bedroom, as if she knew that was Vicki's space.

An almost overwhelming tiredness descended on her and she made her decision. She'd sleep and when she awakened, Dylan would be home again and all would be well.

39

Joseph approached the stoplight with one eye on the rearview mirror. There was no doubt in his mind that the car was following him. He'd seen it as he exited the hospital parking lot; it had turned when he did so many times that it couldn't be coincidence.

The light turned yellow and he slowed as he watched them. They passed under a street light and he got a quick glimpse of a driver and one passenger. He couldn't be certain who the driver was but from the mountain of hair that was unmistakable even in the shadows, he could identify his target. He'd bet his life on it.

Swiftly but thoroughly, he scanned the intersection. He had several weapons to choose from, including a sniper rifle and a pistol. He could simply sit at the stoplight until they pulled up behind him, grab one of the weapons, get out, shoot them, and be back in his vehicle and driving away before anyone was the wiser.

The seconds passed and the car began to slow, as if they didn't want to stop directly behind him. Good move, he thought as his fingers wrapped themselves around the pistol.

The light turned green but he remained where he was. The car stopped at least five car lengths back.

He kept his eyes focused on the rearview mirror. He could slam his own car into reverse, ram the front of theirs, and still jump out and shoot them both. He could use his car to conceal his own body, in the event they also had weapons—which he suspected they did. Brenda Carnegie was too street savvy not to have one.

With his free hand, he reached for the gear shift. Just as he started to place it in Park, he caught a movement out of the corner of his eye: the distinctive colors of an approaching vehicle shouted to the world that they were MP's. They were coming up fast; too fast, he thought, as if they were in pursuit.

The light turned yellow. He took his hand off the gear shift and with his other hand, he slipped the pistol between the seat and the console. As the light turned red, the lights began to flash on the MP's vehicle. He readied himself to move his foot from the brake to the gas pedal.

They didn't slow down as they approached the intersection but began to speed up. He forced himself to relax back into his seat. As they moved into the intersection, they took a hard right turn toward the hospital.

He watched in his rearview mirror as they pulled past the vehicle behind him. He struggled to wait until they had disappeared around a bend before slamming his foot onto the gas pedal and lurching through the intersection, taking a hard left and then an immediate right.

With one eye on the rearview mirror, he could see them fishtailing behind him and coming up fast. He whipped around another corner before circling back and circling again into a wide figure eight. He found himself in a neighborhood; the streets were silent, the houses darkened. He passed one neat lawn after another, the vehicles lined up in the carports like soldiers in formation. All the while, he searched for the perfect location to draw them in and kill them.

Rule Number 1 for a hired assassin was to have an escape route. Rule Number 2 was not to get caught, which led directly back to Rule Number 1. It wasn't enough to stop somewhere, get out and start shooting—most especially on a military installation. Every soldier within hearing range knew what a gun or a rifle sounded like, and every one of them would awaken with a start and be looking out their windows or rushing outside to determine the source.

He sped up, moving expertly now through the neighborhood and onto a main road, both hands on the steering wheel. His speedometer rose above fifty, sixty, and then seventy miles an hour. The car took the corners with the precision of a race car, while he noted Brenda's vehicle swerved into the curves with tires squealing. The sound of their vehicle, he realized, would awaken everyone and bring attention to them both.

Office buildings appeared in the distance and he headed straight for them; the angle at which they were built told him there would likely be side streets and parallel streets onto which he could outmaneuver his pursuers. The speedometer topped seventy-five as he made a near-ninety-degree turn. His rear wheels bounced onto the curb and he silently cursed himself as it sounded a *boom* that echoed in the silent night air.

On another straight-away, he pressed the gas pedal harder until he peaked past eighty miles an hour. A glance into the rearview mirror showed no signs of them, but he didn't slow. He had to get off this installation or find a place to ambush them. He didn't much care which one it was, but he was leaning closer to the ambush. Otherwise, he would simply be delaying what he was hired to do.

He made a sudden left turn followed by an immediate right and found himself on another main road. This one curved around what appeared to be dormitories or barracks but the street was clear. He ignored the lines and the curves and remained as much as possible in the center of the road where he'd be forced to shift to the left or right less frequently.

He caught a movement in the corner of his eye and glancing toward the passenger window, he swore under his breath as he recognized their sedan on a parallel road. They were travelling in the opposite direction but a moment later, they barreled out of a side street a half mile behind him; they'd spotted him, too, and were back in pursuit.

The thought occurred to him that he didn't know why they followed him. Were they intending to kill him, perhaps? The absurd thought almost made him laugh. Many had tried, and all had failed. He would live another day, and he wouldn't be so stupid as to end up in a penitentiary again.

His knuckles were white as he gripped the steering wheel and he leaned forward as if the stance would provide more control. He spotted an intersection up ahead but he didn't slow; his speed now topped ninety miles an hour.

A car was stopped at the intersection perpendicular to him— a cherry red Corvette. No doubt there would be a man driving it, and at this hour of the night, he hoped it was a soldier who was more than half lit; he'd be less likely to call the MP's and he'd be an idiot if he joined in the pursuit.

The green light turned yellow as he approached the intersection. Then seconds before he reached it, his light turned red.

The Corvette moved forward as Joseph careened into the intersection, making a hard left turn inches from the other vehicle's front end. He caught a glimpse of the driver's face, which appeared so close that if their windows had both been rolled down, he might have been able to reach out and slap it as he whipped past. The driver was a young male with cropped hair and wide eyes; he could see the telltale bloodshot look of a man who'd imbibed too much. His reflexes were poor and for a moment, Joseph thought he might turn the car directly into his. He fought the urge to overcorrect and jump the curb as he flew past, but as he glanced into the rearview mirror, he spotted the Corvette crisscrossing the intersection as if someone was still there, inches from his bumper.

Brenda's car flew into the same intersection and tried to take the hard left turn as he did, but the Corvette spun out of control. He heard the impact as both back ends crashed together, but to his dismay, they didn't slow or stop but righted the car and after a violent lurch from side to side, picked up speed to continue the chase.

The Corvette was left in the middle of the intersection, gradually coming to a stop, the back end crumpled.

Joseph moved his eyes from the mirror just in time to see a street sign seemingly appear out of nowhere; the road was curving and he'd been so intent on watching the scene unfold behind him that he hadn't been cognizant of the upcoming curve.

His car jumped the curb as it plowed across a neat lawn before twisting through a low-lying hedge. He heard the crush of branches hitting the car and the rear bounced off uneven terrain as he fought to right the vehicle. The steering wheel seemed to have a mind of its own, and he struggled with both hands as the car lurched into the street before recoiling off another curb, causing him to bounce unmercifully against the driver's door and then the console.

The car fishtailed and then spun completely around. For the briefest of moments, he was facing Brenda's car as it gained ground. Now he knew beyond a shadow of a doubt: Christopher Sandige was driving and Brenda was hanging on as their vehicle lurched and tumbled.

When he got the vehicle righted, he sped down a street going the wrong way, and a glimpse behind him revealed they were still in hot pursuit.

The post gate loomed up ahead. An electronic billboard had been placed beside the road heralding a "100% ID Check In Progress". Lights were flashing on military police vehicles which appeared to be out in force. There was no doubt they were there for him. He swore, his words seeming to echo in the close confines.

No doubt there would be road block barricades; he'd noted the strips across the roadway when he drove onto the post. At a moment's notice and a push of a button, the entire strip would raise and any attempt to drive over it would puncture the tires. He was sandwiched in between the MPs and Christopher Sandige and Brenda Carnegie.

Half a mile before reaching the gate, he slowed and took the last exit, which brought him back onto a main roadway and deeper onto Fort Bragg. He didn't have to glance in his mirror to know that Chris and Brenda were behind him. They were stuck to him like glue.

There was nothing left to do but kill them; but it wouldn't be on the spur of the moment and it wouldn't be in the middle of the street like a Wild West shootout. It would be at the location of his choosing.

He continued taking ninety degree turns and figure eight circles through neighborhood streets, though he'd slowed considerably. He noted they were still behind him but keeping their distance. Why were they following him if not to confront him? He wondered.

He passed a strip shopping center with an attached mall and drove into the back parking lot to scope it out. Too many people were exiting the stores and the worst thing he could do is have a bunch of soldiers as witnesses. They were trained to jump in and defuse threats.

It now became a slow-speed chase as he wove in and out of parking lots. The commissary was closing and employees were crossing the lot in droves. As he reached the far end, he realized Brenda and Chris had been caught behind him as they waited for a group on the crosswalk.

He recognized the opportunity immediately and didn't hesitate to slam his foot to the floor as he reached the main street. Seconds counted and he could put distance between them.

He barreled through a red light and then another, turned left and then right and then left again. One by one, businesses on post were shutting down. He passed a fast food restaurant and then another before spotting a bowling alley up ahead.

He glanced into the mirror but saw no one behind him. They were too smart to lose him, he thought. It was only a matter of time.

He whipped into the bowling alley parking lot and made his way around to the back. One lone vehicle was parked at the far end. Quickly, with his training kicking in, he assessed the potential locations to ambush them. He backed his vehicle under an overhanging tree and then grabbed his rifle from the back seat.

He shut off the engine, turned off the lights and exited the car. Stealthily, he moved onto a knoll just beyond the bowling alley. And he waited.

The seconds ticked by. Though he lay prone on the dormant brown grass, the knoll provided him with a view of two roads.

His heart was still pounding with adrenaline and he took several deep breaths to steady himself. His hands and eyes were ready.

There were no signs of movement on the adjacent roads, no tell-tale lights heralding the approach of vehicles, no sounds other than the occasional owl. The bright lights of the post gate felt like a world away.

The seconds turned to minutes and with each minute that passed, it appeared more unlikely that Chris and Brenda would find him. He debated himself, questioning their motives, wondering if they were just on the other side of the building, lying in wait for him. They weren't hired assassins, he thought smugly, and one didn't instinctively do what he did without the proper training and experience. Still, Brenda was a savvy one; he'd give her that…

Fifteen minutes passed. He scanned the horizon as far as his eye could see.

Five more minutes passed and then ten.

The back door to the bowling alley opened and a lone man wrestled with a group of loaded trash bags. Joseph watched him warily. He was an older man; obviously a civilian judging by his paunch and the labored way in which he moved. He was dressed in a white shirt with the sleeves rolled up despite the nip in the air, and black pants, seeming to struggle to stay on his hips, kept dropping so a few inches at the bottom pooled around his shoes.

Joseph studied him as he dragged the trash bags to the dumpster at the far end of the parking lot, two at a time. He was bald and even from this distance Joseph could make out black eyeglass frames.

The man glanced back at the building and then shook his head as if muttering to himself. He returned to the back door, where he disappeared into the building. A moment later, the lights that announced the bowling alley was open were switched off.

Hurriedly, Joseph came to a crouched position and rushed toward the single vehicle he'd spotted earlier. He half-slid down the knoll to the back of the older model Toyota with one eye on the back door. He squatted by the driver side taillight, noting the rust on the vehicle and the unkempt, obviously unmaintained condition. The thing looked like the doors were ready to fall off. It was perfect.

The back door opened and the man reappeared. He was moving more slowly now as if he'd had a long and exhausting day. He fumbled with his keys as he locked the back door and then fumbled with them some more as he made his way to the car in the corner. With all the attention he paid his keys, Joseph would have thought he'd have the car key out and ready to slide into the vehicle, but when he reached the driver's side door, he was still trying to find the right one.

Joseph silently slipped from behind the car, coming to his feet as he rushed toward the man. Hearing or sensing the movement behind him, the man jerked his head toward the back of the car as the butt of Joseph's rifle hit him full in the face. He crumpled, blood spurting from his nose and mouth, as he hit the pavement.

Quickly, Joseph grabbed his keys and rifled through his pants pockets. He found his wallet easily and opened it just long enough to find the man's identification. Then he stepped over him, found the right key and opened the door.

Less than sixty seconds later, he was driving out of the parking lot with everything from the Mercedes transferred to the trunk of the rattletrap alongside his disguise from the hospital. Behind him, the man still lay prone on the asphalt. He wasn't concerned; no one was likely to find him until morning and by then, he'd be long gone.

He drove just under the speed limit. There was no sign of Brenda and Chris but everywhere he looked, there appeared to be MP's patrolling. Perhaps they picked them up, he thought. He'd worry about that later. He didn't have to remind himself that she was wearing an ankle bracelet; he knew he'd find her again. It was only a matter of time and as she'd continued to elude him, his patience was wearing thin and his resolve thickening.

He spotted the gate up ahead and as the cars did in line in front of him, he dimmed the headlights on the vehicle. He picked up the wallet from the console where he'd dropped it and pulled out the man's identification. Glancing into the rearview mirror, he caught a glimpse of himself without the toupee he'd worn earlier. His shaved head matched the bald man's but the eye color was off; his were brown but the man's were hazel. He noted the birth date and address, his razor sharp memory snapping it into his brain like an item in a lock box.

Two minutes passed and then three. Finally, it was his turn to pull up to the guard.

"Good evening," he said, rolling down the grimy window.

The guard nodded silently in response as he peered into the front seat and behind him into the sorry excuse for a back seat. Then, "Driver's license, please."

Joseph handed him the man's license. "Looks like you've had some excitement on post tonight."

"Your name?" the young man asked curtly.

"Abraham Beanger," he replied smoothly.

"Address?"

He rattled off the address, including the zip code.

"Birth date?"

"February 14, 1960. A Valentine's baby." Joseph smiled.

"What's in the bag?" the young man asked. He did not return his smile.

Joseph glanced to the seat beside him. It was a black leather bag the size and shape of a bowling ball. Beneath it, in the shadows on the floorboard was the medical bag he'd entered the hospital with. "Bowling ball," he answered, reaching for the zipper. "Want to see it?" Before the guard could answer, he zipped it open and revealed an old, faded purple ball.

"What were you doing on post?"

Joseph left the bag open and the ball visible. "I manage the bowling alley. We just closed up a few minutes ago." He glanced at the clock on the dash and hoped it was correct. "Actually, we closed about an hour ago, but I had to clean up and lock up. You know how it is."

"Registration, please."

Joseph unsnapped his seat belt to lean toward the glove compartment. He hoped the man was like the majority of Americans and kept his registration there. He had no Plan B at the ready, and that was beginning to concern him. He could get a shot off and with any luck at all, he'd kill the young man before he knew what hit him. But the gate was teeming with MP's and he knew he couldn't outrun them all.

He found the registration under a pile of napkins from a variety of fast food restaurants and handed it to the guard. The young man perused it and peered at the car as if he was trying to memorize it.

"Open the trunk, please."

Joseph turned off the ignition and removed the key. As he opened the door, he said, "So what's happening? Somebody rob the bank on post?"

The guard shook his head as he accompanied him to the trunk, obviously disinclined to reveal anything. Joseph opened it and stood a foot or two behind him as he shone his flashlight into the trunk. The light skimmed over the computer case and two suitcases. The young man handed him back the registration and license.

He placed them both in his shirt pocket and closed the trunk, slamming it twice before the rusty contraption caught. Then he made his way back to the car door as the guard was already looking past him to the next in line.

"Have a great night," Joseph said amicably as he started up the engine.

The man did not respond but pushed a button for the barricade strips to recede. Joseph waited until he was safely past the guard post before turning on his headlights and he remained just under the speed limit until he was safely off post and heading into Fayetteville.

Then he let out an audible sigh. The first thing he needed to do was ditch this excuse for a car and find another. Right on the heels of that, he needed his team to track down Brenda through her ankle bracelet and formulate another plan. He'd never been assigned a kill that hadn't been carried out, and he'd be damned if this would be the first one.

40

The small building was nearly obscured by a thicket of pine trees, the brown brick blending almost seamlessly with the night sky. The street lamps were far enough that the muted tentacles of light stopped short of the narrow gravel driveway that led to the building. Passersby would be tempted to drive past without ever noticing the non-descript building, which made it perfect for two people who did not want to be found.

Chris' sedan was pulled behind the building, sandwiched by two trees with overhanging branches and completely hidden from the road. The front door was barricaded, having long ago been concealed by outside hedges and inside by file cabinets. A narrow side door was closed and locked and even a close inspection did not betray Brenda's expert hand at picking the lock.

The narrow hallway revealed an older building with dark paneled walls and aged tile floors. Most office doors were closed and locked, though Brenda had applied her skills to Sam's office door, leaving it cracked open. A lamp on the end table cast just enough illumination to dimly reveal a desk and chairs, an overstuffed sofa and a woman's blouse crumpled on the floor.

The blouse was the start of a trail of clothing that led down another passageway; a lace leopard print bra lay on a chipped tile, followed a few feet later by a stiletto heel and then another…

A man's shirt lay crumpled in a partially open doorway, followed by hastily discarded shoes, until finally two sets of slacks, one male and one female, lay intertwined outside a shower stall.

The only sound in the building came from intermingling moans, husky and insistent.

Chris pressed Brenda against the shower wall, weaving his hand through her copper hair as he breathed in the fresh scent of shampoo. Gone were the pine needles and debris that had littered her hair earlier; gone also was the dirt and grime that had covered her skin. The water, which had grown tepid as the minutes rushed past, was now clear as it whirled down their bodies and into the drain.

He reluctantly pulled back from her soft, enticing lips. "I've been wanting to do this to you since yesterday," he whispered as he nibbled her ear.

She responded by tightening her hold on his buttocks, pulling him closer to her as she turned her head toward him. "What took you so long?" she taunted as her lips found his again.

His answer was drowned out by the sound of her moan as his hands cupped her and caressed her. It no longer mattered what had transpired days or even minutes earlier, or what fate might hold for them. There was only this moment; a moment he wished could go on forever. The image of her deep amber eyes, her waves of hair cascading between their chests, her lips, swollen from their passions, would be seared into his memories forever.

They lay entwined in each other's arms, Brenda's leg draped provocatively over Chris' thighs, her head resting on his chest. The radiator in Sam's office eagerly cranked out heat as the lamp cast a yellow glow on their skin, moist from their lovemaking.

Chris' eyes were closed as he lay on his back, one hand cupping a palm full of Brenda's hair while the other absentmindedly ventured up and down her arm. Sleep was just a moment away; a deep, satisfying slumber that he knew would be too brief. But as he began to drift off, an insistent voice in the back of his mind reminded him that they were nude on Sam's couch in Sam's office; the door was open to the hallway; and their clothes still left a trail along the floor. He tried to ignore it, tried vainly to grab the few minutes of sleep he so desperately needed, but the voice grew until it forced him to open his eyes and stare in frustration at the mottled, aged ceiling.

He thought perhaps Brenda had slipped into a slumber more urgently needed than his own; her fingers lay still against his chest and her breathing was rhythmic. Her hair was still slightly damp and he breathed in the soft floral fragrance as he instinctively tightened his hold around her.

She murmured at his movement, shifting her face to peer up at him.

"Did I wake you?" he asked, his voice deep.

"No," she said lazily. "I couldn't sleep."

"We can't stay here, you know."

"No?" She rose slightly as she arched one brow. "Wouldn't it be fun to see the expression on Sam's face when he comes to work?"

"No," he said firmly. "And how's your leg?"

She grew serious. "It'll heal. Anyway, I have a plan."

"Why did I know you would?"

"You're right. We do need to leave."

He shifted so he could see her face better. "We need to get dressed," he corrected. "But we need to stay put until Sam gets here."

"You're too predictable."

"It's the reasonable thing to do."

She rolled atop of him. "Actually, it isn't."

He slid one arm beneath his head. He'd seen that look in her eye before; the gleam spoke of a mind moving at breakneck speed, and which direction it was careening in could be a cause for concern.

"I'm sick and tired of this guy Gabucci coming after me."

"Precisely why we need to be here when Sam arrives."

Her brow arched higher. "So he can what, do what he's been doing?"

Chris remained silent.

"Time for a change in plan." Brenda slid off him and wandered through Sam's office toward her blouse. Despite the sleep deprivation and a gnawing anxiety, his eyes caressed the gentle slope in her slender back and rested on her derriere as she bent to retrieve her clothing. She turned toward him. Catching his appreciative gaze, she smiled coquettishly. "We're turning the tables, Chris."

He remained on his back as he watched her. She half-leaned against the door frame, her eyes shrouded in the shadows. "We're going after him, Chris."

He felt his arm jerk out from under his head as he went straight from lying down to standing up. "Going after *who?*"

He could feel her eyes roaming up and down his body before she answered. "Gabucci. Of course."

Before he could respond, she disappeared down the hall. He caught up with her as she bent to retrieve her bra.

"Are you insane?"

"That's debatable," she answered as she moved toward her shoes.

He grabbed her arm and whirled her around to face him. "You *are* insane," he said, his voice growing louder in the confines of the hallway. "He's a professional assassin. We're amateurs— at least I am, and I think you—well, hell, I don't know what you are."

She pulled away and picked up her shoes before heading toward the bathroom and her slacks.

"Besides, you're injured," he insisted. "I don't know how you've managed to avoid painkillers."

She smiled slyly. "A roll on the couch is all the painkiller this girl needs."

He exhaled in exasperation. "How—? What—?" He ran his hand through his hair. "How?" He repeated.

"How would I do it?" She dropped her clothes on the bathroom counter before picking up her slacks and brushing the dirt off them. "First step is to find him."

He tried to laugh at the absurdity but it came out forced and short.

"That's where my computer expertise comes in."

He perched on the edge of the counter as he watched her dress.

"I can find anybody, anywhere," she said. Her statement was not filled with bravado as he might have expected, but was said evenly as if she was simply stating that she was going to the grocery store for a loaf of bread.

He realized he was gaping, and he forced himself to maintain control. "Fine," he heard himself saying. "But then we phone Sam and let him know where the guy is."

"So Sam can do what? Try to catch him and return him to prison—where he can escape again?" She shook her head. "No, Chris. It's not going down like that."

He felt his lips grow dry and his heartbeat pick up.

"I'm going after him," she continued, pulling on her bra. "I'd like for you to come with me, but I understand if you can't—or you won't."

The silence felt deafening. He watched her shake out her blouse before donning it, her fingers buttoning it hastily before she ran one hand under her hair and tossed it back.

"And what will you do when you find him?"

Her head jerked up, her eyes locking with his. "Murder him," she said. "Of course."

Before he could respond, she stepped to the bathroom door. She started into the hall but stopped with her hand on the door frame as she glanced back at him.

"Of course I'm going with you," he said.

Her eyes dropped to his feet and traveled slowly up his body before stopping to lock eyes with him once more. "Then I suggest you put some clothes on. You might attract attention if you go like that."

41

The bedroom felt ice cold, though when Vicki awakened she heard the distinct sound of the heater forcing air through the vents. She pulled the bedding closer to her neck and instinctively backed up to press herself against Dylan's warm body. But when she couldn't feel him or his warmth, she groggily rolled onto her back and turned her head toward his side of the bed.

The pillow was exactly where she'd placed it hours earlier and the bedding on his side was neatly rolled back, awaiting his return. She felt a void deep inside as she stared at the emptiness; they had become like one and whenever he was gone, she felt his departure like a vacuum. She wouldn't feel quite right again until he'd returned.

Her eyes roamed the bedroom, resting briefly on the open but darkened bathroom entrance. As she continued peering through the darkness, she made out the dresser and then the sofa and chairs in the sitting area, before moving back to the open bedroom door.

The clanking of dog tags reached her ears and she leaned toward her side of the bed to find Shep curled up on the rug beside the bed, sleepily burying her nose beneath her paws. Chloe was curled up beside her, with her head against the dog's and her bushy tail stretching across her body. They looked like they were old buddies.

Vicki had an uneasy feeling in the pit of her stomach. She reached to her nightstand and picked up her cell phone, pushing the button to view the time. It was nearly two o'clock, and Dylan should have been home by now. She toyed with the idea of phoning him but thought better of it; he or Sam would have called if anything was amiss. His work often took him away at odd hours and she didn't want to be considered a nervous Nellie every time he was away.

She placed the phone back on the nightstand and buried herself beneath the covers. She was beginning to tremble with the frigid air but she was in that nether region somewhere between sleep and wakefulness, and she couldn't quite talk herself into rising to check the thermostat or turn up the heat. Instead, she tried to return to sleep with the hope that warmth would come with slumber.

She was just dozing off when the heater kicked off, leaving the house in an eerie silence. Two floors above the kitchen, she was too far away to hear the hum of the refrigerator and the soothing white noise of the fish tanks were far removed. She'd grown accustomed to Dylan's steady breathing in her ear and his strong, muscled arms around her as she slept. Now, for the first time that she could remember, the silence bothered her. It seemed to surround her with a heaviness that grew fuller, closing in on her like a living, sinister thing.

A *tick* sounded from far away, so faintly that it barely registered. Two seconds later, a *tock* sounded in the same gentle fashion. She laid there listening to the grandfather clock as the pendulum methodically swayed back and forth, each swing sounding a *tick* or a *tock*…

It eased her back into slumber, though the trembling was turning to more pronounced shivers as the air that swirled around her grew icier. She could feel her spirit leaving her body, moving into that blue-gray zone of dreams, that black hole from which she may or may not remember where she was going or what she might encounter. Her head sank more deeply into the pillow, her own breathing becoming heavier, the sound helping to lull her to sleep.

Then with a gasp, her eyes flew open.

The sound had grown until it seemed to be levitating directly over the bed. *Tick, tock, tick tock.*

The grandfather clock was broken.

The realization caused her heart to race and though she was still cold, she felt a flush develop across her chest and through her face.

The bedding inched away from her face though she remained perfectly still. Her eyes rolled toward it, watching it pull away from her as if human fingers had grasped it. They moved over her shoulder, leaving it bare, before crawling down her arm. Slowly, she was left bare, her arms still encircling herself in an attempt to get warm, as she stared at the covers. They continued moving over the curves of her body as the *tick, tock, tick, tock* grew louder and more insistent.

When they reached the foot of the bed, the sheet and comforter appeared to pull straight up toward the ceiling.

Vicki bounded to a seated position, her eyes still riveted on the fabric as it hung in mid-air. She felt a presence beside her and as she tore her eyes away from the bedding, she caught sight of Shep sitting at attention, watching the same spectacle that had riveted her. The dog didn't utter a sound but simply stared. Then suddenly, the bedding dropped.

Vicki gasped and jerked her head back to stare at the foot of the bed. But Shep was standing now, her tail wagging as it did when she greeted Dylan. Her head seemed to follow something in the room as it moved from the bed to the open door.

She grasped for the sheet, yanking it toward her to cover her nakedness. A wisp of air brushed against her and as she stared into the darkness, it seemed to grow larger and more luminescent. The larger it grew, the louder the *tick, tock, tick, tock* sounded until it seemed to be thundering in her ears.

She followed the wisp with her eyes as it glided toward the open doorway. Just as it entered the hallway, she caught a glimpse of a long, flowing white gown and straight hair that seemed to fan out behind some unseen force until the snowy locks nearly blended into the gown itself.

Vicki slipped out of the bed, pulling the sheet with her. As she wrapped it around her body, she followed the figure into the hall. It seemed to sense her presence and stopped, hovering inches from the floor.

Then a long arm shielded by the white gown emerged. A bony hand protruded and then a crooked forefinger straightened until it was pointing into the corner of the hall.

Vicki followed with her eyes until they rested on the camera that had been installed with the alarm system.

"Mam?" she asked hesitantly.

The figure did not respond, but continued to point at the camera.

"I see it, Mam," she whispered hoarsely. "I see the camera." Her voice sounded hoarse and not at all herself and she realized her throat had become completely dry.

The figure floated toward the stairs and as Vicki watched, it descended slowly, the hair still billowing in some unseen breeze. She realized her heart had grown calmer though the air around her remained frigid; her brain told her to return to her bedroom, turn on the lights and telephone Dylan. But her heart and her soul urged her to follow the figure as it drifted toward the second floor.

Vicki was halfway down the stairs when the door to Brenda's bedroom swung open. She gasped, her hand instinctively covering her mouth, her own fingers feeling like icicles. She waited for Brenda or Chris to emerge and when they didn't, she moved cautiously forward. It wasn't until she'd taken a few more steps that she realized the figure had disappeared.

Her palms were clammy as she grasped the railing. She struggled to peer through the darkness into Brenda's bedroom— the room that had once been hers.

As she moved toward the open doorway, she remembered other nights—nights in which she was awakened by the sound of footsteps above her, footsteps she believed to belong to Aunt Laurel when the woman was dead and dismembered in a freezer directly above her. Her steps slowed as her mind was flooded with the memory of the bathroom curtains pulling apart, blood oozing down the walls of the bathtub, and a grotesque figure drifting toward her…

It was happening again, she thought. She turned to look for Shep but the dog was not there; she wasn't behind her nor had she gone ahead of her and a glance upstairs did not reveal her sitting outside her bedroom door watching her—or guarding her.

She should continue down the stairs to the main floor, turn on all the lights and sit on the front porch until Dylan came home. But the ghostly figure seemed like a magnet, pulling her into the room even when every inch of her wanted to fight against the forward movement.

Vicki was inside the bedroom before she saw the apparition again; it floated in the far corner, the gown swirling above the floor. The long, flowing white hair almost appeared like a hood; the face that should have been there watching her was darkened so that there didn't seem to be a face there at all.

The arm of the gown wafted up slowly like a piece of clothing on a clothesline caught by the wind. Only when it was completely rigid did a bony hand emerge, the forefinger pointing to the elaborate carved wood above the dresser.

"Talk to me, Mam," Vicki murmured, though if she actually heard the woman's voice, she'd be sorely tempted to run screaming from the room. But the figure did not answer but pointed in earnest toward the dresser.

With one eye on the levitating figure, she flipped on the light.

There was nothing there; no gown and nothing that she might have mistaken for one in the gloom. There was only the naked wall.

She had her hand on the light switch ready to turn it off when her eyes moved to the carved wood around the antique dresser mirror. What had the form been pointing at?

She inched her way toward the mirror almost as if she expected it to come alive and lunge toward her. But as she moved closer, she began to feel foolish; the bright light illuminated everything in the room as though it was day.

She studied the carving and the swirls that formed wood roses around the mirror, now mottled with age and humidity. She turned to walk away when she felt the urge to look behind the dresser. She felt the hairs on her arms begin to stand as she moved ever closer to it before sidling to one side. Peering behind it, she sucked in her breath.

A small black camera was located directly behind the dresser, the cord neatly laid against the wall until it reached the outlet nearly hidden by the large piece of furniture. It was positioned so precisely that from the front of the dresser, the tiny camera lens blended seamlessly into the mahogany carving.

She reached her arm behind the dresser and fumbled for the cord but the furniture was pressed too tightly against the wall and her arm was too short. She tried to push the dresser over or outward, but the monstrous piece of furniture would not budge. Nothing she tried could dislodge the cord, nor could she reach the camera itself.

She backed toward the door, her eyes riveted on the camera. In her peripheral vision, she felt more than saw the images captured by the camera: the chair in the corner, the ottoman, the chest of drawers… and the bed.

Surely Sam would not have done this.

She could envision him alarming the window or focusing a camera on the doors of the house to alert anyone if Brenda attempted to escape. But why? He had been the one to bring her here when she'd been incarcerated in a federal prison—and she was wearing an ankle bracelet.

How could he? She thought as she backed into the doorway. How could he train a camera on her sister's bed, knowing that Chris was there—knowing what they were certainly doing—

A bright light caught her attention, and she jerked her head toward the stairs. The figure was standing next to the front door, pointing into the corner.

"I understand," Vicki said, her voice trembling. "You're showing me the cameras." She hurried to the stairs, ready to descend to the main floor and discover the other cameras that observed their every move; if she could have leapt over the railing to the floor below to speed her discovery, she would have.

But as she rushed to the top of the second flight of stairs, her foot caught in the sheet that she'd so hastily wrapped around her. It seemed to be unfurling on its own and as her foot touched the top step, she stumbled. She cried out as she tried to throw her arms toward the railing to catch herself but her arms were caught in the same fabric, which had tightened around her like a straightjacket. In a split second, her upper body was dangling over the stairs in a final, aggravated suspension before she would be catapulted down the stairs to the floor below.

In an instant, the image of Laurel Maguire rose in her mind—of the woman coming down these same two flights of stairs and falling to her death below; of her lying in the front foyer—the one that stared up at her now. And she was powerless to stop herself.

As if in slow motion, her eyes moved from the floor to the floating apparition just above it. The elongated arm that pointed toward the camera in the far corner swung out in a fluid movement, the palm thrusting forward.

Vicki felt as though she'd been shoved backward, the effort knocking the wind completely out of her. She was propelled backward with such force that once she hit the floor, she slid nearly halfway down the hall. She came to a complete stop and lay there, heaving to catch her breath, her chest hurting so badly she felt certainly that she was bruised.

She might have laid there for a minute or half an hour before she rose to a seated position. The figure still hovered in the downstairs hallway, the hair still blowing. What had been a black hollow in the middle of the hair now seemed to be lightening, though its glow was not as significant as the hair and gown that swirled around it. At the foot of the stairs sat Shep, staring up at Vicki.

She didn't remember the dog leaving the bedroom. Though she'd been distracted in Brenda's bedroom, she certainly would have heard the animal's dog tags clinking as they always did—but she hadn't.

It was then she realized the *tick, tock, tick, tock* continued. She rose unsteadily to her feet, her eyes riveted on the grandfather clock. The hands remained perfectly still, its pendulum silenced.

She gathered the sheet around her once more, taking care to cover only her body and not her legs. Then she made her way to the stairway and descended; her hand racing over an ornate balustrade that felt as though it was made of ice.

Shakily, she nodded as her eyes fell on the camera. "I understand," she said. Her own voice sounded disembodied. She turned to follow the path the camera would encompass and realized it took in both the stairs and the hallway leading back toward the kitchen.

She turned to find the ghostly figure disappearing into the living room. She hurried to the doorway but didn't need to search for the glowing apparition in the gloom; it was gliding toward the center of the bookcases at the far end of the room.

Vicki waited until it had stopped and the finger moved outward from the gown's sleeve, pointing to the highest point on the top shelf.

She turned on the lights to find the apparition gone. Hastily, she grabbed a chair and pulled it to the bookcase, where she tested its sturdiness before climbing onto the seat. She had to stand on tiptoe and strain to see it, but there it was: the lens of a camera atop a book on the top shelf. It was pointed slightly downward and as she turned to look back at the room, she realized that vantage point would view the entire room except for a blind area just underneath it.

She struggled to reach the book under it as the chair wobbled underneath her. She instinctively held her breath until she realized she was beginning to feel light-headed, but the mere act of breathing was enough to prevent her from extending far enough. Finally, the tip of her fingernail caught the bottom edge of the book. She pulled, almost knocking herself off the chair with the effort. The book flew across the room, hitting the floor with a loud thud.

The lens was knocked to the shelf itself and as she watched, the books on either side toppled inward, blocking its view.

She precariously knelt to the chair's seat, her legs shaking more from fear than from the incessant cold. A flash of light caught her attention and she turned to glimpse the gown as it slipped through the living room doorway into the hall.

She forced herself to follow, even though her teeth were chattering and her hands were trembling with an apprehension that grew as the steady *tick, tock, tick, tock* began to sound like thunder in her ears.

She reached the hall as the gown disappeared into the kitchen.

She glanced around for Shep but the dog that had been like a silent guard in the front foyer was nowhere to be seen. She gathered up the sheet around her hips as she dashed down the hall to the kitchen door.

The light was on above the cabinets, casting the old-fashioned kitchen in an eerie shade of fluorescent blue. As her eyes adjusted, she saw the figure hovering at the far end, the finger pointing above the back door.

Vicki hauled a chair from the kitchen table to the back door. The figure flickered and then disappeared as she climbed atop the chair. She couldn't see anything at all. She stood on her tiptoes and stretched until her fingers located the transom above the old door. She felt her way across, her fingers picking up dust particles from ages past.

Then she touched clean wood.

Her heart seemed to stand still as she continued groping. The back of the chair teetered forward as she moved beyond a reasonable range. Just as she was about to give up, she felt it: round, hard and cold.

The chair wobbled dangerously and she gripped the transom as she tried to firmly plant her feet on the chair seat. Then she lowered herself and finally turned around to sit, emotionally drained and emotionally charged.

It was several minutes before she realized the figure was still there, hovering at the door to the kitchen.

"Did I find them all?" Vicki asked.

The apparition turned wordlessly as it moved from the kitchen into the hall.

Vicki rose once more. Her ankles felt so weak that she nearly collapsed. She caught herself on the kitchen table, took a deep breath, and moved back into the hallway, her mind racing.

The ghostly figure hovered near the foot of the stairs until Vicki had nearly reached it. Then it simply disappeared.

Puzzled, she looked around her—down the hall, into the fully lit living room, and into the darkened dining room. She checked the front door; it was still bolted shut. Then she turned to peer upward.

The figure rose two flights above her at the entrance to the master bedroom.

Vicki felt the blood drain from her face. She didn't remember climbing the stairs; one moment she was staring upward at the glowing figure and the next she was clearing the top step on the third floor and moving toward the master bedroom. The figure glided into the bedroom.

As Vicki entered the room, she nearly tripped over Shep. The dog was lying on the rug beside the bed as she had earlier; in fact, she marveled, she didn't appear to have moved. Chloe was still asleep next to her, her head in the same spot against Shep's muzzle, her tail still cascading over Shep's hindquarters. Vicki's head jerked toward the stairs, peering toward the foyer two floors below that was now illuminated from the living room lights she'd kept on. How did—?

A movement caught her eye and she returned her focus to the master bedroom. The ghost hovered at the far end to a bookshelf between two floor-to-ceiling windows.

There was no chair in the bedroom that she could easily maneuver to the bookshelf, but as she considered its location, she realized wherever the camera was located, if it was anywhere on that piece of furniture, it had an unrestricted view of nearly the entire room—and most certainly the bed.

The glowing figure began to flicker. The black chasm began to radiate and for a split second, she glimpsed Mam's face before the entire apparition simply vanished.

The entire house was instantly silenced. Gone was the *tick, tock, tick, tock* that was driving her slowly insane. In its place was the realization that she was in a three-story rambling Victorian home by herself—and a camera was focused on her at that very moment.

When the front door rattled downstairs, she nearly jumped out of her skin. With trembling hands, she rushed to the nightstand and withdrew her pistol. Her fingers were shaking as she removed the safety. As she turned toward the doorway with the pistol in hand, she spotted the alarm's remote control sitting beside her cell phone.

In one fluid movement, she grabbed the remote and pressed the *Panic* button.

42

Dylan burst through the door, his brows creased, his face darkened with rage, and his hands balled into fists ready for a fight. On his heels was Sam with a gun drawn, moving swiftly into the foyer like a member of a SWAT team.

Vicki's name was on his lips when Dylan's eyes landed on her. She stood on the landing on the second floor, her pistol drawn and pointed in the direction of the front foyer, dressed in something that would have looked like a Roman toga—except that he recognized it as one of the sheets off his bed.

"What the h'ail—?"

Vicki lowered the pistol. "I thought—I—" was all she could manage to say.

He strode quickly to the bottom of the stairs. Sam holstered his gun and closed the front door before joining Dylan.

"Did you set off the alarm?" Dylan asked.

"Yes," Vicki said. Shakily, she made her way down the steps.

"Why?" Dylan breathed. His brows were still knit and his face still darkened; his hands trembled with adrenaline and now that he had readied himself for a fight, he wasn't calming down. "Is there someone here or did you think I was an intruder?"

"The cameras—" Vicki placed a hand atop her breast to steady her heart. She was caught between the surreal events that had just unfolded, the relief that Dylan was home again, and the realization that they had been filmed—and might still be.

Dylan grasped her hand and pulled it away from the sheet. "Who the h'ail did this to you?" he bellowed.

"What?" Vicki stepped back, releasing her hand from his grasp.

He clutched at the sheet and pulled it down. Horrified, she clenched it within her fist to keep her breasts from being exposed to Sam. "What are you doing?" Her voice sounded on the verge of hysteria.

"This!" Dylan pointed at her chest. "Who did this to you?"

She tore her eyes away from his to peer downward. In the middle of her chest just above her breasts was the unmistakable, deep red imprint of a hand. "My God," she breathed.

"Answer me, Woman!"

"It's not—not what you think," she managed to say. How could she tell him that Mam had appeared to her? They'd not talked much about her since returning to America; she knew he was still grieving. Yet it was obvious as she looked into eyes filled with outrage that he was ready to hunt down anyone he believed had attacked her.

"Well, then, since you think you know what I'm thinkin', why don't you tell me what I should be thinkin'?" he said.

She pointed to the camera in the front hall. "The cameras are filming us."

His eyes didn't waver from hers. "The cameras are part o' the alarm system. You know that."

She turned her attention to Sam. "Then why are they filming us in bed?"

"What?" Sam's eyes grew wide. Then he stammered, "They're not."

"Oh?" She drew to her full height in righteous indignation. "Then why don't you tell me why there's a camera in my bedroom—that's focused on my bed. *Our* bed," she added, glancing back at Dylan.

He turned to Sam, the thundering adrenaline finding its target. "Tell me this isn't true." His hands released and then balled again into tighter fists.

"I want to see this camera," Sam said, his own anger rising.

———•— ——•—— —••—

Vicki sat in a chair in the formal dining room while Dylan and Sam stood next to her. All three were wide-eyed, their expressions incredulous. They'd selected this room because Mam had not pointed out a camera here but as they gathered, Vicki's eyes continuously moved along the transoms above the windows and the wide door leading into the hallway, and along the built-in cabinets on either side of the fireplace where antique china was carefully arranged.

Sam dialed a number and placed the phone on speaker.

"Bob's Deli," a male voice answered.

Vicki's brows shot up.

"Yeah," Sam said. "I want to order an Italian Sub. Hold the pepperoni and pile on the peppers."

Dylan stepped closer to him, his face reddening. Sam held up one finger.

"Your name?" the voice asked.

"Sam Mazoli."

"Hold please."

While they waited, Sam held his hand over the phone and said, "It's a code."

"Well, I'm certainly glad you'd be tellin' me that," Dylan said. "I couldn't believe you would actually be callous enough after what has occurred to be orderin' food!"

"Bob here." It was another male voice, deeper and so curt that the man sounded as if he was completely no-nonsense.

"Bob, it's Sam Mazoli."

"What's going on?" Bob asked.

"Who did you send to install the alarm I requested?"

"Hold on." It sounded as if the man set the phone on the desk; they could hear noise as though he was rifling through papers. Then he picked up the phone again. "I'm sorry, Sam. We got slammed and we haven't gotten to it yet."

"Excuse me?" Sam held up his finger to prevent Vicki or Dylan from chiming in.

"I promise we'll get to it by next Tuesday at the latest. I see where it's classified as urgent; it's just that we got a lot of orders in—"

"Are you telling me that you did not send anyone to install the alarm?" Sam interjected.

"I apologize, Sam. As I said—"

"Then who installed this alarm?"

There was a brief silence on the other end. "Are you saying someone installed an alarm?" He read off the address.

"That's exactly what I'm saying." Sam pulled out a chair and sat next to Vicki at the oversized mahogany table. "Look, Bob, whoever did this installed cameras focused on the beds of two of our operatives."

"We'd never do that—without the operative's knowledge, that is."

"They were supposed to install cameras around the exterior of the house; you know the type. In addition, they installed cameras inside—they look like they're set to monitor activity in two bedrooms, the kitchen, the living room, and both hallways."

Dylan waved his hand in front of Sam and started to speak.

"Bob," Sam cut in, "I'm here with the two operatives, Vicki Boyd and Dylan Maguire. Dylan wants to say something to you."

"Bob," Dylan said, "remote controls were left in the event we wanted to alert the authorities to an intrusion. Vicki set it off more than thirty minutes ago, and yet no one has shown up yet to investigate. Wouldn't it be customary for law enforcement to respond?"

"Is it still going off?" Bob asked.

"Negative. The alarm sounded for perhaps thirty seconds."

They heard the sound of fingers on a keyboard. Then Bob said, "I have no record of our office installing the alarm—and it would have been this office that handled it. If we had installed it, anything that trips the alarm would have caused the system to electronically notify this office as well as local law enforcement. You would have had our guys there alongside the police."

There was a brief silence as everyone digested this information. Then Sam stated the obvious. "We've been compromised."

"Where are you now?"

"In the house. In a room we don't believe is wired—but I can't be sure."

"Okay," Bob said. He took a deep breath. "Here's what we're going to do. I'm sending a team in; it'll take them about an hour to get there. I'm sending my best. They'll dismantle the whole thing and they'll reverse engineer it—meaning they'll trace the source. We'll know soon who did the installation and where they are."

Dylan nodded and Sam said, "Any advice for us?"

"Try to remain out of view. For the time being, don't talk. Write whatever you need to communicate and then destroy the conversation."

"We'll be waiting." With that, Sam clicked off the phone.

Dylan sat on the edge of the bed and placed his hand on Vicki's leg. Though the bedcovers were between them, she could feel the warmth radiating from his hand. Gone was the rage he'd displayed when he thought she was in harm's way, but his brow was still furrowed with concern.

"It'll be alright," he said soothingly.

"I'm tired of this, Dylan," she answered. Her eyes roamed the bedroom. At his insistence, it had been the first room the technicians searched. They found the camera where Vicki had located it earlier as well as a bug adhered on the underside of a slat in the bed frame and another underneath the coffee table in the sitting area. Though they assured her that there were no more bugs or cameras, she felt as though she'd been physically violated.

He nodded silently. After studying her for a long moment, he reached over and gently brushed a lock of hair off her forehead. "Me own life hasn't been the same since I've become involved w' the CIA, that's for certain… I'm beginnin' to think this sort o' thin' comes w' the territory."

Vicki sighed and stared at the ceiling. "No, Dylan. It isn't the CIA connection. It's the Brenda connection."

He waited for her to continue. When she didn't, he said in a soft voice, "She's your sister."

"Yes," she acknowledged immediately. "But she's trouble. She tried to warn us right off the bat and I didn't listen. Well, now I'm listening."

The heater kicked on and for once, Vicki was appreciative of the white noise. Otherwise, it was too eerie in this rambling old home. The sounds of the technicians downstairs were a reminder that the entire house was being searched, and at least the hum of forced air helped to muffle it somewhat.

"What are you suggestin' we do?" Dylan asked.

She hesitated with the words frozen on her lips. He waited patiently for her to continue, his head slightly cocked and his eyes revealing concern and his own conflicting emotions. Then she said what she'd been dreading but which could no longer be denied. "She can't stay here." Her voice sounded strained. "We're a family now, you and I. And soon we'll have a baby to care for—and protect. And nobody, not even my blood sister, can stay here as long as they're bringing trouble into this house."

He continued to study her before he finally nodded in agreement. "Would you be feelin' like I'm doin' anythin' at'al to force this decision on you?"

"Not at all." She reached for his hand. "You've been patient with her—and me. But this whole notion of being reunited with my sister—it was just some romanticized fantasy—"

"Don't be gettin' too hard on y'self now. How were you to know, as kind and unsullied as you are, that your sister would prove to be just the opposite?"

She squeezed his hand. "I feel guilty."

"You shouldn't. Brenda said it herself right from the beginnin'. And she's repeated it often enough. And this time, even if it isn't her fault, she knows in her heart what she's doin' to our family." He slipped his other hand onto her belly. "She won't resent you, Vicki. She'll know you're just lookin' out for our child."

She nodded silently.

"But there's somethin' you ought to be explainin' to me."

Her eyes widened. "Have I done something—?"

"I want to know who placed their hand on you." He took the hand he held in his and moved it to the reddened imprint just above her breasts. "It doesn't match your hand, and I can't imagine you would've done this to y'self."

"No," she said. She swallowed before continuing. "Do you remember when I first came to live here, how I saw the ghost of a woman so many times?"

His face paled slightly. "Don't be tellin' me 'twas Laurel Maguire who struck you."

"No. In fact, I've not seen her since—well, since I found her body."

"Well, that would be a good thin', 'ey? Because if I felt this house was haunted by that evil old woman, I wouldn't be wantin' to rear me child here." He placed his own hand over the imprint and seemed to be gauging his much longer and fuller fingers to those on her chest.

"No, but—what if…" She swallowed again. "What if you found out that somebody you love was here, and she protected me from falling down the stairs?"

"Someone *I* love?"

She nodded.

"A 'she', you say?"

"Yes."

He kept his eyes focused on hers. "There 'ave only been two women I've ever loved, aside from you."

"I know."

He looked over his shoulder as if someone was there before looking back at her. "So which one would it be?"

"It was Mam." She caught her breath and waited for him to respond.

He continued looking at her with veiled eyes. "Are you sayin' she did that to you?" He nodded toward her chest.

"I—I had gathered the sheet around me and I tripped—"

His face grew pale and he grasped her hand.

"I would have fallen down the stairs, just like Aunt Laurel, but she stopped me, Dylan. She raised her hand and she stopped me. The force was so great that I slid backward down the hall."

He hesitated for a moment before asking, "And you're certain this wasn't your imagination?"

She shook her head. "The thing is, when I was trained as a remote viewer, we learned that there are parallel worlds. People who pass over from this life don't just sit up there on a cloud somewhere and look down on us. They're right here beside us. We just can't see them."

"You learned that in class, did you?"

"I know it sounds strange—"

"Mam often said the same thin'."

"So you believe me?"

He stared at the reddened imprint. "Does she frighten you?"

"Not at all. She protected me, Dylan. Not only that, but it was her who told me there were cameras."

"What are you sayin'?"

"She led me to each one. She wanted me to know—us to know—that we were being watched."

He glanced over his shoulder again. "Is she watchin' us now?"

"I don't know… I don't feel her right now."

"Well. If she comes aroun' again to visit you, will you give 'er a message for me, please? Would you tell 'er that what a man does to the woman he loves is between him and said woman, and she's to stay out o' it? I don't much care for the idea o' performin' for an audience. Especially m' Mam."

Vicki laughed. "That's pretty much what I told her, too."

Dylan smiled. "So. Is that why you wore that hideous getup to bed the other night?"

She nodded sheepishly.

He shook his head as if thinking. "Well. I'll leave it to you to inform the spirits to stay out o' our bedroom." He slapped his knee. "Meanwhile, I'd best be gettin' downstairs to see what sort o' progress the men are makin'."

43

The all-night diner was glaringly bright compared to the darkness of the night as Joseph settled into a corner table, seating himself with his back against the wall and a clear line of sight to the door. He slid his laptop onto the table as a server approached with a menu.

"Coffee," he said before she had a chance to ask. "Black. Do you have Wifi here?"

"Yes," she said, dropping the menu onto the table. "It's public. No password needed."

"Good." He smiled kindly. "My granddaughter emails me every night."

"How sweet." The server appeared to be in her 60's with thinning gray hair and translucent skin.

She seemed to be waiting for more details but when Joseph turned his attention to booting up his laptop, she walked away.

He retrieved an earbud from the case and logged on, switching the audio so any noise emanating from the computer would remain private. He barely noticed when the server returned with a pot of coffee and a cup and saucer but as the aroma of the hot brew reached his nostrils, his hand instinctively went to the cup.

"Can I get you anything else?"

"Not right now," Joseph responded. "Thank you." He smiled again, briefly, before turning his attention back to the computer screen. He hoped his body language indicated that he'd like to be left alone. After a moment that felt too long, the server slipped away.

The rest of the diner was empty except for a middle-aged couple on the other side. They appeared deep in conversation. The server began filling sugar caddies and the short-order cook slipped off his apron and headed down the short hall marked "Rest Rooms".

Joseph turned back to the laptop, logging into the security system. He frowned as he noted one blank screen after another. A strange sensation began moving up his torso; it was a tingle along his skin that almost made him shiver. This was not a mechanical failure. He knew it without a doubt.

Then the living room popped up and he adjusted the sound in his earbud. There were two men in the room; men he did not recognize. He glanced at his watch. It was clearly the middle of the night, obviously too late for the Irishman to have social company. As he watched, the feeling along his skin intensified. These men were not there for pleasure; they were working.

He watched as they turned every piece of furniture upside down, using handheld equipment to aid them in their search. One by one, they located and removed the bugs he'd planted. They never said a word to each other; he could see their faces in the video-camera. Sometimes they would gesture as if they were using a sign language all their own, but no words passed their lips.

Then one turned his attention to the bookcase. Joseph could see the top of his head as he stood directly underneath the camera. It grew larger as he moved up the shelves until he was watching the upper half of his face. Then the eyes locked onto the camera: gray-blue eyes that narrowed as the picture popped and then blackened.

As if on cue, his cell phone rang. It sounded loud and obnoxious in the quiet diner, and he wrestled his hand inside his pocket to retrieve it quickly and stop the infernal noise.

"Yeah?" he answered, his voice barely a hoarse whisper.

"You're too hot."

His breath felt shallow and quick. "I'm not finished."

"Yes you are."

He hesitated. His eyes swept the diner. The server was chatting with the couple across the room and the cook had not yet returned from the rest room.

"All of Fort Bragg is looking for you," the voice continued. It was deep and even and unemotional.

"They won't find me."

"You've been made."

Joseph watched as a police cruiser pulled in front of the diner. He shut the laptop as he watched two officers exit the car and move toward the doors. They were laughing and he relaxed back into the seat.

"They won't recognize me," Joseph said as he watched them enter the double doors.

"You have new orders."

"Proceed."

"Return to Washington."

"I haven't finished here."

"In two days, the President will announce his new Attorney General."

Joseph involuntarily sucked in his breath. It was highly unusual for that much information to be spoken over an unsecured phone line.

"He'll be confirmed with no problems," the caller continued.

"And the girl?"

"We'll use her to our advantage."

He did not need to hear specifics. The detailed information she'd turned over to the FBI said it all. He'd seen every page of it, knew every politician on the list, and was familiar with a good number of the schemes.

The officers had ordered coffee to go and were chatting while the server poured the hot liquid into tall Styrofoam cups. Joseph kept his eyes narrowed as he watched them and listened to the breathing on the other end of the phone.

"Then she'll testify against our opponents," Joseph said.

"Of course she will," the voice answered smoothly. "With a new Attorney General in place, she'll either testify or spend the rest of her life in prison. Which do you think she'll choose?"

Joseph cradled the phone against his shoulder as he slipped the laptop into its case. As he stood, one of the officers casually peered at him.

"I'll be back in Washington before dawn."

"Don't get caught."

"I don't plan to." With that, he clicked off the phone. Slipping it into his pocket, he downed the rest of his coffee and pulled a five dollar bill from his wallet. Then he settled the strap for the computer case over one shoulder and started through the diner toward the front doors.

The second officer stopped talking and both looked in his direction, following his movements with their eyes. The air grew tense and still. The server had finished pouring the coffee and stopped with the pot held in mid-air as she also watched him.

The distance between his table and the door seemed to grow exponentially as he moved slowly through the restaurant. He could feel his pistol against one hip and he shifted the laptop to his other shoulder in preparation for needing it.

One of the officers narrowed his eyes, his hand moving toward his own belt and his own pistol.

Joseph reached the register and leaned over the counter less than three feet from the officers. "Thanks," he said, handing the five dollar bill to the server.

She reached for it, the pot still in her other hand. Scalding hot coffee, Joseph noted.

"Keep the change," he added.

Her eyes widened. "Thank you."

One of the officers turned toward him, his mouth just beginning to open.

"Did you get the email from your granddaughter?" The server asked.

"Yes," Joseph said, smiling broadly. "The recital at her school went well. She received a standing ovation!"

"Good for her! What does she play?"

He strode to the door, the smile still on his face. "Piano," he said as he opened the door. "I'm so proud of her!"

As he turned his back to them, he caught sight of the officer closing his mouth and leaning back just a bit. Thank God for Southern hospitality, Joseph thought as he moved through the double doors and into the brisk night air. Though he'd met that server only minutes before, she'd acted like he was a regular.

He forced himself to stop on the sidewalk and light a cigarette. His hands were steady and he puffed into the night a couple of times before making his way to a white minivan he'd stolen from a car dealership. He took his time setting the laptop into the front seat before moving around the vehicle to the driver's side.

Then he was pulling away, turning away from the Interstate toward the west. Once out of sight, he circled back around until he was driving east. Within ten minutes, he would be on Interstate 95 and heading back to Washington.

But they were wrong, he thought. The purpose for killing her was so she wouldn't talk about any of their associates whose names were on that list. Even if they placed a new Attorney General who was allied with their politics, who was so say he would go along with removing half the names on the list? Who would know with absolute certainty that he would agree to prosecute each of the President's opponents? He'd never had a failed mission before Brenda Carnegie. And though he was headed to Washington as directed, he knew this wasn't over until he'd eliminated her.

44

Chris peered at the paperwork in his hand. The automobile smelled of new leather but with the engine turned off, it was chilling rapidly. He was backed into a corner of a fast food parking lot and the closest street lamp was a good distance away. The restaurant was closed, its lights dimmed, and Brenda had advised him to shut off the engine while she worked, lest a patrolling police vehicle spotted the exhaust rising into the cold air.

"I don't know how you do it," he said, thumbing through the papers.

She was silent except for her fingers tapping on the keyboard. After a moment, she glanced up. "It was easy."

He made a sound that came out as half-laugh and half-cough.

"Really," she continued. "You saw me do it. Sam's laptop was too easy to hack into—for God's sake, he used his cat's name as a password. Who does that anymore?"

"But even so—"

"And hacking into the car rental agency's site, generating the bogus information for this car, that was nothing. Piece of cake."

"But—"

"And hacking into the rental agency's email system and generating an email from the president to the local office, telling

them to leave the key for you to pick up, no questions asked—
that was just icing on the cake."

She returned to typing, and Chris reluctantly placed the
paperwork into the console. "Like I said, I don't know how you
do it—how you know what to do. It's mind boggling."

She shivered involuntarily.

"I should turn the heat on."

"Not yet. I'm almost done."

He leaned against the driver's door and watched her as she
continued typing, her eyes riveted on the screen. It was Sam's
laptop and something told him when he arrived at his office in a
few short hours, he was not going to believe anybody "borrowed"
it. Though they locked up the building when they left, it was
only the door knob and not the deadbolt, since they didn't have
a key. That, too, would be noticed. And of course, there was the
little matter of Brenda having disappeared from the hospital—
and, oh yes, his absence as well.

There was a voice inside him that urged him to telephone
Sam and to insist that Brenda be placed back into some sort of
protective custody. There was another voice, and definitely a
stronger one, that wanted more time alone with her. And if sitting
in a parking lot freezing was part of the deal, he'd take it.

As she worked, he peered out the windows to Interstate 95,
which stretched out before them. They were on the northern
outskirts of Fayetteville, sandwiched in between fast food
restaurants, hotels and gas stations. Brenda had selected this
particular parking lot because their Wifi hadn't required a user
logon or password, and though the restaurant was closed, their
Wifi was definitely on—and fast.

There was scant activity at this time of the morning, though
as he continued to watch the interstate, he realized the number
of tractor-trailers had increased. He glanced at his watch. Dawn
was less than an hour away, and he was astonished that they'd
walked out of Fort Bragg on foot, avoiding the gates and exiting
through a neighborhood, and that they'd been able to hitch a
ride to the rental car agency. He'd kept his jacket collar turned
up and his face tilted away from office cameras, just as Brenda
had instructed him, and he'd retrieved the keys to the new Lincoln

with no questions asked—but wide eyes and a lot of questions hiding behind them.

"We have to move," he said, his voice breaking the silence.

"What is it?" she said, her head popping up.

"Someone is going to question this car," he said. He started the engine. "I have this gut feeling, like we need to be someplace else."

"Fine. Head for Washington."

"Washington—DC?"

"Well, it's not Washington State, that's for sure."

His brows knit.

"I'll explain while you're driving."

He exhaled sharply but eased the car out of the parking lot and onto the service road. In less than two minutes, he was through a stoplight and accelerating on the entrance ramp to I-95.

Brenda waited until he was at a cruising speed before continuing. "He's going to Washington. And he's on this interstate."

His eyes cut over to her before he forced them back to the road. "How could you possibly know that?"

"Want the wiki or the details?"

"The details."

"You're sure?"

"I've got nothing but time."

She turned on the seat heater and leaned back in her seat. "So, I've been thinking. Everybody has been asking me why this guy Gabucci wants me. Why he's after me. And I've been telling everyone that I didn't know. I don't have a clue."

"Have you been lying?"

"No. For once, I've been telling the truth."

He glanced at her again, only to find her watching him with what appeared to be a lot of interest. He felt the heat rising in his cheeks and forced himself to look back at the road.

"So it occurred to me," she continued, "what if he'd killed me?"

"Don't say that."

"Well, he didn't, obviously. And I don't have any plans to die. But what if? What if I wasn't around to badger with questions? What would a homicide detective do?"

"It would have been pretty obvious who did it."

"But what if it wasn't?"

He drove in silence for a moment. "I don't understand."

"Here's the thing," she said, leaning forward with an eager expression. "We have to think like detectives. And when they come upon a scene that they have to solve—like a murder investigation—they move backward in time."

"I still don't understand."

"Stay with me," she said, a lop-sided grin forming. "They start with the approximate time the crime was committed. Well, we know when Gabucci was in my hospital room. And we know where that hospital room was—on a secure military installation."

"Okay," he said slowly.

"So how does one get on a military installation?"

"Same way we got off one? He just walked?"

She shrugged. "Maybe. Or maybe he had access."

"You don't think—he's military?"

She shrugged. "Sam said he works for the highest bidder. It could be the military. Definitely the government."

"You think Joseph Gabucci works for the government? *Our* government?"

"Think about it. Not only did he get on Fort Bragg, but he knew to go to the hospital." Before he could interject, she continued, her voice growing more rapid as she spoke. "There are plenty of maps online, so finding his way to the hospital wouldn't have been such a big deal. But how did he know I was there? How did he know which room I was in?"

"I don't know," he admitted.

"Ah-ha. That's where good detective work comes in. Who knew I was there?"

"Sam, me, Vicki, Dylan—"

"The medical staff, the CIA and the FBI."

"You don't think—"

"Not the medical staff. Possible, but not probable. That leaves the CIA or the FBI."

"Or the military."

"Now you're catching on. Those were military guys sitting outside my room. And they let him in."

"We're assuming, since you were gone."

"We didn't hear gun shots, and there were no MP's rushing to the hospital as we were leaving."

"But there were as we were following him."

She glanced out the side window, her eyes on the darkened shoulder. "I haven't figured that out yet." She turned back and smiled. "Some things take time."

They drove in silence for a few minutes. Chris struggled with the monotony of the interstate, which stretched out straight and flat before them. Only occasional tractor-trailers appeared alongside them, but he'd seen no other vehicles. His mind was miles away, considering the possibilities that Brenda had put before him.

Then he straightened, looking at Brenda for a good long moment. "Then, why are we driving to Washington?"

45

Dylan was two steps behind Sam as they entered the CIA building on Fort Bragg. The sun was barely beginning to peek through the grove of pine trees at the edge of the lawn. The chill in the air reminded him of a brisk spring day in Ireland, but as he glanced at the sky, he realized there was a significant difference: it wasn't raining here.

Sam was bundled into a leather jacket but Dylan enjoyed the nip in the air. He wore a long-sleeved shirt over his muscular arms and torso, but he would have been just as comfortable in short sleeves.

He let the door slam shut behind them as they moved down the hallway toward Sam's office. But before they reached his door, they were met by a middle-aged woman with shoulder-length sandy hair, half-glasses perched near the end of her nose, and a steely-eyed, no-nonsense scowl.

"Were you here last night?" she demanded.

"Good morning," Sam said, brushing past her as he entered his office.

She followed him inside without a glance toward Dylan. "I locked the deadbolt when I left yesterday. Did you unlock it?"

"The door was unlocked."

"Not now," she said, exasperated. "Last night."

Sam shook off his jacket and hung it on a hall tree that looked as though it had seen better days. "Anybody else here?"

"Everyone else is on a mission. It's just you and me this week."

He motioned for Dylan to enter the office. "Are you saying when you got here, the door was unlocked?"

"The deadbolt. The door knob was locked."

"So?"

"So," she said, placing her hands on her hips, "were you here and forgot to lock the deadbolt?"

"Anything missing?"

"Not that I can tell."

"So you forgot to lock it when you left yesterday." Sam's cell phone rang and as he answered it, she let out an annoyed huff. Shaking her head, she pushed past Dylan and returned to her desk down the hall, her footsteps sounding loud against the tiled floors.

Dylan made himself comfortable on the couch while Sam turned his attention to the caller.

"If they're done processing the room," he was saying, "the hospital can clean it up and admit someone else. But I want those toxicology reports, especially on the IV unit." He made his way around to his desk chair. It creaked loudly in protest as he lowered himself into it. "Is that right? Christopher Sandige's fingerprints on the window sill? Interesting…" He strummed his fingers on his desktop. "You're asking me if it's possible? Knowing Brenda Carnegie, yes, I'd say she could climb out that window even as sick as she's got to be."

Dylan spotted the coffee pot on the other side of the room. He rose, picked up the empty carafe and made his way down the hall to the bathroom, where he could fill it with water. Sam's voice became lower as the distance between them grew.

He reached the sink and rinsed out the carafe before patiently refilling it with clean water. As it filled, he idly glanced around the room. A pine needle lay on the floor at his feet and he stooped to pick it up, tossing into the nearby receptacle.

He turned off the water. He hesitated, his hand paused just above the carafe's handle. Something didn't seem right.

He took a deep breath. He cocked his head, his eyes moving upward to catch a glimpse of his own face in the mirror. There was moisture in the air, the kind of humidity left after a steamy shower. His eyes moved beyond his reflection to the bathtub behind him. He once thought it was unusual for an office to have a full bath but now that he'd been working with Sam, he realized there were many sleepless nights and many mornings in which a cold shower and a hot cup of coffee was the only thing that stood between readiness and lethargy.

His eyes traveled to two towels draped over the rod. Leaving the carafe in the sink, he turned toward the tub as his hand reached for the thin terrycloth. It was still damp, as was the other one. The bath walls, he noted, were still spotted with drops that had not yet evaporated.

He returned to the sink, gathered the carafe and reversed his steps, arriving at Sam's office as Sam continued, "Have an analyst review all the tapes—incoming and outgoing traffic, all gates. Keep checking all IDs, no exceptions. They've got to be here somewhere."

Dylan poured the water into the coffee maker, dumped some coffee into the filter, and turned it on. When he turned toward Sam's desk, he found the older man looking under his desk as if he'd lost something. "Yeah, yeah," he was saying. "Full alert. Call me if you find anything." He hung up just as his phone rang again.

"Yeah?" He hesitated, listening. "Interesting… Okay… Hhmmh." After another minute passed by, he hung up.

Dylan poured two cups of coffee. Setting one in front of Sam, he settled onto the couch again, nestling his cup between his hands. The steam rose, tickling his nostrils, as the cup warmed his palms. "Anythin' wrong?"

Sam seemed deep in thought and it was another few seconds before he answered. "The ship—the one that Vicki saw. That was confirmation of its cargo." He fell silent.

"Anythin' you care to share?"

"It was filled with baby food."

"Baby food, y' say?"

Sam looked at his coffee as if seeing it for the first time. He started to raise it to his lips and then set the cup back down. "They confirmed its manufacture, compared it against the manifest... There's no chance the ship was carrying radioactive materials."

Dylan remained silent and after a moment, Sam continued, "They secured the documentation from the submarine. There's no mention of them firing a missile—no training exercise, and definitely no mention of bombing a ship."

"Where does that leave us?"

"In the dark. The thing is, between you and me, and I'd deny I ever said this, but... I think it was one of our subs that bombed that merchant ship." He reached for his coffee again. His fingers stopped just short of it and began strumming his desk. "Angela!" he shouted.

Dylan cocked his head toward the door as Sam repeated her name. "Sounds like she's on the phone," he said when she did not respond. When Sam didn't answer, he said, "You appear to be quite deep in thought."

He shook his head. "Your boy. Shar ma arke Galaid."

Dylan sipped his coffee. "What about 'im?"

"He committed suicide this morning."

He nearly choked on his coffee. Setting down his cup, he cleared his throat. "Suicide?"

Sam nodded.

His mind raced, the image of Sam, his desk and his office seeming to disappear in front of him as he visualized the stark cages filled with men in thin orange jumpsuits pacing their cells or sleeping on mats that didn't appear any softer than the concrete at their feet. In his mind's eye, he saw Galaid sitting across a metal desk from him, his eyes blackened, his nose crooked in a way it hadn't been before, his jaw swollen. And his eyes—those eyes that had been hardened and soulless in their first meetings, beseeching him to remove him from the Americans, tearing up as he pleaded for Dylan to take him into Irish custody.

He remembered his hands shaking as he puffed on a cigarette Dylan provided, his wrists manacled and his ankles tethered to his chair with heavy metal chains. He remembered watching him

as he left his interrogation, his ankles bound so closely together
that he could do no more than shuffle along the sidewalk, his
wrists held in front of him, his eyes downcast.

"How?" Dylan asked.

"How what?"

"How did he commit suicide? By what means?"

Sam's eyes locked onto his. "You don't really want to know."

"Why don't I?"

Sam took a long swallow of his coffee before answering.
"Look. Everyone who dies at a black site commits suicide. Okay?
Leave it at that." Before Dylan could respond, he shouted,
"Angela!"

This time, they heard a chair creak and the heavy footsteps
of an irritated woman marching down the hall. "Your intercom
broken?" she asked as she stood in the doorway.

Sam ignored her question as he strummed his fingers on
the desk. "Where's my laptop?"

They were halfway out the door as Sam continued to bark
into his phone. "That's right. Christopher Sandige." His phone
number rolled off his tongue. "Trace it. Find out where he is.
And trace my damn laptop. Find out what IP she's using. Between
the two, you ought to be able to pinpoint their whereabouts.
Drop everything. This is your highest priority." He snapped off
the connection. "God bless it," he said as they hurried to his car.
"You know how much explaining I have to do now? That laptop
has classified information on it. And it's in the hands of a hacker!"

Before Dylan could respond, he barked, "Get Vicki on the
phone. She's coming with us."

"Where are we goin'?"

"The hell if I know," he snarled as he opened his car door.
"But wherever it is, she's coming!"

46

Chris closed the gas cap on the car and glanced toward the service station across the street. In contrast to the dark and ill-kept station Brenda had insisted on, its competitor was brightly lit, well attended and beckoned to travelers with its large store and restaurants.

He opened the driver's door and popped his head in to find Brenda leaning against the seatback with her eyes closed.

"That's the way I feel, too," he said.

She opened one eye.

"I need coffee. I'm going across the street."

"No." Her voice was urgent and thick with sleep.

He climbed in and started up the car. "I don't know why you insisted on this station, but the coffee's over there." He gestured toward the competitor.

"We can't go there," she said, grabbing the wheel.

"Brenda—"

"Look over there. They've got cameras on each corner. Cameras trained on every gas pump. Trust me; they have cameras inside, too, watching every inch except the restrooms—but definitely the restroom doors."

"But—"

"We can't be seen. They've got to be looking for us."

"Fine."

She dropped her hand from the wheel.

"But I've got to get coffee. We've been up all night and if I don't get caffeine in me soon, we won't make it to Washington."

"Over there." She pointed toward a tiny restaurant down the block. "They've got a drive-thru. I don't recognize the name, so it's not a chain. They're less likely to have cameras."

Wordlessly, he turned toward the restaurant.

A few minutes later, they were cruising north on Interstate 95. North Carolina was behind them, Richmond less than an hour away, and four tall coffees sat between them.

"You never told me," Chris said, "why we're heading to Washington."

"Wiki or details?"

"Details. Always details." He gave her a sideways glance. "I'm an inquisitive sort."

"So you are. Well, while we were sitting at that fast food place—"

"In Fayetteville, when you were on the computer—?"

She nodded. "I was following up on Mr. Joseph Gabucci."

"What do you mean, 'following up'? You didn't—"

"Yes. I did." She grinned. "I started with the Department of Defense. Wasn't hard." She shrugged. "Sam had access to the basic stuff. All I had to do was hack into the more— sensitive—areas."

"What are you saying?"

"I'm saying that Gabucci wasn't there." She motioned a checkmark with her finger. "That means he wasn't likely to be hired by them, so I marked that off my list. I moved on to the CIA."

"You didn't—"

"I did. Wasn't difficult. Sam—"

"Had access."

"Incredible access. He wasn't there, either."

Chris frowned. "Who does that leave?"

"Homeland Security."

"Let me guess. You hacked into their system."

"Of course." She shrugged. "It wasn't difficult."

"Let me guess. Sam—"

"Did *not* have access. At least, to the good stuff."

"And that was…?"

"Emails. You see, by this point, I've confirmed that he isn't an employee; so he's a contractor. A hired hit man."

"But Sam already knew that—or suspected it." He glanced at her. "But you took it a step further, right?"

She picked up a coffee and warmed her hands on the cup before taking a sip. "I did what any computer department can do in any company."

"I'm afraid to ask."

"I accessed all email accounts—each one has a separate folder but they're under a master folder—and I searched on his name in the body of the email." She smiled conspiratorially. "And I found it."

"They weren't audacious enough to—"

"Just once. His name was used one time and one time only. But it was enough for me to follow the string of emails."

The sun was rising to the east, casting a bright glow through the vehicle. Chris adjusted the sun visor before prompting, "Tell me what you found."

"It wasn't much, but it was enough to go on… He's working for Homeland Security. His job is to eliminate 'a target'—doesn't take much imagination to figure out who the target is."

"Why?"

"I don't know—yet. But give me time."

"And Washington?"

"Tomorrow is the election—actually," she said, motioning toward the rising sun, "*today* is the election."

"The Presidential election."

"Ah-ha." She took a deeper drink of her coffee. "And the Attorney General has resigned."

Chris shook his head. "I didn't catch the news last night—"

"I know." She smiled. "We were together. Remember?" He began to blush but she continued, "It wasn't on the news. It won't be released until after the election—tomorrow, to be precise."

"How do you know this?"

"The emails. You'd be surprised at the information people put in emails." She giggled. "It's so absurd—they think they can send an email, delete it, and it's gone forever. They don't realize that *nothing* is ever completely gone."

"But I still don't understand what this has to do with Gabucci."

"The email was cryptic, but I have reason to believe that he's been recalled to Washington."

"What? Why? I mean—he was hell bent on—on—"

"Killing me. You can say it."

"But then, you're saying his assignment was terminated?"

"But wait until next week, next month, ten years from now. I'd always be looking over my shoulder. And I'm done with that. Nope. It's time to turn the tables."

"But—what do you propose we do? We can't drive to the headquarters for Homeland Security and miraculously find him at the door, waiting for us. And what would you do if he was?"

"I still have to work out the details…"

"Then fill me in on the broad plan." He gestured toward the straight interstate, which stretched to the horizon. "We've got a lot of time."

"We get to Washington—within striking distance. I get back on the Internet, I find out exactly what is going down, and with a little bit of luck, I find out where Gabucci is."

"Is that all?" His voice sounded flip.

"—And," she continued, undaunted, "I find out how far up this goes, who is involved, and why they need to have me eliminated."

47

Vicki strapped herself into the seat as Dylan adjusted the ventilation above them, raining a stream of reconstituted air upon them. Sam sat across the aisle, ignoring the flashing words on the screens above them requiring their seatbacks in the upright position. Instead, he spread the contents of his briefcase on the tray, studying each report as his glasses migrated further down his nose.

The sun had been up for several hours but the sky was wintry and so pale that it blended into the gray-white clouds that had settled in above them. The trees at the edge of the runway were stark and forlorn looking; the grass, brown and dormant. November had settled in, heralding the start of the deep autumn, that time of year when all the trees had lost their brilliantly colored leaves and nothing was left but signs of the winter soon to come.

"Mr. Mazoli," the polite male voice of the pilot said through the intercom, "Mr. and Mrs. Maguire, prepare for takeoff."

Vicki and Dylan looked at each other at exactly the same moment.

"He said—" Vicki began.

Dylan burst into laughter. "Aye, and he did. And it will be true, soon enough, 'eh?"

Sam glanced at them over the rim of his glasses before going back to his paperwork.

They taxied onto the runway and Vicki leaned toward the window, catching a glimpse of her vehicle parked in front of the airport office. It was Lumberton's regional airport and it was quiet as they taxied past a few hangars, most with closed doors, before settling in at the end of the runway.

Then they were barreling down another runway, the private plane bumping Sam's papers to the point where he was in serious danger of losing them all over the floor. Then just before the catastrophe occurred, they lifted off. A moment later, they heard the landing gear snapping into the body of the plane.

"Benita returned this morning," Vicki said.

Dylan reclined the seat and unsnapped his seatbelt. "So she did, did she? And I'd be supposin' you told 'er just how much 'er services were missed. I won't be allowin' 'er to go so lightly next time, I'll be tellin' you that for sure."

She smiled. "It's good to have her back. I've missed her home-cooked meals."

"And 'er doin' the laundry."

"And the house-cleaning."

"The dog sittin'."

"The fish keeping."

"If you two lovebirds are finished reminiscing over your housekeeper," Sam said brusquely, "it's time to go to work."

"You'd put me to work in the air, would you?" Dylan asked.

"Not you." Sam pointed at Vicki. "Her."

Vicki reclined in the seat at the rear of the small plane. All of the shades had been drawn and the lights turned off, casting them into darkness. As she closed her eyes and began her deep breathing, the steady drone of the engines threatened to put her to sleep. She used an exercise in focusing to keep her mind alert but her body relaxed, and within a few minutes she had drifted from her normal alpha state into her brain's beta state. Her breathing changed and grew steady and concentrated.

"Find Brenda." Sam's voice came from across the aisle. It was low and even. "Tell me where she's going and what she's planning."

Her brain locked onto the directive. She felt as though she was soaring beside the small plane, watching its wings and then catching sight of the pilot and co-pilot in the cockpit. Then she was gone, like a hypersonic plane leaving a biplane behind; it was there beside her one instant and in another was nothing more than a dot on the horizon behind her.

She found herself sailing above Interstate 95 approaching the busy interchange with the Washington Beltway. She felt like a bird soaring above the bumper-to-bumper traffic and she alternately dipped and rose as she crossed the Beltway and continued north toward the District of Columbia.

A steady *tick, tock* began that was oddly out of place with her mission. The sound did not come from the air, nor was it emanating from the vehicles. Instead, it surrounded her, threatening to take her back to the aircraft and out of the mission.

She tried to focus on staying airborne. Closing her eyes tighter, she envisioned an earpiece and a microphone connecting her to Sam and Dylan. "Please move your watch away from your microphone," she said softly but firmly.

There was no immediate response, and the steady *tick, tock* grew louder.

"Pardon?" It was Sam's voice.

"Your watch. It's distracting."

There was another pause. Then she heard something snap shut. "My watch and Dylan's are in my briefcase. Continue your mission. Report on your position."

"Find the clock and disable it," she said. Her head was beginning to hurt. She was peering down at hundreds, if not thousands of vehicles, stretching for miles to the north and behind her to the south; if she turned to the east or west, the Beltway and the mass of roads that comprised the Metro area were completely bogged down in traffic. Yet one vehicle stood out; a white van that might have been a tradesman's service vehicle.

The *tick, tock* began thrumming in her ears with an intensity that hurt. "Find the clock," she said through gritted teeth.

"There is no clock, Vicki," Sam said. "There are no watches and there is no clock."

There were dozens of white vans just like this one. It was almost nondescript in its plainness; yet whenever she attempted to turn away from it, it drew her back like a lighthouse beacon. The closer she came to it, the louder the *tick, tock* until she wanted to scream in agony.

She reported her position but when she looked to her hand for the familiar GPS to report the exact longitude and latitude, the image was blurred. As she stared at her palm, she realized a shadow was crossing back and forth, back and forth, keeping time with the steady, growing and intense sound.

"A pendulum," she gasped.

"Where?"

"It's a pendulum—the sound." She tried to look beyond the white van but as she glimpsed buildings along the interstate, she reported, "It isn't a clock tower. It's coming from the van."

"License number."

She strained to see the number but felt as though wax paper had been placed over it, obscuring the letters and numbers. "It's blocked. Not physically blocked—someone is preventing me from seeing it."

"That isn't possible, Vicki. Focus."

She labored to read it but her efforts were futile. The traffic was stopping in a gridlock that had become all too familiar to her from her days living in the DC area, and she swooped down beside the van, levitating just outside the passenger door.

She'd expected to see Brenda and Chris. But she found a passenger seat that would have been empty except for a briefcase, a cell phone—and a gun. The sound of the pendulum grew more powerful. It began to accelerate as if its energy was becoming more energetic and frenetic. She felt her own breath growing ragged and short. Sam's voice sounded distant now; it was too far away to hear his words. It became like a drone in the wind as the pendulum circled her.

Her chest felt contracted as if the pendulum had become a boa constrictor; it was steadily squeezing the air out of her. She was dazed, her vision blurred, as the sound came alive like a serpent giving birth to dozens of other serpents, each one crushing the life out of her even while their voices rose in a chorus of pendulum strikes.

"I can't breathe," she managed to say. She tried to raise her hand to her throat, to loosen clothes around her neck, but found that her arms were held against her body and against her will. She was falling now, the vehicles that surrounded her becoming treacherous allies to the pendulum swing, intent on stopping her mission—and her life.

"I can't breathe," she puffed again, each word causing her chest to constrict more.

Somewhere in the back of her mind, she heard Sam's voice and Dylan's voice, climbing over one another before becoming one with the pendulum. And as her vision blurred further and she fought a loss of consciousness, her eyes found the driver.

He turned toward her, casually looking through the passenger window, his black eyes soulless, his face expressionless.

One more word, she thought as she struggled to breathe. Just one more word. It felt like a superhuman effort; a struggle so dire that just expending her energy to say it would spell the end of her existence.

"Gabucci."

48

The lock clicked softly and with a modest smile, Chris slid open the door to his condominium. He motioned for Brenda to enter and then followed her into the foyer.

She found herself in a wide entrance with hardwood floors and walls painted in vertical stripes that alternated between wide beige and thin burgundy. She took a few steps into Chris' home and found herself in a large living room.

"It's chilly in here," Chris said, brushing past her to a fireplace surrounded by stone veneer. With the touch of a button, it roared to life, the gas logs glowing warmly. It cast an inviting glow throughout the large space but Chris nervously opened the drapes that lined an entire wall. The sun shone through the eighth-story windows as if it wasn't late autumn but mid-summer.

Brenda felt as though her feet were frozen in one spot as her eyes roamed around the room. It hadn't occurred to her until this moment that she'd never seen where Chris lived. He'd always been so eager to stay in Vicki's and Dylan's home that she envisioned an apartment with typical bachelor odds and ends that didn't match and weren't quite up to snuff. She'd never envisioned anything like this.

The walls were hand-painted to look like wallpaper with the same beige and burgundy stripes, the darker color so thin that it gave an air of refined class. In the middle of the room, resting on an Oriental rug and facing the fireplace was a leather sofa in a deep wine color. At either end were matching leather chairs.

Chris had disappeared around a corner and she stepped further into the room, pausing to brush her hand against a chenille throw that draped casually over the back of one chair. On the coffee table was a pictorial history book of the White House's finest art. Each end table was identically appointed with porcelain lamps in warm beige.

She continued to a bookcase lining one wall. Interspersed with hard cover books on politics and international history were a myriad of artifacts: a porcelain Chinese dragon, a miniature replica of a Mayan temple, a stein topped with a fragment of the Berlin wall, miniature pyramids and an elegant carafe emblazoned with a Russian czar's motif.

"I turned up the heat," Chris was saying as he joined her. "It wasn't this cold when I left here," he added sheepishly.

"Have you been to all these places?" Brenda asked, motioning toward the artifacts.

He nodded. "There can be quite a bit of travel when you work for a Congressman. Depending on which one you work for, that is."

"Yours obviously liked to travel."

"Several of them did."

"You worked for more than one?"

"I've worked for a few."

"Just a few?"

"Just a few."

She nodded and turned back to the room. At the opposite end of the living room, she could see the corner of a dining room table, the chairs upholstered in the same wine-colored leather as the sofa.

"Can I get you something to drink?"

Her heart said liquor but her head prevailed. "Coffee. Strong."

"Coming right up."

She followed him into a well-appointed kitchen with granite countertops and rich mahogany cabinetry. He poured bottled water into a one-cup coffee maker and popped in a pod of dark breakfast blend. He slipped a mug made of blue glass in place and started the machine.

"It's usually just me here," he said. "One cup of coffee and I'm generally out of here."

"You don't have to explain anything to me."

"Just wanted you to know why I don't have a regular coffee maker."

He started to brush past her when she reached for his arm and pulled him back to her. "You're nervous, aren't you?"

"No. Yes. I guess I am."

"Why?"

"I—I wasn't expecting company."

"Is that what I am? Company?" She smiled and cocked her head.

"No. Yes. It's just… I don't remember the last time anybody else was here."

"Seriously?"

He nodded.

"No dates?"

He shook his head.

"No female friends?"

He shook his head again.

"Come on. A guy like you, and you didn't have women up here in your pad?" She chuckled.

"I never did. No, once, actually. Maybe once—years ago. I work; that's what I do. When I was working, that is…" He hesitated and then wrapped his arms around her and rested his chin on the top of her head. "I didn't have time for a relationship—or so I thought. I got up around four a.m., showered, dressed, grabbed a cup of coffee… And left. I wouldn't get home until midnight, usually."

He motioned toward the refrigerator. "All I have in there is bottled water. Check it yourself."

She pulled away from him to look him in the eye. "Why?"

A look of pain darted across his eyes before he diverted them. "Before I met you, I wanted everything to be… Orderly. Predictable. Habitual… Distant."

"I'm anything but that; any of that."

He looked at her again and this time there was a softening in his warm brown eyes. "I know."

"Am I bad for you, Chris?"

He burst into a laugh that seemed to come straight from his chiseled belly. "On the contrary; you're good for me."

It was her turn to laugh. "I've never been told that before."

He grew serious as he ran his fingers through her hair, brushing it away from her face. "You're passionate. Unpredictable. Random. Gorgeous. Highly intelligent. Street smart." He brushed his lips against hers before looking her in the eye again. "And I love you."

"You know what?" she said silkily. "I love you, too, Christopher Sandige."

His lips sought hers again, lingering over them and pulling her lower lip into his mouth for the briefest of moments before pulling her body against his. She lost herself in his embrace and his warm, moist kiss before reluctantly pulling back.

"You know what," she said, her voice taking on a husky tone, "there's nothing I'd love better than to check out that bachelor bed of yours… But we've got work to do."

He groaned.

"Stay ready for me," she said with a gleam in her eye, "I won't be long."

49

The man was standing at the foot of the steps, patiently waiting as Vicki began her descent. Sam was already nearing the bottom of the steps, and Dylan was directly behind her.

The man was tall and slender, though his face appeared doughy and loose skin hung from his jowls. He extended his hand as Sam's feet touched the tarmac.

"Mr. Mazoli?" As Sam grunted his answer, he continued, "I'm Gerald Barry, from Mr. Croft's office."

Sam shook his hand. "The car?"

"Right here." He motioned to a tan sedan behind him. "I've been instructed to take you wherever you want to go."

"A driver won't be necessary. I'm very familiar with Washington."

"I know you are, sir. Mr. Croft just thought…"

"Tell Croft I appreciate his attention to detail." Sam took the keys from Gerald's outstretched hand and walked briskly to the vehicle. "Do you have a ride back?"

"Yes, sir. I mean, I can get one, sir."

Sam turned to find Vicki closing the gap between them. To his raised eyebrow, she said, "Dylan's getting our luggage."

"Ah. The luggage." He pressed a button on the key fob and the trunk opened. "I'd forgotten I'd instructed you to bring some."

"They're just overnight bags," Vicki said as Dylan joined them. "You said we'd only spend a night, two at the most." Her voice sounded hopeful, but Sam was already climbing into the vehicle.

"Mr. Mazoli," Gerald said, leaning on the open driver's door. "There's just one more thing."

"Yeah?" Sam started the engine as Dylan deposited the luggage in the trunk and opened the door for Vicki.

"The FBI needs Brenda Carnegie in Washington—in their custody, that is."

"Well, that works out to be pretty handy, doesn't it? Seeing as how she's already in Washington."

"Yes, sir. Well, sir, she's to testify beginning next week."

"Testify?"

Dylan climbed in behind Vicki but kept his door ajar so he could listen.

"Corruption cases. She'd agreed to testify…"

"Yes, yes, I know." Sam hesitated. "Do you know what cases?"

Gerald extracted an envelope from his jacket's inside pocket. "Here's the list. They're calling it The Baker's Dozen."

Sam accepted the envelope. Quietly, he opened it and peered at the list of names. Then he returned the list to the envelope and placed it in his jacket. "Anything else?"

"As soon as you apprehend Carnegie, you're to notify the FBI. They'll remove her to a safe house to await her first testimony."

"Am I to show her the list?"

"Yes, sir."

Sam nodded. "Who's the FBI point of contact?"

"The name and phone number is at the bottom of the list. Senior Agent in Charge Humphrey Coten."

"I've known Cot for years."

"Yes, sir."

Sam moved to close his door. "That all?"

"Yes, sir. That's all."

"Tell Mr. Croft—and Agent Coten, if you have the opportunity—that Carnegie will be in FBI custody before noon."

"Yes, sir."

With that, he closed the door and Dylan followed suit behind him. As they drove down the tarmac of the private airport, Sam glanced in his rearview mirror. "I feel like a chauffeur up here."

Dylan pulled Vicki to his side. "I feel better w' m' girl in m' arms, if you don't mind, Sam."

Sam didn't respond. They exited the airport as silence enveloped them. After a moment, Dylan asked, "Can you share the list w' us, I wonder?"

"The list?" Sam repeated absent-mindedly. Then, "Oh, the list. Well, now I know why they're calling it The Baker's Dozen."

"Don't tell me—" Vicki began.

"Yep. Senator Cary Baker tops it."

"No," Vicki breathed.

"You two mind fillin' me in?" Dylan asked. "His name isn't familiar to me."

"That's because you abhor politics," Sam answered. "If you tuned in every now and then, you'd know Baker is one of the most powerful men in Washington. He's been in office for—let's see—I suppose twenty-five years, maybe thirty. He chairs a number of committees. His specialty is international policies, including covert actions."

"Is that so?"

"But he's rumored to be one of the most scrupulous men in Washington," Vicki said. "How can his name top the list?"

"Only your sister can tell us that."

They fell silent once more, each with their own thoughts. Sam joined the gridlock of traffic heading north, only to turn off at the first exit inside the Beltway. As he navigated through neighborhood streets, he said, "That's not our concern. What I am concerned with is this whole pendulum thing you're experiencing, Vicki."

"I don't understand it," she said. Dylan wrapped his arm around her and squeezed her shoulder. "I've never had anything happen like this before… I feel like I'm receiving some sort of coded message from the other side."

"Like Morse code?" Dylan asked.

"No. Not quite. With Morse code, there's a series of dots and dashes. This is exactly the same sound, over and over again. It's the sound of a metronome, swinging from one end to the other. The sound of the ticking has been getting louder and louder… At first, when it happened at home, I thought it was the grandfather clock. Then I realized the clock was broken. When I discovered all the cameras, the sound of the pendulum was deafening. I'm dreaming of it… And during this last mission, I heard it grow louder as I approached Gabucci."

"It's a clue of some sort," Sam stated the obvious.

"But of what?" Dylan asked. "The only time I've ever heard of a metronome is on top of a piano, keeping time." He looked down at Vicki. "Is it tied to music, somehow?"

"Paying the piper?" Sam asked.

"No… I can't explain it, but if it was something like that, why am I not hearing a piper? Why a pendulum?"

"A pendulum… a pendulum. What else are they used for?"

"There's a pendulum at the Smithsonian. It ticks down the time."

"Are your visions tellin' us, mayhap, that we're out o' time? Or we're runnin' out o' time?"

"Maybe so." Vicki paused. "Maybe that's it."

"It's tellin' you, mayhap, that the mission is urgent. That time is o' the essence."

Sam pulled onto a winding driveway leading to a guard post. He rolled down his window as the guard stepped out to greet them. Beyond the post, the drive wound up a hill. Even from this vantage point, Vicki could see twin buildings with a balcony on every other floor.

"Name?" The guard asked.

"Sam Mazoli." He pulled his CIA identification out of his pocket and showed it to the guard. "Official business."

The guard studied the identification for a few seconds before peering over Sam's shoulder into the back seat.

"They're CIA as well," Sam said before he could ask. "Do you need to see their identifications?"

"No, sir. Are you going to the administrative office?"

"Yes. That's right."

"I'll get you a parking pass, sir."

A brief moment later, the guard was handing Sam a parking pass and directing him to the administrative office suited on the first floor of one of the buildings. Then he opened the gate and Sam drove through, following the drive up the hill.

"Where are we?" Vicki asked.

"Chris' condo. He lives on the eighth floor—top floor, from the looks of things."

They passed tennis courts on their left and a putting green on the right.

"Are we going to the administrative offices first?" Vicki asked.

"Of course not," Sam said. "That guard didn't need to know where we're going."

He paused at a t-intersection where a sign directed drivers to Building 205 on the left and 207 on the right. He turned to the left, following the drive past a swimming pool covered by a winter tarp. He parked in the visitors section and turned off the engine.

"How do we know they're here?" Dylan asked.

Sam pulled his smart phone from his pocket and tapped into an app. "I had my office trace Chris' cell phone. His GPS has led us straight here." He peered at the phone for a moment before returning it to his pocket. "And they haven't moved."

50

Brenda slipped one leg underneath her as she sipped the hot coffee. She sat at the dining room table in a plush white bathrobe with Sam's laptop on the table in front of her. Despite the urge to track down Joseph Gabucci, other urges had become more insistent and she had to admit, she was much more relaxed than she'd been just an hour earlier. As the laptop booted, she caught a glimpse of Chris zipping up a pair of jeans as he made his way down the hall toward her.

He smiled as he stopped beside her chair. He leaned toward her, twisting her long copper locks through one hand as he kissed her on the top of her head. Then he glanced at the computer screen. "What are you doing?"

"Hacking into Homeland Security emails again. Trying to find out more about this guy Gabucci—maybe where he is, and why he's intent on killing me." She clicked through a few screens before glancing back at Chris. "If you're planning to watch me, you're going to be bored silly."

"I could never be bored watching you." He dropped her hair. "But that coffee does smell awfully good. I think I'll get myself a cup."

"Beat you to it," she said. "It's sitting in the coffee maker. Should still be hot."

"You're a darling." He started toward the kitchen before stopping and turning back to her. "You mind if I turn on the television? Today's election day, and it's a hard habit to break..."

She chuckled. "Go ahead. You know I'm a news junkie."

A moment later, he returned with his cup of coffee in hand. The voices of political pundits wafted in from the living room, rotating between the presidential election and potential tipping points in Congress.

He dropped a stack of mail on the dining room table. "Mind if I join you?"

"Please do," Brenda muttered, her eyes on the screen.

He pulled out a chair. "My neighbor Ray collects my mail while I'm gone. He places it on a table in my kitchen."

"Hhmm."

"Looks like I have quite a stack this time."

"Ah-ha," she answered, her eyes still on the screen.

He separated the junk mail from the important stuff and found himself looking at one pile several inches thick and another pile consisting of three bills—his cell phone, his cable and his electric bill. That was his life, he thought as he looked at it. He could leave for weeks or months at a time and as long as he contacted his creditors ahead of time or paid online, nobody missed him.

He watched Brenda, her eyes unblinking as she concentrated on the screen, her fingers tapping steadily on the keyboard. Until now, he thought. Now he had Brenda. For whatever time was left to them—no, he thought, that was not the way to think about it. They had the rest of their lives; he'd do whatever he had to in order to ensure that. She wouldn't go to prison and Gabucci would never find her again. Whatever strings he had to pull, whatever favors he had to call in, he would do it for her.

He rose abruptly and picked up the junk mail.

She looked up. "You okay?"

"Better than okay," he said. "Look, there's a chute just outside my door for recyclables. I'm just going to step out for a minute, drop these down, and I'll be right back."

"You don't have to explain anything to me, you know. It's your home."

"I know." He stopped short of saying he wanted it to be their home. The words were there, on the tip of his tongue, along with his declaration of undying love for her. Then she turned her attention back to the computer and the moment was gone.

Maybe it was just the sex. He read once that men often declared their love for a woman during sex; there was some sort of chemical in the brain that confused sex with love at the oddest moment… No; it was more than sex. Much more.

"Do you mind if I open a window?" she asked. "It's quite warm in here."

"Of course. I'll open the balcony door," he said. "I probably overcompensated for the chill, between the fireplace and turning up the heat."

She rose and her bathrobe fell open. She raced her fingers along his cheek. "Or maybe you've warmed me up quite nicely. I'll get the door. You take care of your mail."

He nodded and when she dropped her hand, he took a deep breath and started through the living room to the front hall. If he hesitated just a few seconds, he thought, they'd end up right back in bed. Which wasn't such a bad idea, he thought.

He reached the door and hesitated as a blast of cool air reached him. He half-turned to find Brenda stepping onto the balcony. With his hand resting on the door knob, he watched the breeze as it caught her hair. She pulled the bathrobe tighter around her as she peered over the balcony.

He was certain that oversized bathrobe looked a helluva lot better on her than it ever did on him. The balcony was completely private; the seven floors below him consisted of two-story condominiums, each with a balcony on the lowest floor. It meant that even if someone was on a balcony below them, they were unlikely to hear one another. And each floor consisted of only four units, one on each side, so there were no neighbors stepping out on their balconies while he was enjoying his—or if they were, he'd never know it. It was one of the features that attracted him to this particular set of buildings; he coveted his privacy and the peace and quiet after the relentless commotion that seemed to accompany politics.

She leaned over the balcony, and he found himself smiling as her bare legs peeked from under the bathrobe. This side of the building overlooked the swimming pool. In warmer months, the water sparkled like the Caribbean against the blue walls of the pool. Now he knew it would look forlorn, abandoned; covered as it was by a black tarp.

He sighed. Then he opened the door, careful to keep it from shutting behind him; the door had an automatic lock, which was meant to be a security feature but had turned into a nuisance.

He bent his head as he slowed the movement of the door and out of the corner of his eye he spotted something dark emerging out of nowhere. It punched through the space where his head had been just a fraction of a second earlier, and with nothing to stop it, it plunged into the door, smashing it open.

He had barely enough time to register it swinging full, crashing against the wall in his apartment, before the dark object swung again. Instinctively, he ducked, one arm rising in front of his head, taking the full brunt of its hostility. Then he was slung against the wall. The man seemed to be everywhere at once and somehow in the mêlée he realized the darkest object that kept swinging at him was a pistol. In the back of his mind the refrain began: I'm being pistol-whipped. I'm being pistol-whipped.

He heard Brenda call out to him and in the next instant he knew he had to close the door, even if it locked him out. He grappled with his assailant, placing himself in between the doorway and the man. Somehow he managed to grab the pistol with both his hands and he banged it relentlessly against the wall, trying to dislodge it from his hands.

They bobbed and weaved in a circle, joined together. Each time the door began to swing shut, the man managed to bound toward it, pushing it open again. With a guttural shout, Chris drove him to the opposite side of the hall, where he continued to pound his hand against the wall, working his fingers in between his and the trigger, trying desperately to dislodge it.

Through their grunts and shouts, he realized a door had opened down the hall and he felt more than saw his neighbor, Old Mrs. Cravise, peering out only to immediately slam the door shut and bolt it. He wanted to call out to her to phone 911, but his words remained stuck in his throat, the energy to expel them caught up in the urgency of staying alive.

They tangled and snarled up and down the hall. The man's bald head began to wrinkle and he realized with sudden clarity that he was wearing a mask. With a superhuman effort, he managed to slam him against the trash chute to look into his eyes. They were black, as cold as iron, without a hint of emotion. He'd seen those eyes before in a hallway similar to this one; a hotel hallway on the weekend he'd first met Brenda.

The realization shone through his confusion and his instincts became razor sharp. The man was strong; uncommonly tough for someone who had to be thirty years older than he. With a roar, he banged the pistol against the trash chute, his teeth alternately gritting and parting just enough to bellow his growing rage.

In a fraction of a second, the gun dislodged and before either could grab it, it careened down the trash chute with a clatter that seemed to grow as it descended eight floors. Without the object in Gabucci's hands, Chris realized they were both slick with sweat and suddenly it was as if he was trying to hold onto an oiled pig. The man's hands slipped out of his grasp and he ducked past him, rushing for the apartment door.

Chris lunged at him, catching his foot as they both tumbled through the door. He caught sight of Brenda standing on the balcony, wide-eyed, as he found himself holding a shoe in his hand. He scrambled up to see Joseph lurching through the living room at breakneck speed. As he rushed to catch up with him, he realized there was only the one door to the balcony and it was open—and Brenda was caught without any means of escape.

He heard shouts behind him and recognized Dylan's Irish brogue as he and Sam charged in. They moved forward like a wall, nearly shoulder to shoulder, as Gabucci descended on Brenda. His arm enfolded her neck for a split second before they were both tumbling, Brenda's limbs striking out like a scalded cat against him, her nails driving into his eyes and face as he screamed in torment.

"Out o' the way!" He heard Dylan shout and as he dove for the concrete balcony floor, a gunshot rang out above him.

Then Gabucci grabbed Brenda by the bathrobe and hurled both of them over the rail.

Chris lunged for her, crying out as if his voice could stop them, his hand encircling her ankle just as she dived out of sight. In the blink of an eye, Sam and Dylan were beside him, grasping her calf and then both calves and then her knees.

Then a guttural cry pierced the air. It sounded like a chorus of men in a torture chamber and as their bodies were wrenched against the railing, Chris caught sight of Joseph tumbling through the air like a mannequin, still holding onto Brenda's bathrobe.

There were hands everywhere as they hauled Brenda's nude body over the rail. Uncharacteristically silent as she collapsed on the balcony, she looked pale and as Chris bent to her side, she grabbed him with trembling hands.

In the distance, he heard the sound of police sirens and he looked up to find Dylan and Sam peering over the railing.

"I'll go down," Dylan announced, the adrenaline forcing the words out in a breathless shout. He was through the door, his long legs taking the living room in a few strides before disappearing into the hall.

His bedspread was shoved through the door at him, and he hauled Brenda to her feet as Vicki descended on them, wrapping her sister in the warmth of the bedding. As she led her into the apartment, Chris joined Sam at the railing.

Eight floors below, Joseph Gabucci's body lay sprawled in the middle of the swimming pool cover. Flat on his back, spread-eagled, he looked like a child making angels in the snow.

Chris pulled back. As he looked into Sam's eyes, he realized he had begun to shake. He ran his hand through his hair in a futile attempt to calm himself. His words tumbled out. "I've never been so glad to see anybody in my whole life."

Sam poked his finger at his chest. "What the hell were you thinking?"

Chris shook his head. "I—I don't even know what I'm thinking now."

Sam wiped the perspiration off his brow, though the wind was chilling. They both peered through the glass at Brenda, sitting on the sofa with Vicki by her side, her arms around her in a vise grip.

There was shouting down below and Sam returned to the railing. "He was just there!"

Chris rushed to join Sam. Eight floors below, Dylan stood with his arms out in the universal sign of "what the hell?" and as Chris' eyes drifted toward the pool, he realized what his friend was trying to ask them.

In the center of the tarp lay the bathrobe—and no one and nothing else.

Sam was through the door in a flash. "Close that door," he barked, pointing at the balcony door as Chris entered the living room. "Lock it. Nobody goes out there again." He crossed the living room. "Bolt this door. Nobody gets in here without me or Dylan. Nobody leaves." He stopped just a step before the doorway. "Got that?"

"Yes," they all said in unison.

"*Do not* disobey me!" He shouted. Then he was gone, the door slamming shut behind him.

Chris was at the door in an instant, bolting and chaining it. He returned to the living room to find Vicki locking the balcony door before closing the heavy drapes, plunging them into darkness.

51

Vicki entered the living room with two plates laden with pancakes. Chris sat on the sofa, his eyes on the television screen but his face blank as though he was miles away. Dylan sat in one of the leather chairs, his hands cupped in front of him as if he was deep in thought. Sam stood a few feet away on his cell phone.

It had been two hours since Joseph Gabucci had plunged over the balcony. Police, FBI and CIA still combed the grounds, leaving no inch unturned. But it seemed that he'd vanished into thin air.

Vicki handed a plate to Dylan and one to Chris. "It's not much," she said apologetically, "but you didn't give us much to work with, Chris." She smiled weakly.

"I don't often eat at home," he mumbled.

"Apparently," Brenda said as she joined them with three more plates. She handed one off to Sam, who was clicking off his cell phone, before giving one to Vicki. She had changed back into her own clothing. As she joined Chris on the sofa, he nearly dropped his plate in an effort to hold her hand.

"Stop fawning over me," Brenda said.

He returned his hand to his plate, half-heartedly picking up his fork.

"No, fawn over me," she retorted.

Chris smiled as his hand came to rest on her knee.

"Here's the plan," Sam said, stuffing a hunk of pancake in his mouth. "We're to stay put. The FBI is readying a safe house for Brenda. Until then, we're as safe here as anywhere. They've already dispatched agents for extra security and they'll stay with us until you're moved."

"You 'ave a nice place 'ere, Chris," Dylan said as he dove into the pancakes.

He glanced around. "I guess. It was always just a place to lay my head."

"Until you laid me?" Brenda asked slyly.

"I don't understand you all being so flip," Vicki said, waving Dylan not to get up as she perched on the broad chair arm. "I still don't believe what happened."

They fell silent for a moment and then Dylan said, "What did he say?"

"Who?" Sam asked.

"Him," he repeated, pointing at the television.

Chris grabbed the remote and turned up the sound. "DVR," he said, pausing the image. "Even with live TV, I can rewind." He pushed a button and the image of the television reporter reversed.

"There," Dylan said. "Right there."

He hit *play* as the newscaster said, "This just in. The White House has announced that Armed Forces have killed the mastermind behind the series of ship bombings. In a shoot-out in Somalia, Special Forces have confirmed the death of Shar ma arke Galaid." A photograph of Galaid appeared on the screen, which appeared to have been taken in a training camp when the man was much younger. "Galaid has been wanted for a series of terrorist activities, including plane hijackings. In recent years, he became the head of the Somalian arm of Al-Qaeda and began masterminding piracy on the high seas. Earlier this year, he trained and directed teams in blowing up merchant ships. The plan was to create economic chaos in the United States through shortages…"

Chris chuckled. "Well, that didn't work."

"What do you mean?" Dylan asked.

"The President's plan, of course," Chris said, becoming animated. "By shifting the manufacturing of goods to the United States, he stopped the impact that the ship bombings would have on our commerce. What this guy was doing no longer mattered."

"Galaid was killed when Special Forces stormed a building this morning, along with several senior operatives," the reporter continued. They flashed several photographs across the screen. "They caught the men completely by surprise. Though their instructions were to 'kill or capture' the shoot-out that ensued led to all of the terrorists' deaths. There were no injuries or fatalities among the Special Forces units…"

Dylan's eyes met Sam's. "Galaid was killed *this morning*, in *Somalia*, in a surprise attack."

Sam waved his hand as if to dismiss him.

Dylan started to say something else but then clamped his mouth shut. Then as the report continued, he repeated in a louder voice, "He was killed today. In Somalia."

"What's going on here?" Brenda asked, her eyes darting between Dylan and Sam.

"Dylan," Sam said, his usual brusque voice even deeper, "I'm warning you. Watch your step. That mission is classified."

"Their mission?" He thumbed toward the television. "Or mine?"

"Both." They stared at each other for a moment. "Watch your step."

Dylan fell silent. After an awkward moment where they all looked at each other or self-consciously looked away, he settled back into his chair and poked at his pancake, which was growing cold.

"This is a pivotal day for the President," the newscaster continued. "Eliminating the threat to merchant ships in addition to boosting our economy by bringing jobs back home is a double win. And here to tell us about the election turnout is White House correspondent and host of *Politics Today*, Jeremy Doon."

As if the volume wasn't loud enough, Chris turned it up higher. His face lit up like a child on Christmas morning. Catching the others looking at him with amused expressions, he said, "Politics. It's in my blood."

"Polls will remain open for several more hours," the political pundit began, "but we are already predicting a solid win for a second term. It's a landslide, with exit polls showing the President topping 88% while his opponent has simply not been able to gain traction…"

Vicki stood and began collecting empty plates. "Anybody want more?" she asked.

Dylan shook his head absent-mindedly.

"You've hardly touched yours," she said. "You've got to be hungry."

"When the ship bombings began this summer," the reporter continued, "it was a wake-up call to politicians, especially the incumbent. He rose to national prominence during his first presidential campaign four years ago, on a promise to bring jobs back home and get our economy back to the profitable boom it experienced some twenty years ago…"

Vicki hesitated, the empty plates in her hand, while Brenda and Chris sat riveted to the edges of their seats. Even Dylan was paying close attention.

"This election proves that it really is all about jobs. His opponent argued that we needed a global economy, but the only ones who wanted to hear that have been the wealthiest one percent, who earn more money by taking their businesses overseas… It's obvious that the American people have rebelled against that and are showing up at the polls in record numbers to vote—not only for the incumbent—but for the economic future of this country."

Vicki started toward the kitchen door.

Chris slapped his knee. "And that's how the pendulum swings!" he said excitedly.

"What?"

Vicki froze at the door to the kitchen. Somehow, she had turned completely around to face Chris without even being conscious of her turnabout.

Sam stood by the windows, his plate in his hand, his mouth full of pancake, but his mouth was no longer moving.

And Dylan was on the edge of his seat, his plate thrust out so it was mere inches from Chris.

Chris looked from one to the other. "What'd I say?"

The room was completely silent. If the newscaster or reporter had continued to speak, no one heard them. All eyes were on Chris.

Then Dylan began to stammer. "Wh-what did you say?"

"What *did* I say?"

"Something about a pendulum swinging?"

"Oh," he said, muting the television, "it's an old expression."

Vicki returned to the living room, the plates still in her hands, her eyes unblinking.

"Enlighten me," Dylan said. His face appeared to have turned to stone.

"Well, you know what a pendulum is." He waved a finger in the air until it was on his right. "There's a philosophy—not just with politics but with, I guess, just about anything... Well, when the pendulum swings too far to the right—" He swung his finger toward his left "—then it will swing to an equal distance to the left. The further to the right, the further it swings back to the left. And vice versa."

"Why did you say that just now?"

"'That's the way the pendulum swings?' Because, well," he glanced at Sam, who motioned for him to continue. "Well, there's been a swing toward moving all our manufacturing—and a good number of services, as well, to other countries. Some feel—a good many feel, apparently—that this policy has come at the expense of the American worker. We've had no jobs because—well, because every other country has them. The American worker has been competing against the Chinese worker, the Mexican worker... You get my drift."

He leaned in earnestly. "Did you know that 46 percent of the wealth in the entire world is owned by only 85 people on the entire planet? The rich get richer, filthy rich, while the average individual struggles to put food on the table."

Sam had somehow managed to swallow his food. He set his plate down on the end table. "So when you said, 'that's the way the pendulum swings—'"

"I was referring to the abrupt change in policy. Ever since the ship bombings, the president's policies on bringing home the jobs we once had has taken hold. Every member of Congress who supported his policies is riding on a landslide win. Every member who opposed it—"

"Is being voted out of office," Brenda finished.

Sam reached to his jacket's inside pocket and handed Chris a piece of paper. "Take a look at these names."

Chris unfolded the paper, his eyes roaming quizzically from one to the other. When he looked at the list, his eyes widened.

"Recognize anybody?" Sam asked.

"Well, yes. Of course." He pointed to the list. "These are all Senators, Representatives… There's a high-profile governor on the list."

"Are you familiar with their politics?" Sam asked. His voice had become so smooth it sounded deadly.

Chris looked at the list again. "They're all of the same party."

"The party that wanted to keep the jobs overseas?" Dylan asked.

He studied the list for a moment. "Yes. I believe they did."

Sam narrowed his eyes. "And none of them belong to the President's party, do they?"

"What's going on here?" Brenda asked. All eyes remained on Chris. "Does anybody care to fill me in?"

Sam slipped the list out of Chris' fingers and deposited it in Brenda's lap. "They're the first on *your* list of crooked politicians." As she studied the list, he added, "And something tells me you won't be required to testify unless they've just been reelected."

52

They met in an unlikely place: Chris' bedroom. Vicki and Brenda sat side-by-side on the bed, Vicki's fingers intertwined with her sister's. Three chairs had been pulled up around them; Chris sat near the foot of the bed, Dylan was nearest the middle, and Sam's chair was empty as he stood beside them. The room had been darkened, the draperies pulled tight, and when it was time, Vicki knew that her sister would move away from the bed and she would be lying prone upon it, watched by them all.

"Before we begin," Sam said, looking at each in turn, "it's important that everybody here understands a few things." He waited for his words to sink in, and was met by four sets of expectant eyes.

"This is a mission we're about to embark on," he continued.

"Sounds dramatic," Brenda said flippantly.

He locked his eyes on hers, his expression deadpan. "It's a classified mission. For Your Eyes Only. Do you know what that means?" Without waiting for an answer, he said, "It means there are five people in this country—in this world—who are going to know about this." He pointed to each in turn. "If any one of you ever, and I do mean *ever*, disclose what is about to transpire here, it will be considered an act of treason."

"Aren't you being a little melodramatic here?" Chris asked hesitantly.

Sam glared at him.

"I'd be thinkin'," Dylan said in a low voice, "that if I were you, I'd be withdrawin' that question."

"I understand," Chris said. "This is serious."

Sam reached for Vicki's hands. As her fingers slipped from Brenda's, she joined Chris as Vicki concentrated on Sam's words.

"Vicki, you are going to the person or persons who bombed those ships. Wherever they are; whatever they are doing. Latitude and longitude mean nothing. Follow the source, and report back to me."

She nodded. The air grew chilly, although five of them were in such close proximity that she should have been warm.

Sam dropped his hands from hers and settled into the chair nearest her head. "Whenever you're ready."

She took a deep breath before lying back on the bed. She tried to clear her mind of the others in the room, of the low hum of the heater, and of the events that threatened to keep her thoughts swirling. Sam had planted the intent with his words, and she knew she only needed to step out of her own way, to allow her subconscious to thread its path through the universe. Faith dictated that she would find her way to the right place.

The room grew bright, but she knew it was not Chris' bedroom that flooded her senses with light but another room, miles away. A man stood at a large picture window, staring at the landscape just beyond the building. As she honed in on him, she relayed what she saw back to Sam: he was dressed in an immaculate navy suit, his short hair stopping well above a starched white collar. He looked to be in his fifties; a ring on his right hand spoke of wealth and privilege. She could even smell his cologne; a crisp, almost overpowering scent of balsam and orange.

She knew even before she realized where she was standing, who she was watching. He was without a doubt the most recognizable—and the most powerful—man in the world: the President of the United States.

He half-turned toward the room, and she caught a glimpse of the landscape just beyond the window: flawlessly manicured hedges, winter cabbage, a flash of color in an otherwise stark winter scene.

She pulled back, her eyes taking in the rest of the room; its distinctive oval shape, the rug laid precisely in the middle with the unmistakable presidential seal, the stiff, formal couches on either side.

He was speaking and now as he turned completely toward the room, she tried to concentrate on his words.

"The day after tomorrow," he was saying, "I'll announce the appointment of the new Attorney General, Isaac Campbell."

"There will be opposition." The voice came from the direction of the couches some distance from the President, and Vicki turned to find the White House Chief of Staff leaning forward in his seat, his eyes on his superior.

"There will be no opposition," the President countered. He fingered his ring, swirling it around his finger as he spoke. "We have the list. Anyone who opposes his nomination will receive a nice little visit with a nice little package of facts we have on them. Anyone who opposes him will be ruined."

"They'll be ruined anyway," the other man countered. His smile was sly, a bit crooked, and it never reached his eyes.

"Yes. But they won't know it—not just yet."

"When will they issue the first set of indictments?"

"As soon as he takes office. We'll rush through the nomination citing national security concerns."

"And Carnegie?"

"She's going into FBI custody today. She'll be cut off from everybody—they'll ensure she won't have any opportunity to communicate anything she knows. That is, until we need her testimony."

"We have confirmation on the allegations in the list," the Chief of Staff said, steepling his hands. "We really don't need her testimony… The FBI has been independently verifying the illegal activities of each politician. She amassed quite a list."

"There was only one copy of the list to my understanding." The President tapped his fingers on his desk. "She had it stored online. The FBI has it maintained in their sole possession, and they've removed the copy she had."

"Are we sure there was only one?"

"I have complete assurances."

A *tick, tock* began to sound in the back of Vicki's mind. It was so foreign from the conversation that was unfolding in front of her that she almost asked the others in the room to remove their watches or move further from her. But in the next instance, she realized it was the pendulum, beginning its steady movement yet again.

"And the bombings?" the Chief of Staff asked.

"Shar ma arke Galaid. It's already been reported in all the news media that he masterminded the attacks. Now he's been killed, and the attacks stop."

"And we improve the economy overnight."

"It's what the American people want, isn't it? So we've given it to them. On a silver platter, I might add… And while they're enjoying the first economic boon we've had in decades, I'll be quietly destroying our political opponents."

The other man nearly snickered. "What's our next step?"

The President's eyes dropped to his desk, and the sound of the pendulum grew so loudly that Vicki was tempted to place her hands over her ears to stop the intrusive sound. Her eyes were drawn to his fingertips and she realized they rested on an open folder. "Destroy the files on the ship bombings." He flipped the folder closed. "Starting with this one."

As the Chief of Staff rose from his seat and began to cross the room, Vicki peered past the President's shoulder to stare at the folder. Across the neat brown dossier was a single word, printed in large block letters: PENDULUM.

In that instant, the steady *tick, tock* that had threatened to hijack her mission stopped abruptly. She was left with the silence of the room, the soft steps of the Chief of Staff crossing the thick rug, and his fingers wrapping themselves around the folder. "Consider it done."

Vicki's eyes opened to find four people sitting alongside the bed, each person's face paler than the one before them, each person's eyes riveted on her. For a long moment, no one spoke. Their expressions said it all.

After a long, awkward moment, she rose to a seated position.

"What are our orders?" It was Dylan's voice that broke the silence. He was studying Sam's face, and all turned toward him for his response.

Sam sat silently, as if he hadn't heard Dylan's question. He stared at the corner of the bed but the look in his eyes revealed that his thoughts were miles away. The stillness grew. A different sort of *tick, tock* sounded; it spoke of the passage of time, the lengthening of the shadows, and the inevitable moment in which the FBI would arrive on Chris' doorstep to whisk Brenda away.

Finally, he spoke. His eyes remained on the bed, and his words were hushed. "We do nothing."

For a moment, no one spoke. Vicki's eyes met Dylan's, his furrowed brows displaying his confusion. Chris opened his mouth but then half-closed it. Brenda's face paled.

"Pardon me, Sam," Dylan said finally. "But what exactly are you meanin', when you say we do nothin'?"

Sam looked up as if seeing them there for the first time.

"We do nothing." His voice was flat, the usual brusqueness absent.

"Can't you—aren't you plannin' to run it up the chain, the way you usually handle a mission?"

Sam's head cocked. "Run it up *what* chain? The chain of command? The chain that ends with the President?"

As his words sank in, a pall descended upon them.

"How would I know," Sam continued, "who the good guys are? There could be thousands of them and just one—just one— who sees the report, who knows we spied on the President of the United States, and we're all through."

"But—"

"You think what we've been through with Brenda hasn't been enough? Each of us would carry a bounty on our heads— a bounty that would only be satisfied when each of us has been *eliminated*." The word hung in the air.

"The FBI is coming to pick up Brenda," Vicki said quietly. "How do we know that she's not the first to be eliminated? How do we know that they won't still come after each of us in turn?"

Sam rose and crossed to the other side of the room, where he pulled back the drapes and stared out the window. After a few moments, he turned back to them. "We're going to fake our mission."

"How?"

"I've had Dylan working with Shar ma arke Galaid, trying to get information out of him." He turned toward Dylan. "Your last time with him, he confessed, did he not?"

"He did."

"Then we close the case."

"He's dead—it's already been closed, 'asn't it now?"

"Yes, he's dead. And yes, they've released information to the media that he was the mastermind. Now we follow it up with our own conclusive report. We agree with everything they've already concluded."

"For what purpose?" Dylan breathed.

Sam took a few steps toward them. "To live another day."

"What're you sayin'?"

"I'm saying that we agree with the President. Shar ma arke Galaid was the mastermind of those ship bombings. He was killed in a raid in Somalia. End of story. Case closed."

"But you know it isn't true," Dylan said in a hoarse whisper. "It wouldn't be right."

"Right has nothing to do with it. You can be right and wear crosshairs on your forehead. Is that the kind of life you want to lead? Looking over your shoulder every minute of every day, knowing that someone will track you down when you least suspect it? Think of Vicki, Dylan. Think of your child. Blame it on Galaid and put it behind you."

"And what about Brenda?" Vicki asked.

Brenda had been uncharacteristically subdued, watching events unfold in front of her and listening quietly to Dylan's impassioned debate. Now she tilted her chin upward. "It leaves me where I've always been, doesn't it?" she asked. "In Joseph Gabucci's crosshairs."

"I've been sending reports up the chain of every mission Vicki's done—as standard operating procedure. Now I'll write up a report that states that Gabucci is working for one of our enemies—Iran, Russia, North Korea, take your pick—because Brenda has information about *that* world leader."

"But she doesn't."

Brenda did not agree, and all eyes turned to her.

"Do you?"

She shrugged. "It's out there to be found. And if you're saying you want me to find something, I will."

"But when?" Vicki pressed. "The FBI could be here any minute to take her into protective custody. What opportunity would she have? And how would we know, if she's kept incommunicado?"

"We can't prevent what they have intended for her," Sam said. To everyone's protests, he added, "They don't intend to kill her. If they did, they wouldn't send an FBI envoy to collect her. They'd send an assassin."

"Like Gabucci?" Brenda quipped.

"I'll write a report that makes them believe you have international information that could tip the scales. In the meantime, I'll call my old friend Coten and ask him to personally oversee your safety."

"And just how good a friend is he to you?" Dylan asked, his eyes narrowed.

"We'll find out, won't we? Look, we don't have a lot of options here…" Sam squeezed the bridge of his nose. "Our only recourse is to lead our own government to the conclusion that we are not a threat—not to the President, not to his political party, and not to anyone who had anything to do with the ship bombings."

"And Brenda's list?"

Sam turned to her. "You have to act worthy of an Oscar. You must convince them that you have no political affiliations. You must convince them that you are willing to testify against any name they put in front of you. And you must convince them that you don't care about any of the other names."

Vicki started to protest but Brenda interrupted her. "I get it. If I play their game, I survive."

"That's the long and the short of it."

"Just one question," Brenda said. "How do I know when the agents lead me out of here that Gabucci isn't waiting for me on some rooftop, waiting to blow me away?"

Sam sighed. "We don't know. But now it's up to me. I write reports that are read by analysts, that go up the chain, and eventually—if they're important enough—are read by the men at the top. So, as I see it, I have two reports to write. One, closing the case of Shar ma arke Galaid. The second one, my higher priority, as I see it—to stack the cards in Brenda's favor, to show that she's one of *them*, even if she isn't."

"But where does all this lead?" Dylan said.

"I can answer that," Chris said. He'd been silent as he watched the others debate. "We can't win in this political climate. It's a fool's errand to think we have any chance. The President is winning by a landslide. Even if his methods are corrupt, his message has gotten through to the American people. Think of the alternative if we somehow managed to persuade the American public that he should be impeached. And even so, it wouldn't happen overnight. He'd still be sworn into a second term. It could take years before anything was proven. He'd stonewall us every step of the way."

Chris stood. "So we wait. We play their game, as Sam suggested. And when the winds shift, we'll still be here."

A long moment of silence ensued. Finally, Sam said, "I've got to call Coten. And I have some reports to write." With that, he left the room, his footsteps heavy on the hardwood floor.

Dylan reached for Vicki's hand. Taking it in his, he walked her through the room, leaving Chris and Brenda behind. They entered the hallway to the sound of Sam's voice on his cell phone.

"It isn't right," Dylan whispered to Vicki.

53

They were gathered in the hallway when Sam opened the door to Chris' condominium. "We're ready," he said. He took a deep breath as he closed the door behind him. "Here's what's going to happen, so listen up. We've got a van and two escort vehicles. I'm driving the van. Agent Coten will be up front with me. Dylan, you're in the back with Brenda." He turned back around and placed his hand on the doorknob. "Let's do it."

"What about—" Vicki began.

"Us?" Chris finished.

"You two are staying behind."

Vicki's eyes met Brenda's and filled with tears. "I don't know when I'll see you again."

"Don't get all mushy on me," Brenda said.

"Brenda," Chris said, pulling her into his arms. "I love you. Whatever happens, know that I love you."

Sam opened the door and stepped into the hallway.

"You know I love you, too," Brenda whispered. "You're a good guy, Chris. God only knows what you've ever seen in me..."

"Don't talk that way," he admonished. "We'll get through this. And I'll be waiting for you."

"Where are you taking her?" Vicki asked, wiping the tears from her cheeks.

Sam stepped back to the doorway. "Langley."

"CIA Headquarters?" Brenda asked, her eyes widening.

"Agent Coten is going as far as the Langley gates. Once we're through, Dylan and I are taking you to a facility that isn't on any maps—the building doesn't exist, if you get my drift."

"You're not—" Vicki began.

"Yes. That's precisely where she's going. Your old room."

"Really?" Vicki settled back on her heels. Then she turned to Brenda. "You'll be safe there."

"We'll have a special task force assigned to her. Word came down from the Director that the President himself wants assurances that she'll be kept safe and ready to testify." They exchanged glances and then Sam added, "Let's go. We've got men waiting downstairs."

"Sam," Brenda began. "I need to speak to Vicki."

"Then make it quick."

"Can she—is it possible for her to go with me?"

"No. Absolutely not." Sam avoided their eyes as he peered down the hall.

"He's right," Dylan said quietly. "It's too dangerous for you, Vicki. Think 'o the child."

"Are you sure?" Vicki asked. "Langley isn't far—maybe fifteen miles, if that."

"The distance doesn't matter. If you've got something to say to her, say it now." Sam's voice turned gruff.

"Please, Sam. You'll have me in a van, and you've already said we'll be escorted. He won't try anything—if he's still alive. He fell from eight stories, for Christ's sake. He's got to have broken bones." Brenda's voice was uncharacteristically on the edge of begging.

"What would you say in a van that you can't say right here?" Sam said, exasperated.

She hesitated. "You wouldn't understand. It's sister stuff."

"You're right. I wouldn't understand." Sam glanced up and down the hall. "Oh, alright. But hurry it up. We're wasting time."

Brenda rushed back to Chris, falling into his arms and kissing him with a passion more appropriate in private, but neither appeared self-conscious. As they reluctantly parted, her fingers trailed along his arm to his fingertips, as though she was reluctant to break physical contact with him. Then with a loud sigh, she abruptly turned and followed Sam to the elevator, where an agent stood waiting.

Vicki and Dylan followed close behind. As they entered the elevator, Vicki glanced back at Chris, who was standing alone in his doorway. She felt guilty for leaving him; if anyone should have accompanied Brenda, it should have been the man she loved—the man who loved her.

Then Dylan's hand was on the small of her back, pushing her gently into the elevator.

Seconds later, they found themselves in the underground garage. An off-white van waited, the door open to the back. An FBI Agent around Sam's age stood waiting. "Agent Coten," he said, gesturing for them to enter the back. Dylan briefly introduced himself and pointed out Brenda and Vicki as they settled in. Then he climbed in behind them.

There were no side windows and the back window was small and positioned higher than a normal van, so that one would have to nearly stand in order to see out. It also, Vicki realized, would prevent anyone from seeing how many were in the van— or who they were. Rising to her feet, she glanced through the window, catching a glimpse of a government vehicle behind them with two agents in the front seats. Glancing in the other direction, an identical vehicle was parked in front of them, also with two agents.

Sam climbed into the driver's seat as Coten settled in beside him. They were separated from the back by a sheet of Plexiglas that stretched from the floor to the ceiling. But when Coten spoke, his voice carried through an intercom system. He announced the time of their departure, their current position, and their destination.

Vicki glanced at Dylan, who was checking his weapon. She wondered if Coten had been speaking to the men in the other vehicles, or if their movements were being reported up the chain of command.

Then all three vehicles began moving through the garage. They exited to a red-orange glow from a dramatic sunset, driving past Chris' apartment building toward the main road. Brenda tried to peer through the back window, perhaps to see if Chris was standing on his balcony, but Dylan waved her back down.

They sat in silence for a moment. Then Vicki said, "Depending on which route they take, we could be there in less than fifteen minutes. You said you wanted to tell me something?"

Brenda pushed her hands in her pockets and looked at the van floor for a moment. When she looked up, her eyes were teary but her mouth was set. "I know you've always blamed yourself for Mom and Dad dying," she stated.

Vicki's eyes met hers but she remained silent.

"There was nothing you could have done," Brenda continued. "I remember it well. You tried. You really tried. It was one of those things that was just—meant to be."

Her hands moved within her pockets as if she was nervous. "I think—I think everybody has a destiny in mind for them."

Vicki glanced at Dylan. He was listening intently, but remained silent.

"Your destiny, Vicki," Brenda continued, "was obviously to use your gift—this incredible psychic gift that you possess." She smiled slyly at Dylan. "And to meet him." She sighed. "I wish I'd met him first, Vicki. You've got quite a catch there."

"You're talking like we're never going to see each other again," Vicki said, brushing a tear from her eye.

"I'm not one for theatrics," Brenda said. "I just wanted you to know that I love you. And we'll always be sisters, wherever we are. However far apart we are."

"I'll see you again," Vicki said. "You'll be in my old room— Sam said so. It's not so bad. I grew up there. Dylan was there for a time, too."

"My time wasn't so pleasant," he said in a low voice. The van was speeding up, and Dylan half-stood to glance out the back window.

"Vicki," Brenda said, pulling her hand from her pocket. "In your mission, the President said that they had all the copies of the list I'd put together."

"Yes." As she looked into her sister's eyes, she realized why Brenda had wanted her to come along and why she'd needed to talk to her.

She pushed a piece of paper into her hands. "There are multiple copies, Vicki. And they're all right there, at your fingertips."

Vicki started to open the folded paper, but Brenda stopped her.

"Don't. Keep it. Look at it when you're alone. I uploaded it to multiple websites, hosted all over the world. The user names and passwords are all right there."

"You mean—"

"Whenever you need it, *if* ever you need it, you'll have it."

"But this—"

Her words were interrupted by a sudden surge to the right and the grinding of metal against metal. Dylan jumped from the left side of the van to the right just as it crumpled inward. Vicki screamed involuntarily, her voice sounding loud and harsh in the small confines of the van. Brenda grabbed her, throwing her to the floor before joining her.

The vehicle gathered speed, and as Vicki looked up from the floor, she saw Dylan peering out the back window. "Where the h'ail is the follow vehicle?" he demanded, his brogue thick with adrenaline.

The van careened to the right again, flinging them to one side. "Stay down!" Dylan demanded as he lurched forward. He grabbed the seat back to steady himself as he looked through the Plexiglas. "It's a white pickup truck," he said to them. "Stay down. They're tryin' to drive us off the road."

A white pickup... Vicki placed her hands over her head and closed her eyes. Sam's and Coten's voices climbed over each other as they tried to avoid another collision. Her cheek felt the stiff bristles of the floor mat but her mind raced back to a dream— a dream she'd nearly forgotten. It had been just Brenda and herself in a car, and they'd been chased by Joseph Gabucci in a white truck. As she remembered her dream and how he'd run them off the road and Brenda had been pinned against the steering wheel, she fought to keep her breathing under control and her nerves steady.

"We're on the George Washington Parkway," Dylan stated as they barreled onto the entrance ramp.

The Parkway… In her mind's eye, she pictured the gently winding road alongside the Potomac River; the embankments and the river itself, churning, deep and dark.

She began to rise up on her forearms.

"Stay down, Vicki!" Dylan's order was terse and husky.

"I've seen it!" She tried to keep her voice from sounding shrill and hysterical, but her voice sounded anything but calm.

"Seen what?"

"I know what's going to happen!"

The entire van was thrust far to the right and the sound of gravel crunching under the tires merged with metal crushing and tires squealing. Through the glass, she saw Sam gripping the wheel in both hands, struggling to keep the van from lurching off the road. They zigzagged ferociously, their bodies bouncing from the back-and-forth of pavement versus gravel shoulder, and twice they sank into something soft before veering back toward the roadway.

"This can't happen!" Vicki screamed, coming to her feet.

"Get down, Vicki," Brenda yelled, grasping at her legs. But her sister was quick, outmaneuvering her. She reached Dylan's side, and he quickly placed a hand on her shoulder and forced her into the seat beside him. He remained standing, his other hand firmly grasping his pistol, his eyes darting from Sam and Coten to glimpses of the white truck as it tried to cut them off.

"Listen to me," Vicki urged. "Tell them—" She looked up ahead. Along the skyline were highrises; each seeming to rise higher than the previous one. One remained under construction, the parking garage rimmed with temporary wooden rails.

"Tell them what?" Dylan demanded.

"That parking garage—go there." She pointed as they continued to lurch.

He tried to follow the direction. "Are you daft?"

"Trust me. We have to go *up*."

He bit his bottom lip and then banged on the glass. "Can you hear me?"

"Affirmative!" Sam shouted.

"Go to the parking garage. Go up."

"Are you crazy?"

"Ooh, this is gonna sound lame," Dylan said under his breath. Then he shouted, "Vicki had a vision. Go *up!*"

The van gained momentum. As Vicki watched from her seat, she spotted the truck dropping back behind them before speeding up and crashing into the back of the van. She heard Brenda's voice expel rapidly as her sister's body twisted across the floor. She wanted to help her, to stop her from banging against the metal supports for the seats, but it took all her strength to hold on herself, to keep herself from falling atop of her or lurching through the air.

Brenda's arm shot out, grabbing ahold of a metal support, revealing a long gash in her upper arm. Her eye caught Vicki's and she said, "It's nothing. Just watch out for yourself!"

A car was stopped ahead and Sam careened around it as the truck pressed inward, squeezing them between the two vehicles. They dragged the car several yards, the sound of metal gnawing against metal growing to a fever pitch. Then the car disengaged, falling back behind them into the middle of the intersection.

Dylan looked back through the van. "Where the h'ail is the follow vehicle?" His voice was filled with rage as he looked out the back window before turning toward the front.

The sky grew dark as the tall buildings on either side blotted out the remnants of the sunset. They jumped the sidewalk, two wheels shifting upward as the opposite two remained on the pavement. The tilt of the van caused them all to plummet toward the left, toward the badly mangled metal and closer to the onslaught. Vicki screamed out in frustration as she held onto the seat with all her strength. Brenda continued to slide dangerously close and Dylan jumped forward, dragging her back.

They were inches from the truck—and he was inches from them. A shot rang out and then two, but they couldn't determine where they were originating. Coten remained in the front passenger seat, speaking into a microphone, calling for assistance.

Though Vicki was not an arms expert, she knew he wouldn't have a clear shot—Sam's head was in the way, and to shoot through the glass would be too foolish for him to attempt. It had to be Gabucci firing—but how could he drive the truck and shoot at the same time?

The truck smashed into them again; this time, she thought she heard something dragging beneath them. A glance toward the back window revealed sparks. Parts were falling off the van, she realized as her heart dropped. She looked toward the front. The parking garage was still a distance away—and in between they were dangerously close to the water's edge.

"Listen to me, Vicki," Dylan shouted to be heard above the maelstrom. "If we go into the water, I'll open this door. Get out, and swim underwater as far as you can. Do not put your head above water. Are you understandin' me? Go deep. Stay deep."

Vicki nodded, even as she closed her eyes tight to keep from screaming again.

"Did you hear me, Brenda?"

"Yes!" she shouted.

"You do the same. Whate'er happens, go deep, stay deep, and swim as far from shore as possible."

Vicki's bottom lip trembled. "What about you?"

He avoided her eyes. "Don't you be worryin' about me," he said. "Go deep. Stay deep. Fight the instinct to come to the surface."

The van veered off the roadway again, thudding onto soft dirt before shakily swinging back to the left. Then again they rolled off the pavement. Sam was shouting now and a glance toward the front revealed him fighting the steering wheel, ramming the truck back to the left so he could regain traction.

Then they swerved sharply back to the right and for a moment, everything seemed to be in slow motion: the tilt of the van as the right tires hit soft dirt, the water's edge, appearing cold and dark and deadly; something flying through the air and Dylan's torso bounding off one side of the van, his voice sounding deafening as the breath was knocked from him.

In the next moment, Sam was heroically forcing the wheels back to the left, even while the sound of metal clattering grew around them. Then he took a dramatic turn to the right.

They were all slung violently forward. Vicki held her breath, expecting the sudden splash of the water beneath them, the dragging down of the vehicle, Dylan wrestling to open the door... But as they continued to the right, she realized the tires had not hit soft dirt but were clanging against metal as they ascended. She opened her eyes and looked through the Plexiglas and saw nothing but sky.

The stars were out in abundance and a full moon stared down at them. It looked so large that she could see the impressions, the variegated colors; she thought she could almost reach out and touch it. How odd, she thought, that this should be the last thing I see on earth.

With a boom, the van leveled out and they were tossed toward the other side. It was then that she realized they were climbing the parking garage. The concrete had been poured but the edges had nothing but flimsy wood rails marking the sudden drop; it looked far more intimidating than it had appeared from a distance, and Vicki began to question her instincts.

Behind them, the truck kept pace. Each time it was near enough to strike from behind, they'd reach the next level and Sam swerved like a rabbit to stay out of his range.

Then the sky opened up again. This time it was full; complete. This time, it was all-encompassing. It wrapped around them like they were on the peak of a mountain.

The thought that they had reached the top flew through Vicki's mind, and she realized she had no other plan than this.

As the van swerved violently around the last incline, the door suddenly opened and Dylan jumped.

Vicki screamed, instinctively rushing toward the open door, but Brenda grabbed her, pulling her back. The air spilled in— cold and biting. It swirled around them as the van screeched to a halt.

The truck jumped off the pavement as it reached the top. Six shots rang out, followed by loud booms. Then Coten was leaping out of the front seat and more shots split the night air.

Vicki was dragged to the floor, her face pressed into the floor mat, her sister's body laid across hers.

She heard the sound of an engine accelerating and then the sound of something huge and heavy hitting the surface of the water. She bounded up, shaking off Brenda's efforts to keep her pinned down, and flew out the side door.

She found Dylan lying on his back, his torso upright, his pistol held in both hands. The truck was nowhere to be seen. She was caught between wanting to rush to his aid and taking in her surroundings, her mind confused with all she saw—and didn't see.

The top floor of the parking garage was flat and stark, bare except for the van that lay mangled atop it. Crudely erected two-by-fours were nailed haphazardly around the perimeter; it was more, she realized, to keep someone from stepping backward into an abyss than to prevent a vehicle from plummeting over.

As Dylan rose, she caught sight of Coten standing at the edge of the concrete. The railing was missing there, and one piece dangled on the side, a remnant of the sudden collision. She rushed to the edge before Dylan grabbed her arm and pulled her back.

The truck was nearly submerged.

"Get back," he ordered her. "He could begin shooting."

Realizing her folly, she backed away from the concrete. Somewhere, in the back of her mind, she heard Sam on his phone, calling for divers and backup. In the distance she heard sirens. Brenda's voice came to her, but she couldn't make out the words; they seemed disembodied.

She found herself next to the opposite side, watching government vehicles like the ones assigned to be the lead car and follow car, coming up the garage ramp from the street. She watched the blue lights flashing off the glass of area buildings as they approached, their sirens growing into a chorus as they neared.

"It's over," she said to no one in particular. She looked at the vastness of the sky around her, at the stars twinkling and the moon gazing down upon her. "It's all over."

54

Vicki adjusted the heat in the hotel room before peering out the window. The tenth floor room provided a perfect view of 15th Street. It was late morning and only muted winter sunlight wound its way around the row of skyscrapers. She watched a lady's hat blow off in the blustery wind, and she shivered as she observed the heavy coats, the scarves, and the knee-length boots. Winter had definitely arrived in Washington, D.C.

She turned back to the room. She supposed it was a standard issue hotel room; the building was old but the rooms had recently been renovated. They were booked into a room with a king-sized bed and a sitting area with a round table and chairs. The walls were patterned in deep blue and ivory; the carpet was navy, and the spread was striped in navy and cream—all enough to cast the room in a shadowy veil. The air was dry and despite turning down the heat, it still felt like they were roasting.

Chris and Dylan didn't appear to notice, however, as Chris pulled a hooded sweatshirt over his head.

Dylan held out a Bluetooth earpiece.

"That guy must have nine lives," Chris said as he accepted the earpiece and placed it in his ear.

"To say the least," Dylan said. "I don't rightly know how he managed to survive the fall from your apartment. Then to have 'im plummet into the Potomac River the way he did and still manage to get away…"

"But you shot him, right? You had to have shot him."

"Ooh, no." Dylan placed an earpiece in his own ear as he continued, "I knew it would be a miracle if I managed to shoot through the cab and actually hit 'im. So as he came up the ramp, I aimed for the tires."

"The tires, huh? Good thinking."

"He was movin' so fast, you know, and as he came around the corner at the top—well, once the tires blew out, he just didn't manage to stay in control."

"I think he drowned," Vicki said as she joined them. "He never came up to the surface, and the place was swarming with police. The divers were there within minutes. They raised the truck, but there was no sign of him. Sam said they expected his body to wash up downstream."

Chris added a thin jacket over his sweatshirt, followed by another one. "Thanks for keeping Brenda safe."

"She was just bruised up a bit," Dylan said. "We all were. Anyway, she's safe now. She'll remain at Langley in between her testimony—if it ever happens." They locked eyes for a moment and then they both looked away as if they were a bit self-conscious.

Chris cleared his throat as he pulled the hood over his head. "How do I look?"

"Like a homeless man," Vicki stated flatly.

"Good. Then it works."

Dylan handed him something that looked like a gym bag that had seen better days.

"Where'd you get this?"

"Salvation Army. Think it'll work?"

Chris unzipped it. He looked at the contents for a moment and then crumpled the bag, keeping it unzipped. "It's good."

"There's one thin' I'm not quite comprehendin'," Dylan said. "The President's name isn't on Brenda's list."

"And you're wondering why the President has such a special interest in it?" Chris asked. "Politics, pure and simple. His allies are on it, and he needs to squelch that or he loses control of the

House and Senate. His enemies are on it, and he feels the need to—"

"Annihilate them," Dylan finished.

Chris shrugged. "It's the way politics are played now. It isn't enough to beat your opponent. You must destroy their career."

"And Brenda was seen as a threat because she held the information—not only the list on paper, but in her memory," Vicki added.

Dylan nodded silently as he looked him over once more: the scuffed boots, the worn jeans with a hole near the knee that revealed long johns, and then at the layers of jackets with the hood protruding from two levels beneath. He glanced at his watch. "It's time."

Dylan and Vicki stood side-by-side at the hotel window. The street below remained full of activity as a steady stream of people entered and exited office buildings, walked briskly along the wide sidewalks and crossed the street in between a continuous line of vehicles. Even with the window closed and the heater humming, they could hear the chorus of engines and the cars honking each time the light changed or someone tried to weave in and out of adjoining lanes.

The restaurants that dotted the street grew steadily busier as the clock ticked toward noon.

"Where is it?" Dylan breathed. He used his binoculars to scan the street in both directions. Then, "The limousine is turnin' the corner, two blocks down."

He shifted the binoculars so he was peering at the figure of what appeared to be a homeless man, sitting on the pavement at the edge of the block, his back against a granite building. The man rose, keeping his head down. The hood shielded his face from view.

Then he switched to the building foyer. The glass doors afforded him a decent view of the lobby. A security guard sat behind a desk, chatting with another guard nearer the door. They were gatekeepers, he thought, meant to keep people like them from reaching the man they most needed to see.

"He's just exited the elevator," Dylan said. He scanned between the lobby and Chris, who had moved from the building to a trash receptacle near the street. He appeared to be going through it as if looking for something to eat. He did not turn toward the building but kept his back to the man who was moving through the revolving door.

"He's on the sidewalk," Dylan stated. He glanced down the street. "The limo is pullin' up. It appears like it's goin' to stop about four yards from you."

Chris' head moved upward only slightly. His face remained in shadows but Dylan knew he was watching intently. Then he began to move, slowly and deliberately, pulling the gym bag closer to his side.

The man who had exited the building was smartly dressed, his black business coat reaching below his knees to reveal navy blue dress slacks. Dylan was sure his shoes were shined like patent leather. He did not wear a hat, though the weather was frigid; instead, his light hair danced in the growing wind. He raised a hand to brush it back as the limousine stopped in front of a handicapped zone.

He was a mere five feet from the vehicle. The driver did not appear as though he intended to get out and open the door. The man quickened his step, reaching for the door handle.

Chris bumped into him, startling the man, who instinctively turned to look at him. He did not appear as though he wanted to stop. The gym bag jostled in between them, and then Chris was gone, moving down the street in the opposite direction of the limousine, blending in with the growing crowds escaping their offices for the lunch hour.

"He has the package." The voice came through Dylan's earpiece loud and clear.

Dylan shifted the binoculars back to the limousine. The man was climbing into the back seat. The moon roof provided a shadowy view and he adjusted the binoculars until he spotted the envelope in the man's hands. While the driver waited for the traffic to move so he could proceed, the man opened the envelope to reveal a folder. He stared at the words on the front of it for the briefest of moments before opening it. He thumbed through the pages, slowly at first and then rapidly. He leaned toward the driver, said something, and then looked behind him in the direction Chris had gone.

Dylan scanned the street but there was no sign of Chris. He'd either moved into an adjoining building or he'd turned a corner—or he was lost in the sea of bodies.

He turned his attention back to the man. After a moment of trying vainly to spot the man who had provided him the documents, he looked at them again. Then he closed the folder and looked again at the words that had been typed neatly on the cover: The Pendulum Files.

Then the limousine was pulling away from the building with *The Washington Post* emblazoned across its granite walls, merging with the traffic that was never-ending.

"Do you think he understands what he has?" Vicki asked softly.

"If anyone is likely to understand it," Dylan said, "it would have to be him."

"What do you think he'll do with it?"

"We'll have to wait and see now, won't we?"

"You know when Brenda's list is made public, there are going to be questions."

"Aye, and so there will be. But I removed the passwords from each o' the websites so it's all public knowledge now. There'll be no need for her to testify. The public outcry will require investigations into each o' the allegations and the trail is there for anyone to follow."

"But does he know that?"

"There was a typed note in w' the list. He has 72 hours afore the search engines will likely pick up on the open status o' the websites. Then it's anyone's game. And it's my guess that he'll want the *Post* to get a jump on the competition."

"And the President's mission, marked *Pendulum*?"

"Not a mention o' it, otherwise Sam would have our necks. Only the title on the front o' it, and bein' a top-notch investigative reporter himself, I'd say he'll want to know what it refers to."

Vicki exhaled. "So."

Dylan put down the binoculars and turned back to the room. "So." He reached an arm around Vicki, pulling her to him.

"What do we do now?" she asked, kissing him on the tip of his nose.

"Well, seein' as how Chris is goin' back to his apartment… Sam and Brenda are presumably busy… and it's too late in the day for us to drive all the way back home…"

"And we do have this hotel room for the whole night," Vicki added.

"Then I'd say we need to take full advantage o' it. Besides, there are a few things I've been meanin' to chat w' you about, but events seemed to 'ave prevented it."

"Oh? What kind of things?" She brushed her lips across his.

"Oh, plans for a weddin'," he said, smiling as he returned her kisses. "And a proper honeymoon."

She pulled back. "Oh? What do you have in mind?"

He bent and scooped her up in his arms. "Right this moment, what I 'ave in mind is lovin' you. Afterward, we'll talk about makin' it legal."

As he deposited her gently on the bed, Vicki closed her eyes with a contented sigh. He was tempted to think that it was all coming to an end—the days of watching over their shoulders, of Brenda's secret list, of assassins and black sites. But tomorrow, there would be another mission, and next week, another. And there was still the matter of the valuables he'd found in Aunt Laurel's home that he felt certain had been stolen by the Nazis in World War II—just like the treasures he'd spotted during his mission in Ireland. And, he thought as he leaned forward to kiss the woman he loved, they would soon be returning to his homeland for their honeymoon.

But for tonight, none of that mattered. For tonight, it was just the two of them.

About the Author

p.m.terrell is the pen name for Patricia McClelland Terrell, the award-winning, internationally acclaimed author of more than eighteen books in four genres: contemporary suspense, historical suspense, computer how-to and non-fiction.

Prior to writing full-time, she founded two computer companies in the Washington, DC Metropolitan Area: McClelland Enterprises, Inc. and Continental Software Development Corporation. Among her clients were the Central Intelligence Agency, United States Secret Service, U.S. Information Agency, and Department of Defense. Her specialties were in white collar computer crimes and computer intelligence.

A full-time author since 2002, *Black Swamp Mysteries* is her first series, inspired by the success of *Exit 22*, released in 2008. *Vicki's Key* was a top five finalist in the 2012 International Book Awards and 2012 USA Book Awards nominee. The series has several main characters whose lives are forever intertwined through events or family ties: Dylan Maguire, Vicki Boyd, Brenda Carnegie, Christopher Sandige, Alec Brodie and Sandy Stuart.

Her historical suspense, *River Passage*, was a 2010 Best Fiction and Drama Winner. It was determined to be so historically accurate that a copy of the book resides at the Nashville Government Metropolitan Archives in Nashville, Tennessee.

She is also the co-founder of The Book 'Em Foundation, an organization committed to raising public awareness of the correlation between high crime rates and high illiteracy rates. She is the organizer of Book 'Em North Carolina, an annual event held in the real town of Lumberton, North Carolina, to raise funds to increase literacy and reduce crime. For more information on this event and the literacy campaigns funded by it, visit www.bookemnc.org.

She sits on the boards of the Friends of the Robeson

County Public Library and the Robeson County Arts Council. She has also served on the boards of Crime Stoppers and Crime Solvers and became the first female president of the Chesterfield County-Colonial Heights Crime Solvers in Virginia.

For more information visit the author's website at www.pmterrell.com, follow her on Twitter at @pmterrell, her blog at www.pmterrell.blogspot.com, and on Facebook under author.p.m.terrell.

www.ingramcontent.com/pod-product-compliance
Lightning Source LLC
Chambersburg PA
CBHW070915260626
47162CB00007B/2685